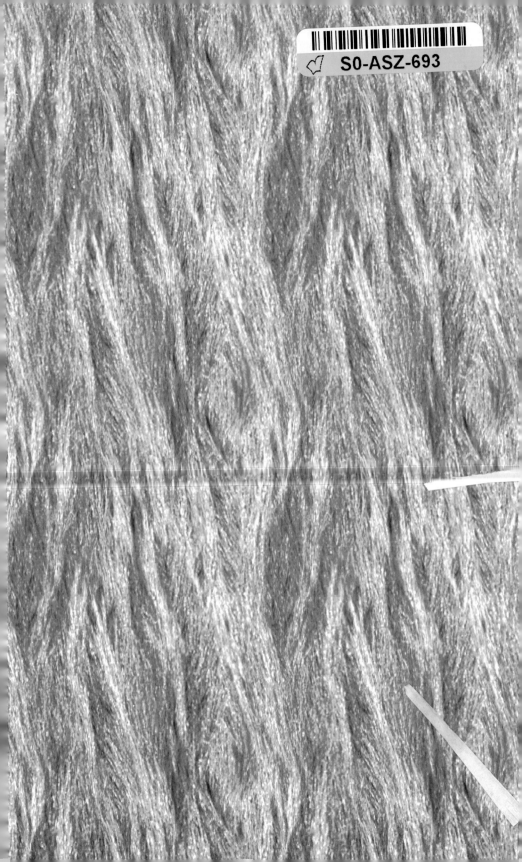

MICHAEL MOORCOCK'S
ELRIC:
TALES OF THE WHITE WOLF

Published by:

White Wolf Inc.
4598 Stonegate Industrial Boulevard
Stone Mountain, Georgia 30083

White Wolf Fiction

Editor: Stewart Wieck
Assistant Editor: Staley Krause
Copy Editor: Robert Hatch
Sales: Michael Krause
Marketing: Wes Harris
Art Director: Richard Thomas
Graphic Designer: Michelle Prahler

an original anthology
edited by Edward E. Kramer and Richard Gilliam

C O N T E N T S

Dedication

This book is dedicated to Linda and Michael Moorcock, with love, respect and admiration. May the *Chronic Outlaw* live on within us all...

Acknowledgments

The editors would like to thank Paul Cashman for his assistance in story continuity, and Stewart Wieck for finally bringing the *White Wolf* home.

INTRODUCTION TO TALES OF THE WHITE WOLF

BY MICHAEL MOORCOCK

Dear Reader,

Long ago, before the dawn of time, when all my old friends and heroes were still alive and I was an enthusiastic teenager editing a magazine called *Tarzan Adventures*, I was asked, I thought, to write a story about Conan the Barbarian, creation of Robert E. Howard, who committed suicide in Texas in 1936, some four years before I was born. I was already in touch with L. Sprague de Camp, a writer whose own reputation was chiefly for humorous fiction but who had a huge admiration for Howard and had helped initiate a new series of Conan stories which continue to this day.

To tell you the truth, by the time I began to write my Conan story I was a little jaded with barbarians, sorceresses, legendary mystical jewels and unstable vamps and felt that Howard's wonderful Conan novel *The Hour of the Dragon* had taken the character as far as he could reasonably go. So when John Carnell, editor of *Science Fantasy* magazine, told me that he didn't actually want a Conan story but "something along the same lines," I offered him Elric, the character I had been writing about in private and discussing with my friend the author and illustrator James Cawthorn.

I was actually tired of sword-and-sorcery as the genre then existed. I admired the work of C.L. Moore, Leigh Brackett and Fritz Leiber and continued to respect the vitality and invention of Howard, but I had little time for the likes of Tolkien and Lewis, whom I regarded as bad popular children's writers whose moral attitudes were highly questionable and whose particular syntheses had none of William

6

Morris' vision, Howard's manic originality or Leiber's sophisticated flair. I was, I suppose, bored with the form itself. So when Carnell commissioned the first Elric story I decided I would try to do something as different as possible from everything which then existed.

I was, of course, familiar with Morris, Cabell, Dunsany and the other literary writers who had influenced Leiber, and while some of their irony no doubt informed my stories, I was still attracted to the muscular tale-spinning of Howard and Edgar Rice Burroughs. I greatly admired Poul Anderson's *The Broken Sword* (still one of the great classics of the genre, particularly in its original version) and Fletcher Pratt's *The Well of the Unicorn*, but my tastes had by that time expanded to include all kinds of mythology, including Hindu and Zoroastrian, as well as the work of modern visionary writers like Huxley, Brecht and Camus. I was already thoroughly familiar with the nineteenth-century romantics like Byron, Shelley and Swinburne and the Gothic tales of Radcliffe, Lewis, Maturin and Le Fanu, and I was fired by the visionary qualities I found in Dickens, James, Conrad and my contemporary hero Mervyn Peake, so my particular synthesis had sufficient novelty to find favor with a readership used to the best that writers like Ballard, Sturgeon, Aldiss and Dick were already offering. I should say, however, that I never consciously planned anything revolutionary or novel. I was merely trying to write a good supernatural adventure story which would bring a bit of freshness to the form and entertain readers enough so that Carnell would commission a couple more stories. Not expecting to write more than a few novelettes, I was determined to pay homage to another childhood hero, Anthony Skene, who had written about a villainous albino known as Monsieur Zenith — "Sexton Blake's greatest adversary" (as the pulp magazine *Union Jack*, which featured Blake's adventures from the 1890s to the 1930s, would have it).

Admittedly I had been infected by the first book I had ever bought with my own money, Bunyan's *Pilgrim's Progress*, and was probably incapable of writing anything which didn't have at least a little allegory in it. My ambitions changed as the series (beginning with *The Dreaming City*) went on and I began to use it to explore some of the themes which continue to recur in my literary as well as my genre fiction, so that by the time I wrote the four parts of the novel published as *Stormbringer*, in response to readers' interest, I was doing quite a bit more with the form than I had originally set out to do.

A couple of years after *Stormbringer* I began to adapt the themes and the plots of the Elric stories to a more contemporary hero, Jerry Cornelius. By then, of course, the Eternal Champion and the Multiverse, two of my earliest creations, also existed and both Elric and Jerry were already perceived as aspects of the same personality, as they were of mine.

Ironically, although a number of writers borrowed from Elric and the title *Stormbringer* was used by two rock-and-roll bands for their album titles, while other performers from Marc Bolan to Hawkwind produced their homages, it was Jerry Cornelius who first inspired other people to write their own stories about him. These began to appear in *New Worlds*, which I was then editing, in the late sixties. They were eventually reprinted in a book called *The Nature of the Catastrophe* in 1971 and most recently in an expanded collection called *The New Nature of the Catastrophe* with work by James Sallis, Norman Spinrad, Langdon Jones, M. John Harrison, Brian W. Aldiss and others. But it was only recently that, thanks to the inspiration of Ed Kramer, a collection of Elric stories was proposed. When Ed first suggested it I was a little uncertain about the idea. Elric is, after all, an elderly chap, well past thirty, and I was not sure that any other writers would find sufficient mileage in him. I was, as you'll read here, very wrong. After all, I can still find new themes and ideas for the series, so I should not have been surprised that others could do so, too. What perhaps did surprise me was the originality, wit and imagination that so many of the writers here display — how many new angles they bring to the series and how much fresh inspiration they have given me (I've already asked Tad Williams if he minds me writing some more about the Gypsy Prince...).

What impresses me most about these stories is their vitality, the individuality of the writers, the range of their talent and the extraordinary variety of their work. I had really not expected anything this good. All the writers here have built reputations in their own right and bring their own special vision to the stories. There is no dilution, therefore, of the original material — but there is considerable amplification and complement. Neither have the writers let themselves be limited by one form. From Neil Gaiman to Nancy Collins, they have brought their own voices, their own visions and their own concerns to Elric, and this I find especially stimulating.

I hope you discover these stories to be as thoroughly absorbing and inspiring as I did.

Yours sincerely,

Michael Moorcock
Lost Pines, Texas
May 1994.

THE WHITE WOLF'S SONG

BY MICHAEL MOORCOCK

Come, Mephistophilis, let us dispute again,
And argue of divine Astrology.
Tell me, are there many Heavens above the moon?
Are all celestial bodies but one globe,
As is the substance of this centric earth?
　　— Christopher Marlowe, *The Tragical History of Doctor Faustus*

I.

AN UNUSUAL OCCURRENCE ON THE XANARDWYS ROAD

The rider was lean, almost etiolated, but subtly muscled. His ascetic features were sensitive, his skin milk-white. From deep cavities within that half-starved face moody crimson eyes burned like the flowers of Hell. Once or twice he turned in his saddle to look back.

A tribe of Alofian hermaphrodites at his heels, the man rode eastward across the Dakwinsi Steppe, hoping to reach fabled Xanardwys before the snows blocked the pass.

His pale silver mare, hardiest of all Bastans, was bred to this terrain and had as determined a hold on life as the sickly albino who had to sustain himself by drugs or the stolen life-stuff of his fellows.

Drawing the black sealskin snow-cloak about him, the man set his face against the weather. His name was Elric and he was a prince in his own country, the last of his long line and without legitimate issue, an outcast almost everywhere in a world coming to hate and resent his alien kind as the power of Melniboné faded and the strength of the Young Kingdoms grew. He did not much care for his own safety but he was determined to live, to return to his island kingdom and be re-united with his sweet cousin Cymoril, whom he would one day marry. It was this ambition alone which drove him on through the blizzard.

Clinging to his horse's mane as the sturdy beast plodded through the deepening drifts which threatened to bury the world, Elric's senses grew as numb as his flesh. The mare moved slowly across the ridges, keeping to the high ground, heading always away from the afternoon sun. At night Elric dug them both a snow-hole and wrapped them in his lined canvases. He carried the equipment of the Kardik, whose hunting grounds these were.

Elric no longer dreamed. He was almost entirely without conscious thought. Yet still his horse moved steadily towards Xanardwys, where hot springs brought eternal summer and where scarlet roses bloomed against the snow.

Towards evening on the fifth day of his journey, Elric became aware of an extra edge of coldness in the air. Though the great crimson disc of the setting sun threw long shadows over the white landscape, its light did not penetrate far. It now appeared to Elric that a vast wall of ice loomed up ahead, like the sides of a gigantic, supernatural fortress. There was something insubstantial about it. Perhaps Elric had discovered one of those monumental mirages which, according to the Kardik, heralded the inevitable doom of any witness.

Elric had faced more than one inevitable doom and felt no terror for this one, but his curiosity aroused him from the semi-stupor into which he had fallen. As they approached the towering ice he saw himself and his horse in perfect reflection. He smiled a grim smile, shocked by his own gauntness. He looked twice his real age and felt a hundred times older. Encounters with the supernatural had a habit of draining the spirit, as others whom he had met could readily testify....

Steadily his reflection grew larger until without warning he was swallowed by it — suddenly united with his own image! Then he was riding through a quiet, green dale which, he sincerely hoped, was the Valley of Xanardwys. He looked over his shoulder and saw a blue cloud billowing down a hillside and disappearing. Perhaps the mirror effect had something to do with the freakish weather of this region? He was profoundly relieved that Xanardwys — or at least its valley — was proving a somewhat substantial legend. He dismissed all questions concerning the phenomenon which had brought him here and pressed on in good spirits.

All around were the signs of spring — the warm, scented air, the bright wild-flowers, the budding trees and shrubs, the lush grass — and he marvelled at a wonderful paradox of geography which, according to the tales he'd heard, had saved many fugitives and travelers. Soon he must come to the ivory spires and ebony roofs of the city herself where he would rest, buy provisions, shelter and then continue his journey to Elwher, which lay beyond all the maps of his world.

The valley was narrow with steeply rising sides, like a tunnel, roots and branches of dark green trees tangling overhead in the soft earth. Elric felt a welcome sense of security and he drew deep breaths, relishing the sweet fecundity all around. This luxury of nature after the punishing ice brought him fresh vitality and new hope. Even his mare had developed a livelier gait.

However, when after an hour or two the sides grew yet steeper and narrower, the albino prince began to puzzle. He had never encountered such a natural phenomenon and indeed was beginning to believe that this gorgeous wealth of spring might be, after all, supernatural in origin. But then, even as he considered turning back and taking heed of a prudence he usually ignored, the sides of the valley began to sink to gentler rolling hills, widening to reveal in the distance a misty outline which must surely be that of Xanardwys.

After pausing to drink at a sparkling stream, Elric and his mare continued on. Now they crossed a vast stretch of greensward flanked by distant mountains, punctuated by stands of trees, flowery meadows, ponds and rivers. Slowly they came closer to the domestic reassurance of Xanardwys' rural rooftops.

Elric drew in a deep, contented sigh.

A great roaring erupted suddenly in Elric's ears and he was blinded as a new sun rose rapidly into the western sky, shrieking and wailing like a soul escaped from hell, multicolored flames forming a pulsing aura. Then the sound became a single, deep, sonorous chord, slowly fading.

Elric's horse stood mesmerized, as if turned to ice. The albino dismounted, cursing and throwing up his arm to protect his eyes. The broad rays stretched for miles across the landscape, bursting from the pulsing globe and carrying with them huge shapes, dark and writhing, seeming to struggle and fight even as they fell. And now the air was filled with an utterly horrifying noise, like the beating of a million pairs of monstrous wings. Trumpets bellowed, the brazen voices of an army, heralding an even more horrible sound — the despairing moan of a whole world's souls voicing their agony, the fading shouts and dying cries of warriors in the last, weary stages of a battle.

Peering into the troubled vivacity of that mighty light, Elric felt heavy, muscular, gigantic forms, stinking with a sweet, bestial, almost overpowering odor, landing with massive thuds, shaking the ground with such force that the entire terrain threatened to collapse. This rain of monsters did not cease. It was only the purest of luck which saved Elric from being crushed under one of the falling bodies. He had the impression of metal ringing and clashing, of voices screaming and calling, of wings beating, beating, beating, like the wings of moths against a window, in a kind of frantic hopelessness. And still the monsters continued to fall out of a sky whose light changed subtly now, growing deeper and more stable until the entire world was illuminated by a steady, scarlet glare against which flying, falling shapes moved in black silhouette — wings, helmets, armor, swords — twisted in the postures of defeat. Now the predominant smell reminded Elric of the Fall and the sweet odor of rot, of the summer's riches returning to their origins, and still mingled with this was the foetid stink of angry brutes.

As the light became gentler and the great disc began to fade, Elric grew aware of other colors and more details. The stink alone threatened to steal his senses — the snorting, acrid breath of titanic beasts, threatening sudden death and alarming every revitalized fiber of his being. Elric glimpsed brazen scales, huge silvery feathers, hideously beautiful insect eyes and mouths, wondrously distorted, half-crystalline bodies and faces, like Leviathan and all his kin, emerging after millions of years from beneath a sea which had encrusted them with myriad colors and asymmetrical forms, made them moving monuments in coral, with faceted eyes which stared up in blind anguish at a sky through which still plunged, wings flapping, fluttering, folded or too damaged to bear their weight, the godlike forms of their supernatural kind. Clashing rows of massive fangs and uttering sounds whose depth and force alone was sufficient to shake the whole valley, to topple Xanardwys' towers, crack her walls and send her townsfolk fleeing with black blood boiling from every orifice, the monsters continued to fall.

Only Elric, inured to the supernatural, his senses and his body tuned to alien orchestrations, did not suffer the fate of those poor, unlucky creatures.

For mile upon mile in all directions, through light now turning to a bloody pink flecked with brass and copper, the landscape was crowded with the fallen titans: some on their knees; some supporting themselves upon swords, spears or shields; some stumbling blindly before collapsing over the bodies of their comrades; some lying still and breathing slowly, resting with wary relief as their eyes scanned the heavens. And still the mighty angels fell.

Elric, with all his experience, all the years of mystic study, could not imagine the immensity of the battle from which they fled. He, whose own patron Chaos Duke had the power to destroy all mortal enemies, attempted to imagine the collective power of this myriad army, each common soldier of which might belong to Hell's aristocracy. For these were the very Lords of Chaos, each one of whom had a vast and complex constituency. Of that, Elric was certain.

He realized that his heart was beating rapidly and he was breathing in brief, painful gasps. Deliberately he took control of himself, convinced that the mere presence of that battered host must ultimately kill him. Determined, at least, to experience all he could before he was consumed by the casual power of the monsters, Elric was about to step forward when he heard a voice behind him. It was human, it was sardonic, and its accent was subtly queer, but it used the High Speech of Old Melniboné.

"I've seen a few miracles in my travels, sir, but by heavens, it must be the first time I've witnessed a shower of angels. Can you explain it, sir? Or are you as mystified as me?"

II.

A DILEMMA DISCOVERED IN XANARDWYS

The stranger was roughly the same height and build as Elric, with delicate, tanned features and pale blue eyes, sharp as steel. He wore the loose, baggy, cream-colored clothing of some outland barbarian, belted with brown leather and a pouch which doubtless holstered some weapon or charm. He wore a broad-brimmed hat the color of his shirt and breeches and he carried over his right shoulder another strange-looking weapon, or perhaps a musical instrument, all walnut, brass and steel. "Are you a denizen of these parts, sir, or have you been dragged, like me, through some damnable chaos vortex against your will? I am Count Renark von Bek, late of the Rim. And you, sir?"

"Prince Elric of Melniboné. I believed myself in Xanardwys, but now I doubt it. I am lost, sir. What do you make of this?"

"If I were to call upon the mythology and religion of my ancestors, I would say we looked at the defeated Host of Chaos, the very archangels who banded with Lucifer to challenge the power of God. All peoples tell their own stories of such a war amongst the angels, doubtless echoes of some true event. So they say, sir. Do you travel the moonbeams, as I do?"

"The question's meaningless to me." Elric's attention was focused upon just one of the thousands of Chaos Lords. They lay everywhere now, darkening the hills and plains as far as the horizon. He had recognized certain aspects of the creature well enough to identify him as Arioch, his own patron Duke of Hell.

Count von Bek became curious. "What do you see, Prince Elric?

The albino paused, his mind troubled. There was a mystery to all this which he could not understand and which he was too terrified to want to understand. He yearned with all his being to be elsewhere, anywhere but here; yet his feet were already moving, taking him through the groaning ranks whose huge bodies towered above him, seeking out his patron. "Lord Arioch? Lord Arioch?"

A frail, distant voice. "Ah, sweetest of my slaves. I thought thee dead. Has thou brought me sustenance, darling heart? Sweetmeats for thy lord?"

There was no mistaking Lord Arioch's tone, but the voice had never been weaker. Was Lord Arioch already considering his own paradoxical death?

"I have no blood, no souls for thee today, great Duke." Elric made his way towards a massive figure lying panting across a hillside. "I am as weak as thee."

"Then I love thee not. Begone...." The voice became nothing but fading echoes, even as Elric approached its source. "Go back, Elric. Go back to whence ye came.... It is not thy time.... Thou shouldst not be here.... Beware.... Obey me or I shall...." But the threat was empty and both knew it. Arioch had used all his strength.

"I would gladly obey thee, Duke Arioch." Elric spoke feelingly. "For I have a notion that even an adept in sorcery could not survive long in a world where so much Chaos dwells. But I know not how. I came here by an accident. I thought myself in Xanardwys."

There was a pause, then a painful gasp of words. "This... is... Xanardwys... but not that of thy realm. There is no... hope... here. Go... go... back. There... is... no hope.... This is the very end of Time.... It is cold... so... cold.... Thy destiny... does... not... lie... here...."

"Lord Arioch?" Elric's voice was urgent. "I told thee... I know not how to return."

The massive head lowered, regarding him with the complex eyes of the fly, but no sound came from his sweet, red lips of youth. Duke Arioch's skin was like shifting mercury, roiling upon his body, giving off sparks and auras and sudden bursts of brilliant, multicolored dust, reflecting the invisible fires of hell. And Elric knew that if his patron had manifested himself in all his original glory, not in this sickly form, Elric's very soul would have been consumed by the demon's presence. Duke Arioch was even now gathering his strength to speak again. "Thy sword... has... the... power... to carve a gateway... to... the road home...." The vast mouth opened to drag in whatever atmosphere sustained its monstrous body. Silver teeth rattled like a hundred thousand arrows; the red mouth erupted with heat and stink, sufficient to drive the albino back. Oddly colored wisps of flame poured from the nostrils. The voice was full of weary irony. "Thou art... too... valuable to me, sweet Elric.... Now I need all my allies... even mortals. This battle... must be... our last... against... against the power... of... the... Balance... and those who have... allied themselves... with it... those vile servants of Singularity... who would reduce all the substance of... the multiverse... to one, dull, coherent agony of boredom...."

This speech took the last of his energy. One final gasp, a painful gesture. "Sing the song... the sword's song... sing together... that power will breath thee into... the roads...."

"Lord Arioch, I cannot understand thee. I must know more."

But the huge eyes had grown dull and it seemed some kind of lid had folded over them. Lord Arioch slept, or faded into death. And Elric wondered at the power that could bring low one of the great Chaos Lords. What power could extinguish the life-stuff of invulnerable immortals? Was that the power of the Balance? Or merely the power of Law... which the Lords of Entropy called "The Singularity"? Elric had only a glimmering of the motives and ambitions of those mighty forces.

He turned to find von Bek standing beside him. The man's face was grim and he held his strange instrument in his two hands, as if to defend himself. "What did the brute tell you, Prince Elric?"

Elric had spoken a form of High Melnibonéan, developed through the millennia as a means of intercourse between mortal and demon. "Little that was concrete. I believe we should head for what remains of the city. These weary lords of hell seem to have no interest in it."

Count Renark agreed. The landscape still resounded with the titanic clank of sword against shield and the thunderous descent of an armored body, the smack of great wings and the stink of their breath. The stink was unavoidable, for what they expelled — dust, vapors, showers of fluttering flames and noxious gases of all descriptions — shrouded the whole world. Like mice running amongst the feet of elephants, the two men stumbled through shadows, avoiding the slow, weary movements of the defeated host. All around them the effects of Chaos grew manifest. Ordinary rocks and trees were warping and changing. Overhead the sky was a raging cacophony of lightnings, bellowings, and agitated, brilliantly colored clouds. Yet somehow they reached the fallen walls of Xanardwys. Here corpses were already transforming, taking on something of the shapes of those who had brought this catastrophe with them when they fell through the multiverse, tearing the very fabric of reality as they descended, ruined and defeated.

Elric knew that soon these corpses would become re-animated with the random Chaos energy which, while insufficient to help the Chaos Lords themselves, was more than enough to give a semblance of life to a thing which had been mortal.

Even as von Bek and Elric watched, they saw the body of a young woman liquefy and then reform itself so that it still had something human about it but was now predominantly a mixture of bird and ape.

"Everywhere Chaos comes," said Elric to his companion. "It is always the same. These people died in agony and now they are not even allowed the dignity of death...."

"You're a sentimentalist, sir," Count Renark spoke a little ironically.

"I have no feeling for these folk," Elric assured him with rather too much haste. "I merely mourn the waste of it all." Stepping over metamorphosing bodies and fallen architecture, which also began to alter its shape, the two men reached a small, domed structure of marble and copper, seemingly untouched by the rest of Chaos.

"Some kind of temple, no doubt," said von Bek.

"And almost certainly defended by sorcery," added the albino, "for no other building remains in one place. We had best approach with a little caution."

And he placed a hand up on his runesword, which stirred and murmured and seemed to moan for blood. Von Bek glanced towards the sword and a small shudder passed through his body. Then he led the way towards the temple. Elric wondered if this were some kind of entrance back to his own world. Had that been what Arioch meant? "These are singularly unpleasant manifestations of Chaos," Count von Bek was saying. "This, surely, is Chaos gone sour — all that was virtue turned to vice. I have seen it more than once — in individuals as in civilizations."

"You have traveled much, Count von Bek?"

"It was for many years my profession to wander, as it were, between worlds. I play the Game of Time, sir. As, I presume, do you."

"I play no games, sir. Does your experience tell you if this building marks a route away from this realm and back to my own?"

"I could not quite say, sir. Not knowing your realm, for instance."

"Sorcery protects this place," said the albino, reaching for the hilt of his runesword. But Stormbringer uttered a small warning sound, as if to tell him that it could not be employed against this odd magic. Count von Bek had stepped closer and was inspecting the walls.

"See here, Prince Elric. There is a science at work. Look. Something alien to Chaos, perhaps?" He indicated seams in the surface of the building and, taking out a small folding knife, he scratched at it, revealing metal. "This place has always had a supernatural purpose."

As if the traveler had triggered some mechanism, the dome above them began to spin, a pale blue aura spreading from it and encompassing them before they could retreat. They stood unmoving as a door in the base opened and a human figure regarded them. It was a creature almost as bizarre as any Elric had seen

16

before, with the same style of clothing as von Bek, but with a peaked, grubby white cap on its unruly hair, stubble upon its chin, its eyes bloodshot but sardonically intelligent, a piece of charred root (doubtless some tribal talisman) still smoldering in the corner of his mouth. "Greetings, dear sirs. You seem as much in a pickle over this business as I am. Don't it remind you a bit of Milton, what? 'Cherub and Seraph rolling in the flood, with scattered arms and ensigns'? Paradise lost, indeed, my dear comrades in adversity. And I would guess that is not all we are about to lose.... Will you step inside?"

The eccentric stranger introduced himself as Captain Quelch, a soldier of fortune, who had been in the middle of a successful arms sale when he had found himself falling through space, to arrive within the building. "I have a feeling it's this old fellow's fault, gentlemen."

The interior was simple. It was bathed in a blue light from above and contained no furniture or evidence of ritual. There was a plain geometric design on the floor and colored windows set high near the roof.

The place was filled with children of all ages, gathered around an old man who lay near the center of the temple, on the tiles.

He was clearly dying. He beckoned for Elric to approach. It was as if he, like the lords of Chaos, had been drained of all his life-stuff. Elric knelt down and asked if there were anything he needed, but the old man shook his head. "Only a promise, sir. I am Patrius, High Priest of Donblas the Justice Maker. I was able to save these, of all Xanardwys' population, because they were attending my class. I drew on the properties of this temple to throw a protection around us. But the effort of making such desperate and powerful magic has killed me, I fear. All I wish now is that you take the children to safety. Find a way out of this world, for soon it must collapse into unformed matter, into the primal stuff of Chaos. It is inevitable. There is no hope for this realm, sir. Chaos devours us."

A dark-skinned girl began to weep at this and the old man reached out his hand to comfort her.

"She weeps for her parents," said the old man. "She weeps for what became of them and what they will become. All these children have second sight. I have tutored them in the ways of the multiverse. Take them to the roads, sir. They will survive, I am sure. It is all you need do. Lead them to the roads!"

A silence fell. The old man died.

Elric murmured to von Bek — "Roads? He entrusts me with a task that's meaningless to me."

"Not to me, Prince Elric." Von Bek was looking warily in Captain Quelch's direction. The man had climbed a stone stair and stood peering out of the windows in the direction of the defeated legions of hell. He seemed to be talking to himself in a foreign language.

"You understood the elder? You know a way out of this doomed place?"

"Aye, Prince Elric. I told you. I am an adept. A *jugadero*. I play the Game of Time and roam the roads between the worlds. I sense that you are a comrade — perhaps even more than that —and that you are unconscious of your destiny. It is not my place to reveal anything to you more than what I must — but if you would join with me in the Game of Time, become a *muckhamir*, then you have only to say."

"My interest is in returning to my own sphere and to the woman I love," said Elric simply. He reached out a long-fingered, bone-white hand, on which throbbed a single Actorios, and touched the hair of the sobbing child. It was a gesture which gave the watching von Bek much insight into the character of this moody lord. The girl looked up, her eyes desperate for reassurance, but she found little hope in the ruby orbs of the alien creature who stared down at her, his expression full of loss, of yearning for some impossible ambition. Yet she spoke: "Will you save us, sir?"

"Madam," said the Prince of Ruins, with a small smile and a bow, "I regret that I am in a poor position to save myself, let alone an entire college of tyro seers, but it is in my self-interest that we should all be free of this. That you can be sure of...."

Captain Quelch came down the steps with an awkward swagger and a hearty, if unconvincing, chuckle. "We'll be out of this in no time, little lady, be certain of that."

But it was Elric to whom the young woman still looked and it was to Elric she spoke. "I am called Far-Seeing and First-of-Her-Kind. The former name explains my skills. The latter explains my future and is mysterious to me. You have the means of saving us, sir. That I can see."

"A young witch!" Captain Quelch chuckled again, this time with an odd note, almost of self-reference. "Well, my dear. We are certainly saved, with so much sorcery at our disposal!"

Elric met the eyes of Far-Seeing and was almost shocked by the beauty he saw there. She was, he knew, part of his destiny. But perhaps not yet. Perhaps not ever, if he failed to escape the doom which came relentlessly to Xanardwys. They were in no immediate danger from the Chaos Lords; only from the demons' unconscious influence, which gave foul vitality to the very folk they had killed, transforming them into travesties. Casually, unknowingly, the aristocracy of hell was destroying its own sanctuary, as mortals, equally unknowingly, poison their own wells with their waste. Such brute behavior horrified Elric and made him despair. Perhaps after all, we were mere toys in the hands of mad, immortal beasts? Beasts without conscience or motive.

This was no time for abstract introspection! Even as he looked behind him, Elric saw the walls of the temple begin to shudder, lose substance, and then reform. But those within had nowhere to flee. They heard grunts and howls from outside.

Shambling Chaos creatures pawed at the building, their sensibilities too crude to be challenged by argument, science or sorcery. The revived citizens of Xanardwys now knew only blind need, a horrible hunger to devour any form of flesh. By that means alone could they keep even this faint grip of life and what they had once been. They were driven by the knowledge of utter and everlasting extermination; their souls unjustly damned, mere fodder for the Lords of Hell.

Once, Elric's folk had made a pact with Chaos in all her vital glory, in all her power and magnificent creativity. They had seen only the golden promise of Chaos, not the vile decadence which greed and blind ambition could make of it. Yet, when they had discovered Evil and married that to Chaos, then the true immorality of their actions had become plain to all save themselves. They had lost the will to see beyond their own culture and convictions, their own needs and brute survival. Their decadence was all too evident to the Young Kingdoms and to one sickly inheritor of the Ruby Throne, Elric; who, yearning to know how his great people had turned to cruel and melancholy incest, had left his inheritance in the keeping of his cousin; had left the woman he loved beyond life to seek an answer to his questions.... But, he reflected, instead he had come to Xanardwys to die.

Renark von Bek was running for the steps, his weapon in his hands. Even as he reached the top a creature, flapping on leathery wings in parody of the Chaos Lords, burst through the window. Von Bek threw his weapon to his shoulder. There was a sharp report and the creature screamed, falling backwards with a great, ragged wound in its head. "Elephant shot," called von Bek. "I carry nothing else, these days." Quelch seemed to understand him and approve.

While he could not grasp the nature of the weapon, Elric was grateful for it, for now the door of the temple bulged inward.

He felt a soft hand on his wrist. He looked down to see the girl staring up at him. "Your sword must sing its song," she said. "This I know. Your sword must sing its song — and you must sing with it. You must sing together. It will give us our road." Her eyes were unfocused. She saw into the future, as Arioch had done, or was it the past? She spoke distantly. Elric knew he was in the presence of a great natural psychic — but still her words hardly made sense to him.

"Aye — the sword will be singing, my lady, soon enough," he said as he caressed her hair, longing for his youth, his happiness and his Cymoril. "But I fear you'll not favor the tune Stormbringer plays." Gently he pushed her to go with the children and comfort them. Then his right arm swung like a heavy pendulum and his right gauntlet settled upon the black hilt of his runesword until, with a single, sudden movement, he drew the blade from its scabbard and Stormbringer gave a yelp of glee, like a thirsty hound craving blood.

"These souls are mine, Lord Arioch!"

But he knew that, ironically, he would be stealing a little of his patron's own life-stuff; for that was what animated these Chaos creatures, their bizarre deformities creating an obscene forest of flesh as they pressed through the doorway of the temple. That energy which had already destroyed this realm also gave a semblance of life to the creeping half-things which now confronted Elric and von Bek. Captain Quelch, claiming that he had no weapon, had gone to stand with the children, his arms out in a parody of protection. "Good luck with that elephant gun, old man," he said to Count von Bek, who lifted the weapon to his shoulder, took careful aim, squeezed the trigger and, in his own words, "put a couple of pounds of Purdy's best into the blighters." There was a hideous splash of ichor and soft flesh. Elric stepped away fastidiously as his companion again took aim and again pounded the horrible creatures back from the door. "Though I think it fair to warn you, Prince Elric, that I only have a couple more of these left. After that, it's down to the old Smith and Wesson, I'm afraid." And he tapped the pouch at his belt.

But the weapon was needed elsewhere as, against all the windows high in the walls, there came a rattling of scales and a scratching of claws and von Bek fell back to cover the center while Elric stepped forward, his black runesword moaning with anticipation, pulsing with dark fire, its runes writhing and skipping in the unholy metal, the whole terrible weapon independent within the grip of its wielder, possessed of a profound and sinister life of its own, rising and falling now as the white prince moved against the Chaos creatures, drinking their life-stuff. What remained of their souls passed directly into the deficient body of the Melnibonéan, whose own eyes blazed in that unwholesome glory, whose own lips were drawn back in a wolfish snarl, his body splashed from head to foot with the filthy fluids of his post-human antagonists.

The sword began to utter a great, triumphant dirge as its thirst was satisfied, and Elric howled too, the ancient battle shouts of his people, calling upon the aristocracy of hell, upon its patron demons, and upon Lord Arioch, as the malformed corpses piled themselves higher and higher in the doorway, while von Bek's weapons banged and cracked, defending the windows.

"These things will keep attacking us," called von Bek. "There's no end to them. We must escape. It is our only hope, else we shall be overwhelmed soon enough."

Elric agreed. He leaned, panting, on his blade, regarding his hideous work, his eyes cold with a death-light, his face a martial mask. "I have a distaste for this kind of butchery," he said. "But I know nothing else to do."

"You must take the sword to the center," said a pure, liquid voice. It was the girl, Far-Seeing.

She left the group, pushing past an uncertain Captain Quelch and reaching fearlessly out to the pulsing sword, its alien metal streaming with corrupted blood. "To the center."

Von Bek, Captain Quelch and the other children stared in amazed silence as the girl's hand settled upon that awful blade, drawing it and its wielder through their parting ranks to where the corpse of the old man lay.

"The center lies beneath his heart," said Far-Seeing. "You must pierce his heart and drive the sword beyond his heart. Then the sword will sing and you will sing, too."

"I know nothing of any sword song," said Elric again, but his protest was a ritual one. He found himself trusting the tranquil certainty of the girl, her deft movements, the way she guided him until he stood straddling the peaceful body of the master wizard.

"He is rich with the best of Law," said Far-Seeing. "And it is that stuff which, for a while, will fill your sword and make it work for us, perhaps even against its own interests."

"You know much of my sword, my lady," said Elric, puzzled.

The girl closed her eyes. "I am against the sword and I am of the sword and my name is Swift Thorn." Her voice was a chant, as if another occupied her body. She had no notion of the meaning of the words which issued from her. "I am for the sword and I replace the sword. I am of the sisters. I am of the Just. It is our destiny to turn the ebony to silver, to seek the light, to create justice."

Von Bek leaned forward. Far-Seeing's words seemed to have important meaning to him and yet he was clearly astonished at hearing them at all. He passed his hand before her eyes.

All attention was on her. Even Quelch's face had grown serious, while outside came the sounds of the Chaos creatures preparing for a fresh attack.

Then she was transformed, her face glowing with a pink-gold radiance, bars of silver light streaming from hair that seemed on fire, her rich, dark skin vibrant with supernatural life. "Strike!" she cried. "Strike, Prince Elric. Strike to the heart, to the center! Strike now or our future is forever forbidden us!"

There came a guttural cough from the doorway. They had an impression of a jewelled eye, a wriggling red mouth, and they knew that some rogue Chaos Lord, scenting blood and souls, had determined to taste them for himself.

III.

WALKING BETWEEN THE WORLDS

"STRIKE! O, MY LORD! STRIKE!"

The girl's voice rang out, a pure, golden chord against the cacophony of Chaos, and she guided the black sword's fleshly iron towards the old man's heart.

"Strike, my lord. And sing your song!"

Then she made a movement with her palms and the runesword plunged downwards, plunged into the heart, plunged through sinew and bone and flesh into the very stone beneath and suddenly, through that white alchemy, a pale blue flame began to burn within the blade, gradually turning to pewter and fiery bronze, then to a brilliant, steady, silver.

Von Bek gasped. "The sword of the archangel himself!"

But Elric had no time to ask what he meant for now the transformed runesword burned brighter still, blinding the children who whimpered and fell back before it, making Captain Quelch curse and grumble that he was endangered, while the girl was suddenly gone, leaving only her voice behind, lifted in a song of extraordinary beauty and spiritual purity; a song which seemed to ring from the steel itself; a song so wonderful, speaking of such joys and fulfillment, that Elric felt his heart lifting, even as the Chaos Lord's long, grey tongue flicked at his heels. From somewhere within him all the longing he had known, all the sadness and the grief and the loneliness, all his aspirations and dreams, his times of intense happiness, his loves and his hatreds, his affections and his dislikes, all were voiced in the same music which issued from his throat, as if his whole being had been concentrated into this single song. It was a victory and a plea. It was a celebration and an agony. It was nothing more nor less than the Song of Elric, the song of a single, lonely individual in an uncertain world, the song of a troubled intellect and a generous heart, of the last lord of his people, the brooding prince of ruins, the White Wolf of Melniboné.

And most of all, it was a song of love, of yearning idealism and desperate sadness for the fate of the world.

The silver light blazed brighter still and at its center, where the old man's body had been and where the blade still stood, there now hovered a chalice of finely wrought gold and silver, its rim and base emblazoned with precious stones which themselves emitted powerful rays. Elric, barely able to cling to the sword as the white energy poured through him, heard Count von Bek cry out in recognition. And then the vision was gone. And blackness, fine and silky as a butcher's familiar, spread away in all directions, as if they stood at the very beginning of Time, before the coming of the Light.

Then, as they watched, it seemed that spiders spun gleaming web after web upon that black void, filling it with their argent silk.

They saw shapes emerging, connected by the webs, filling the vacuum, crowding it, enriching it with wonder and color, countless mighty spheres and curving roads and an infinite wealth of experience.

"This," said Renark von Bek, "is what we can make of Chaos. Here is the multiverse; those webs you see are the wide roads that pass between the realms. We call them 'moonbeams' and it is here that creatures trade from world to world and where ships arrive from the Second Ether, bringing cargoes of terrible, exquisite stuffs, not meant for mortal eyes. Here are the infinite realms, all the possibilities, all the best and the worst that can be in God's creation...."

"You do your deity credit, sir," said Elric. "This is too much for me. I doubt my brain is trained enough to accept it all."

Von Bek made a graceful movement of his hand, like an elegant showman.

Forms of every kind blossomed before him, stretching to infinity — nameless colors, flaming and shimmering and glowing, or dull and distant and cold — complex spiderwebs stretching through all dimensions, one connected with another, glinting, quivering and delicate, yet bearing the cargo and traffic of countless millions of realms.

"There are your moonbeams, sir." Von Bek was grinning like an ape and relishing this vast, varied, yet ultimately ordered multiverse, forever fecund, forever reproducing, forever expanding its materials derived from the raw, unreasoning, unpredictable stuff of Chaos, which mighty alchemy made concrete. This was the ultimate actuality, the fundamental reality on which all other realities were based, which most mortals only glimpsed in visions, in dreams, in an echo from deep within. "The webs between the worlds are the great roads we tread to pass from one realm of the multiverse to another."

Spheres blossomed and erupted, reformed and blossomed again. Swirling, half-familiar images reproduced themselves over and over in every possible variety and at every scale. Elric saw worlds in the shape of trees, galaxies like flowers, star systems which had grown together, root and branch, so tangled that they had become one huge, irregular planet; universes which were steely oceans; universes of unstable fire; universes of desolation and cold evil; universes of pulsing color whose beings passed through flames to take benign and holy shapes; universes of gods and angels and devils; universes of vital tranquillity; universes of shame, of outrage, of humiliation and contemplative courtesy; universes of perpetually raging Chaos, of exhausted, sterile Law; all dominated by a sentience which they themselves had spawned. The multiverse had become entirely dependent for its existence on the reasoning powers, the desires and terrors, the courage and moral resolve of its inhabitants. One could no longer exist without the other.

And still a presence could be sensed behind all this: the presence which held in its hand the scales of justice, the Cosmic Balance, forever tilting this way or that, toward Law or toward Chaos, and always stabilized by the struggles of mortal beings and their supernatural counterparts, their unseen, unknown sisters and brothers in all the mysterious realms of the multiverse.

"Have you heard of a Guild of Adepts calling itself 'the Just'?" asked von Bek, still as stone and drinking in this familiar vision, this infinite constituency, as another might kneel upon his native earth. Since his companions did not reply, he continued, "Well, my friends, I am of that persuasion. I trained in Alexandria and Marrakech. I have learned to walk between the realms. I have learned to play the *Zaitjuego*, the Game of Time. Grateful as I am for your wizardry, sir, you should know that your skills draw unconsciously upon all this. You are able to perform certain rituals, describe certain openings through which you summon aid from other realms. You define these allies in terms of unsophisticated, even primitive superstition. You, sir, with all your learning and experience, do little else. But if you come with me and play the great Game of Time, I will show you all the wonders of this multiverse. I will teach you how to explore it and manipulate it and remember it — for without training, without the long years in which one learns the craft of *muckhamir*, the mortal mind cannot grasp and contain all it witnesses."

"I have things to do in my own realm," Elric told him. "I have responsibilities and duties."

"I respect your decision, sir," said von Bek with a bow, "though I regret it. You would have made a noble player in the Game. Yet, however unconsciously, I think you have always played and will continue to play, whether you are aware of it or not."

"Well, sir," said Elric, "I believe you intend to honor me and I thank you. Now I would appreciate it if you would put me on the right road to my realm."

"I'll take you back there myself, sir. It's the least I can do."

Elric would not, as von Bek had predicted, remember the details of his journey between the realms. It would come to seem little more than a vague dream, yet now he had the impression of constant proliferation, of the natural and supernatural worlds blending and becoming a single whole. Monstrous beings prowled empty spaces of their own making. Whole nations and races and worlds experienced their histories in the time it took Elric to put one foot in front of another upon the silver moonbeams, that delicate, complicated lacework of roads.

Shapes grew and decayed, translated and transmogrified, becoming at once profoundly familiar and disturbingly strange. He was aware of passing other travelers upon the silver roads; he was aware of complex societies and unlikely creatures, of communicating with some of them. Walking with a steady, determined gait, von Bek led the albino onward. "Time is not measured as you measure it," the guide sensor explained. "Indeed, it is scarcely measured at all. One rarely requires it as one walks between the worlds."

"But what is this — this multiverse?" Elric shook his head. "It's too much for me, sir. I doubt my brain is trained enough to accept it at all!"

"I can help you. I can take you to the *medersim* of Alexandria or of Cairo, of Marrakech and Malador, there to learn the skills of the adept, to learn all the moves in the great Game of Time."

Again the albino shook his head.

With a shrug von Bek returned his attention to the children. "But what are we to do with these?"

"They'll be safe enough with me, old boy." Captain Quelch spoke from behind them. The floor of the temple alone remained, hovering in space, with the children gathered upon it. At their center now stood Far-Seeing, smiling, her arms extended in a gesture of protection. "We'll find a safe little harbor, my dears."

"Have you power over all this, Count Renark?" Elric asked

"It is within the power of all mortals to manipulate the multiverse, to create reality, to make justice and order out of the raw stuff of Chaos. Yet without Chaos there would be no Creation, and perhaps no Creator. That is the simple truth of all existence, Lord Elric. The promise of immortality. It is possible to affect one's own destiny. That is the hope Chaos offers us." Von Bek kept a wary eye upon Quelch, who seemed aggrieved:

"If you'll forgive me interrupting this philosophical discourse, old sport, I must admit to being concerned for my own safety and future and that of the little children for whom I now have responsibility. You gentlemen have affairs of multiversal magnitude to concern you, but I am the only guardian of these orphans. What are we to do? Where are we to go?" There were tears in Quelch's eyes. His own plight had moved him to some deep emotion.

The girl called Far-Seeing laughed outright at Captain Quelch's protestations. "We need no such guardianship as yours, my lord."

Captain Quelch made a crooked grin and reached towards her.

Whereupon the temple floor vanished and they all stood upon a broad, bright road, stretching through the multicolored multitude of spheres and planes, that great spectrum of unguessable dimensions, staring at Quelch.

"I'll take the children, sir," said Count von Bek. "I have an idea I know where they will be safe and where they can improve their skills without interference."

"What are you suggesting, sir?" Captain Quelch bridled as if accused. "Do you find me insufficiently responsible...?"

"Your motives are suspect my lord." Again Far-Seeing spoke, her pure tones seeming to fill the whole multiverse. "I suspect you want us only that you may eat us."

Elric, baffled by the girl's words, glanced at von Bek, who shrugged in helpless uncertainty. There was a confrontation taking place between the child and the man.

"To eat you, my dear? Ha, ha! I'm old Captain Quelch, not some cannibal troll."

The white road blazed on every side.

Elric felt frail and vulnerable beneath the gaze of that multiplicity of spheres and realms. He could barely keep his sanity in the face of so many sudden changes, so much new knowledge. He thought that Captain Quelch's features twisted, faded a little and then became quite a different shape, with eyes that reminded him of Arioch's. Then, just as von Bek realized the same thing, Elric knew they had been duped. This creature could still change its shape!

A Chaos Lord, no doubt, who had not been as badly wounded as the others, who had scented the life-stuff within the temple and found a way of admittance. Perhaps it was Quelch who had drained the old man of life and had failed to feed on the children only because the girl unconsciously resisted him. The children gathered around her, forming a compact circle. Their eyes glared into those of an insect, into the very face of the Fly. Now Quelch's body shifted and trembled and quaked and cracked and took its true, bizarrely baroque shape, all asymmetrical carapace and coruscating scales, brass feathery wings, the same obscene stink which had filled the Xanardwys Valley; as if he could keep his human shape no longer, must burst back into his true form, hungering for souls, craving every scrap of mortal essence to feed his depleted veins.

"If you seek to escape your Conqueror's vengeance, my lord, you are mistaken," said the girl. "You are already condemned. See what you have become. See what you would feed off to sustain your life. Look upon what you would destroy — upon what you once wished to be. Look upon all this and remember, Lord Demon, that this is what you have turned your back upon. It is not yours. We are not yours. You cannot feed off us. Here we are free and powerful as you. But you never deceived me, for I am called Far-Seeing and First-of-Her-Kind and now I sense my destiny, which is to live my own tale. For it is by our stories that we create the reality of the multiverse and by our faith that we sustain it. Your tale is almost ended, great Lord of Chaos —"

And at this she was surprised by the great beast's bawling mockery, its only remaining weapon against her. It shook with mephitic mirth, its scales clattering and switching. It clutched at a minor triumph.

"It is you who are mistaken, my Lady Far-Seeing. I am not of Chaos! I am Chaos' enemy. I fought well but was caught up with them as they fell. Their master is not my master. I serve the great Singularity, the Harbinger of Final Order, the Original Insect. I am Quelch and I am, foolish girl, *a Lord of Law!* It is my party which would *abolish* Chaos. We fight for complete control of the Cosmic Balance. Nothing less. Those Chaos Engineers, those adventurers, those rebellious rogues and corsairs who have so plagued the Second Ether, I am their nemesis!" The monstrous head turned, almost craftily. "Can you not see how different I am?"

In truth, Elric and von Bek could see only similarity. This Quelch of Law was identical in appearance to Arioch of Chaos. Even their hatreds and ambitions seemed alike.

"It is sometimes impossible to understand the differences between the parties," murmured von Bek to Elric. "They have fought so long they have become almost the same thing. This, I think, is decadence. It is time, I suspect, for the Conjunction." He explained nothing and Elric desired to know no more.

Lord Quelch now towered above them, constantly licking lips glittering with fiery saliva, scratching at his crystalline carapace, his moody, insect eyes searching the reaches of the multiverse, perhaps for allies.

"I can call upon the Authority of the Great Singularity," Lord Quelch boasted. "You are powerless. I must feed. I must continue my work. Now I will eat you."

One reptilian foot stepped forward, then another as he bore down upon the gathered children, while Far-Seeing stared back bravely in an attitude of challenge. Then von Bek and Elric had moved between the monster and its intended prey. Stormbringer still shone with the remaining grey-green light of its white sorcery, still murmured and whispered in Elric's grasp.

Lord Quelch turned his attention upon the albino prince. "You took what was mine. I am a Lord of Law. The old man had what I must have. I must survive. I must continue to exist. The fate of the multiverse depends upon it. What is that to the sacrifice of a few young occultists? Law believes in the power of reason, the measurement and control of all natural forces, the husbandry of our resources. I must continue the fight against Chaos. Once millions gave themselves up in ecstacy to my cause."

"Once, perhaps, your cause was worthy of their sacrifice," said von Bek quietly. "But too much blood has been spilt in this terrible war. Those of you who refuse to speak of reconciliation are little more than brutes and deserve nothing of the rest of us, save our pity and our contempt."

Elric wondered at this exchange. Even when reading the most obscure of his people's grimoires, he could never have imagined witnessing such a confrontation between a mortal and a demigod.

Lord Quelch snarled again. Again he turned his hungry insect's eyes upon his intended prey. "Just one or two, perhaps?"

Neither Elric nor von Bek were required to defend the children. Quelch was cowering before the gaze of Far-Seeing, increasingly frightened, as if he only now understood the power he was confronting. "I am hungry," he said.

"You must look elsewhere for your sustenance, my lord." Far-Seeing and her children still stared directly up into his face, as if challenging him to attack.

But the Lord of Law crept backwards along the moonbeam road. "I would be mortal again," he said. "What you saw was my mortal self. He still exists. Do you know him? Las Cascadas?" It seemed as if he made a pathetic attempt at familiarity, to win them to his cause through sympathy, but Quelch knew he had failed. "We shall destroy Chaos and all who serve her." He glared at Elric and his companion. "The Singularity shall triumph over Entropy. Death will be checked. We shall abolish Death in all his forms. I am Quelch, a great Lord of Law. You must serve me. It is for the Cause...."

Watching him lope away down that long, curving moonbeam road through the multiverse, Elric felt a certain pity for a creature which had abandoned every ideal, every part of its faith, every moral principle, in order to survive for a few more centuries, scavenging off the very souls it claimed to protect.

"What ails that creature, von Bek?"

"They are not immortal but they are almost immortal," said von Bek. "The multiverse does not exist in infinity but in quasi-infinity. These are not deliberate paradoxes. Our great archangels fight for control of the Balance. They represent two perfectly reasonable schools of thought and, indeed, are almost the same in habit and belief. Yet they fight — Chaos against Law, Entropy against Stasis — and these arguments are mirrored in all our mortal histories, our daily lives, and are connected in profound but complex ways. Over all this hangs the Cosmic Balance, tilting this way and that but always restoring itself. A wasteful means of maintaining the multiverse, you might say. I think our role is to find less wasteful ways of achieving the same end, to create Order without losing the creativity and fecundity of Chaos. Soon, according to other adepts I have met, there will be a great Conjunction of the multiversal realms, a moment of maximum stability, and it is at this time that the very nature of reality can be changed."

Elric clapped his hands to his head. "Sir, I beg you! Cease! I stand here, in the middle of some astral realm, about to tread a moonbeam into near-infinity, and every part of me, physical and spiritual, tells me that I must be irredeemably insane."

"No," said Renark von Bek. "What you behold is the ultimate sanity, the ultimate variety, and perhaps the ultimate order. Come, I will take you home."

Von Bek turned to the children and addressed Far-Seeing. "Would you care for a military escort, my lady?"

Her smile was quiet. "I think I have no further use for swords. Not for the moment. But I thank you, sir."

Already she was leading her flock away from them, up the steep curve of the moonbeam and into a haze of blue-flecked light. "I thank you for your song, Prince Elric. For the singing of it you will, in time, be repaid a hundredfold. But I think you will not remember the singing of your song, which brought the Grail to us three, who are, perhaps, its guardians and its beneficiaries. It was the sword which found the Grail and the Grail which led us through. Thank you, sir. You say you are not of the Just, yet I think you are unknowingly of that company. Farewell."

"Where do you go, Far-Seeing?" asked Melniboné's lord.

"I seek a galaxy they call The Rose, whose planets form one mighty garden. I have seen it in a vision. We shall be the first human creatures to settle it, if it will accept us."

"I wish you good fortune, my lady," said Count Renark with a bow.

"And you, sir, as you play the great Game of Time. Good luck to you, also." Then the child turned her back on them and led her weary flock towards its destiny.

"Can you not see the possibilities?" Von Bek still sought to tempt Elric to his Cause. "The variety — every curiosity satisfied — and new ones whetted? Friend Elric, I offer you the quasi-infinity of the multiverse, of the First and Second Ethers, and the thrilling life of a trained *mukhamir*, a player in the great Game."

"I am a poor gambler, sir." As if fearing he would not remember them, Elric drank in the wonders all about him: the crowded, constantly swirling, constantly changing multiverse; realm upon realm of reality, most of which knew only the merest hint of the great order in which they played a tiny, but never insignificant, part. He looked down at the misty stuff beneath his feet, which felt as firm as thrice-tempered Imrryrian steel, and he marvelled at the paradoxes, the conflicts of logic. It was almost impossible for his mind to grasp anything but a hint of what this meant. He understood even so that every action taken in the mortal realms was repeated and echoed in the supernatural and vice versa. Every action of every creature in existence had meaning, significance and consequence.

"I once witnessed a fight between archangels and dragons," von Bek was saying, leading the albino gently down the moonbeam to where it crossed another. "We will go this way."

"How do you know where you are? How are time and distance measured here?" Elric was reduced to almost childlike questions. Now he understood what his grimoires had only ever hinted at, unable or unwilling to describe this super-reality. Yet he could not blame his predecessors for their failures. The multiverse defied description. It could, indeed, only be hinted at. There was no language, no logic, no experience which allowed this terrifying and rapturous reality.

"We travel by other means and other instincts," von Bek assured him. "If you would join us, you will learn how to navigate not merely the First Ether, but also the Second."

"You have agreed, Count Renark, to guide me back to my own realm." Elric was flattered by this strange man's attempts to recruit him.

Von Bek clapped his companion upon the back. "Fair enough." They loped down the moonbeams at a soldier's pace. Elric caught glimpses of worlds, of landscapes, hints of scenes, familiar scents and sounds, completely alien sights, seemingly all at random. For a while he felt his grasp on sanity weakening and, as he walked, the tears streamed down his face. He wept for a loss he could not remember. He wept for the mother he had never known and the father who had refused to know him. He wept for all those who suffered and who would suffer in the useless wars which swept his world and most others. He wept in a mixture of self-pity and a compassion which embraced the multiverse. And then a sense of peace blanketed him.

Stormbringer was still in his hand, unscabbarded. He did not wish to sheathe the blade until the last of that strange Law-light was gone from it. At this moment he understood how the conflict in him between his loyalty to Chaos and his yearning for Law was no simple one and perhaps would never be resolved. Perhaps there was no need to resolve the conflict. Perhaps, however, it could be reconciled.

They walked between the worlds.

They walked for timeless miles, taking this path and then another through the great silver lattice of the moonbeam roads, while everywhere the multiverse blossomed and warped and erupted and glowed, a million worlds in the making, a million realms decaying, and countless billions of mortal souls full of aspiration and despair, and they talked intimately, in low voices, enjoying conversations which only one of them would remember. It seemed sometimes to Elric that he and Count von Bek were the same being, both echoes of some lost original.

And it seemed sometimes that they were free forever of the common bounds of time or space, of pressing human concerns, free to explore the wonderful abstraction of it all, the incredible physicality of this suprareality which they could experience with senses themselves transformed and attuned to the new stimuli.

They became reconciled to the notion that little by little their bodies would fade and their spirits blend with the stuff of the multiverse, to find true immortality as a fragment of legend, a hint of a myth, a mark made upon our everlasting cosmic history, which is perhaps the best that most of us will ever know — to have played a part, no matter how small, in that great game, the glorious Game of Time....

GO ASK ELRIC

BY TAD WILLIAMS

Up From the Skies was rattling the windows. Sammy never played Hendrix at less than concert volume, no matter the hour, whether his parents were home or not. It was one of the things Pogo admired about him.

"Church," Sammy said, and took another hit on the bong. He puffed out his cheeks like a trumpet player, trying to hold in a cough.

"Yeah. Man was God," Pogo said, nodding. "*Is* God." He started to reach for the bong, but decided that too much dope would interfere with the rush when the acid hit.

"You know he'd hate it now," Sammy said. "All this shit. Gerald Ford. Hardly any acid. *Disco.*" He waved his hand in a loose-wristed gesture that summed up and dismissed the entire decade of the Seventies to this halfway point. "He'd be bummed."

"Fuckin' A." Pogo flopped back into the beanbag chair and contemplated the decor of Sammy's room. Roger Dean album covers, an M.C. Escher drawing with self-absorbing chameleons, and three different portraits of Jimi Hendrix were thumbtacked to the walls. The walls behind the pictures and all of the ceiling had been painted black and covered with whirlpools of white stars — the artistic end-product of a weekend's speedathon. The northwest-corner stars were little more than blobs. Sunday afternoon, Pogo remembered, when they started to come down.

It was a cool look, he thought. Like floating in outer space, but with posters.

As he watched, the stars shimmered slightly and the sable field behind them seemed to recede.

"Man! You feeling it?"

Sammy nodded. "Gettin' buzzy." He leafed through his sideways stack of records, motor-coordination already starting to short-circuit. *"Dark Side of the Moon.* Sick of it. *Surrealistic Pillow?* That's pretty trippy. *'Go ask Alice, when she's ten feet tall...',* " he sang in the familar — and tuneless — Key of Sammy. He stared at the cover, then dropped it back and riffled further. "How about *Close to the Edge?"*

"Nah. More Hendrix. *Electric Ladyland."*

Sammy tried to stand up, laughed, and crawled to the turntable. As the needle came down on the wrenching wah-wah of *Voodoo Chile* Pogo smiled a tiny smile. He needed the Hendrix right now. Jimi was a friend, in a way no one he had ever met in real life could be. Jimi was... well, maybe not God exactly, but... something. Something. He raised his eyes to the picture over Sammy's bed. The Man, flanked by his Experience — black Jesus and two pasty thieves, all wearing haloes of frizzy hair. Hendrix was smiling that little half-smile, that *you can't judge me brother until you've been where I've been* smirk. And his eyes... Jimi... he *knew.*

"Whoah," Sammy whispered from somewhere nearby. The room was getting dark, as though the sun was setting, but Pogo felt fairly sure it was still early afternoon, and the summer twilight hours away.

"Yeah." He chuckled, although nothing was funny yet. Hendrix was watching him. "Here comes the rush."

And as the stars reached out for him — *Laughing Sam's Dice,* Pogo thought, *that one's all about stars and acid, Jimi was hip to stars* — he felt himself drifting, like a rudderless boat in a sea of pack ice. Something was pulling at his mind, something he wanted to articulate and share.

"Sammy, check it out. Hendrix, man...." The thought was elusive, but he knew it was important. "Like, the stars, man — he was saying that the stars are playing dice with the world, man, with the whole universe. And that when you take acid, the acid... it takes you out there. Where the dice are rolling."

If Sammy replied, Pogo couldn't hear him. He couldn't see him either. The bright stars were burning before his eyes, and the interstitial blackness was empty beyond imagining. Pogo felt himself sliding forward, pulled as though by slow, slow gravity.

This is some really fucking good shit, he thought. Then he plunged into a silent white bonfire.

⊕

It was black — no, more than black. It was negative black, an absence of

34

illumination so complete that even the memory of light was tainted.

That movie about Jimi's life, Pogo remembered, and was relieved to have at least his own thoughts for company. *That guy said Hendrix was somewhere between sleep and death, and he just chose a different trip — just floated on out. Did that happen to me? Am I dead?*

He had a dim inner vision of himself, Pogo Cashman, lying on Sammy's floor. Would there be ambulance men? Sammy's parents? But Sammy wouldn't even come down for hours, so it might be hours until he noticed his friend was dead.

In a strangely unworried way, Pogo hoped Sammy wouldn't find him during the teeth-grinding, gray, post-trip state. That would bum him out for a long time, and Sammy was a good guy.

Jesus, it was dark. And silent. And empty.

So am I dead? Because if it's gonna be like this for eternity, it's really boring.

What if he had just gone blind and deaf? That would be more in line with the horror-stories about bad acid trips he'd heard. But that would be almost as fucked as being dead. No tunes, no movies. Well, at least he wouldn't have to go to school. Maybe he could learn to play pinball, like in *Tommy.*

As for the first time he seriously contemplated what entertainment pinball might provide to the deaf, dumb and blind, the darkness was effaced by a dim smear of light.

Coming down, he thought with some relief. *Maybe I should have smoked some of that Colombian and cut the rush a little. This shit is pretty intense....*

The light bloomed, shimmered, then stabilized in a pattern of concentric rings. Several moments passed before he recognized what he was seeing. He stood in a long stone corridor, like something out of a Dracula movie — torches in brackets, moss-bearded walls, puddles of water throwing back ghostlight from the torch flames. It was a long tunnel, winding away out of his sight some hundred yards ahead.

What the fuck...?

Pogo looked down and was relieved to find his very own body still attached to him, unchanged since Sammy's room — desert boots, patched Levis, his *Rock and Roll Animal* shirt covering the merest beginning of a hard-won beergut.

So when you die, you get to keep your Lou Reed t-shirt. Mysterious and weird are the ways of God... or whatever they say.

But the longer he stood on this spot, the more restless he felt. Something was calling him — no, not calling, but drawing him, as a cool breeze might summon him to a window on a hot day. Tickling at his thoughts. Something lay ahead of him, down the corridor. Somebody there wanted him — was calling to him. Somebody....

Hendrix. The thought was electrifying. *I was thinking about Jimi. It must be him — like his spirit or something. He's got a message for humankind. And I'll be his messenger.*

He hurried down the corridor, absently noting that, just as in the Dracula movies, his footfalls echoed unpleasantly and small furry things scuttled out of his path, vanishing into the shadows.

If I'm gonna be his messenger, he'll have to teach me how to play guitar like him. So I can make people listen. I'll take Jimi's message all over the world, and I'll jam with Page and Clapton and all those guys.

He entertained a vision of Jeff Beck shaking hair out of his eyes and saying, "Fuckin' 'ell, Pogo, you really make that axe sing — Jimi chose the right cat," as they stood basking in rapturous applause on the stage at Wembley (or one of those other big English places), both of them covered in manly jam-sweat.

Pete Townsend suddenly appeared beside them, his whippet face screwed up with anxiety. "You said you'd get high with me, Pogo, and tell me about Jimi. You promised."

Beck's angry, proprietorial reply was interrupted by a squeak and crunch. Pogo looked down to discover he had trodden on one of the furry scuttlers. In the torchlight he could see it was not a rat, but the bloody mess on his bootsole was not amenable to a more precise identification.

Jeff and Pete and the rest did not return, but that scarcely mattered: Pogo's thoughts were quite taken up with what stood before him.

The black iron door was flush with the wall of the corridor, taller than Pogo and covered with bumpy designs — writhing demons and monsters, he saw when he leaned closer. It was quite solid beneath his hands, and quite immovable. Yet the feeling of being needed pressed him even more strongly, and he had no doubt that its source lay on the other side.

"Anybody in there?" he called, but even with his ear at the keyhole he heard no reply. He stepped back, looking for a crowbar or other heavy instrument (or even better, a spare key), but except for the torches and the scuttlers, which seemed more numerous now, the corridor was empty.

Jimi Hendrix stood on the far side, Pogo felt sure, with a message just for him from beyond the grave. And free guitar lessons thrown in. The situation was weird enough already that a simple locked door couldn't stop him — could it?

"When logic and proportion / have fallen sloppy dead...."

The tune had been running through his head off and on, largely unnoticed, since Sammy had sort-of sung it — but now the words of the old Airplane drug song seemed peculiarly appropriate. Down a hole, like Alice in Wonderland, caught in a bad acid trip. What did Alice do? For a little girl who'd probably never heard of Owsley or Haight-Ashbury — Pogo had the dim idea the original book had been written a long time ago, like around World War One or Two — she'd always seemed to get through all right. Of course she'd had magic cookies and stuff, which made her...

...shrink....

Suddenly, the door was getting bigger. The keyhole was several feet above his head and climbing. At the same time, water was rising around his knees. And the walls were getting farther and farther away....

Holy shit! I'm shrinking! Bitchin'!

If he could stop the process at some point, that was. If not, it might become a bummer of major proportions.

As the crack at the bottom of the door rose up past him — the black iron portal itself now loomed as large as the Chrysler Building — Pogo waded through the puddle beneath it, making a face as the scummy water sloshed around his chest. Once the broad expanse of door was past, he floundered out of the bilge onto a spit of muddy dirt and thought very hard about growing. When it worked, he was almost as surprised as the first time.

Pogo watched his surroundings draw down around him like a film run in reverse, the walls shrinking like a sweater-sleeve washed in hot water. When the process slowed and then halted, he ran his hands over himself to make sure everything had returned to its correct size — he briefly wondered if he could enlarge just selected parts of his body as well, which might help him finally get some chicks — and then looked around.

There was only one torch here, fighting hard against the dank air; the wide room was mostly sunk in shadows. A few clumps of muddy straw lay on the floor; out of them, like Easter eggs in plastic grass nests, peeped skulls and other bits of human bone.

Pogo could tell a bad scene when he saw one. "Whooo," he said respectfully. "Torture chamber. Grim, man."

As if in response, something rattled in the shadows at the far side of the chamber. Pogo squinted, but could see nothing. He slid the torch out of the bracket and moved closer. The feeling of being summoned was stronger than before, although in no way unpleasant. His heart beat faster as he saw a shape against the wall... a human shape. Jimi, the Man himself, the Electric Gypsy — it must be! He had summoned Pogo Cashman across time and space and all kinds of other shit. He had... he had...

He had the wrong color skin, for one thing.

The man hanging in chains against the stone wall was white — not just Caucasian, but without pigment, as white as Casper the Friendly Ghost. Even his long hair was as colorless as milk or new snow. He did wear a strange, rockstar-ish assortment of rags and tatters, but his eyes, staring from darkened sockets, were ruby red. It was not Hendrix at all, Pogo realized. It was...

"...Johnny Winter?"

The pale man blinked. "Arioch. You have come at last."

He didn't *sound* like Johnny Winter, Pogo reflected. The blues guitarist was from Texas, and this guy sounded more like Peter Cushing or one of those other guys in the old Hammer horror movies. But he wasn't speaking English, either, which was the weirdest thing. Pogo could understand him perfectly well, but a part of his brain could hear words that not only weren't English, they didn't even sound human.

"Do not torment me with silence, my lord!" the white-faced man cried. "I am willing to strike a bargain for my freedom. I will happily give you the blood and souls of those who have prisoned me here, for a start."

Pogo goggled, still confused by the dual-language trick.

"Arioch!" The pale man struggled helplessly against his chains, then slumped. "Ah, I see you are in a playful mood. The length of time you took to respond and the bizarre shape you have assumed should have warned me. Please, Lord of the Seven Darks, I have abided by our bargain, even at such times as you have turned it against me. Free me now or leave me to suffer, if you please."

"Ummm," Pogo began. "Uh, I'm not... whoever you think I am. I'm Pogo Cashman. From Reseda, California. And I'm pretty high. Does that make any sense?"

⊕

Elric was beginning to believe that this might not be Arioch after all. Even the Hell-duke's unpredictable humors did not usually extend so far. This strange, shabby creature must then be either some further trick by Elric's tormentors, or a soul come unmoored from its own sphere which had drifted into this one, perhaps because of his summoning. Certainly the fact that Elric could understand the language the stranger called *Pogokhashman* spoke, while knowing simultaneously that it was no human tongue he had ever encountered, showed that something was amiss.

"Whatever you are, do you come to torment oft-tormented Elric? Or, if you are no enemy, can you free me?"

The young man eyed the heavy iron manacles on the albino's wrists and frowned. "Wow, I don't think so, man. Sorry. Bummer."

The meaning was clear, though some of the terms were obscure. "Then find something heavy enough to crush my skull and release me from this misery," breathed the Melnibonéan. "I am rapidly growing weaker, and since apparently I am unable to summon aid, I will be helpless at the hands of one who has not the right to touch the shadow of a Dragon Emperor, much less toy with one for his amusement." And as he thought about Badichar Chon's grinning, gap-toothed face, a red wave of hatred rolled over him; he rocked in his manacles, hissing. "Better I should leave him only my corpse. An empty victory for him, and there is little in this life I will miss."

The stranger stared back at him, more than a bit alarmed. He brushed a none-too-clean hank of hair from his eyes. "You want me to... kill you? Um... is there anything else I could do for you instead? Make you a snack? Get you something to drink?" He looked around as though expecting the Priest-King to have supplied his dungeon with springs of fresh water.

The albino wondered again whether the idiot apparition might not be a further cruelty from his captor, but if it were, it smacked of a subtlety the Chon had not exhibited previously. He struggled to maintain his flagging patience. "If you cannot free me, friend, then leave me to suffer in peace. Thrice-cursed Badichar Chon has taken Stormbringer, and without the strength it gives to me, my own treacherous body will soon accomplish the executioner's work without assistance."

"Storm...?"

"Stormbringer. My dark twin, my pet demon. My sword."

The strange youth nodded. "Got it. Your sword. Y'know, this is pretty weird, this whole set-up. Like a J.R.R. Tolkien calendar or something. Are there hobbits here, too?"

Elric shook his head, surfeited with nonsense. "Go now. One who has sat upon the Dragon Throne prefers to suffer in private. It would be a kindness."

"Would it help if I got this sword for you?"

The albino's laugh was sharp and painful. "Help? Perhaps. But the Chon would be unlikely to give it to you, and the two-score killers of his Topaz Guard might have something to say on the subject of your taking it."

"Hey, everything flows, man. Just try to stay cool."

The youth turned and walked back toward the front of the cell. Elric's dimming sight could not follow him into the shadows there, but he did not hear the door open. Even in his pain and long-simmering fury, he had a moment's pause. Still, whether the stranger was a demon, a hallucination, or truly some hapless traveler lured between the spheres by Elric's desperate summons, the Melnibonéan doubted he would see him again.

⊕

Curiouser and curiouser. Who said that?

Pogo grew back to his normal height on the far side of the door. This was certainly the strangest trip he had ever taken, and it wasn't getting any more normal as it progressed. Still, he had told the pale man he'd fetch his sword, and who knew how long it would be until the acid started to wear off? Better get on it.

He chose a corridor direction from the somewhat limited menu and set off. The stone passageway wound along for quite a distance, featureless but for the occasional torch. Pogo was embarrassed by the meagerness of his own imagination.

Sammy went on a spaceship that time when we did the four-way Windowpane, with all those blue insects flying it and giant donut creatures and everything. 'Course, he reads more science fiction than I do — all those guys with the funny names like Moorcock and Phil Dick. Sounds like they should be writing stroke-books instead.

Still, if his imagination hadn't particularly extended itself in terms of dungeon decor, he was impressed by the relentless real-ness of the experience. The air was unquestionably dank, and what his desert boots were squelching through definitely looked, smelled, and sounded like the foulest of mud. And that Elric guy, with his built-in mime make-up, had been pretty convincing too.

The corridor opened at last into a stairwell, which alleviated the boredom somewhat. Pogo climbed for what seemed no little time. He was still terribly disappointed that it had not been Jimi Hendrix who had summoned him. He had been so *certain*....

A few more steps brought him to a landing which opened out in several directions, and for the first time he could hear sounds other than his own crepe-soled footfalls. He picked one of the arched doorways at random. Within moments he found himself surrounded by people, rather a shocking amount of them — perhaps he had undercredited his own powers of creativity — all bustling about, all dressed like they were trying out for *The Thief of Baghdad* or some other Saturday morning movie of his youth. Shaven-headed, mustachioed men hurried past, bearing rolled carpets on their shoulders. Small groups of women, veiled to a disappointing degree, whispered to each other as they walked close to the walls. In one large room that opened off the hallway, dozens of sweating, flour-covered people seemed to be cooking a fantastically large meal. The din was incredible.

None of them seemed to pay much attention to Pogo. He was not invisible — no one bumped him and several actively avoided him — but nobody allowed themselves more than a swift glance before continuing briskly with whatever task consumed their attention. He forced a few to stop so he could ask them the whereabouts of a magic sword, but they gave him no reply, sliding away like cheerleaders avoiding a drunken loser at a party.

As Pogo walked on, the hallway widened and became more lavishly decorated, the walls scribed with flowing patterns of blossoming trees and flying birds. He saw fewer and fewer people until, after he had walked what he estimated was about twice the distance from his house to Xavier Cugat High School, he found himself in a section of the vast palace — or whatever it was — that was empty. Except for him. And the whispering.

He followed the rustling noise farther down the corridor, peeking into open rooms on either side; all were abandoned and deserted, though they looked as though they were in regular use. At last he found himself at the doorway of a large chamber that *was* in use. It was from here the whispering came.

In the center of a huge, high-roofed room stood a stone dais. Atop the dais, mumbling and hissing amongst themselves, stood half-a-dozen bearded men in robes of dramatic colors and wild design, each garment different, as though the men were in some sort of fashion competition. They were standing in a ragged circle, intently examining a black sword which lay atop the stone like a frozen snake.

All around the dais, facing outward, stood several dozen grim-faced men in gleaming armor studded with brown jewels, each with a long, nasty-looking spear in one hand and a curving, equally nasty-looking sword scabbarded at his waist.

Those must be the guard-guys Elric was talking about, he reasoned. _And that sword those other dudes are looking at must be Stormbanger, or whatever it is.

His good-acid-trip confidence began to pale a little. Surely even if they couldn't really hurt him — it was only a hallucination, after all — getting whacked with all those sharp things could turn the trip into a real bummer, and possibly even make him feel kind of queasy for a couple of days after he came down.

After a moment's consideration, then a single careful thought, he felt himself begin to shrink once more.

It was strange walking along the groove between the tiles and seeing the edges stretch, valley-like, over his head. It was even stranger staring up between the legs of the colossal Topaz Guardsmen, each one now as tall as a the pylons of a bridge.

Be pretty cool to do this right underneath Diana Darwent and her jockette friends. If they were wearing skirts.

He laughed, then froze in place, afraid that he might be heard and noticed. After a moment's reflection — had *he* ever heard a bug laughing? — he hiked on.

Climbing up onto the dais was difficult, but at his present size there were irregularities in the stone that offered good handholds. The robed and bearded men around the sword were talking, and just as with Elric, he could understand them perfectly — or at least their words, although their voices were thunderously loud and rumbled like the bass notes at a Deep Purple concert. Their meaning was a little less clear.

"It is a coagulated form of Etheric Vapor. Were it not for the binding rituals, it would re-transmogrify into Vapor Absolute and evaporate. If we could just try the Splitting Spell once more...."

"Your reasoning is as thin as a viper's skinny bottom, Dalwezzar. Etheric Vapor plays no part here. It is a perfectly ordinary sword which has been drawn through a Multiversal Nexus, and hence its individual monads have... er... turned inside-out. More or less."

"You two! If you would ever look at something without trying to make it fit those hobby-horse ideas of yours, those addle-brained pseudo-certainties you cosset and fondle in your lonely beds as though they were catamites.... Badichar Chon needs *answers*. Bah! Never send a Theoretical Thaumaturge to do a Practical Thaumaturge's job."

As he was listening to this, albeit uncomprehendingly, and pondering how he could get to the sword itself — he was putting aside the "and then what?" question for a little while — something large and dark moved over him like a storm cloud.

"And what is this? Look, Dalwezzar, a homunculus! Now tell me how your Etheric Vapor nonsense explains the breeding of homunculi by the Study Object! Ha! If there were ever a proof that this is a product of a Multiversal Nexus...."

Pogo looked up in shock as he realized that the homo-whatever they were talking about was him. As he wondered whether it was his desert boots — he had told his mom he wanted real hiking boots, but she had told him if he wanted a pair of sixty-dollar Vibram-soled shoes just to stand around the parking lot, he could damn well get a job — a pair of tweezers the size of a lamp-post closed on his shirt and hoisted him into the air.

He was jerked upward to hang before something so full of holes, so covered with hairs like burnt tree-trunks, that for a moment he thought he had been kidnapped by a public campground. Several more moments passed before he could tell what it was —a giant face.

"Quick, get the killing jar!" The fumes from the yawning, snaggle-toothed cave were enough to make Pogo swear off onions for life. "Ah, Dalwezzar, you will cringe in embarrassment when this is published! You will shriek and writhe! 'Etheric Vapor' will be a term of academic scorn for centuries to come!"

"Pig! Of course you want to put it in the killing jar! Were I allowed to boil it alive, you would see that this too is a pure distillation of the Vapor! Give it to me!"

A gristly thing like a giant pink squid reached up and snatched at the tweezers. Pogo felt himself being whipped back and forth through the air as though on a malfunctioning carnival ride. The material of his t-shirt began to shred.

Oh shitshitshit, he thought in a panic. *Small bad! Small bad! Big good!*

The robed and bearded men suddenly began to shrivel around him, as did the room itself, even the serried ranks of Topaz Guards. Within moments, the entire half-dozen Learned Men had disappeared. Or rather, as Pogo realized after a bit, they were still around, but he was sitting on them. He could hear their dying cries from beneath the back pocket of his Levis, and feel their thrashing final moments against his posterior. It was pretty gross, but he couldn't get up, since his head was now wedged against the tiled ceiling.

The Topaz Guards, hardened combat veterans to a man, stared at the sudden appearance of a forty-five-foot tall California teenager in a Lou Reed shirt, then screamed and fled the great chamber. By the time the last spear had clattered to the floor, Pogo was alone.

Something was giving him a distinctly painful sensation in his hindquarters. He reached around behind himself, shuddering as he scraped loose a wet unpleasantness in a robe, and tried to remove the pricking object.

As soon as his fingers touched the black sword, he found himself normal-sized once more, the transition so painfully swift that for some minutes he could only sit, head spinning, among the unwholesome remnants of what had once been Badichar Chon's College of Thaumaturges.

Elric looked up at the sound, a thin yet painful scraping. Something was happening in the darkness near the door of his cell. He felt so weak it was difficult to focus his eyes, let alone muster any interest.

"Uh, hey, are you okay?"

It was the strange young man again. He had appeared out of the darkness as mysteriously as he had vanished. Elric gave a hapless shrug which gently rattled his chains. "I have been happier," he admitted.

"It's stuck halfway under. It'll fit, I just have to pull on it some more. Too bad nobody around here ever heard of a kitty-door. That woulda been perfect."

Having finished this obscure announcement, the stranger turned and headed back toward the front of the cell. There was some kind of stain on the seat of his pants. It looked like blood.

After a further interlude of scraping, the apparition returned. Elric's eyes widened.

"This must be it, right?" He held Stormbringer cradled in his arms. He had clearly never handled a sword.

"By my ancestors, how did you...?" Elric could feel the runeblade's nearness like a cool wind on his face.

"Long story. Look, could you take it? It feels kind of weird. No offense."

Elric's white fingers strained at the hilt, which the strange man obligingly brought near. As his palm closed around it he felt a tiny trickle of energy, but within moments even that ended. Elric still felt very feeble.

"There is something wrong. Perhaps it has been too long since the blade has taken a life. It does not strengthen me the way it should." He twisted his wrist; even with the slight additional strength it had given him, he could not lift it upright. "It is hungry for souls."

The stranger — what had he called himself? Pogokhashman? — squinted suspiciously. "Like, take it to a James Brown concert or something. But don't point it at me, okay? That thing's weirder than shit."

The Melnibonéan slumped. "Of course, my friend. I would not harm you, especially when you have done me such an unexpected good. But without Stormbringer's power, I am still as prisoned as I was before. And if the Chon has been alerted to its theft, he will approach me very carefully; I will not be given an opportunity to blood it." He paused, staring at the black blade. "But if it were hungry for soul-energy — depleted — then I do not understand why it did not try to force me to kill you. Usually it is like an ill-bred mastiff, always lunging at my friends."

Pogokhashman shrugged.

Frustration welled up in Elric. To think that the last scion of his proud people should come to this: slowly starving to death in a cell, prisoner of a low-level satrap, his blade in his hand and yet useless to him!

"Ah, Duke Arioch!" he screamed suddenly. "Fate has played a clever trick on me this time! Why have you not come to gloat? Your love of irony should draw you like a tick to hot blood! Come, Arioch, and enjoy my plight! Come, Chaos Lord!"

And, as the echoes of Elric's voice settled into the damp walls and mired floor, Arioch came.

The light of the torch seemed to bend; the cell darkened but for one spot, where the straw glowed as if afire. In that place the shadows became a buzzing cloud of flies, which drew into a tight spiral, then circled more closely still until they composed a moving tube of glinting, humming darkness. The tube widened, then unfolded, becoming a beautiful young man in a strange suit of red velvet. He wore a cylindrical hat with a wide brim, and his hair was nearly as pale as Elric's own.

"Arioch! You have come after all."

The Hell-duke eyed him with amusement. "Ah, sweet Elric. I find you in yet another dreadful predicament."

Backed against the wall, Pogokhashman was staring, goggle-eyed. "I know you!" he said. "You're that guy in the Rolling Stones. But Sammy said you drowned in your swimming pool." He regarded him a moment longer. "Nice tux."

Arioch turned to survey the stranger, his look of benign indifference unchanged. "Hmmm," he said, his musical voice as langorous as the song of a summer beehive. "Your taste in companions is still inimitably your own, my little Melnibonéan."

Elric felt compelled to defend Pogokhashman, obscure and alien though he might be. "This man has done me a great service. He has returned Stormbringer to me."

"Ah, yes. Stormbringer. Which was taken from you by ambush, yes?" Arioch walked delicately through the muck of the cell-floor as though trying to keep the hems of his flared scarlet pantaloons clean. "Your runeblade was snatched from you by Badichar Chon, I believe the fellow's name is, and subjected to much experimenting by his pet wizards. And now it doesn't... function properly, is that it?" He spoke with the solicitude of Elric's old torturer Doctor Jest sympathizing with a prisoner over some heinous outrage which Jest himself had perpetrated.

"Yes. Yes! It does not overcome my weakness. I cannot break free."

"No doubt that is because of the Splitting Spell... and the Chronophage."

Elric frowned. "I have never heard of either of these things."

"The first is very simple — primitive even." Arioch crossed his legs as a tailor might, and hovered a yard and a half above the cell floor. Across the cell, Pogokhashman's face split in a wide, incredulous grin. "You wielded more powerful magicks yourself when you were but a child princeling. Badichar Chon searched far and wide to fill his College of Thaumaturges... but his is rather a backwater kingdom after all; the candidates were of a somewhat low order. Still, the Splitting Spell they used in an effort to unlock Stormbringer's secrets was crudely effective, although in their ignorance they did not even recognize their success. They managed to partially unbind its energies — just for a moment of course, but in one of those delightful coincidences that are the bane of less flexible sorts than myself, it happened to be just the proper moment: a part of your runeblade's essence was drawn away."

"Drawn away by what? And what of this Chronophage? Some demon or wizard who robbed Stormbringer of its power?"

Arioch smiled and floated higher, until he was far above Elric's head. A tube appeared in his hand, pulled out of some crack in reality, and the Chaos Lord brought its brass mouthpiece to his lips and inhaled. After a moment he blew out a great ring of blue smoke which drifted above his head and hung there.

"It would never do to tell you too much, pretty Elric," he said. "It is antithetical to Chaos to rob individuals of their initiative."

"Games, Duke Arioch, always games. Well, then, I will find Badichar Chon's wizards and discover what they have done with their ham-handed spells."

Arioch grinned around the brass mouthpiece. "You will not have to look far, I think." He inclined his head toward Pogokhashman. Smoke wafted from his nostrils. "Turn around, you."

The stranger stared at Arioch, then slowly pivoted until the stain on his backside came into view.

"If you have any questions for the College of Thaumaturges," chuckled Arioch, "you may ask them now."

"It was... um... an accident," Pogokhashman said quietly.

Elric shook his head. "I understand nothing."

Arioch blew another smoke-ring. "You must find Stormbringer's stolen essence; it will lead you to the Chronophage. That is enough to begin. Farewell, my tragic underling."

"Wait!" The Melnibonéan leaned forward; his chains clanked. "I am still trapped here, too weak to escape...."

"Which will make your adventure all the more *piquant*." Arioch abruptly began to grow transparent, then disappeared. The last of the smoke-rings followed him into oblivion a few seconds later.

"A thousand curses!" Elric howled at the empty air, then let his chin droop to his chest. Even anger sapped him; he could feel his remaining strength sifting away like sand through spread fingers. "Betrayed once more. My family's bargain with Chaos has again proved to be a dubious one."

"Wow, man, sorry." Pogokhashman came forward and awkwardly patted the albino's shoulder. "I'm not too clear on all this, but it sounds like a bummer." He paused for a moment, then dug in his pocket. "Would these help any?"

Elric goggled at the ring of iron keys. "What... where...?"

Pogokhashman shrugged. "One of those Topless Guards dropped 'em. When they all ran away."

"Ran away...?"

"Long story, man, like I told you." The youth began trying the keys in the thick iron lock on Elric's shackles. The third one clicked, then clicked again, and the shackles fell away.

Elric was having trouble encompassing all that had happened to him. He stared at his unlikely savior and shook his head. "I thank you, Pogokashman. If I can ever repay you...."

"I just hope you get your sword fixed. Or whatever that swimming-pool guy was saying."

Elric held Stormbringer before him. It was still his living blade, but its essence was quiet, as though it slept. He shook it experimentally, then turned to his companion. "And somehow, I gather, you have destroyed the College of Thaumaturges — the Chon's wizards?"

The look of embarrassment returned. "Didn't mean to. I kind of sat on them."

Elric shook his head, but did not pursue the matter. "Then I shall have to find some other method of seeking Stormbringer's lost essence. You seem to be full of hidden powers, my friend. Can you help me? I am far in your debt already."

"I don't think so, man. I mean, I'm not even sure how I got here in the first place. We just took some acid, Sammy and me, and I was thinking about... well, anyway, I don't think so."

"Then I must try to solve the riddle." Secretly, Elric felt a little relieved. The ease with which this stranger had defeated the Chon's wizards and handpicked guard and then retrieved Stormbringer made the Melnibonéan feel embarrassingly helpless. His sickly constitution had often placed him in such a position, but he did not hate it any the less for its familiarity. Now, even though his predicament was desperate, at least he would stand or fall by his own devices.

He wracked his mind for a spell that would allow him to trace Stormbringer's stolen essence. This process was made slightly more difficult by his own light-headed weakness, and also by Pogokhashman, who strolled up and down the length of the cell whistling and humming, his feet crunching through the rotted straw. Elric winced, but persevered, and at last a wisp of memory rose from the depths.

"Bring me the torch," he called. His new companion went and drew it from the bracket, then stood in obvious amazement as the albino pushed his long-fingered right hand into the flames.

"What... uh...?"

"*Silence!*" Elric hissed through clenched teeth. When he deemed a long enough moment had passed, he snatched it out again. The pain was dreadful, but it was necessary: between his own feebleness and Stormbringer's strange torpor, Elric needed to strengthen the connection to his sword. He grasped the runeblade's hilt in his raw, agonized hand; ignoring the pain as well as he could, he closed his eyes and felt for the restlessly slumbering core of Stormbringer.

⊕

"In flame and blood our pact was sealed,"

⊕

He intoned in a tongue that had been ancient before Imrryr was raised above the waves. He thought he could perceive a vague stirring in the internal darkness.

⊕

"*With death and souls the bargain fed.*
Now lost to me is my dark friend,
Its secrets all concealed.

⊕

"In blood our pact was first annealed,
With death and souls the bond was made.
Let light now burn away the shade,
Let all now be revealed.

⊕

"By all the ancient lore I wield,
By all who wait at my command,
By my heart's blood and my right hand,
Now let the breach be healed!"

⊕

When he had finished the incantation he paused, listening for something soundless, looking for something that had no shape. In a further shadow, deeper than the blackness behind his eyelids, something was indeed stirring. He felt for it, and sensed its incompleteness: Stormbringer itself was searching for what was lost. The questing *something* that was the remnant of the blade's essence uncoiled and began to draw away from him. He seized at it with his mind, and could feel himself being pulled along.

"Pogokhashman," he croaked, eyes still tightly shut. "Take my hand!"

Something grasped his left hand, even as he felt himself being sucked down through his own thoughts, down a darkly pulsing rabbit-hole into nothingness.

⊕

Curiouser and curiouser, my ass! This is just plain ... weird.

Pogo had grabbed Elric's white hand — not without some trepidation; he had been half-certain the albino was going to push *his* fingers into the torch as well. An instant later, he was off to Wonderland.

Or something. Actually, what made it frightening is that it wasn't really *anything*. The closest comparison Pogo could make was the light-show ride down to Jupiter in *2001*. But that had been a day at the beach compared to this.

Bodiless yet achingly cold, he was tumbling like a meteor through shouting darkness. Streamers of thinly-colored something-or-other flared past him, but although they looked like ragged clouds, he could sense that they were somehow alive, that it was their voices which raged and bellowed in his ears, enraged by his relative warmth and mobility. He could also sense that, if they caught him, they would do things to him he wouldn't like at all.

Pogo closed his eyes, but it made no difference. Either he truly had no body — he couldn't see his hands, his legs, or even his faintly embarrassing suede desert boots — and hence had no eyes, or the place he was, the things that shouted at him, were all behind his eyelids... in his brain.

But if the bits with Elric and the dungeon and that Rolling Stones guy, if they had all been a hallucination too, how come they felt real and this part felt crazy?

Pogo had just decided that it was time to contemplate seriously coming down from this whole trip, and was wondering how to do it, when he popped through a hole in a much more normal-looking sky and tumbled to a halt on an endless, grassy plain. A single hill loomed in the distance; otherwise the place was incredibly boring, like the kind of state park even his parents would drive through without stopping. Elric rose to his knees beside him, clutching Stormbringer in his blistered right hand. The albino looked very real and quite weary.

"We are here, Pogokhashman — wherever 'here' may be."

"You mean you don't know?"

"No more than you. Stormbringer, not I, has led us to this place."

Considering all that had gone before, this new wrinkle worried Pogo rather more than it should have. He found himself longing for the shadowy dungeon, which had begun to feel quite familiar, almost homey. Could you get lost in an acid hallucination, somehow get off the proper track and go permanently astray? He dimly remembered from Cub Scouts that when you were lost in the woods you were supposed to stay in one place until people found you.

But somehow I don't think that Mr. McNulty would've shown up with a compass and a canteen and taken me home even if I'd stayed in the dungeon.

"Bummer," he said aloud, with considerable feeling. "So what do we do now?"

Before Elric could answer, a booming crash knocked them both to the ground, which itself trembled as if in sympathy. A vast globe of light bloomed on the distant hilltop, spreading and reddening.

"Whoah! Nukes?" Pogo asked, but he didn't really want to know.

A moment later there was a rustling in the grass. Pogo looked down, then leaped to his feet with a shout of alarm. The plain was alive with serpents and rodents, hundreds, maybe thousands of them, and they were all moving in a single direction with the speed of complete terror.

"They're runnin' from the bomb on the hill!" he shouted, and searched his memory for nuclear attack information. "Duck and cover!"

Elric, too, was on his feet, shaking loose a cluster of panicked ground-squirrels from his boot. "I do not know what should frighten these creatures so," he called above the whipsaw hissing of the grass, "and do not recognize the word you used, but they are running *toward* the hill."

Pogo turned. The albino was right. The rush of small creatures bent the grass like a heavy wind; there were insects, too, flashing like dull jewels as they flew and hopped — all speeding toward the hill, where the globe of red light still hung, although it seemed to be fading.

"Look, Pogokhashman!" Elric now pointed in the opposite direction. Pogo turned again, frowning. His neck was beginning to hurt.

A dark line had appeared on the far horizon, a moving band of shadow. It was from this that the local fauna were beating such a hasty retreat. As he and

Elric stared, the line moved closer. It was hard to see clearly at such a distance, harder still because of the clouds of dust and chaff thrown up by the fleeing animals. Pogo squinted, and was glad for the concealing dust. What he could see was quite unpleasant.

"It's weird-looking guys in armor. And — Jesus! — there's a whole *shitload* of 'em. Thousands!"

"If they are not a Chaos horde, they are a marvelous imitation," Elric said grimly. "See, they are twisted and malformed."

"Yeah. Ugly, too."

Elric pushed Stormbringer into his belt and clutched Pogo's shoulder. "They are too many to fight, especially with my runeblade in its diminished state. In any case, we are too exposed here, and we know nothing of this world."

"What you're saying is: 'Let's run away,' right? Good idea."

Elric seemed about to try to explain something, but instead turned and began loping toward the hill. Pogo hurried to catch up.

This is just like gym class, he thought, feeling a stitch already beginning to develop in his side. *But at least in gym, you get to wear sneakers. What kind of a stupid acid trip is this, anyway?*

It was difficult to run through the living sea of animals, but Pogo had already accustomed himself in the dungeon to stepping on furry things. Besides, one look back convinced him that the pursuing horde of beast-men would happily do the same to him. Gasping for breath, pumping his elbows with a determination that would have made his PE teacher Mr. Takagawa stare in disbelief, he sprinted toward the solitary hill.

Elric faltered, and Pogo suddenly realized how difficult this must be for a man who until minutes ago had been hanging in chains. He grabbed the albino's elbow — it was astonishing how thin he was beneath his tattered shirt — and half-tugged him along, which made their progress even more agonizingly slow. Pogo was now feeling so frightened that a part of him considered just letting the pale man fall so he could run at full speed.

Once, back in junior high school, he had left Sammy lying with a twisted ankle after they had rung Old Jacobsen's doorbell and run. Sammy got caught, and had to go to the emergency room too. Pogo had never felt good about that.

"C'mon, dude, we're almost there," he panted. The albino struggled on.

Something was echoing in Pogo's ears as they reached the skirts of the hill, a mysterious, almost pleasant buzzing too low and soft to identify. There was something in the way it vibrated in the bones of his skull that he knew he should recognize, but he was too busy dragging Elric and dodging high-speed rodentia to give it proper consideration.

They began to clamber up the slope. The greater number of fleeing animals parted and passed around the hill like a wave around a jetty, but enough accompanied Pogo and Elric to continue to make their progress difficult. One large, white, long-eared creature ran right between Pogo's legs and bounded up the slope ahead of him. He was almost certain it had been carrying a pocket-watch.

Never... had... acid... like this. Even his thoughts were short of breath.

The red glow hovering over the hilltop had almost disappeared. Pogo was trying both to dodge around the few bedraggled trees dotting the slope and to observe the peak when something suddenly hit him hard in the back and toppled him forward.

Before he could do more than register the pain in his skinned palms and note that Elric too was lying on the ground beside him, something very sharp poked the back of his neck.

"The first of the Hell-troop," a voice said. "And not the homeliest of the lot, I'll be bound — although these two still have little to brag about. Do you think the prince will want to see them?"

"No. He is deep in his spells. I say we skewer them here and then finish the barricade."

A certain breathlessness lay beneath the hard words. Despite his own fast-beating heart, Pogo recognized that these men were frightened.

Well, if they're waiting here to fight the Munsters Fan Club, that's not much of a surprise.

"We are not enemies," Elric said hoarsely. "We are not part of the Chaos horde, we are fleeing it."

"They speak!"

"Yeah," Pogo offered, "but we'd probably do it better if we weren't eatin' turf, man."

The pointy thing was withdrawn from his nape; as Pogo clambered slowly to his feet, he identified it as the business end of a very long spear. The man on the other end and his companion looked much like the guards Pogo had met at the Chon's palace, except not so stylishly dressed; they wore ragged chain-mail, dented helmets, and expressions of worried fatigue.

"You are not mortal men," one of their captors said suspiciously.

"We are, whatever you may think of our appearance," Elric assured him. "Now, if you are part of a force that opposes that oncoming horde, and if, as it appears, there is no bargaining with them, then we will fight at your side."

"We will?" Pogo thought the "run away" idea had been much superior.

Elric turned to him. The prospect of a fight appeared to have revived the albino somewhat, although he still seemed dreadfully weak. "We cannot outpace them forever. If we must make a stand, it should be here, with other brave souls."

"Whatever, man." Pogo was again giving serious thought to coming down. The problem was, he couldn't figure out how to do it. Everything seemed rather dreadfully and inescapably real. When he closed his eyes, he could still hear Elric and the soldiers talking.

"If you are truly allies, you are strange-looking ones. We should take you to our lord."

"And who is he?"

"Why, Shemci Ucndrijj, the Gypsy Prince himself!" The man seemed to expect a gasp of startlement from Elric. When he spoke again, he sounded disappointed. "You have not heard of him?"

"I am certain he is a man of great bravery, to command such loyalty," Elric said. "Take us to him, please."

Pogo opened his eyes: it was useless. Same stupid place, same stupid trip. Same ravening army of beast-men moving rapidly across the plain toward them.

The soldiers led them up the hill at a jog. The cries of the oncoming horde echoed louder and louder, and so did the strange, vibratory almost-sounds that Pogo had noticed earlier.

The horde was baying for blood, its voices as discordant as a group of frat boys opening the dozenth keg on a Friday night. Pogo stumbled ahead, growing less and less enchanted with the products of his own imagination every moment. They passed other soldiers, sullen and fearful, who turned to watch them. At last they reached the top of the hill, bare but for a copse of trees and a small group of armored men. At the center, holding in his hand a blade that looked as though it had been carved from a single piece of ivory, stood the Gypsy Prince.

Pogo teetered to a stop, goggle-eyed.

⊕

Elric strode forward from between the men who had captured them, lifting his hands in a gesture of peace as he approached the Gypsy Prince. There was little time to be wasted on mistrust. "We come as allies, sir. I am Elric of Melniboné, and this is Pogokhashman of... of...." He waited for his companion to add the proper details, then noticed that Pogo was no longer within his peripheral vision. He looked down.

The young man had fallen to his knees, his arms extended before him in an attitude of worship. For one so casual in other ways, he seemed quite formal about meeting royalty. Elric felt a moment's ill-humor that he, who had once sat the Dragon Throne itself, had received no such obeisance. Still, hanging in chains was undoubtedly a curb to good first impressions....

"*Jimi!*" shrieked Pogokhashman, and banged his forehead against the ground. "Oh my god, Jimi, it's *you!* I knew it! Man, I *knew* it! Sammy will be *so bummed* he missed this!"

Startled, Elric took a step away, then turned to survey the Gypsy Prince, who seemed just as disconcerted as the albino.

Shemei Uendrijj was a handsome, dark-skinned man no older than Elric. His wild, curly, black hair was restrained by a scarf tied about his forehead, and he was clad in bright but mismatched finery that made him look something like a corsair of the Vilmir Straits — in fact, he dressed much as Elric did. Stranger still, as the dark Gypsy Prince was in some ways a reverse image of the albino, his bone-white sword was a distorted mirror-version of Stormbringer.

Was that why the runesword had drawn them here?

"Your friend seems to know me." Uendrijj's voice was soft and lazy, but with hidden strength; given speech, thought Elric, so might a leopard speak. "But I confess I do not know him. Rise, man!" he called to Pogokhashman. "If I have forgotten you, that is my shame, but there is much to occupy my thoughts today." He turned to Elric, and as his gaze slid down to Stormbringer, his eyes widened a trifle, but in speculation rather than worry. "If you are allies, you are welcome. But I fear you have joined what will surely be the losing side." He smiled despite his gloomy words. Elric could not help liking him.

"We will be proud to fight alongside you, whatever the case," the Melnibonéan replied. He glanced at Pogokhashman, who still looked like someone in a narcotic dream. "I have fought against such a Chaos troop before. They are not unbeatable."

The Gypsy Prince raised an eyebrow. "Ah, but they are merely the outrunners. The Chronophage is our true, and direst, enemy."

Startled, Elric opened his mouth, eager to question Uendrijj, but before he could utter a word a ragged shout came rolling up the hillside from below.

"They come! They *come!*"

The Gypsy Prince turned to Elric. His mustachioed upper lip twitched in another smile. "I sense we might have much to talk about, you and I, but I fear we are about to be interrupted." He lifted his sword. "Ah, Cloudhurler, again we stand in a strange place as death rushes upon us. I should never have allowed my destiny to become entangled with yours."

A strange, low humming came from the white blade, a kind of vibratory music unlike anything Elric had ever heard, although with some inexplicable similarities to Stormbringer's own battle-song. Pogokhashman lifted his head and shook it dreamily, as though the sword spoke to him in some deep manner.

The baying of the horde was growing louder. The dark tide of their armored forms swirled around the base of the hill. "But who or what is this Chronophage?" Elric shouted. "Is it the master of these creatures?"

"No!" Uendrijj beckoned for his soldiers to gather around. "It is a... a force. A blasphemy, a thing that should not be. It devours all in its path. These creatures, these mad Chaos-things, run ahead of it, seizing a last opportunity to smash and rend and murder before the greater destroyer comes."

A small troop of attackers had burst through the barricade at the bottom of the hill and were rushing up the slope. Their leader, whose sagging skin seemed to have melted and run like candle-wax, swung a long iron bar studded with rusting spikes. His cohorts, their faces and limbs also distorted, hopped and limped after him, barking like maddened dogs.

Elric lifted Stormbringer as the beast-men approached. His weakness made it feel very heavy; he was barely able to deflect the melted man's flailing bar. Neither did he feel the runeblade's usual sentience, its familiar battle-lust. As the bar whistled toward him again, Elric ducked under it and jabbed up into his foe's throat. It seemed an effort even to pierce the runneled flesh, but at last the runesword sank in and a shower of watery blood spattered the albino's face. Stormbringer did not drink the creature's soul. It was as lifeless as any old iron blade.

Two of the melted man's companions came shambling forward as Elric struggled to free his blade. A flick of white sheen from one side and the nearer limped on a few steps without a head before crumpling to the ground. Elric darted a quick look, but Uendrijj had already moved away again, carrying his ivory sword to the support of some of his hard-pressed soldiers. The second beast-man moved in more slowly, hefting a huge, crude axe. His mouth seemed to have slipped down to his neck, where it gaped wetly.

The axe rose and began to fall even as Elric at last yanked Stormbringer free. He whirled, knowing he could not bring it up in time to prevent the blow. The beast-man's teeth were bared in a grin of triumph, gleaming from the hole in his throat. A moment later, he shot into the air and vanished. His axe thumped onto the ground.

A giant nearly ten times Elric's height stood where the bar-wielder had been, his vast hand shielding his eyes against the sun's glare.

"Cool," said the giant. "He's really flying!" He winced. "Whoah. Splatcity."

As the albino stared upward in shock, he was nearly beheaded by another member of the horde who ran forward whirling a long, weighted chain. As Elric began to duck, the creature abruptly disappeared beneath the odd, rubbery sole of the giant's boot.

"Pogokhashman...?"

"Yeah," the giant boomed. "Sorry, 'Ric. I got kinda startled at first, and got small. You almost stepped on me." He examined the underside of his boot. "Ick. I woulda looked like *that*."

Elric smiled wearily. "I am too weak to be much amazed, but you are amazing, nevertheless. I begin to get some idea of how you defeated the Chon's guardsmen."

"Yeah. Hang on for a minute, okay?"

As the Melnibonéan watched, Pogokhashman squinted as if in deep concentration, then grew even larger. Stepping carefully over Uendrijj's soldiers, he crossed to the copse of trees, uprooted one of the largest and oldest, then returned to the battle, holding the tree by the roots. Using it as something between a war-club and a broom, within moments he had scraped, slammed, and swept most of the beast-men from the hilltop, tumbling them broken and shrieking back down onto the plain, where the rest of the horde cowered in open astonishment. When Uendrijj and his men had dispatched the few remaining enemies, a relative calm fell over the hill. The horde of beastmen below seemed in no hurry to resume their assault.

"I think I should shrink back again," Pogokhashman said, setting down his tree. A few squirrels crept out of its upper branches and wobbled away in search of a quieter home. "I'm getting kinda dizzy."

The Gypsy Prince turned from posting a fresh set of sentries. "I do not know what the source of your magic is, brave youth, but I think as long as you retain that size, the enemy will hesitate before attacking again."

"I'll try. Maybe if I sit down." Pogokhashman sank to the ground, where he sat crosslegged. Even with his chin resting on his fists, he was still as large as a moderately tall building.

"I have never seen the like." The prince shook his head in admiration.

"We must talk while we have the opportunity, Shemei Uendrijj," Elric said. "There are mysteries to be unraveled on both sides, but you know more of this situation than we do. What is the Chronophage?"

"Rest yourself, friend Elric, for you look ill and tired. I will tell you." Uendrijj looked down at the sea of deformed creatures surrounding their tiny island. "I will make my tale brief."

The Chronophage, he explained hurriedly, was not a living thing but a force of nature — or rather a force of *un*-nature, as his own magicians had told him when it first manifested.

"It was brought about by some unprecedented slippage or sparking of the multiverse. We know not what caused it, but only that it threatens all life, all thought... *everything*. It is a mindless hunger that eats Time itself — where it has passed, nothing remains but swirling, unfathomable emptiness. Even the Lords of Law are helpless against it."

"As must be the Lords of Chaos as well," Elric said thoughtfully. "In his backhanded manner, my patron Arioch has manipulated me into fighting a battle which he cannot himself fight."

"You are a servant of Chaos?" asked Uendrijj, a little startled. "But I have been taught that its underlings are as soulless as the deformed beasts we fight."

"I am an often-unwilling servant." Elric explained his family's age-old pact with Arioch and his kin. "And both Chaos and Law manifest themselves differently in different spheres."

"I myself am not always happy in my service to Law," admitted Uendrijj. "I fear the stultifying world my masters would make should they ever triumph — but they are weak in my world, and to maintain a balance under which mortals can live, their cause must be supported." He continued, explaining that his people had first heard rumors of the Chronophage from the fleeing survivors of worlds where it had already struck, and how at last he, the prince, had been forced to the temple of Law to beg for supernatural aid. There Donblas herself, the living Goddess of Serene Peace, had told him that the Chronophage threatened not just humankind, but the continued existence of the entire multiverse.

"So I retrieved Cloudhurler, my singing sword, from the place where it hung. I had sworn an oath that I would not draw it again, since it had served me treacherously during my pacification of the Merymmen, the Undersea People, leading me to inadvertent murder. But human oaths mean little set against the safety of Time itself."

As he spoke, he looked at gleaming Cloudhurler with an expression Elric knew all too well.

"I chose this deserted site, a world my magicians discovered, as the place to make a stand against the Chronophage. We are few, as you have seen: the rest of my armies are helping my people to flee to another world through portals the wizards have made. Numbers will not avail me here, but I fear that neither will flight save my people if I fail."

"And your sword?" Elric leaned closer. "I was brought here by my own blade, in quest for its lost essence. Like yours, Stormbringer is more than a mere weapon.

Could there be some reason having to do with your sword that we were drawn here?"

The prince frowned. "It is possible. My chief mage, Jazh Jandlar, assisted me in a spell designed to use Cloudhurler to summon supernatural allies — it has served me that way before, though never reliably. But no allies answered my summons."

Elric sat up, pondering. "So you used your blade to call for help. I used my own summoning to call my patron, Duke Arioch of Chaos, to help me regain my lost sword Stormbringer — but at the very moment I did so, my enemy's chief magicians were tampering with the substance of my runeblade. And now we are both here, in this empty place. That makes for too many coincidences. I think I see the manipulation of the Lords of the Higher Planes at work here." He looked up at Pogokhashman, who was trying to scrape something off the sole of his yards-long shoe. "I received an ally — that strange youth. Could it be that *you* received something of the essence of Stormbringer?"

The Gypsy Prince stared at him for a moment, then drew his white blade, which was discolored with various shades of beast-man ichor. "I have noticed a certain... restlessness in it, but the Singing Sword has ever been an unpredictable companion; I thought perhaps it responded to the presence of the Chronophage."

Something had been stirring in the depths of Stormbringer for several moments, as faint but arresting as an almost inaudible cry of pain. Elric lifted his runeblade and gently laid it against Cloudhurler's white length. Suddenly, the sensation of sentience flared; at the same moment, Uendrijj reeled back as if he had been struck.

"By the Root, the Black Cat, and D'Modzho Feltarr!" breathed the prince. "Something is indeed alive in that sword of yours. I felt it as though it clawed at my soul."

The albino did not speak, but gritted his teeth, suppressing a scream. Stormbringer's lost power was flooding back into the blade and into him as well, boiling through his veins like a river of molten metal. Sweat beaded on his brow and his muscles trembled convulsively. Uendrijj lifted a brown, long-fingered hand as though to aid him, but hesitated, not sure what was happening.

As Stormbringer's stolen essence flowed out of the white sword and through his own black blade, Elric felt something of Cloudhurler, and of its master as well. When at last the inrush stopped, his body throbbed with new strength. He boomed out a laugh, startling Uendrijj again.

"O Gypsy Prince, I sense that we have far more in common than just the possession of such weapons! You have been the victim of many of the same cosmic jests that have made *my* life a misery."

Before Uendrijj could reply, the moon-wide face of Pogokhashman suddenly tilted down toward them.

"Hey, those weirdos are coming at us again," the giant boomed. "Think you better get ready, man."

Elric sprang to his feet. Now that his strength had returned, the prospect of combat almost delighted him. He reminded himself that some of the anticipation was Stormbringer's own inhuman battle-glee; it would not do to become careless. "Come, Uendrijj, my more-than-brother! We have work to do!"

The Gypsy Prince unfolded himself more slowly, but with considerable grace. "I am glad to see you looking healthier, friend Elric."

"Here they come," called Pogokhashman, rising to his full, towering height. "God-*damn* they're ugly!"

⊕

Having screwed up their courage to face the giant, the beast-men came on now without stopping, a seemingly unending tide of brutal, unthinking bloodlust. Despite their bravery and steadfastness, Uendrijj's soldiery were dragged down one by one; some of those overcome did not die for hours, and their screams seemed to darken the air like shadows. Before the long afternoon had waned, only Elric, the prince, and the giant youth still stood against the horde.

As the sun fell into the West behind the ceaseless tide of attackers, the albino and the Gypsy Prince fought on, side by side. Elric shouted and roared, siphoning strength from his defeated enemies. Uendrijj chanted, plying his ivory sword with the fierce calm of a warrior monk. The swords gave voice, too, all through the long afternoon, Stormbringer's exultant howl was capped and counterpointed by Cloudhurler's complex, cascading song, as though the two weapons performed some arch-exotic concert piece. For hour upon hour the blades sang and their duochrome flicker scythed the awkward beast-men like a field of flowers... but these flowers had fierce thorns: both Elric and Shemei Uendrijj sustained many small wounds.

Pogokhashman retained his giant's form, although in the few brief glimpses he could snatch, Elric could see that his companion's strength was flagging. The youth stationed himself just far enough away to avoid treading on his allies by accident, but close enough that he could protect them when they were too hard-pressed. Despite great weariness, he flailed about him with splintering tree trunks, shouting *"It's hit deep to center-field! It could be... yes! It's a bye-bye baby!"* and other incomprehensible battle-cries, and causing vast carnage among the Chaos army. But still the horde came on. Their numbers seemed endless.

Uendrijj had stooped to pick up his ivory sword, which had slipped from his blood-slicked hands. Elric stood over him, keeping a small knot of attackers at bay. Stormbringer had drunk deep of the half-souls of beast-men, but it still thirsted. Elric was almost drunk on stolen vitality. If he were to die, it would be laughing, bathed in the gore of his enemies.

"I think you enjoy this," Uendrijj shouted above the din as he straightened up. "I wish I could say the same, but it is only horrible, wearisome slaughter."

Elric brought Stormbringer down in an almost invisibly swift arc, crushing the gray, jackal-eared head of one of their attackers. "War is only life speeding at a faster pace, O Prince!" he cried, although he did not know exactly what he meant. Before he could say more, Pogokhashman's rumbling voice filled the air.

"The sun! Whoah, man — check it out!"

Elric looked up to the far horizon. The sun hung there, a flat red disc, but something huge and dark had moved across its face. But this was no mere eclipse, unless an eclipse had arms.

"*The Chronophage!*" screamed Uendrijj, and drove into the beast-men before him, clearing an opening.

"Lift us up, Pogokhashman," Elric shouted to his companion. The giant youth squelched through the intervening foes and lifted his two allies in a palm the size of a barge.

The many-armed shape on the far horizon was an empty, lightless black that burned at the edges, as though an octopus-shaped hole had been scorched through the substance of reality. As they watched, the tentacles lashed across the sky; where they passed, nothing remained but sucking blackness. Lightning began to flicker all through the firmament.

The beast-men shrieked, a terrible howling that forced Elric to cover his ears, then the whole horde turned and fled down the far side of the hill, swarming and hobbling like scorched ants. They no longer seemed to care whether they destroyed Elric and his allies or not, but were only intent on staying ahead of the all-devouring Chronophage. Within moments the hill was empty but for the giant and the two men in his hand. The Chaos horde had become a fast-diminishing cloud of dust moving toward the eastern horizon.

"The greater enemy is here," said Uendrijj. "True doom is at hand."

⊕

As he gasped, struggling to regain his breath, Pogo decided that Jimi's remark was rather unnecessary. The giant, flaming squid-thing was pretty hard to miss.

But it *wasn't* Jimi, though. Not exactly. It was hard to keep that straight when it looked like you were holding Mister Electric Ladyland himself in your sweaty palm, but this guy was some other Hendrix — a reincarnation or something. Still, it had been very satisfying to discover that he had been right after all: the Man *had* been calling him. Those eyes, that sly smile — however he talked, it was still Jimi.

"So what do we do now?" he asked. He hurt all over and his arm was so tired it trembled. He reflected briefly on how embarrassing it would be to drop the multiverse's greatest guitar player on his head. "There isn't any such thing as 911 in this world, is there? I mean, a SWAT unit would be kinda comforting right now."

Elric and Jimi winced. Pogo felt bad; he'd have to remember how loud his voice was in this giant size. Not that he'd be able to stay this way much longer. His muscles were throbbing like the first day of gym class, and he already had the grandaddy of all hangovers.

"We go forward — probably to die," said Hendrix. It was weird hearing the same Educational TV-type speech that Elric used coming out of Jimi's mouth, but Pogo had finally gotten used to it.

"We have stood together," said Elric. "We will fall together, too."

Pogo made a face. Elric with his strength back was a pretty bitchin' act — more than a little scary, too — but you could carry this King Arthur stuff too far. "How about we win and we *don't* die? I like that idea better."

Elric's blood-flecked smile was painful to see. "It has been a rare pleasure knowing you, Pogokhashman. But what the Lords of the Higher Planes themselves cannot defeat...."

"But I was listening! You said those High Plains dudes brought you guys together on purpose, or something like that! Why would they do that if you couldn't win? Seems like there must be easier ways to get you two rubbed out if that's all they wanted."

Hendrix and Elric exchanged glances. "Perhaps there is something in what he says," Jimi said slowly. "Perhaps...."

"I mean look at you two! You're like... mirror images, kinda. I mean, maybe you're supposed to... I don't know... form a supergroup! Like Blind Faith!" He darted a look at the western horizon. The Chronophage was spreading. Bits of the land itself had begun to disappear, as if they had been gnawed by rats the size of continents.

Elric stared hard at Pogo, then turned to Jimi. "Raise your blade again, Uendrijj," he said.

Jimi hesitated, then lifted the white sword. Elric pushed Stormbringer forward until the tips touched. "I have long since given up any kind of faith, blind or otherwise," the albino said, "but perhaps...."

The place where the swords met began to glow with a deep blue light. As Pogo watched, hypnotized, the blue spread and enveloped both men. Pogo could feel a tingling in his palm where they stood. There was a sudden azure flash, bright as a gas-flame turned up to "infinity." When Pogo could see again, only one figure remained in his hand. It wasn't Elric.

It wasn't Jimi, either.

She was tall and slender and absolutely naked, her skin a beautiful coffee-and-cream color, her hair streaked both black and white. Beneath her long lashes were eyes like golden coins. In her hand she held a slim gray sword.

"*It is not a moment too soon,*" she said in a voice as naturally melodious as birdsong.

Pogo stared, slack-jawed and dry-lipped. He felt big, dumb, and sweaty — and seventy feet tall made for a lot of all three. He had never developed a swifter crush, not even the one on Miss Brinkman, his fifth-grade teacher, who had worn tartan miniskirts. "Um, who... who *are* you?"

"*I am the place where Law and Chaos come together, Pogo Cashman,*" she said, "*— summoned by the joining of two sundered souls. I am that place, that moment, where seeming opposites are reconciled. Wrong needs right to exist; night must have its sibling day. The red queen and the white are in truth inseparable.*" She raised her arms and held the sword over her head. It was oddly unreflective. "*You might call me Harmony — or Memory, or even History. I am that which holds the fabric of Time together — its guardian.*"

"Kind of like Glinda from the Wizard of Oz?"

"*You have played your part. Now I am free to play mine.*" As she spoke, she rose from his hand like a wind-tossed dandelion seed, and hovered. He wanted to look at her body — she was exquisite — but it seemed wrong, like wanting to touch up the Virgin Mary or something. She smiled as if she sensed his thought. Just the sight made his heart skip two beats.

"*Your time here is almost done,*" she said. "*But the multiverse holds many adventures for you... if you only look for them.*"

Abruptly she turned and was gone, flying just like a comic-book heroine toward the hideous smear on the horizon, the gray sword lifted before her. Pogo thought she was unutterably, heartbreakingly beautiful. At the same time, she sort of reminded him of the hood ornament on a Rolls Royce.

He quickly lost sight of her against the pulsating black of the Chronophage, although he felt as though a part of him had gone with her. Deciding there was nothing more he could do, Pogo sat down on the ground, then allowed himself to shrink back to his normal size. He sighed with pleasure as his natural stature returned: it was like taking off the world's tightest pair of shoes.

Something flickered on the horizon. As Pogo stared, still dizzy from changing sizes, the Chronophage writhed; then a searing streak of light moved across one of the tentacles. A soundless howl tremoloed through Pogo, a noiseless vibration that shook his very bones. The great black arm withered and vanished; where it had been, the sun seemed to be growing back.

More streaks of light, like the contrails of science fiction spaceships, ripped across the Chronophage. Pogo found himself back on his feet again and cheering. One by one the other arms shriveled and disappeared, and the blighted sky and earth began to return.

When the arms had all gone, there was a moment when the rest of the Chronophage's black body began to swell, growing larger and larger against the sky until the sun was once more obscured. Pogo's heart pounded. Then a star, a sparkling point of white light, bloomed in the midst of the darkness. An even deeper shuddering ran through Pogo as the Chronophage erupted in great shreds of tearing black. He was shaken so hard that for a moment everything swam away from him, and as he tumbled into oblivion he wondered if in fact the battle had been lost after all.

⊕

When Pogo opened his eyes again, Elric and Jimi were lying on the ground beside him. The sky contained nothing more sinister than a few clouds and the setting sun.

The albino struggled to sit up. Beside him, Jimi was slower to rise. Despite their weariness, a single look at the horizon showed both men that they had triumphed. Elric embraced the dark prince, then turned to Pogo, full of questions, but as the albino reached out a thin white hand to him, Pogo realized he could see the grass through it. Elric saw, too.

"I am being drawn back to my world," he cried. "I sense that you and I are not to remain too long together in the same place, Shemei Uendrijj." He looked at something Pogo could not see, and grinned wolfishly. "Ah, it seems that at least I will be granted my revenge against Badichar Chon. Hah! That is something!" He raised a nearly transparent Stormbringer in salute. "Farewell, Pogokhashman. You have performed a great service, and for more than just me. If we do not meet again, remember you have Elric of Melniboné's undying gratitude!"

"Same to you. Take it easy, dude!" Pogo was genuinely sorry to see the albino go. He stood watching, his eyes suspiciously itchy, as Elric began to fade. "Wait a sec," he said suddenly. "Elric — how do I get back?"

"*Farewell...*" The albino's voice still echoed, but he was gone.

Pogo slumped to the ground, stunned. He was marooned. Like Alice, but down the rabbit-hole forever with no way out. And no ruby slippers.

No, that was Oz again. Anyway, he was stuck.

A hand touched his shoulder.

"I am sorry you have lost your companion, Pogokhashman," Jimi said. "But I would be honored if you would return with me to my world. You will be acclaimed as a hero. There is much that is beautiful there."

"Yeah...?" This was better than nothing, that was for sure. Still, though the necessities of the moment had distracted him, he had not realized until now just how much he had been longing for his true home. "Suppose so. Is there stuff to do?"

"To do?" Uendrijj laughed. "Aye, much and much. There are places to see — the febrile and primitive swamps of Baahyo, the glittering buildings and fragrant alleys of Noj Arleenz and Jhiga-Go. There is music to be heard — I am myself known as something of a harpist, when I am allowed some peace from battle. And women, beautiful women...."

"Women? I *did* think this whole trip was kinda short on chicks...." He remembered the creature called Harmony, and felt a moment of sweetly painful mourning. "And... and would you teach me to play?""Certainly," Uendrijj said, smiling. "Come, take my hand! You shall be my companion, then, Pogokhashman — *the whole multiverse shall know your name....*"

But as Pogo's hand closed about his, Jimi, too, became faint, passing into translucency. The plain on which they stood became dim as well. For a moment Pogo suspected that he and Jimi were merely undergoing more magical travel, but his last diminishing sight showed him that the Gypsy Prince still gripped the hand of *another* Pogo, who was disappearing along with him as the world fell away....

⊕

"Man! That was some *intense* acid, huh?" Sammy was bouncing around the room like a hamster whose wheel was out for repairs. "You wouldn't believe what happened to me while you were lying there all out of it! I looked out the window and the mailman looked like some kind of monster! Unbelievable! And the street was, like, *bubbling....*"

Pogo leaned back in the beanbag nursing a joint. Sammy's non-stop monologue was as reassuring as the sound of night traffic to a city-dweller.

"Sounds good, man," he drawled, and stared up from the spots of blood on the soles of his desert boots to the poster of Jimi Hendrix on the wall. Was it really true, then? That somewhere in the multiverse an albino guy with a magic sword was remembering his time with Pogo? And, even weirder and cooler, that somewhere else in the multiverse, Jimi — the Man himself — and his new buddy Pogo Cashman were having adventures together?

Sammy put *Surrealistic Pillow* on the stereo, skipping as always to his favorite song. *"One pill makes you larger…"* he tunelessly crooned, anticipating the actual beginning of the vocals by several seconds — something that usually drove Pogo mildly crazy.

"Sounds good, man," Pogo said, smiling.

Sammy wandered over to take the joint from him, then stood contemplating the poster of Jimi with his white guitar. "I wonder what 'Stratocaster' means, anyway?" Sammy said hoarsely, his lungs full of smoke.

" 'Cloudhurler'."

"Cloudhurler?" Sammy stared at him, then belched out a smoky laugh. "Man, you're too high. Naw, it must have something to do with, like… broadcasting. You know, radio or something."

"S'pose so," said Pogo. "Throw me those potato chips, will you?"

"Here." Sammy dropped the bag into his lap. "Feed your head." He chuckled. *White Rabbit* was building toward its chugging climax. " 'Feed your head' — get it?"

"Yeah," said Pogo. "Got it."

NOW CRACKS A NOBLE HEART

BY DAVID M. HONIGSBERG

The sun was setting when he reached the place, a slender figure clad in black armor astride a jet-black charger which stamped impatiently, restlessly. The scene before him was similar to others he could easily call to mind, the remembrance of battles he had fought or instigated.

He swept a strand of silken white hair from his eyes as he spurred his mount into the vale. The beast picked its way through the masses of wounded and dying knights, their limbs broken or severed, their bodies lying at impossible angles, their cries ringing in the ears of the albino prince who rode through their ranks. His crimson eyes searched the terrain, hoping that in the last light of day he would find the man he had ridden to see, a man he feared he was too late to save.

The runesword at his side murmured in frustration, sensing the flickering souls of so many nearby. Yet Elric, though weakened by his long ride, did not draw the blade, though he knew it could provide him with the nourishment he so needed. No, there were other matters to tend to. He rode onward, downward, noting that the bodies of the fallen grew more numerous with every step. Still there was no movement, nothing he could see nor sense which would tell him if his journey were for naught.

A breeze stirred the air and the banner of Medraut fluttered sluggishly, its cloth flecked with mud and blood, its edges tattered, torn. Elric knew that he would find Medraut and his uncle, the king, near that standard. He turned his horse's head and rode towards the beacon.

Within moments he could see both prince and king, pretender and monarch. Medraut lay gasping for breath, transfixed by his enemy's spear, blood still slowly trickling from the wound. Arthur sat no more than forty yards from his nephew, propped against a pile of saddlebags. Elric could see that he fared no better than did Medraut. His helm was split, his skull dented. As Elric approached, the last denizen of the Dreaming City of Imrryr nearing the last denizens of Camelot, Arthur stirred. Speaking to Bedwyr, who stood beside him, in words too low for Elric to hear, he handed the man his sword. As Bedwyr took his leave, Arthur turned his attention to Elric.

"You are too late, I fear," the king informed him, his voice soft, yet full of power. "My time is come. There is nothing more to do here, my friend. Would that your quest had been successful. We might not be sharing this doleful sight."

"I would that it were so, too, Arthur." Elric dismounted and knelt beside the fallen king. "I was able to hold Morgaine's sorceries at bay but was unable to find Myrddin, though I called upon all the forces which I command. The powers that bind him are stronger than I imagined. He is beyond my reach and only he could have saved this day."

"You must not feel responsible, Elric. If Morgaine had not sent the viper to the field of parley, the good men you see about you," he gestured weakly, encompassing the entire field of Camlann, "would still be hale and hearty, feasting in the great hall at Camelot or at rest with their lady-loves. Now, there is nothing." His voice trailed off as he gazed into the dusk.

A coughing sound caught Elric's attention. "I might have been incapable of preventing this, but I can certainly help to finish it," he told the fallen king. He drew the runesword from its scabbard as he rose and moved towards the sound, towards Medraut's banner. Bedwyr passed him, empty-handed, making his way back to Arthur's side. Elric watched for a moment as he bent down to talk to the king. The wind shifted, barely carrying their words to him.

"I saw nothing but the wind upon the waters," Bedwyr was saying.

"Then you have not done as I asked," Arthur replied. "Go you again, and do my bidding. Throw it in and return to me."

Bedwyr stood and walked away from Arthur, a troubled look upon his face. Elric knew that something was happening to which he was not a party, but resumed his course to Medraut's banner.

The usurper was close to death, his face almost as pale as Elric's. The albino stood before him, his scarlet eyes glowing in the pale light of a rising moon, Stormbringer thrumming hungrily in his hand. Medraut looked up, eyes wide as he recognized the apparition.

"Ah, Death. You have come for me, have you not? Come to take my soul to your master."

"Come for you, aye," Elric responded. "But the death I bring is far worse than you can conceive. There is no tomorrow for your soul, I fear."

Medraut laughed, his arrogance reasserting itself in the face of disaster. "You have no power over me. This day shall live forever, for this is the day that the great King Arthur fell at the hands of his nephew; the day that a dream died."

"You underestimate his worth, I think," Elric patiently spoke. "That this day, this field, this Camlann, will be spoken of forever, it is true. But while your uncle will live in the hopeful dreams of many, your name will be cursed more than you can possibly comprehend. If that is the fame that you desire, then you have found it."

"Spare me your soliloquies, fiend." Medraut spat weakly towards Elric's feet. "The forces I serve are more powerful and more fearsome than any you could know."

Elric smiled at the brave words. "You know not of what you speak, I am afraid. Until you know what it is to serve a Lord of Chaos, your words are boastful emptiness. If you have not felt the power of the runesword course through your body, you cannot speak with wisdom of things such as fear. You may serve dark lords. I do not doubt this. Yet their power fades to nothing when compared to the forces I can control. You have done nothing but to destroy that which was good and decent here. Your punishment shall be swift, and just."

With these words he plunged the runesword into the prince's body, next to the wound which Arthur had dealt him, and watched in mute satisfaction as Medraut realized that his very soul was being pulled into the black blade.

Elric felt Medraut's vitality pass into him, strengthening him, making it possible for him to voice the runes of an ancient spell which opened the gates between the universes and which called forth surcease for the king.

The albino returned his blade to its scabbard, sensing its reluctance to be sheathed, and returned to Arthur's side. The king was feverish and murmured to himself.

"Where is Bedwyr?" Elric asked, and Arthur turned in the direction of the voice.

The king's voice was weak as he answered. "I have sent him to do something you could not, for you would not be able to handle Caliburn. He must return it to its source. Thrice I have bade him do this, and twice he has failed me. I pray that he has done it, for I can feel my life slipping away with each breath."

"You will not die, Arthur. You will sleep, a dreamless sleep, awaiting the day you are called again." He stood and looked towards a glimmer in the darkness. "Even now your conveyance approaches, a barge which plows the multiverse, here to take you to Tanelorn."

"Your words confuse me, Elric; you speak of things that I cannot fathom, things that Myrddin tried to teach me, but which I could not grasp. Forgive me."

Elric said nothing, but watched as the shimmering barge settled beside the fallen king. Three willowy women, their features very much like his own Melnibonéan countenance, gently lifted Arthur and placed him upon a bed of soft pillows. The magical transport then set off, to sail the seas of time and space until it reached the peace of Tanelorn.

Panting with exertion, Bedwyr reached Elric's side almost as the king's barge was out of sight. Elric did not turn to face the man but asked, "Did you do it?"

Tears in his eyes, Bedwyr nodded. "I threw the sword as far as I could; before it touched the river, a woman's hand reached out to pluck it from the air. She held it aloft in triumph for a moment before pulling it down beneath the waves. I shall never forget the sight." He looked after the barge. "Nor this. Where is it taking him?"

"To a place you call Avallach," Elric answered as the barge twinkled out of sight. "To a rest I fear I shall never know."

The two men stood together in silence for a moment, each lost in his own thoughts. Then, with no more than a nod of farewell, Elric mounted his horse and rode away from the death in Camlann, back to the land of the living, leaving Bedwyr in the twilight.

A DEVIL UNKNOWN

BY ROLAND J. GREEN AND FRIEDA A. MURRAY

"Your wine is excellent, Messer Leonardo."

The voice was cultured, even a nobleman's. The accent hinted of a man who had learned Italian well, but only as an adult.

The hand clasping the hammered silver cup was bone-white, as was the face above it. It seemed balanced on the edge of despair, that face; only the blood-red eyes gave it life. It was the face of one who had sought answers to questions better left unasked.

The artist, sketching the soldier he had invited to his studio, thought he had never seen a more perfect model for the Archangel on the verge of his fall.

"I would be a poor host otherwise, messire."

"Nonetheless, this is a vintage equal to any in Melniboné. Not to be mistaken for one, but quite equal."

Again that name. It seemed this well-bred soldier of such astonishing appearance expected Leonardo to know it and to be flattered by the comparison. Would he take ignorance as an insult, the artist wondered, or would he answer more questions?

Eh, well, sitting is tiring work. It loosens the tongue.

"And where lies your homeland, this Melniboné?" the artist asked.

⊕

Elric, the hereditary emperor of ten-thousand-year-old Melniboné, considered the question. How to explain to this artist, be he never so courteous, that Elric's

71

homeland lay on an entirely different plane? The emperor's magic had been equal to rendering his speech into the local tongue and the local speech into the common tongue of the Young Kingdoms of his own plane, but there was no spell to put knowledge or new ideas in a man's mind. If there were, many tasks both common and imperial would be easier.

"You would not find it on your maps," Elric replied. "Certainly no ship of your people could reach it."

"It lies beyond the limits of the Portuguese voyages?"

Elric presumed that the Portuguese were another, seafaring people. He hoped that their tongue was similar to that of this city, Milan, or that he would not need to speak with them. He could not use too many spells merely to make himself understood, without weakening himself for other purposes.

"Then I win my wager with Messer Beppo," the artist said. "He swore you were Circassian."

"By all means, let him think that if he wishes." Elric's voice held a warning note that he hoped would not be taken for anger. He hoped to return to Melniboné long before he needed to supply a detailed account of his origins to anyone in Milan.

"How did you get here, then?"

"By sorcery, messire."

Elric had been about to return to Melniboné and resume (or possibly retake, if Cousin Yyrkoon proved obdurate in giving up his regency) the Ruby Throne. To do that, he needed an ample supply of the drugs that maintained his strength.

Climbing a hill in Hrolmar known locally as Medicine Mount, he had discovered an abundance of the necessary herbs. He had also discovered a multiversal gate. It was new and weak, wandering about within the confines of a mountain meadow some five hundred paces broad, barely detectable even by Elric's sorcery-attuned senses.

Indeed, he would have ignored the gate — save that something on the other side had attracted the attention of Stormbringer. The black sword neither fully awoke nor remained quiet. But Elric had remained aware of it, rather as a New Kingdom warrior might be aware of fleas under his armor. This turned curiosity to annoyance. To put an end to that annoyance, Elric had stepped through the gate.

He had found himself on the outskirts of an unknown city. The strange sights and sounds, the need to orient himself, and finally hunger had distracted him from tracking to its source what had touched Stormbringer.

He had begun to contemplate going beyond the walls or spending the night on the streets, neither of which pleased him. For a city hardly as civilized as many in the New Kingdoms, Milan seemed unperturbed by Elric's appearance. Nonetheless, he had received sufficient stares to know that sooner or later he would be reported to the rulers, the protectors of the public peace, or the local criminals. The end of that would be the slaughter of innocents and flight from Milan with the matter of the call to Stormbringer unresolved.

Then an artist had offered him supper in return for the privilege of sketching him. Elric could detect neither power nor treachery in the man, and had seen no reason to refuse. Nor could he find fault with the artist's hospitality.

"What sort of sorcery is needed for this journey?" the artist asked. His tone mingled curiosity and skepticism. "Do you have flying garters for long distances, or can you merely wish yourself from place to place?"

"After a fashion," Elric replied. Stormbringer could transport him — if he fed it enough. He would prefer if the artist's curiosity did not extend to the black sword. The artist appeared to be robust, if not a seasoned fighter; a quarrel might end with Stormbringer drawn and feeding.

Poor repayment for anyone's hospitality.

⊕

The artist's fingers continued to work steadily, but the pace of his thoughts increased. He had had much success in irrigating the Lombardy plains, and had gained the name of sorcerer for the mechanical toys he had made at two courts. But all the lore of alchemy had not enabled him to manufacture gold, and he had to walk or ride like anyone else when he wished to go somewhere.

The soldier's words carried conviction. Even were he no more than a gifted storyteller, he might be used to ferret out rivals for the regent's favor. That was a necessary task for any artist with a place at court; he could no more survive without friendly and well-placed ears than without charcoal or paint. And if there were any chance of this tale being true....

"You may sleep in my studio tonight, if you wish," offered the artist. "Or my steward can direct you to an inn, at my expense."

"Your studio will serve," replied the soldier. Now his voice held weariness, but it did not lose its magisterial dignity. "It is quiet."

And indeed, until the artist rose to go, not another word was said.

⊕

Behind him, Elric heard the horns blow for the closing of the city gates. As

73

his own destination lay ahead, he merely noted that returning before dawn, without attracting undesired attention, might be difficult. But if tonight he found what he sought, he might not need to return to Milan at all.

Two meals, a night's sleep on a comfortable pallet, and a generous dose of strengthening drugs had left Elric fit to resume his search for that which had awakened Stormbringer. The day was clear, and in the harsh winter sunlight Milan had lost any exotic aspects it might have possessed. The mountains on the northern horizon retained theirs; Elric had small experience with snow-crowned peaks.

Stormbringer was a less-than-perfect guide, but Elric could tell when he was drawing away from or coming closer to the source of the black sword's annoyance and his. It was near twilight when he reached a venerable building. It was half-ruined, although not far from it rose new buildings in various stages of construction. The door was sound and locked, but the albino half-drew Stormbringer and bade it open the door.

A moment later he was staring at five men in red robes and face-concealing hoods, gathered around a brazier.

"O mighty Heramael —" began one.

"Hush!" said another, then continued. "Emperor Lucifer —"

Elric, realizing that he had interrupted a rite of summoning, began to feel amused. With a slight smile, he asked, "What am I expected to do for you?"

After a brief pause, the last man who had spoken found his voice. "Do you accept the pact?"

"Speak on," Elric replied.

"I conjure you, Lucifer, by Aqua, Ariel, Arioch, Delphe, Majon, Mathom, Tagle, that you strengthen and restore to full health of body and mind Gian Galeazzo Sforza, the most puissant Duke of Milan! And especially I conjure you, who brought lechery into the world, that you bring fire to his loins that he may beget healthy sons upon Isabella, his wife. Restore his fiery humors! Strengthen his blood!"

Elric felt an instant of ironic pity that such a request should be made of him, whose own blood was so weak that his father had called him accursed, and who needed drugs and sorcery to maintain the strength for common tasks. It could not be this pitiful invocation that had created a multiversal gate, then reached through it with enough strength to awaken Stormbringer.

The sorcerer-emperor considered simply letting the black sword take them all. But that would serve the Lords of Chaos without thought or limit. Not even Elric's patron, Duke Arioch of Hell, had that kind of service from him.

"Bring this duke to me," ordered Elric. "Now go — if you would save your souls!"

He laid his hand on the runesword's hilt, and the men departed with more haste than dignity.

The sorcerer glanced around the site of the late rite. He saw and sensed nothing: no rune of power, no geomantic figure capable of confining a Lord of Chaos. Ink, parchment, and the brazier remained, nothing more. Yet Chaos had been summoned.

And why had he given that last order? the emperor asked himself. Did he desire to see a counterpart on this plane, another sickly ruler?

Footsteps cautiously approached the door. Elric moved out of the direct line of sight but took no other precaution.

The man who entered was surely one of those who had just fled, though he was now dressed in breeches and a leather jerkin. He was in every respect unremarkable. Even the dagger at his belt might have been purchased from any one of a hundred shops in the Street of the Armorers.

Under Elric's red-eyed gaze, the man spoke freely.

"I know not what you are, man or demon, sorcerer or mountebank," the man said. "But by any power above or below, if you keep bargains, I would make one with you."

Elric smiled. "You should add 'beyond,'" he said. "What do you want?"

"Those others, they want to heal the duke," the man said. His voice was as devoid of character as everything else about him. "*Perbacco!* Let the *cochon* die! You can do that."

"How do you know?" Elric asked.

"Anyone can kill. Demons or sorcerers can kill easily."

"You know that much. But why should I kill for you?"

The man shrugged. "Whatever you are, you won't be staying in Milan. Why not gain — whatever it is you want — before you leave?"

"Anyone can kill. Must they then leave the city?"

"Yes." The tone lacked conviction.

"If you plan to stay in the city," Elric asked, "what are you doing here?" He did not trouble to hide his doubt. Expecting this man to lead him to the summoning of Chaos was asking much.

"Doctors, what do they know? They tried to balance the *caccastechi's* humors! All Milan knows he hasn't enough fire to kindle his own tallow."

"If you want to escape *my* humor, you will tell me precisely what you were trying to do. Now."

"They tried to balance his humors," the man repeated. "Called on the spirits to build up his fire and water. Me, I just told the spirits to come and do as they pleased. Forget about balance."

"You stupid, stupid man," the albino prince said softly.

So, it was as simple as that. Someone had tried to counter an orderly if ineffective spell, and had opened a door to the Lords of Chaos. Someone who probably did not on most occasions have at his command magic enough to curl a single hair of his scanty beard!

The man grew sullen. "If you think you can do better —" he growled.

"I will do better," promised Elric. A perverse desire to help his counterpart was growing in him. "What is it to you whether this duke lives or dies?"

"What is it to *you?*" the man growled.

"If you want to bargain —" Elric began.

"If my own man is duke, it's better for me."

Elric felt weary. Another petty intrigue, worthy of a sailor's tavern by the harbor of some New Kingdom town. His sympathy for the unknown but sickly duke grew.

"Bring this duke to me, and you shall see what I can do."

⊕

"So this Elric spoke to none all day," Leonardo said. "But by the time the gates shut, he was at the old chapel of Sanct' Spiritu."

The man addressed, a handsome lord with a pale face and dark hair, shrugged. "So he had no trouble finding the haunts of those intriguing *puttini*. Was a rite enacted last night?"

"So I was told, but he frightened everyone away."

Lodovico Sforza, the Regent of Milan, laughed. "Come, messire, do you really believe that the owner of a face like that —" he indicated the sketch the artist had shown him "— is a saint in disguise, come to cleanse *our* temples?"

The lord stared at the sketch again. "It's unique. It demands white marble, if you please. I'll not balk at rubies for the eyes. That should impress Ferrara, or even, God willing, the Florentines."

"A thousand thanks, Your Highness, and I will begin at once." Leonardo did not care to promise a date of completion at this time. He had less experience with marble than with other media. But he had promised Il Moro that, no matter what the art, he could practice it as well as it could be practiced, and he had no wish to annoy his patron with petty details.

"There is more, however," Leonardo continued. "Afterward, Messer Elric spoke with one calling himself Giovanni di Tuscania. A *ribaldo* who trades in secrets, Your Highness, probably for more than one master. My servant was certain, however, that Elric desired to see Duke Gian in person."

"Perhaps he should," Lodovico Sforza replied. Leonardo felt his mouth open, but the Regent continued impatiently, "Come, messire. If this man is here for any *malatesta*" — the artist winced at the clumsy pun — "it isn't one requiring concealment. Not with that face. Why shouldn't the duke face down one plot and free up men to deal with the nine-and-forty others infesting Milan alone? To say nothing of all the rest of Italy down to Sicily! Finesse is hardly required, this time."

Indeed not, Leonardo thought. *It would take but one accident to make you Duke of Milan.*

He bowed, and took a formal leave.

⊕

"It is true, my lord," Giovanni di Tuscania said. "We are to perform the rite tonight. The duke will be there."

"Impossible," grumbled the aggressively handsome lord to whom he was reporting. "Il Moro will never risk his nephew's safety for such a trifle. It has to be some kind of trap."

"Which it should be possible to turn on Il Moro," Giovanni replied. His voice was brisk and firm, so unlike his previous manner of speaking that some might have suspected sorcery in the change.

The lord, familiar with this and many other artifices, merely considered it one more barrier to the discovery of his presence in Milan. It would not readily occur to most that the Duke of Orléans, cousin to the King of France, might be secretly in the city he had claimed.

Giovanni continued. "Were Lodovico known to have been associated with black sorcery, and if Gian Galeazzo were to die —"

"Not even the Pope would uphold him," the French duke interrupted. He laughed. "Imagine, the Pope favoring our cause without a fortune in bribes! With Il Moro discredited, and no other Sforza heir, Milan would face chaos, a return to the Viscontis, or...."

"Indeed, my lord."

Louis d'Orléans' smile widened. If Milan fell into his hand without fighting, its wealth would be intact; likewise its *condottiere*. The Italian sell-swords were a mixed blessing, but the wealth could hire enough Swiss and Germans to put the throne of France itself within his reach.

⊕

Elric spent the day strolling about, studying the Milanese from a safe distance. The day was overcast and disagreeably chilly for one of his thin blood, but it provided a good excuse to go cloaked and hooded. He stopped for a midday meal in a small inn, where no one gave his shrouded form or the coins provided by Messer Leonardo a second look.

His impulse to help his fellow sufferer had faded, but he determined to return to the ruin that night to see if anyone appeared. If no one did, he would return to the city in the morning and finish off that chaos-caller. That was all he had come to do, and if he stayed longer the black sword might need more than one life to send him back to his own place.

At dusk he reentered the ruin. He had been there long enough for true night to fall when men came. Five wore the red robes and masks of the night before. There was also a young man in dull scarlet accompanied by four others, obviously guards, in plain leather.

Elric sat on a wooden seat that had once had a high back. It might have been the seat of a high priest, although he could detect no lingering traces of power.

He bade the others disperse themselves around the walls. They did so, eyeing him (or perhaps his seat) uneasily.

He called forward the young man in dull scarlet, trying to sense his condition more clearly. He was weak, indeed, but was he the duke?

"If you are not Gian Galeazzo Sforza, Duke of Milan," the sorcerer intoned, "your life is forfeit."

"Yes, yes, I am M-Milan," the young man stammered.

"Stand there," said Elric. "The rest of you, be still."

With the ink left from the night before, Elric drew a rune around the young man. It was the rune of fire. Then he bade the duke lie upon it.

⊕

Outside, the regent and the artist watched. "Will you not stop this now?" the artist asked.

"So far, it is but mummery," Il Moro replied.

Elric reseated himself and began the calling of fire elementals. They seemed more distant from this plane than from that of his home, and he dared not put his whole being into the calling. He needed only the gentlest of elementals, with the healing power of fire, not the destructive.

But fire was fire, never easy to control. When a fire elemental was present, Chaos was always closer than even a servant of Chaos could wish.

Elric called in the ancient High Tongue of Melniboné. He had no further need to command his audience to stand still; they were frozen like images.

⊕

Outside, sweat broke out on the faces of those who watched and listened.

"Now, my lord?" the artist asked.

"It is still mummery," the regent replied. "Come, messire. When you perform an experiment, are you not prepared to wait for results?"

The artist had no answer.

⊕

All within the room felt the rising heat. Elric saw with relief that those whom he called were present.

"By the bond between your folk and mine, ancient and honored, I ask you to strengthen him whom you see on the rune. Heal what may be healed. Do no harm."

Being no healer, Elric could not be more specific. These people had wished fire for a healing; fire they would have.

The duke lay shivering on the rune for some minutes. Elric would not have ventured to guess if it were from fear or cold.

More minutes, and the young duke's taut limbs eased. He began to breathe easily and deeply. The sense of easing seemed to flow outward from him and pass around the men by the walls.

Until it reached Giovanni di Tuscania, under his red hood.

⊕

Outside, the artist saw the trance take all in the chamber. Was the power in the words, or in the soldier who uttered them?

Then he saw one of the red-robed figures raise his arms and cry out, "Princes and Powers, come! Work your own will!"

The figure launched himself toward the man on the rune, a gleam of metal showing as his sleeve cleared his hand. The artist vaulted onto the windowsill and launched himself into the chamber.

⊕

Elric struggled to maintain control.

He thanked the elementals and dismissed them to their own plane. The fire had strengthened him too, or else he and all in the ruin would have burned.

He could feel Chaos growing, drawing strength from the walls around and the ground beneath. His senses, bred of a line that had served the Lords of Chaos for ten thousand years, showed him that this land, like any mortal one, held its balance of Law and Chaos. But this one had known more Chaos than Law for a thousand years; moreover, its lords and princes, instead of strengthening Law, had served Chaos. By now, wizards as petty as the red-robed ones could summon Chaos, and it would answer.

Stormbringer yearned to be free. Elric began to draw the runesword, then stopped when he saw the face of his artist-host above the young man on the floor. The red-robed chaos-caller lay still.

"Does he live?" Elric asked.

"The duke does," answered the other. "This one is dead — a broken neck." He spoke with assurance, and Elric remembered the finely wrought anatomical drawings in the artist's studio. One who could portray a neck so well likely enough knew how to break one.

Elric knew sorrow, but also resignation.

"Take your duke and leave," he commanded in an imperial tone.

He accompanied the artist to the window by which he had entered, then stood by while the artist lowered the duke to the ground outside. The lord of Melniboné stood well back; the artist had not come alone, and a chance arrow shot through the window could unleash more Chaos than anyone save its Lords would care to face. A thousand questions blazed in the artist's eyes; he asked only one.

"Your sorcery is real. How shall I know it if I meet it again?"

"By its results, messire."

Elric turned his back to the window. He kept his hand on the sword at his hip for perhaps ten breaths. Then he drew it, giving a great cry of relief, as the

Chaos in the sword and the Chaos around him met.

"Blood and souls for Duke Arioch of Hell!"

The runesword fed, scarcely needing Elric's hand to wield it. The first to die was a guard. Stormbringer split his skull before he had a chance to look surprised, and when it was done the guard had no face to show any emotion, had he been alive to show it.

The sword leaped to one of the red-robes. He died with his chest cleft from one shoulder down and across to his loins. He sensed his death, enough to cry out before he had no lungs to hold the breath for the cry.

The black sword wreaked its way around the room, singing as it slew. All four guards and the five celebrants fed their souls to Stormbringer and their strength to Elric in the time a hungry man might have taken to eat a light meal.

With the strength of nine, Elric called on Stormbringer to take him to his home plane.

It did. One with the sword, Elric was not fully aware of anything until he sensed stillness around him. He opened his eyes. He was no longer in the blood-streaked ruin, nor did any mountains loom on the horizon.

Stormbringer too was still, the stillness of full feeding. The call that had nagged at Elric for three days was ended.

The albino looked about him. He had gone through the gate in Hrolmar. From Hrolmar to the Isle of the Purple Towns was but fair traveling, and from the Isle he could have taken ship for the Dragon Isle.

This was not Hrolmar. He could see in the distance a misty horizon that meant the sea, but he knew not where he was nor how far from Melniboné.

⊕

"The duke is sleeping normally, Your Highness," the physician said. "With the amount of wine he appears to have taken, I doubt he will awake before morning."

The regent nodded. "Thank you, Messer Ambrogio." His tone held dismissal.

When Ambrogio was gone, the regent looked wryly at his nephew. Gian Galeazzo was drunk, all right, but Lodovico had provided the wine — as soon as his artist and chief engineer, who was also an anatomist, had assured Il Moro that it was safe to do so.

He had also fired, with his own hands, the ruins of Sanct' Spiritu. Bare stone for the most part, it had burned as fiercely as if it had been stuffed with tinder and pitch. Even the mortar in the walls seemed to blaze, or at least to melt, and in the end hardly one blackened stone remained upon another.

In the shadows beyond the circle of light around the dying chapel, Il Moro and his little party had slipped away, unseen by those drawn by the blaze.

"'By its results,'" Messer Leonardo quoted. "The next time I meet a sorcerer, perhaps he will stay long enough for me to study him and his methods." He also looked at the man on the bed, then at the regent. "Do you still want the bust, Your Highness?"

"No!" Il Moro replied. Then, realizing that he had revealed more than he cared to, he added, "I do not even wish the sketch. You will have the price of the marble, and more, for your work tonight. But as for sorcerers in Milan, in the future I must treat them as heretics and enemies of the Church."

The artist acknowledged both the bribe and the warning with a wry grin. "Sticking with the devil you know, Your Highness?"

Il Moro smiled for the first time since returning to the city. "Indeed, Messer Leonardo."

⊕

Historical Note:
Elric visited Milan in the winter of 1489-90.
In the autumn of 1490, the Duchess of Milan, Isabella d'Este, bore a son.
It might even have been her husband's.

KINGSFIRE

BY RICHARD LEE BYERS

The elf — or so I judged him to be — knelt beside a creek, his snow-white hair blowing in the chill November wind and a huge sword, dull black like an iron kettle, clasped in his pallid hands. He struggled to lift it, then sobbed when its point fell back to the ground. The five ragged brigands surrounding him hooted and closed in.

That particular morning I felt so bitter, so angry at myself and the world both, that for a heartbeat I told myself it was none of my affair, that I ought simply to turn and ride away. Then I couched my lance and kicked Ebony into a gallop. My tattered cloak flapped and the destrier's hooves threw up brown leaves as we hurtled down the slope. One of the rogues, a stocky, black-bearded man with scars on both cheeks, spun around and started to shout. My lance punched into his breast and out the other side of his body.

Now ignoring their intended prey, whom they no doubt deemed too decrepit to pose a threat, the remaining outlaws snarled and ran at me. I frantically dropped my lance and snatched for my sword, drew it just in time to receive their attack.

Ebony kicked at someone who'd circled behind us. A brigand with a ruddy, swollen-looking nose swung an axe at my thigh. I caught the blow on my shield, then slashed at him. He jumped away, slipped, and stumbled farther backward toward the pale man.

Trembling, teeth gritted, the elf finally managed to raise his blade. The bandit fell on it, spitting himself. A ghastly keening, a shrill screech one moment and a bone-shaking basso roar the next, filled the air.

As the outlaws whirled to see what was howling, the ivory-skinned man sprang up and pounced at them, wielding his ponderous weapon one-handed. Its raven blade now shone like polished obsidian, and runes glowed like embers down its length.

Fearless as ever, even in the face of something unnatural, Ebony bore me forward into the fray, but he might as well not have bothered. The elf hacked one knave open from throat to groin and beheaded the other two, all before I could strike another blow.

The black sword slashed and thrust aimlessly for another moment, reminding me strangely of a mastiff tugging at its leash. Then the pale man grimaced, and the muscles in his arms and shoulders bunched. The keening died, and the blade grew still. Its owner flicked his wrist, a motion which threw every speck of gore off his weapon, then rammed it back into its scabbard.

I felt my heart thumping like a drum beating quick time and realized I was as unnerved by the elf's unearthly appearance and demeanor as by the fact that I'd just risked my life. I swallowed away the dryness in my mouth. "I wish I could clean my arms that easily," I said. "Are you all right? You looked weak when I first saw you."

"I'd traveled a long way without sustenance," he answered in a cultured baritone voice. "I'm fine now, and I thank you for saving my life. My name is Elric."

I wondered how, if he'd been starving before, he could have recovered without eating, but I was afraid he'd think me discourteous if I probed any further. And I didn't want to offend him. I saw now that his garments, though worn and grimy as my own, were made of dyed, intricately tooled leather and velvet brocade, and I hoped that he might be in a position to reward me. I sheathed my sword, dismounted, pulled off my gauntlet, and offered my hand. "Martin Rivers, knight bachelor, my lord."

His grip was firm, and his hand felt like anyone else's. The contact was reassuring, demonstrating that, no matter how uncanny he seemed, at least he was made of flesh and blood. "What place is this?" he asked.

"We're not far east of Augsburg," I answered in surprise. If he was so confused that he didn't know that, perhaps he hadn't recovered after all. "Where" — I faltered, groping for words —"where do you want to be? Where are you going?"

His crimson eyes glittered in his lean, patrician face. "Oh, I'm on another quest," he said sardonically. "A virtuous queen and her virtuous realm require deliverance from the fiendish hordes of Chaos, and I seek the magic that will hurl the abominations back. Unfortunately, I suspect that the saintly damsel-monarch and a goodly portion of her court will perish in the course of invoking its power, but that isn't my problem, is it? Certainly it can't blacken my reputation any further. And what's *your* quest?"

I blinked, bemused. I hadn't thought of my errand in those terms. Quests were for fey creatures like himself, or heroes who lived in another age, not ordinary fellows like me, and yet the word fit. "I'm looking for something magical too," I told him. "Kingsfire." He arched an eyebrow in inquiry, and foolishly, I felt a bit deflated. But perhaps he'd never ventured out of Faerie before, and so knew nothing of mortal history. "Richard Lionheart's lost sword."

His eyes narrowed. "Ah," he replied, and looked at the corpses scattered at our feet. "Was this rabble seeking it too?" He touched the black sword's hilt. "Did they think this was it?"

Reminded of the bodies' presence, I stooped and began to loot their purses, discovering without surprise, but to my disgust nonetheless, that they only had a few clipped coins among them. "Possibly," I said, "though supposedly Kingsfire shines *red* from point to guard."

"Or perhaps they merely took me for something loathly," he said. "One called me a devil, and another accused me of lacking a soul." From his contemptuous tone, I gathered he was used to it.

"I imagine they took you for an elf," I said uncertainly. "I did myself."

"But you helped me."

I shrugged. "I've known folk with a trace of Faerie blood. They were no wickeder than anyone else. Besides, it was five hale against one who seemed infirm."

"Well, as it happens, I'm *not* an elf." He smiled unpleasantly. "I'm a Melnibonéan, and I'll hazard that that's something considerably fouler. Nevertheless, I recognize my debts." My heart leaped up. "I've no money" — my spirits sank again —"but I'd gladly aid you on your quest. If you care to throw in with one called Betrayer and Kinslayer."

I sensed that he might truly be mad or evil, and was certainly perilous to know. But the way he flaunted it, as though with perverse, self-pitying pride, irked and amused me, made me want to keep him at my side out of sheer contrariness. Besides, whether he was an elf, some other sort of Faerie creature, or merely a traveler from some distant kingdom where, perhaps, everyone had ashen skin and scarlet eyes, he clearly carried an enchanted glaive, and might well possess skills that could help me greatly. "What of your own task?"

"I seem to be stranded for the moment," he said, and once again I wondered what he meant. "I might as well keep busy until I find passage."

"In that case, I'm honored to accept you as my comrade."

I then offered him half of my meager plunder, which he declined with a wave of his slender hand. When I dragged my lance out of the scarred bandit's corpse, I discovered that the oaken shaft had split. If my fortunes improved I could purchase another, but for now I'd have to do without. Muttering an oath, I snapped the head off, wiped it clean, and stowed it in one of Ebony's saddlebags. Then we set off down the creek bed. I led the horse, to rest him and to facilitate discourse with my new companion.

The brook gurgled, my mail clinked, and pebbles crunched under our feet. Elric kept looking from side to side, smiling, his nostrils flaring, evidently savoring the sight of the squirrels bounding along the bare branches and the scent of the moldering leaves. He was lightly dressed, but the cold didn't seem to trouble him. "Do you have some reason to think the sword nearby," he asked after a while, "or are you simply seeking at random?"

I bristled, thinking he was implying I was a fool, then remembered that he seemed to be more or less seeking at random himself. "Kingsfire vanished mysteriously a century and a half ago," I told him, "when Richard was imprisoned in Durrenstein Castle, not all that far from here. Allegedly, the sword possessed miraculous powers, and adventurers have sought it fruitlessly ever since. Well, three weeks ago, an angel of the Lord appeared in front of Augsburg Cathedral and announced that the blade abided in the lands to the east, inside a fortress made of wood, and that the man who found it would become the greatest knight of the age. The forest was full of treasure hunters an hour later. Could you" — I hesitated, for most men, if they didn't bear a drop of Faerie blood, would take the suggestion I was about to make as an accusation that they'd sold their souls to Satan — "could you cast a spell to guide us to the blade ahead of them?"

Elric nodded as if my request was wholly unremarkable. "My sorcery is weak here, but perhaps I can manage. Stand back a few paces, and don't speak till I finish."

I led Ebony away, sat down with my back against a rowan. The Melnibonéan grasped his sword hilt, then swayed. His eyelids drooped and his features slackened till he seemed asleep on his feet. A babble of grating syllables, as hideous and inhuman as the shrieking of his weapon, erupted from his throat. A moment later, a curl of blue-green vapor coalesced before him.

His eyes opened. He whispered to the mist, and it stretched and squirmed, reminding me of a kitten having its belly scratched. Then it floated off between two trees. "Come on," said Elric, "we have to follow. If it loses sight of us, it's likely to forget its errand."

I jumped up, grabbed my shield and Ebony's lead line, and trotted to catch up with him. "What is it?"

"A sylph," he replied, "a minor spirit of the air."

"Does it know where Kingsfire is?"

"No, but it has senses we lack, and, with luck, it will detect the weapon's emanations."

We trailed the sylph for an hour, then stumbled onto a glade that reeked of blood. The bodies of three men-at-arms lay scattered about the sward, all beheaded and thoroughly dismembered, slashed apart with long cuts from a heavy sword or pole arm. Evidently their slayer so relished butchery that he'd hacked them into pieces after they fell.

Elric said, "Lord of the Seven Darks! Is someone waging a war you neglected to mention?" My stomach churning, I shook my head. "Then, even by my exacting standards, this realm of yours is a dangerous place."

"Not my realm. I'm English. I think some treasure hunter's murdering his rivals."

"Or Kingsfire has a guardian. The object of a quest frequently does. I don't mean to impugn your courage, but if you aren't accustomed to this kind of thing you may want to reassess how keenly you covet the sword."

"Keenly enough," I said, for all that I suspected my resolution branded me a dunce. I stooped to rob the corpses, swearing when a dozen ants swarmed up my fingers. Despite his avowed poverty, Elric once again declined to participate, less, I sensed, out of respect for the fallen, a sentiment which in better times I might have permitted myself, than because he was too fastidious to paw through gore.

My pilferage accomplished, we set out after the sylph again. After a while Elric asked if "the Lionheart" was a great man.

I started to say yes, of course, as almost any knight would, then paused, recalling the history my mother and tutors had taught me. Richard's rebellion against his father and thus his own people, and his negligent, ruinous governance. His legendary rages, and the massacre of the prisoners at Acre. "He was a superb fighter and a skilled commander," I said at last. "He spent his whole reign winning victories against the Saracens and French."

The pale wizard nodded thoughtfully, his slanted eyes hooded, and I had the discomfiting feeling that he'd heard my thoughts as clearly as the words I'd spoken aloud. Then he pointed. "Another dead man." And so it was, cut into several fragments like the others. As the day wore on, we found a dozen more.

Around dusk, the mist-creature began to flit excitedly back and forth. It shot up to Elric, circled his head twice, and darted away again. "Has it found Kingsfire?" I asked.

"Not yet, but it's found something." The sylph led us down a slope, through a stand of yews, and onto a narrow, overgrown trail that ran between two standing stones. I glanced between the moss-covered menhirs, then blinked and looked again, certain that my eyes were playing tricks. But beyond the monoliths the path meandered up a hillside that didn't seem to exist unless one was peering between them.

"My God," I said, "a portal to Faerie."

Elric grinned. "You've brought me luck, my friend. If we hadn't been seeking Kingsfire, Xiombarg knows how long I would have wandered before I stumbled on a gate from your plane to the next."

As I've already indicated, I didn't fear even pureblood faeries the way many Christians do. Still, at that moment I remembered all the bogle tales I'd ever heard about the fate of mortals who intruded on the Fair Folk uninvited, and a chill slid up my spine. "Is the sword *in there?*"

He nodded, his demonic eyes glinting. "Afraid?"

I took a deep breath. "Not enough to turn back." He smiled, whether in approval or mockery I couldn't tell, and gestured to the sylph. It floated between the stones, and we followed.

My first good look at the fabled land of Faerie, which scarcely a living man had ever seen, was both ominous and disappointing. Trouveres sing about a Summer Country where the weather is always pleasant and everything is verdant and lovely, albeit often with a malevolent, dangerous beauty. But the realm beyond the menhirs was even colder than the one we'd just departed, as though we'd walked from autumn into winter. The grass was brittle and brown, the trees bare and excruciatingly gnarled, like bodies twisted and maimed by a master torturer. A shroud of dark-gray clouds obscured the sunset, and a faint stink of corruption hung in the air. Elric grimaced and said, "I've seen more fearful vistas, but few drearier," and I agreed with him.

A few minutes later, we found the bodies of two frail-looking gnomes, hairless, gray-skinned creatures with beetle-browed, spotted heads that reminded me of toadstools. The murderer had mutilated them as thoroughly as their human counterparts.

We made camp when night fell, and discovered that we'd have to dispense with a fire. The sticks on the ground looked suitable for burning, but squished to sodden mash when we picked them up. So we simply bundled up as best we could, even Elric now shivering as the air grew steadily colder. Somewhat to my surprise, he consented to share my stale black bread, dried apples, and the last of my sour yellow wine; evidently he didn't subsist entirely on magic.

"What did this garrulous 'angel of the Lord' look like?" he asked as we finished our repast.

"I didn't see it," I said, "only heard about it."

He cocked his head quizzically, his countenance a deathly blue-green in the foxfire of the sylph hovering above us. "You seem too hardheaded to embark on a quest on the strength of what was, to you, no more than a tavern tale."

I shrugged. "It's not as if I had anything else to do. The year I won my spurs, the pope — both popes, actually — called for a truce, and, their kingdoms ravaged by decades of war and plague, the princes of Christendom agreed to it. I suppose that was a blessing for most folk, but not for newly dubbed knights lacking both reputations and connections. I couldn't find a lord willing to add me to his retinue, so I supported myself by tourneying. That was all right so long as I won, but this year I started to lose, until now I don't dare enter the lists again. I don't have the money to ransom Ebony" — hearing his name, the destrier snorted — "and my arms if someone else unhorses me."

"But now you stand to reverse your fortunes with a single stroke," Elric said. "What will you do when you hold the Lionheart's sword? Conquer the world?"

I laughed. "No, a kingdom will content me, as long as it's wealthy and comes with a beautiful queen."

He frowned, and I belatedly remembered the queen he served, the one likely to perish if his own quest succeeded. "You know," he murmured, "I've possessed the kind of power you seek." The black blade purred, and I felt the hair on the back of my neck stand on end. "It carries its own set of griefs and dire imperatives. However strait your circumstances, you have freedom, and clean hands. I hope you appreciate — "

My fists clenched. "I *appreciate* that I haven't sent my mother a penny in months. She's living on charity if she hasn't starved. I appreciate that my servant — my *friend* — Geoff lies sick with the ague, and I can't afford the physick he needs to recover. And I appreciate that soon I'll have no choice but to *sell* my steed and mail, and after that I won't be a knight anymore. I don't care to hear you discourse on the benefits of poverty, Lord Elric, for I don't believe you're conversant with the subject. Whatever your sins and calamities, it's plain *you* grew up rich, and even if your purse has occasionally emptied since, I doubt you've ever had much trouble filling it. Hell, I imagine you can conjure gold out of the ground if you need to!"

He sat silent for several heartbeats, then said, "I apologize. You're right. No one knows how onerous another man's burden is, and I'm presumptuous to tender advice unbidden. I'll take the first watch." He rose and strode away.

I watched him for a time, a shadow slipping through the contorted trees, then fell into a doze. The next thing I knew, a hand was gripping my shoulder.

"Wake up," Elric whispered. "I heard footsteps."

"The killer?"

"I don't know," he said with a reckless grin. "Let's go find out."

I threw off my blanket, jumped to my feet, and snatched up my sword and shield. Then we walked into the darkness.

As we advanced, I heard something tramping through the brush. A second later a horn blew, a tinny blat like the toot of a child's toy trumpet. Pursuing the sounds, quickening our pace, we trotted toward a massive willow. Unlike most of the trees in the dying forest, this one retained a portion of its foliage.

"Do you *see* anything?" Elric asked.

"No," I replied. Then the willow's limbs crashed down on our heads, coiled around our bodies and wrenched us into the air.

We carried our blades in our hands, but, clasped in the willow's embrace, we couldn't swing them. Its grip tightened agonizingly, inexorably, its bark abrading my skin, till I feared it would crush us to pulp. A band of squealing goblins like those whose corpses we'd discovered scurried out of the bushes and lifted long spears to skewer us.

I sucked in a breath and whistled with all my might. Hoofbeats pounded, then Ebony exploded into the midst of the gnomes, rearing, biting, battering, kicking backward. The dwarfish creatures screamed and scattered.

Elric bellowed another cacophonous incantation. The sylph streaked out of the dark and sped around and around us, somehow creating a roaring vortex. Suddenly, I couldn't catch my breath. For a few moments I was afraid I was going to suffocate, but then the whirlwind tore the branches clutching us to splinters and dispersed as abruptly as it formed. My comrade and I fell heavily to the ground, and the tree froze into immobility again. Glancing up, I saw that our misty ally had disappeared, and realized it had given its life to save us.

His white face a mask of rage, Elric raised his sword and stalked after the gnomes. Gripping his shoulder, I gasped, "No need to kill them."

He sneered. "Are you craven? They tried to murder us. They've been murdering your people by the score."

"I don't think so," I said. "For one thing, we found dead goblins too. For another, they lack the stature, the brawn, and the proper weapons to inflict the wounds we saw. I wouldn't be surprised if they only attacked us because they saw a tall figure with a huge sword prowling through the night and mistook you for the killer. And even if that's not the case, where's the honor in slaughtering them needlessly? My God, they're puny, they wouldn't stand a chance in a fair fight."

The fury drained out of his face. "You're right." The black sword snarled. The white-haired sorcerer shuddered as if with palsy, his hands trembling so that for a second I doubted he'd be able to slip the weapon back into its sheath.

"Are you all right?" I asked.

"Yes," he said, averting his gaze. "Stormbringer has a will of its own, and it likes to kill. Sometimes, if I disappoint it, I have to exert myself to remind it which of us is master."

Not knowing what to say to that, I returned to the situation at hand. "I wonder if the goblins know who the murderer is. I wish we could persuade them to talk to us."

"So do I, but it doesn't seem likely."

"Oh, I don't know. I'll wager they're listening to us right now. What if we pledge not to harm them, and lay down our arms?"

He gaped at me. "For whatever reason, they *did* just try to kill us."

I grinned back. "Afraid?" He burst out laughing, pulled his baldric over his head, and laid the black sword Stormbringer on the ground. Secure in the knowledge that Ebony would guard them till we returned, I set my own blade and shield beside it. Then Elric took my arm and we strolled farther into the trees.

When we'd walked about fifty paces, the goblins crept warily into view, encircling us with lances leveled. Behind them cowered other sorts of faeries, goat-legged fauns and a woman no larger than a mouse, with an extra set of arms, feelers sprouting from her chitinous brow, and veined, translucent wings.

After a moment another gnome, this one unarmed, pushed through the ring of spearmen. From the sigils painted on his hands and head, and the clanking amulets dangling from his neck, I surmised he was the magician who'd animated the willow. "I'm called Blue Morel," he said in a reedy voice.

"This is Sir Martin Rivers of England," my companion replied, "and I'm Prince Elric of Melniboné. Do you have a quarrel with us?"

"No," Blue Morel said, "and we beg pardon. Sir Martin was correct. When we glimpsed you, we thought Tyrith had found our hiding place, so we drew you into the trap we had prepared. Once we noticed there were two of you we should have realized our mistake, but by that time we were too panicked to reason."

"Who is Tyrith?" I asked.

"Until he went mad, he was king of the forest," the goblin said. "Now he stalks the wood, and your earthly wood beyond, killing everyone he finds, and infecting our land itself with his morbidity."

"Tyrith's most likely an elemental," Elric told me, "albeit of different ilk than our poor sylph, his essence and well-being, or lack of it, linked to his particular domain." He turned back to Blue Morel. "I believe I can guess the rest. Unable to overcome the king yourselves, you remembered he stole his sword from a mortal monarch. So, knowing most of Martin's people mistrust faeries too much to heed their blandishments or pleas, you summoned a spirit that could pass for a seraph and dispatched it to Augsburg to announce that the blade could be found in the lands to the east, all in the hope that some human knight puissant enough to vanquish your oppressor would come seeking it and slay him in the course of claiming his prize."

Blue Morel nodded. "I realize it was despicable to lure your folk to their deaths. But we're desperate."

I stared at Elric. "How did you know?"

"I didn't, really, but once we discovered that one of these wights is a nigromancer, it seemed the most likely possibility. In my experience, genuine divinities rarely appear to the general populace unless they intend to annihilate it. So now that you know the truth, what do we do?"

"Finish what we started," I replied. "I don't care whether God's will or a faerie's deceits led me here. Kingsfire is still Kingsfire. Any captain in Europe will offer a high place to the man who recovers it, and warriors and investors will flock to me if I decide to found a company of my own." Also, I pitied the Fair Folk and wanted to help them.

I expected Elric to advance the hypothesis, impossible to dismiss out of hand once one grasped something of Stormbringer's peculiar nature, that it was ownership of Richard's sword that had driven Tyrith mad. Indeed, I had counter-arguments marshaled in my head. But he simply said, "Then if Blue Morel will direct us to Tyrith's famous wooden castle, let's be off. If His Majesty isn't home, we'll lie in wait."

The faeries cheered.

We reached Tyrith's fortress around midnight. In the darkness it was solid black, a pillar of shadow in the center of an enormous clearing. Surely it was an edifice only an entity "linked to his particular domain" could have erected, for it was both a keep and a colossal, living tree. In happier times it had probably been magnificent, but now it was as gnarled and blighted as the rest of the ailing forest.

Leaving Ebony outside, Elric and I warily advanced through a lofty double gate, both leaves warped and the one on the right hanging askew, into a cavernous hall. A whitish sap or ichor oozed from cracks in the walls and ceiling, and the maggoty, segmented bodies of twoscore faeries lay scattered among the broken tables and benches. The reeks of animal and vegetable putrescence combined to form the most sickening stench I'd ever smelled, and for a few seconds I was sure I was going to vomit.

Elric swallowed. "Let's keep moving," he said.

So we started to search the stygian keep, the smoldering runes on Stormbringer's blade, occasionally augmented by sprays of luminous blossoms sprouting from sconces and patches of phosphorescent fungus, providing just enough light to see by. Everywhere we found further evidence of Tyrith's dementia and the tree-castle's decline. Fey servants cut down at their labors. More shattered furniture, broken statues, shredded books. Sections of floor decaying into slime, cancerous tangles of wood blocking corridors and stairs, sheets of mold rioting across paintings and tapestries.

Until, after what seemed an eternity, we heard a high, sweet music up ahead. A sound too pure to flow from a human throat, unlike but somehow akin to Stormbringer's dreadful wail.

I repressed a shiver, then forced myself to slink forward, Elric creeping at my side. Rounding a corner, we found the door from which the singing issued.

Beyond it was a large bedchamber, its ornately carved canopy bed, sumptuous carpets and intricately woven wall-hangings as ruinous as everything else in the citadel. Inhumanly tall and gaunt, naked and filthy, Tyrith was pacing restlessly back and forth, his pale green skin and emerald hair attesting to his kinship with the land as eloquently as his deformities — one arm longer than the other, scabrous, barklike tumors on his breast and thighs, pustulant lesions on his genitals — demonstrated the virulence of his affliction. He carried the crooning sword on his shoulder. Despite its name, I didn't think Kingsfire's crimson radiance much resembled flame. It looked more like a splash of blood, or the color of Elric's eyes.

"Tyrith of Faerie," the Melnibonéan quavered, startling me so badly that I jumped. "I call on you to yield yourself to us. I swear by my gods, we have no wish to harm y— " The mad king screamed and charged us.

I blocked his first blow with my shield. The next instant, Elric leaped at him and drove him backward. Blades rang, exchanging blows too fast to follow, howling a dissonant duet. Then Stormbringer flickered in and out of Tyrith's breast. The elemental fell, his green blood gushing. Its voice failing, Kingsfire flew from his hand to clatter on the floor.

I started toward it, then hesitated. What if it *had* driven Tyrith insane?

Well, even if it had, the process had taken a hundred and fifty years. I wouldn't live that long. Sneering at my timidity, I advanced again.

But Elric reached Kingsfire first, lifted it off the floor and released it. Crooning again, it floated unsupported. The Melnibonéan gripped his own glaive in both hands, swung it over his head and whipped it down. Stormbringer roared. The ruby sword screamed, and shattered into a hundred pieces.

Aghast, I could only assume that Elric had played me for a fool, that Kingsfire — the destruction of Kingsfire — had been the goal of his own quest all along. I shouted, "Whoreson!" and came on guard.

The pale wizard whirled, his teeth bared and his scarlet eyes blazing with a rage as mad as Tyrith's. And at that moment, my own wrath crumbling into dismay, I penetrated a secret that had hitherto eluded me.

Stormbringer absorbed the strength, perhaps the very souls, of those it slew, passing along a measure of this stolen vitality to its possessor. Alas, the more life it drank, the greater its influence over Elric became, and now, gorged on Kingsfire's essence, it ruled him. Delighting in death, it was eager to kill again, and I was the only prey at hand.

More terrified of losing my life to that raven blade than I'd ever been of any other peril, I cut at Elric's head. He sidestepped with pantherish celerity, then hacked at me, shearing away the top half of my shield.

After the first few seconds, I knew I couldn't defeat him, not fighting chivalrously. Perhaps I was as skillful a swordsman, but I couldn't match the ogreish strength now coursing through his arm. So I cast away the remainder of my shield, which was virtually useless in any case, to empty my hand, and retreated toward a certain section of floor.

Stormbringer wailed and bellowed, flashed at me again and again, and for a moment I was certain that I'd never reach my objective. Then I trod in something slippery. Dropping beneath a blow that could have decapitated me, I scooped up a wad of the ubiquitous muck and threw it at Elric's eyes.

Luck was with me. I hit them square, then lunged to run him through. Stormbringer deflected the thrust and slashed unerringly at my face. Caught by surprise, I barely managed to parry, but the stroke snapped my sword at the hilt.

As I scrambled backward, dodging blow after blow so narrowly that the black blade often glanced, screeching, off my armor, I realized my mistake. Stormbringer was a living thing with senses of its own. Useless to blind the swordsman unless one blinded the glaive as well.

So I shouted a war-cry and hurled myself forward, right past him, speed and surprise my only defenses. The keening sword slashed through the air behind me. Then I tumbled through the wreckage of the canopy bed, grabbing a double handful of rotting sheet just before I rolled off the other side.

When Elric dove after me, I swept the covers over him and Stormbringer both, then kicked at his knee. The joint crunched, and man and weapon screamed. I wheeled and dashed for the door.

A second later, I heard him pursuing. His steps were uneven, but with his plundered stamina he could hobble as fast as I could run. So, gasping, my own strength beginning to fail, slipping in puddles of slime and tripping over corpses and rubble, I sprinted through the labyrinth of dark hallways, Stormbringer constantly baying at my back. Much of the time, I was certain I'd forgotten the way out.

But at last the gate yawned before me. Shrieking Ebony's name, I staggered into the starlight. The horse raced to me instantly and started running for the edge of the clearing the second I clambered onto his back.

Elric burst out of the keep and charged, nearly closing the gap between us. But then the destrier surged forward, running faster than he'd ever run before, leaving my nemesis — and its fleshy slave — behind.

Even when Stormbringer's wailing faded I wanted to keep galloping, but I knew that if I did the horse would surely step in a hole. And so, despite my dread, we slowed to a walk, but we didn't stop to rest until we reached the other side of the standing stones.

I was still so frightened that I didn't think I could possibly sleep. But I was exhausted as well, and once I sat down, I soon fell into slumber.

I dreamed I was King Richard on Crusade. My most recent battle won, I sat enthroned, Kingsfire lying naked across my thighs and a sea of prisoners, men, women, children, and babes, cowering before me.

For a moment, I was inclined to grant them mercy. Then the red sword sang a lilting arpeggio, and I realized how richly the entire pack, filthy infidels with the temerity to defy a Christian sovereign, deserved to die. It would be weak to spare them, politic — even gratifying — to make them an example.

As my men-at-arms kindled the autos-da-fé, I awoke in a sweat. After I collected myself, I felt as if I'd come to my senses after a long delirium. How could I have contemplated gambling my reason and character? If something corrupted them, I wouldn't be the same person anymore. And even though times were hard, why had I so lusted after magic? I already possessed sharp wits, martial training, a staunch supporter in Geoff, and a splendid mount. Many a chap had founded a fortune on less.

Once I decided I was glad I hadn't gained Kingsfire, I began to doubt that Elric had truly desired to rape its power. It seemed more likely that he'd broken the sword to save me from myself.

Or perhaps because he couldn't break his own.

Shortly after I rode back into Augsburg, a lickerish abbot engaged me to repel vengeful cuckolds. Geoff and I spent a comfortable winter in his employ, and the following spring, war broke out from Cadiz to Constantinople.

THE GATE OF DREAMING

BY BRAD STRICKLAND

In which Elric journeys to a hostile land and finds there the threat of release.

A thin-armed, thin-legged boy climbed a smooth dome of stone, its sun-washed surface burning his bare hands and feet. The hot, dry air cracked his lips and nostrils and dried his tears before they could spill. He toiled at last to the top, found the bowl-shaped depression his master had told him about, and paused to gaze at the desert of Akrador.

It was a country which killed. Low, wind-eroded hills glared bone-white in the sun; a level desert of pebbles the coppery color of old blood stretched away from the hills in all directions until heat-shimmer hid its horizon. The trade track was no visible trail, and only the sentinels, as traders called the man-high piles of stone half a thousandpace apart, marked the route. For three days and nights no beasts or men had appeared on the trail. The boy's master lay dying in a shallow cavern scooped by the wind from the white stone of one of the hills. His last hope, their last hope, lay now in the untutored boy's attempt to work a great spell at this uncanny spot, this place where lightning had dug itself a nest.

The boy closed his eyes, feeling them throb as he shut out the killing desert. *Breathe deeply,* the old man had told him. *You must think of the words, their weight and their shapes. You must see in your mind what you wish to happen. You must call upon the force you will find around you and make what you call for real.*

He had never tried such a complicated work of magic before, but he sensed the power the old man had spoken of here: It sizzled in his hair and along the skin of his arms and legs, latent magical energy pouring from the stone itself. It was his task to harness that force, to turn it to his own ends, to find salvation for the old man and for himself. He trembled in the heat.

Then, his mind as clear as he could make it, he began to whisper the spell in a hoarse, soft tumble of words, a carefully-ordered chant. He called simply for a hero with the means to save them from the desert.

He felt the power surge around him. For a dizzy moment he tasted salt on his lips, the spray of some cold sea. He opened his eyes and cried out, stumbling.

The boy was perhaps eight years old.

He who shared the hilltop with the boy might have been any age.

⊕

The albino warrior reeled. One instant he had been standing alone on the deck of a ship plying a mist-shrouded sea, pondering the doom that was leading him toward a confrontation with Agak and Gagak, whoever they might be. The next moment Elric nearly fell, for he had adjusted his balance to the roll and pitch of the ship, and that had ceased with a silent roar and a blinding blaze of light.

Elric gasped furnace-hot air. His hand went instinctively to the hilt of Stormbringer.

He found his balance and shielded his eyes. He stood atop a stone hill, in the midst of a desert, beneath a pitiless copper sky, and before him knelt a tanned and scrawny child. The child, a boy, said something in a strange tongue.

"I do not understand," Elric told him. He frowned, troubled, for beneath his grip the pulse of Stormbringer was faint, almost not there. "Who are you, and what is this place?"

The boy said something else in an unknown tongue and then he pushed himself to his feet. He descended the slope a little way and turned, looking up.

Elric took a deep breath of the desert air. He had none of the drugs that sustained him — they were belowdecks, aboard the ship, wherever the ship might be — and the whisper of Stormbringer's dire power was so thin, so weak, that he felt apprehensive. "You want me to follow you," he said.

The boy painfully climbed back up and stretched out a bony hand. Elric disdained to touch it. He gestured with his head. "Go. I will follow. There is naught else to do."

The descent was not a difficult one, but the boy staggered and stumbled as if barely able to stay on his feet. He kept glancing back anxiously at the warrior. For his part, Elric felt already an increasing fatigue, the weight of weariness that was his curse, and yet he had no great trouble in following the child. They came at last to an overhang of stone, a deep crevice leading back into darkness. The boy went into the cavern and, his senses alert, Elric followed.

Not far from the mouth of the cavern a man lay on smooth yellow sand. He was an elderly man with a tangle of gray beard, and his clothing was of strange fashion and material: a loose green robe, much soiled and torn, and a turban-like headdress of red. The old man opened deep-sunken eyes, and Elric saw that he was fighting death. The boy spoke something to the elder, and the man spoke to Elric, who shook his head.

With a frown, the man closed his eyes and appeared to lose himself in thought. Then he spoke again. Elric felt a strange sensation, as if a cool breeze had blown momentarily over him. "There," the man said. "Is that better?"

"It is better," Elric said. "You worked some magic."

"Yes. A simple spell to allow us to understand each other."

"You are a sorcerer?"

"I am," the man said. "My name is Chavrain. Are you a hero?"

"I am Elric."

The old man sighed and closed his eyes. "I sense some strangeness about you. You are not — human, are you?"

"I am Elric."

Chavrain was silent for a long time. Then he sighed and spoke again, weakly: "You find my charge and me in perilous circumstances. Weeks ago I concluded an agreement with the lad's parents to take him to the wizard-schools of Vanislach for training. He has the strongest inherent magic I have ever seen in a child, but it is wild, unharnessed. We joined a small spice caravan following the trade track to the realms of Markelan, but bandits waylaid us. The guards died in defense of the caravan, and the bandits killed or took all of the sapads. The surviving merchants cast us loose, taking all our food and water. And so you find us here."

"Here?" Elric asked.

A faint smile played on the old wizard's blistered lips. "Ah. My apprentice summoned you from Elsewhere. I see. 'Here' is Akrador, the great desert. We are perhaps three days' walk west of the Weeping Stones and water; but without aid, we have no hope of making the journey."

Elric inclined his head as if listening, but what he heard was an unaccustomed stillness. "Is this one of the planes of Earth?" he asked.

"Earth? The name is not known to me."

"This world is truly different from anything I have known," Elric said. "The forces of Law and Chaos seem far from here, a memory of an echo."

"I do not know what you mean," Chavrain said.

"It is no matter. What resources do you have?"

They did not have much. The boy had skinned and dressed a haunch of sapad, a beast of burden whose meat was tough, stringy, and all but tasteless. A few days' supply of the meat, two flat and empty water skins, and the clothing they wore constituted all of the supplies the two of them — now the three — could claim. "How long since you have had water?" Elric asked.

The old man closed his eyes and thought. "Two days now, and part of a third."

Elric leaned against one of the smooth-worn walls of the cavern. It was incongruously cool to the touch. He explored his own feelings: he felt somewhat weak, but nothing so weak as he should have felt under the circumstances. Staring out at the desert glare, he murmured, "Can you reach this place you spoke of, this Weeping Stones? Have you the strength?"

Chavrain whispered, "No. I die even now. Before sunset, without water."

"But with water — ?"

"Yes. With water, I could recover. With water, the boy and I might actually live."

"Do you have an incantation for — ?"

"No, Elric," Chavrain said. "No weather magic. Only the power of finding that which is lost. That is my study."

"The boy?"

"Alas, he can work only the spells I shape for him. I spent two days formulating the finding of a hero. I shall die before I can devise another spell."

Elric frowned. "I do not know what you wish of me, old man."

Chavrain opened his eyes. "Take the boy eastward. You will come to the grasslands of Markelan, to the settlements along the River Kothorn. Find there a member of my brotherhood and entrust the boy to him. That will fulfill the spell and will release its hold on you. Then you may return to your home."

"Not to my home," said Elric grimly.

"Then to the place from whence you were summoned. It is a week's march — "

Elric interrupted: "That is impossible."

Chavrain turned his head. For a long while the old wizard regarded the albino. "You lack strength," he murmured. "You could not make the journey, no more than could I."

"No."

The old man frowned. "I do not understand. I formulated the spell carefully, and I sent the boy to a place of power, a lightning-touched hilltop. The summoning should have brought a hero capable of — " He fell silent.

All this time the boy had crouched quietly in a recess of the cave, his large brown eyes intent on the form of his master. He crept out and tentatively touched the old man's face. The wizard gave the boy a weary look. "Did you carry out the chant as I told you?"

In a harsh, dry, choking whisper, the boy said, "Yes."

"Then I do not understand."

Elric looked at the two impassively. He calculated his strength. A day's walk — possible. Two — doubtful. Three — no. Three would kill him. And, he thought to himself, the boy as well. But there might be one way....

"Old man," Elric said at last, "would you give your life that the boy might live?"

"That is a question without meaning."

"Perhaps it is. But say it had meaning; then would you give your life for his?"

Chavrain closed his eyes. "My life is near its end anyway. Yes, if I knew he would live, then I would surrender my own life."

"Then," Elric said, fingering the hilt of his runesword, "there may be a way."

In a few words Elric told Chavrain of Stormbringer, of how it drank souls and gave the life-force of its victims to him who wielded it. "With your strength and that which is left me," the warrior-prince concluded, "I might be able to take the boy eastward."

Chavrain nodded his understanding. He sighed. "So be it," he murmured.

"Very well." Elric drew the blade.

And paused, for Stormbringer felt oddly lifeless in his grip. Yet its dark blade flickered with a pale glow, like heat lightning glimpsed on a distant horizon. It was a different kind of magic than its wonted thirst for souls, and the very difference caused Elric to hesitate.

The cavern grew dark. The boy, crouched beside the old man, raised himself on hands and feet, then slowly stood.

From outside the cavern came a howl of wind and a clash of rain.

The boy cried aloud, ran to the cavern mouth, and stepped into a downpour. Elric stood over the old wizard, Stormbringer in his grip, waiting.

The boy, hair plastered to his scalp, dark skin glistening, cupped hands brimming, stumbled back to his master. He dribbled the water into the old man's mouth, then ran for more. "The water skins," the old man croaked. "Fill them — "

Streams cascaded down the face of the hillside in that torrential downpour, and filling both skins was the work of only a few moments. The old man drank deeply, and the boy re-filled the skin. Chavrain breathed hard, propped himself on his elbows, and murmured what sounded like a prayer.

Elric did that which he had never before done: he sheathed Stormbringer before it had tasted a foe's blood or had stolen a soul. He shivered.

From outside the cavern the sounds of rainfall, wind and thunder died away.

"You are indeed the hero we sought," Chavrain said.

Elric shook his head. "The rain was no gift of mine."

"But it was. Of your sword."

"Stormbringer does not give such gifts."

"The name of your blade is — Stormbringer?"

Chavrain rose a little more and sat upright. "This is the sorcery of Thaumia, friend Elric. The magic of the names of things, and the power of their names. The sword is called Stormbringer — and in this world it brings storms."

The boy had drunk his fill. He offered the water skin to Elric, who waved it away. "A strange world," Elric said. "And a kinder one than my own, it seems."

"Yes," Chavrain said. "I feel it is. I feel that in your own world your sword is also your curse and your doom."

"It may be so."

"Then you have a choice, friend Elric. I think you may choose to remain here, in this world, and escape your fate."

"No one may do that."

"One may try."

For a moment Elric was silent. Through his mind ran the weary panorama of the endless war between Law and Chaos, a war that raged throughout the whole of existence — save perhaps here, in this backwater of creation. Here a warrior might escape their dominion, might even escape his old vows. And yet —

And yet escape meant bidding farewell to his beloved Cymoril, to the Ruby Throne, to the eternal struggle. Elric stirred like one awakening from a deep sleep. "Old man, you show me a gate that is not there. It is a gate of dreams, an illusion."

"Is it? You might try its existence, friend Elric. You might venture through the gate."

Elric thought long. "It is a tempting offer," he said. "But my blood is not made for these climes, nor for this strange magic. For what it is worth, I am glad to have done you some service." The albino warrior walked out into an afternoon fresh with the scent of rain.

He took a long, regretful breath of that rain-washed air, closed his eyes, and felt the deck pitch beneath his feet. When he opened his eyes again, he stood at the rail of a ship sailing on a mist-shrouded sea.

From behind him a voice said, "Have you dreamed, Elric?" It was Corum of the brocaded eyepatch and the silver gauntlet, he who insisted that Elric had fought side by side with him at the Tower of Voilodion Ghagnasdiak — or would fight there. He joined Elric and stared morosely out at the mists. "You have the look of one who has lately dreamed."

"Perhaps I have," Elric said.

"A fair dream, I hope."

"Too fair to be anything other than a dream."

Corum nodded. "Yet, fair or foul, all existence is a dream," he said. It was an opinion he had expressed before.

⊕

The boy and the wizard reached the Weeping Stones at dawn after their third night of travel. By then their water skins were empty, and they drank gratefully of the brackish water pooled between the upright stones. "Here we will wait," Chavrain said. "We have food for several days, and ere long a caravan will pass this way. I have hopes of seeing you enschooled yet, you young rascal."

"Chavrain," said the boy, "was he really a Hero? Did he really come from a different world? What is it like there? Why was he so sorrowful? Why did he not stay, if he suffers a doom? Why —?"

Chavrain sighed. It had been like this since the albino had walked out of the cavern and vanished. "All men make choices," he said. "And friend Elric made his, I think, long before your summoning."

"But why would he give us a chance of living if he himself faced doom?"

"That is the mark of his heroism, boy. A hero accepts fate. He does not fight vainly against it."

"But why did he not stay to — "

"I wish indeed he had stayed," Chavrain growled, "if only for the fact that you were quiet in his presence. Remember what Devalo advised his apprentice: 'A pebble of silence is worth a mountain of noise.'"

"But I want to know — "

"Enough," said Chavrain.

"But, sir, I want to — "

"Enough, young Barach!" said Chavrain.

THE LITTLEST STORMBRINGER

BY BRAD LINAWEAVER AND WILLIAM ALAN RITCH

Hear nothing that we do not wish you to hear. See nothing that we do not wish you to see. Believe nothing that we do not wish you to believe. Think nothing that we do not wish you to think.
— Dr. Paul Joseph Goebbels

"Heroes are braver than the *Volk?*" The lad who was speaking had the nickname of Thick Wilhelm. We all hated him. Not that he'd ever said anything deliberately subversive. He was just dirt-dumb stupid.

Our troopleader had figured out poor Wilhelm's limitations and no longer punished the rest of us for a *Dummkopf's* lapses. With dedication worthy of the *Führer*, Herr Krieck made an attempt at explanation, while the rest of us tried not to snicker or to laugh out loud: "The hero is the fulfillment of the *Volk*, Wilhelm," said Krieck. "Without the Folk Spirit arising from the purity of the race, there is no hero to manifest these values in terms of honor and loyalty and personality."

The sky was as blue as our troopleader's eyes. A cool breeze brought the fresh scent of oak leaves to all of us. I don't know about the rest of them, but my mind was taken far away by the *Wandervogel* spirit. That was something no teacher could encapsulate in words, and as a top honors student with aspirations to be an educator, I had a strong sense of limitations.

As a long time veteran of Eckart Camp, I'd learned the tricks of pretending to pay attention when my mind was far away. Sometimes I suspected the camp leaders were capable of similar feats when listening to our daily reports. The troopleader had memorized a number of inspirational phrases from Karl Schenzinger's *The Hitler Youth Named Quex,* the most popular novel (by direct order) in the Third Reich. When Herr Krieck used these phrases, I doubted whether he actually listened to himself. There were certain advantages to doing things by rote.

Schenzinger's book had already sold millions of copies before the war. Since our hard-earned victory in '44, the figure had skyrocketed. The liberated countries of a United Europe devoured the Reich's books and movies, not only because they were encouraged to do so, but because Germany made the best entertainment outside of Hollywood. (This was easy enough to prove. Like most teenagers, I'd seen my fair share of Hollywood movies on the black market. Our U.F.A. movies were good, too, but slower-paced.)

Anyway, the troopleader cut the lesson short. Wilhelm remained unenlightened and the rest of us had been entertained. We picked up our packs and returned to camp, enjoying the beautiful, warm summer day, the birds singing in the trees, the clean, cold sound of a crashing waterfall... and most of all, anticipating the fun we would have beating up Wilhelm before dinner.

Only Wilhelm was lucky this time. He'd been complaining about a stomach ache all day, and that kept him from the activities preceding the evening meal. He received permission from Irene to go to bed early. Irene was the camp nurse. She didn't approve of Aryan illness, which usually meant something was really wrong with the boy who dared face her.

Eckart Camp was the most prestigious Hitler Youth camp in Burgundy — and overseen by elite members of the SS. We were divided into three divisions: the oldest boys, who were already young men as far as the SS was concerned; the mid-range adolescents that included me, of course; and the kids. No girls were allowed, but they had their own camp just beyond the lake. (Some of the older boys would sneak across for late-night meetings with future mothers of the Reich; but when they were caught they would be taken away for punishment.)

My little brother, Otto, was attending for the first time. As a seasoned veteran of summer camp, I had enjoyed lording it over him... at first. But something strange had happened in the past week. I'd caught him reading. The book was not one of the banned titles. He'd gotten it out of the Official Library. But it was one of the most scholarly works on Burgundian magick and race history, so far above what I took to be Otto's reading level that, well, I'd have trouble with it!

At first I thought he was only trying to impress me. Every young boy hopes that one day he might join the inner circle of the SS, and be a Nazi of such importance as to share a dual citizenship between Burgundy and the Reich. I didn't doubt that Otto had the necessary physical attributes to make a fine soldier. But he'd never struck me as any sort of scholar. The first time I tried to tease him about such matters, he quoted some abstruse material from Alfred Rosenberg and then added: "The Reich has many enemies and we are always in need of an Eternal Champion."

⊕

The evening started out normally enough. At the beginning of summer I'd volunteered to read stories for the younger boys. Otto had asked me to do selections from a popular children's book: largely, I think, because the main character was named Otto! Tonight I turned to Chapter Five from *The Littlest Stormtrooper:*

⊕

This was Otto's best Christmas ever! Good old Uncle Neckel had given him a huge picture book. "Oh, thank you, Uncle," said the boy with a grin as big as his older relative's well-fed stomach. "Why, it's *The Big Book of Jewish Lies,"* Otto read the title page slowly, savoring each word as if it were a fine candy. "But it's so long...."

"That's only Volume One, my lad," came the kindly voice, as the old man put a firm hand on the boy's shoulder. Since Otto's father had died, his uncle had done what he could to fill the void. Otto's mother approved with all the honest decency in her wholesome peasant soul. The boy needed a father figure close at hand to provide guidance, as the *Führer* guided the course of the whole nation.

Besides, Uncle Neckel had recently been retired from his position in Himmler's elite unit of the SS and was feeling a bit useless. He needed Otto as much as Otto needed him.

"Ah, me," he said to his nephew as he lit up his ornate pipe, "we put our heart into eliminating enemies of the Reich in the old days, but to hear these new officers talk, you'd think we never gave good service. I admit the current methods are more efficient, if all you care about is speed and quantity, but what about caring that you do your best for the *Führer*? These youngsters don't respect veterans and a lifetime of duty...."

⊕

Every eye in the room was riveted to me as I read the scene, even acting out the different parts and changing my voice accordingly. I was really starting to identify with the characters when we were interrupted by the world beyond the barracks window. There was a flash of lightning, followed by a thunderbolt a fraction of a second later that sounded as if a Berlin blockbuster bomb had just been dropped next to us. What made the experience all the more unnerving was that the night sky was perfectly clear —without a cloud in sight.

This was only the beginning of a night of surprises. I happened to have been glancing at my younger brother when the lightning struck. A few seconds crawled by before I observed the complete absence of surprise on my little brother's face! In fact, he was smiling calmly while the rest of us had nearly jumped out of our skins. Then I noticed that, besides Otto, there were two other boys exchanging knowing glances suggesting some kind of shared secret.

Eckart Camp did not encourage secrets. Except those of our leaders, of course.

"What was that?" asked Roland, a frail boy who was always getting sick and bringing down the wrath of Nurse Irene.

Before I could answer, Otto surprised me by volunteering, "Lords of Chaos cannot stand against the True Hero. Jewish demons would avenge their people and bring ruin on True Law and True Order. The Champion will save us."

This was my kid brother talking? He'd never sounded like that before. I assumed he must be quoting that old book he'd been studying. The two other boys were nodding their heads and chuckling in a manner that made me think of Gestapo men. I had the strange feeling that I was dreaming, even though I knew I was awake.

"Fritz," my younger brother addressed me, completely forgetting the formality due an older member of the camp and an assistant counselor. "Do you think we could conclude tonight's lesson with a look at the Eternal Warrior?" After getting out that mouthful he smiled in a sickening manner.

I've never been good at handling stuff that comes at me, as the Americans say, from left field; and I don't mean only Bolsheviks. Otto had always chosen the easiest lessons. *The Littlest Stormtrooper* was a readily accessible work. In contrast, the study of folklore was a demanding discipline. Coming straight down from

Alfred Rosenberg's Cultural Ministry through Hans Schemm's Office for Youth Literature and on to the Reich Youth Organization, the National Socialist Teacher's Association, the Reich Division of Youth Literature and the Party Control Office, and further down to the Reich Youth Library, the study of myths and legends meant hard study, endless tests, unbelievable amounts of memorization and more work after that. (And to think they used to complain about the bureaucracy of the Weimar Republic.)

Not that I'm complaining. I'm not complaining! It's just that kids never asked for this. Yet here was Otto... asking for it.

"Well, I guess we've survived a close swing of Thor's hammer," I said, smiling. "Maybe this would be a good time to review the relationship of Volk-ish rituals to the Sagas." That just happened to be what I was studying for my next major examination. Many of the boys groaned, but not the cryptic trio. They seemed to be enjoying themselves immensely.

Two hours later the younger boys at Eckart Camp were put to bed. When it was time for my age group to follow their example, I snuck out of the sleeping quarters. I couldn't sleep tonight! Something was gnawing at my peace of mind.

The reason I always enjoyed going to camp was to get away from my parents. They did everything the Third Reich exhorted parents not to do. They worried all the time. They complained all the time. The Hitler Youth offered the best escape from the crap at home. But now, for the first time, I found myself really worrying about my kid brother. A Nazi summer camp was not a good place to stand out from the crowd or to be different in any appreciable way. Otto had never shown any dangerous signs of individualism before, but social atomism begins small. And what's a big brother for, if not to suppress ambition in his younger siblings?

The night air was refreshingly cool after a hot day. Something drew me in the direction of the hill where the lightning had struck. Something else told me that I would not be alone.

Otto and the other two were already there, carrying torches that gave off a heavy black smoke. I'd never imagined that such young boys could be this resourceful. "He's here," said Otto in a hushed voice.

They surrounded a figure lying prone on the ground. Crouched behind a tree, I did not have a good angle to see more, but I decided to be patient rather than present myself to them. This was the strangest situation I could have imagined, hiding from my own brother. But as soon as the figure sat up and I saw his face in the flickering light, I entered a realm beyond my imagination.

"I am Lord Elric of Melniboné," he announced.

⊕

It was early summer, yet the gentle hills were covered in a quilt of snow and ice. Elric, the prince of doomed Imrryr, the Dreaming City, stood silently watching the latest snowfall. The icy winds whipped his long white hair about his shoulders. The snowflakes clung to his plaster skin, blending in but not melting. Were it not for his gaily colored clothes, he would be invisible. Or so thought his companion, the Prince Swain, lord of this bleak land.

"Apopka was once a bright and prosperous land." The young prince's words disrupted Elric's dour reverie. "Our crops once thrived. Cities of commerce dotted the valleys. Our musical halls were well known throughout the world. Now this." He waved at the desolation. "It has been two years since the winters came. Barely we survived the first year due to large storehouses of grain and preserved vegetables. But, when the spring failed to come the second time.... The people began to die. Those who could, left. Our towns emptied."

Prince Swain paused, as if he expected Elric to speak. The grim albino was silent. The prince exhaled a fog of ice and continued his saga.

"I have contacted many magicians. Each thought a different cause, a different theory, a different sacrifice to be made. Nothing helped. That is when I contacted you. Magick is different for you, Lord of Melniboné. It flows through your veins and the veins of your ancestors. Mere humans only touch the Magick. You live it!"

Elric acknowledged the statement with a nod, nothing more.

"I have nothing left, but I would give all to restore my land. I would give my life itself!"

"Your life?" roared Elric. "Think you something that feckless could affect the forces dominating your land? Your life! Would you give your very soul?"

Shocked by the sudden violence of Elric's questions, Prince Swain staggered, amazed and inarticulate.

"I... I... I guess. I suppose.... Yes. I would."

A ghastly smile etched itself across Elric's face. His hand rested on the bejeweled hilt of his sheathed sword. "I was sure that would be your answer." Elric drew his black runesword before Prince Swain could react. "Hear me: a prince is the soul of his land and the land is the soul of a prince. Were there another way, I would not, but...."

The ebony blade began to sing in anticipation as Elric held it in check. Prince Swain was afraid, but the blood of his ancestors roared in his veins. He stood erect, nodding toward Elric.

Without the guidance of Elric's hand, the sword leaped through the air and buried itself in the prince's chest. The pain was much less than he had expected. But then Stormbringer began to feed on his soul.

"No...." he began but his words were halted by the sword's thirst.

"Now, Hellsword, you have fed. Let us do our duty to brave Prince Swain."

The sword twisted from Elric's hand and rose above his head. It made mystical passes in the snowy air. Suddenly the wind rushed about the great sword. Darkness radiated from the ebony blade. Into the black maelstrom Stormbringer vanished.

Elric felt its tug, he heard its siren song bidding him to follow. With all his heart, Elric wanted to resist; but his promise to Prince Swain and his weakness without the damned blade made him leap into the vortex. Thus through the black hole Elric entered the land of Burgundy.

✦

"Welcome, Eternal Champion," said Otto, bowing. There was something so ridiculous about seeing a kid brother adopting the mannerisms of a pompous old man that I almost laughed out loud; but fortunately I restrained myself.

"You are the Nordic superman," said one of the other boys. As the figure stood up I was impressed at his height, towering over the three boys like a great white tree. Unless it was a trick of the light, I had never seen such whiteness this side of a snow bank. The face was bleached of all color, and the hair hung about his shoulders like a pale, white spider. As he surveyed his surroundings, I saw him full on and was shocked to see sickly pink eyes where I had expected the sparkle of Aryan blue.

"Where is it?" he asked one of the boys. No one answered. Reaching out a long arm, he touched Otto, who backed away, breaking the small circle that hemmed in the strange visitor. As he stepped closer to me I had an unobstructed view of the man's hand, which was as pale as the rest of him.

He repeated his questions with one alteration: "Where are *you?*" For one chilling moment I thought the apparition was asking about me as he stared straight in my direction. But then the head turned, pink eyes searching for someone, or something, else.

He took a few steps and faltered, almost losing his balance. Suddenly I could look beyond the imposing aspect of this man and recognize that he was desperately ill. And then I realized that he must be an albino, with all the health problems of that condition. I had read about such things. Irene, the Nazi nurse, would not consider this man a worthy symbol of the race. But then, since when were people symbols?

Otto and the others did not rush forward to help him. With predictable National Socialist discipline they did nothing to help someone they supposedly admired. Which once again raised the question as to who was this remarkable personage to be consorting with three young members of the Hitler Youth? As if in answer to my unspoken query, the alabaster man cried out: "Show yourself, you evil thorn of destiny! I cannot see your ebony blade in the darkness of this alien night. I have followed you here. Do not abandon me now."

There was a shrill whistling sound behind me. Against my better judgment I turned slowly around and saw a sight as bizarre as the presence of the man. A sword was sticking up from the ground as if an exclamation point, with a blade so black as to be invisible except for the flickering torchlight outlining it. I had never seen a larger two-handed broadsword, and I had taken the tour of the museum of the Teutonic Knights! The hilt was easy to see, however: encrusted with jewels, winking in the crimson light as if a chandelier from one of Berlin's finest ballrooms. And the most peculiar aspect was that the whistling almost sounded like some kind of song.

The man stumbled weakly toward the sword as if it were the staff of life. And I was right in line between them. Naturally I attempted a strategic retreat. Unfortunately, the move turned out to be a personal Stalingrad.

"Halt!" cried out a commanding voice. I came to attention. Damned training! A few seconds later I realized that the voice had not come from the man but from Otto! I was going to have to do something about my kid brother.

The man saw me. Or rather he seemed to be looking straight through me at the weird weapon that made so much noise. He brushed past me and I felt his cold, clammy skin on my cheek. The clothes he wore felt as smooth as silk, but heavier; and a purple cape flapped around his thin frame.

"What?" Otto said as he noticed me, but said nothing else after realizing I had joined the select little circle. We were all in suspense about the stranger and what he was about to do.

"Is that which we seek here, runeblade?" asked the man as he grasped the hilt and held the sword up against the night.

The sword continued to emit some kind of music, but he cocked his head as if listening to a message. "So," he addressed the blade, "you would feed on the souls of these children?"

That didn't sound very promising. Nor did the sight of the man seeming to grow in stature and strength as he held the blade. I grabbed Otto by the arm and pulled him close. "What the hell have you done?" I hissed in his ear. "Who is this man?"

The other boys hung back, as much from me as from Elric of Melniboné. Otto swallowed hard and said, "We practiced rituals in the book to bring the Eternal Champion."

"We chose a sacrifice the camp wouldn't miss," said the second boy.

"We're sure he was a virgin," added the third, with no sense of the absurdity of a boy his young age making such an observation.

"What do you mean?" I asked, squeezing Otto's arm hard enough to hurt him. I kept glancing over at the strange man who seemed to be engaged in an argument with his sword. The idea that a sword could be speaking to him in some fashion suddenly seemed no more ridiculous than the other events of the evening. I didn't like the tone of his voice, or the scraps of phrases that I heard him use: "death" and "soul eating" and "power!"

Receiving no answer to my question but a terrified look, I pressed on: "Who is this sacrifice you speak of, Otto?"

"We sacrificed Thick Wilhelm," he blurted out.

"A slow-acting poison," added one of the others.

"When they check the beds tomorrow morning, they'll find he died in his sleep," Otto continued, "at the exact moment the lightning came down and brought us the Eternal Champion."

There was no way I could have grown up in the Third Reich and not have been exposed to a full helping of the occult stuff. But I'd never believed it. I assumed the occult was part of the initiation, like a game to be played with secret words and handshakes for the elite members of the club. None of the Reich's scientists believed the moon was made of ice, for instance, but that didn't eliminate the crazy idea from the Burgundian Creed. Listening to my little brother's confession, and watching the pale warrior wield his black sword, I suddenly realized that I could believe in anything.

"What have you done?" I asked in a defeated tone of voice. The only answer came from the man who now approached us, the frightening sword held at his side, but no less threatening for that.

"What is the name of this world which speaks so strange a tongue?" he asked, none of us perplexed by his flawless German in the presence of far greater magick.

"You are in the Third Reich," said Otto.

"This is the planet Earth," I expanded the point, "in the twentieth century, A.D.!"

"This is Stormbringer," said the man, as if introducing a companion. "He was called by you, and I followed."

"I am Otto," said Otto. The others began to introduce themselves but the man didn't seem to hear.

"Cursed blade!" he shouted. "I had my chance to be free of you but the bond is too tight, and I cannot do battle with the Lords of Chaos alone. And you are always hungry!"

"Excuse me," I made an attempt to get his attention. "Lord Elric," remembering his name, "are you the pure hero of the Aryan race?"

"What nonsense is this?" he said. "Which among you is the wizard who brought me hence? Where is the ravisher of Apopka?"

Under the circumstances, Otto was the closest thing to the fulfillment of his request and even if it were not a prudent action on his part, my brother had the courage to step forward. "I will serve the Third Reich and the purity of Nordic man," he said.

"By Arioch," said the man, "this puny one sounds like an ancient Theocrat. What powers protect you, and what will we feed Stormbringer ere I return to my own world?"

Otto wasn't fazed. "Does your sword have a taste for Jews?" he asked.

"My demon has a taste for souls," was the answer.

One of the other boys pulled at Otto's sleeve and said, "That might be a problem if Jews don't have any souls."

Suddenly the sword quivered with a life of its own, and every muscle in Elric's right arm quivered and twitched as if an invisible army marched upon his body. "You offer soulless bodies!" he screamed. "Are you insane? Are you —" he addressed the boy who had spoken, "— are you one of these Jews?"

"I'm no Jew," the boy exclaimed.

"Good," said Lord Elric of Melniboné as he swung the five-foot blade and split the boy wide open from the crown of his head to his collarbone. As blood and brains splattered over every one of us and the victim dropped his torch, I had a very clear view of the weapon. There were runes engraved near the hilt. The analytical part of my mind seized on this observation as if discovering the most interesting thing in the universe. I'd never seen bloody death before and it didn't seem nearly as romantic and heroic as I'd been expected to believe.

While I turned inward, Otto had the opposite reaction. He screamed and attempted to run away. The man, no longer weak or unsure of himself, moved with the speed of a great white wolf. He grabbed Otto with his free hand and said, "Don't play the coward with me. I know the tricks of wily magicians and the forms they take. Stormbringer has fed on one of your underlings, buying us a little time in which to speak. Now don't offer me soulless bodies after this!"

Otto opened and closed his mouth as if speaking. The only trouble was that no words came out. Fear will play its little tricks. For some reason I will never understand, I was not afraid. But I understood that the only thing standing between life and death for my brother and myself was the quality of my thinking. I dared not say I was the master here. I'd seen the fate of an underling, and I didn't want that gory fate befalling Otto. On the other hand, I had to take on the mantle of authority if I hoped to bargain with this monster.

"We brought you here for good cause," I said, stressing the "we." I wished that I'd spent more time studying the occult. My head was full of an ocean of Nazi verbiage but the words were mostly political. I needed the right words. "Your world and ours," I ventured, "face similar dangers. We thought you might help us."

"In return for the souls of your enemies," he finished. "Where are they?"

"We've gotten rid of them," said the other boy. This was not the wisest statement he could have made. At least this time I had some idea of what to expect and covered Otto's eyes so he wouldn't have to witness the next execution, or feeding, that the black sword insisted upon. Even so, blood splashed on my hand and some of it got on my younger brother's face. Otto was trembling so violently that I feared the inevitability of a wrong move from him next. But so long as terror stilled his tongue I had confidence that I could talk my way out of the problem. *Why, it's like a job interview with Heydrich or Himmler,* I told myself.

When the first torch dropped, it sputtered out. This second one threatened to set the hill ablaze, so I told Otto to stand still and risked letting go of him so I'd be free to stamp out the burning grass. Then I raised the still-burning torch and had a better view than ever of this implacable madman. His face was as stone. He waited.

"Do you think we would call you here for no reason?" I asked, desperately trying to think of what my next move would be. "You say you fight chaos. So do we. The Jews may be gone from Europe but...." I realized I'd better come up with something good. "But they have left demons behind that sap the vitality of our people and threaten the future prosperity of this world."

I took a deep breath and waited. He seemed to be considering what I had said. Then he spoke slowly and with great force: "Yes, I sense that dark, magickal forces are at work here. The Law of Balance is more important than even Law or Chaos. I sense that your world has been thrown badly out of balance. Aha!" He stepped so close that I felt I would vanish into the abyss of his flaming eyes. "How clever of you," he said.

"You understand," I replied without the faintest idea of what he meant.

"Stormbringer knows what to do with other demons, don't you, black one?" he asked his sword, the dark blade still running with young German blood. "Mayhap the demon you would have us face is the one that I, myself, seek."

"And which would provide you the route home for your trouble," I threw out the thought in wild hope that my gamble would save Otto, save me, save the Reich and save the world... instead of meriting a sword through my head as reward for a slight miscalculation.

"You are the clever one," he said. "So this other one is but your underling as well," he added, eyeing Otto as if he were a fluffy piece of pastry. "Let Stormbringer feed a third time and we will see how we fare against the demon."

Oh, shit, came to mind.

"No, he is my equal. We perform our rituals together. You have fed twice on our servants. We have no other souls to offer." I hated sounding as cheap as a pawnbroker but the time had come for serious bargaining.

"You bargain well," he said. "Very well, I must avenge the Prince of Apopka. Call up this demon and we will settle the matter."

Oh, shit.

"Come now," I said, "you know that no more is required of us." I found it hard to breathe and my heart was pounding so hard that I thought it would burst. "You and your sword have all the magick you need. And you said that you sensed the powers that pervade this region. You have fed. Now do battle against a worthy foe!"

Anger flashed across his face and I was certain that I was a dead man. He held up the black sword, blood dripping off the hilt onto his pale fist. I wondered if I could fend off his first blow with the torch, but I never found out how I would have fared against this mighty warrior. He communed with the sword, and muttered to it, then nodded. Part of me wanted to believe that he was insane, but everything else that had happened eliminated that possibility. Somehow the sword was speaking to Elric.

"Very well," he said. "We will find the demon." No sooner had he spoken those words than the clear night vanished in roiling clouds, and a terrific wind tore at our faces and garments. Embracing Otto with all my strength, I waited. And I prayed. I did not pray to the Nordic gods, either, but to the god of my parents.

A demon came. White as Elric, flabby and large, with beady eyes and a hooked nose, it had the appearance of one of Julius Streicher's anti-Semitic cartoons. The thing was huge, at least twenty feet tall. The width was impossible to estimate as it kept spreading out from the waist as if it were oil poured on water.

Elric raised the incredible sword and went forth to do battle. A giant projection of the sword, worthy of the huge foe, grew in the air where Elric pointed the runeblade. I would never doubt the existence of the supernatural again.

As the spectacle spread across the sky, Otto found his tongue and stopped trembling. "I was right," he cried, as if he were the *Führer* on that bright day when V-weapons and atomic bombs turned the tide for Germany. "The Eternal Champion will destroy the Jewish Demon!"

The demon made its first sound then. The thing laughed, ignoring Elric and Stormbringer. "So you think I'm a desert deity, boy? I'm part of the mountains, ice in my veins, a Yuletide snowman fashioned from hate as cold as your leader's heart."

Elric paused in his advance, listening to the demon's pedigree. But the warrior did not turn, did not let down his guard for one second. Again, Elric waited.

Otto, with the return of courage, also received the gift of impatience. "What are you saying? You're a thing from the Talmud and the Torah, a Moses monster." Again, I was impressed that little Otto had been doing his homework.

The pale blob of horror had a different opinion: "I am of Asgard, you little fool. I am a frost giant and I am here to reward you with a gruesome death for bothering me."

"Annihilator of Apopka!" Elric cried in a voice ten times his size. "Winter fiend! Ice bringer! You dare defile my land, my world?"

I wasn't sure what he was shouting about, but Elric seemed to have a private grudge to settle with the demon that had little to do with Otto or me.

Elric swung his sword at shadows, while above him the Spirit Sword did battle with the giant. Surprised by the presence of our Eternal Champion, the giant bellowed in pain when the sword struck his shoulder. The scream was more like the rumbling of the world than a sound. Now I knew what it must feel like to be at the site of our W-bomb tests.

The frost giant halted only temporarily. It had weapons of his own. Its massive arm, an oak of snow, made a pass through the air. Every cubic centimeter of air turned to snow and fell upon the odd albino. It didn't affect him. Instead the snow melted about his body as if he were a white-hot slab of steel.

"Arioch!" cried the warrior. I could not tell if this was an oath, a prayer, or a summoning. "Arioch! The bones of my ancestors are dedicated to you! Hear me now. I face the despoiler of our world!"

Already glowing, Elric's skin grew brighter. First neon, then incandescent, he was soon glowing like a welding arc. The giant lashed at him, ice forming in its wake. The bright champion cut through the ice with his runesword, and its projected brother dug into the giant's chest.

Far away, at the camp, they must have thought that a terrible storm raged in the hills. Or maybe, more accurately, they thought they were in the middle of World War III.

"Perhaps we should go," Otto insisted at my side. It was a good idea from my little brother, but I found I could not move. My spirit was bound to this battle. I really didn't know which side to root for. If the frost giant was really from Asgard, he was of my people. But if Elric was our Champion, then it was to him that I owed my allegiance. I needed a leader to tell me what to think. Or a scorecard.

"I grow weary of this battle," roared the mountain of ice. "To me your puny flame is like a firefly to a blizzard. I will douse it into lump of coal."

"I say thee, nay!" bellowed Elric as he leapt into the air. Whether he was levitating or being carried aloft by his sword I did not know, for I was suddenly struck by the absurdity of the situation. I felt like I was in one of those Thor comic books that the Ministry of Youth published. White-haired Elric as the super-hero and his black blade taking the place of Thor's hammer.

I began to laugh. I admit I was becoming hysterical. My laughter became louder and more maniacal. This was a bad thing. It disturbed the giant, who threw a stalactite of ice my way.

Laughter and fear froze my legs. Fortunately, Otto thought faster than I. He chanted three words in what sounded like Old High German, and the fatal icicle melted before me. I was deluged by a column of ice-water, but it was certainly better than being impaled. My brother had mastered the black arts well.

Distracted by my averted doom, I did not see what happened next. I heard a sound like a thousand lightning bolts striking at once. I looked up to see Elric's black sword embedded in the center of the monster's forehead. The giant groaned and writhed but it could not stop its essence, its very *whiteness*, pulsating into the sword. With each gulp, the sword glowed briefly white, but then emerged impossibly blacker than before. In a few seconds the demon shrank to nothingness; or rather, into the blade.

When the frost giant was gone, the runesword sprang to life in Elric's hand, bobbing up and down as if sniffing for new victims. Fighting against his own hand, the white warrior sheathed his mighty sword. He faced us and spoke:

"I will not give thanks, for you deserve none. But your unwitting distraction allowed me more easily to defeat the Winter. For that, I have spared your souls from Stormbringer's appetite. I return to Apopka to hasten the belated spring. I leave you to your own dark destinies."

He strode away from us into the woods. Seconds later, lightning filled the air and calm summer returned to the woods.

⊕

We fell asleep, too exhausted to return to the camp. A few hours later the dawn woke us with golden clouds worthy to be a crown for Zarathustra. I cradled Otto in my arms, truly proud of him for the first time in my life.

"No one will ever believe this," I said, "but we must explain the death of your comrades. I know! We'll say a maniac did this and he escaped. After all, Elric took his weapon and there's no way we could have butchered the boys without...."

He stared at me with an expression I had never seen before. "We must tell the truth," he said solemnly.

"Otto, no one will believe us."

"I don't mean tell just anyone! We must tell those who will believe. The inner circle of Burgundy."

He had a point. Now that I'd seen the proof that magick worked, there was a very real possibility that high-ranking SS occultists would believe. "Maybe in time," I said, half to myself, "if we approach the right people carefully, and you remember which spells did the trick. Of course, we'll keep what the demon said a secret between you and me."

Otto pulled away from me and stood up. "No," he said, "the Fatherland is wrong. Wrong about the Jews. The demon was our demon, not a Jewish one. We must tell the whole truth."

I gave him every chance to come to his senses. He was only a kid, after all. And he was my brother. If he'd even pretended to be reasonable I would have let it go. But he kept repeating his threat to tell the SS the truth about the Jews.

After what I'd seen that night, it wasn't very hard to strangle Otto. The lack of blood made murdering him a lot easier. I'd simply blame all three deaths on the lone maniac. I wouldn't even mention Thick Wilhelm's death by poison unless I could turn that to my advantage. Nurse Irene was so incompetent she'd probably put Wilhelm's death down to natural causes, anyway.

I left Otto's body next to the other two. They might wonder why he wasn't butchered, but there's no telling why a madman does what he does. I even cried over him and said a prayer my parents would approve.

He opened my eyes to a universe of possibilities that I never would have entered otherwise. I'm glad for that. And I will always miss him. But he left me no choice. I'll keep his memory unblemished, and no one will ever know that he would not have made a very good Nazi.

PROVIDENCE

B Y   K E V I N   T.   S T E I N

I bleed from many minor wounds; precious blood flowing down arms, leg, side, slicking the marble and forcing a cautious stance. Burning eyes glance unbidden to the thin lines of crimson, thin in amount and consistency. No phantom gauge but the blood purports swiftness of sword, strength of stroke.

Stormbringer softly moans, tired, hungry, heavy in pale hands that slow with another parry against the thin blade of Harlequin, opponent, Fate's Clown. Black and white diamonds of the automaton's raiments match the lozenges on the cold floor of this great palace where skill and runeblade were sold as balance for the scale of escape. Hypnotic blur of contrary color forces the blade to slow again, yet the moan of the weapon brings senses back to the attack, scoring another scratch.

Swift Harlequin dodges aside and with right épée feints; left, lunges. Spinning, a storm of royal blood fuses black with white, Stormbringer arcing in straining hand against failing will to strike the weapon away, wrenching muscle and tendon. Minutes ago there might have been pain; hours, agony. Now there is naught but nothing, a burn that is cold and a thought that is desperate.

The kingdom entered, disguised as somewhere, the lands of ancestors, Tanelorn, so many others, yet there is no escape without the Fight of Fools, no flight from personal Hell. There is no extrication from Fate, the Sword Lords have the perseverance of the gods they strive to become. Pacts were attempted, made to escape this intrigued land, but there is always forced return to elemental hearths, wet and cold or hot with flame, no true flight of arrow. Safe philosophers accede that struggle is all, yet they do not wield black blade nor spill their life on thirsty sands.

Pressing the attack, three vicious cuts left right down, Harlequin dodging and its face stares blankly into my eyes and never breaks. Mechanical, and ticking in blurring thought only, a perfect machine in this strange land where the collusions of court are the rule of life and even those out of the game are players in some way. The heavy pommel strikes jaw and the Clown staggers but stabs forth with both blades, striking thigh and air. A stumble gives time enough for recovery, cherished advantage lost.

A lifetime's defensive fight, guided, prodded, kicked. There is little thought for the next defense, little thought in defense of the battles brought to unwilling pieces; the black blade cuts air and cries silently, catching both épées. And, like that, there is a life of running and fighting and searching for peace that never appears. Memories of other lives that are shadows against dreams; desires being the shadows of dreams and thereby the stuff of gossamer and less than nothing. Black jewel, gods' hand and eye, seas of ice: they all find what they desire, whether death or not. Stormbringer hungers where my hand is fatigued; when the thin frame tires the runeblade leads and there is no recourse but to follow. And friends die.

The machine pauses a moment after a backpedal, tightening stance and loosening limbs. The air seems hot and stale and heavy sweat stains thin armor on heaving shoulders. The black blade will not let swordhands lower a degree, knowing Harlequin is a subtle opponent, a mocking fighter, an agent of change. There is great envy for this strange automaton: It is unfeeling and purposeful, a single thought clutched jealously in gear and gauge. It knows the pain of its mechanics, understands maneuvers and manipulations, sees perfect avenues of entrance and escape. A thin white frame is no vessel for such gifts; portents cannot be read till their time has passed.

The air shrieks at drawn and whirling steel, two blades the girth of leaves that black-magicked blade cannot destroy. The Clown steps forward once, performs, steps forward, slashes, retreats. Runeblade parries and cuts, drawing blood from the automaton as red as that which already stains the cold tile. It has many cuts and wounds but does not slow, Fate's Fighter, perhaps better than Kinslayer, White Wolf. How the memories burn of friends killed at the end of the howling ghost of a weapon; though their names, even faces do not clear to mind. How many have been murdered, and how many more shall follow? This question arises often, but to seek an answer would invite only Despair, an opponent that needs to rest, strong as the will is weak.

Many bets are made on the lines at the side, though the number of spectators is small. This event is for the eyes of this kingdom's greatest players: king, queen, a friend and daughter. The two attendants who offer aid to the white stranger look on with whispers and gibes. They have no names to give, and laugh and say they are dead. Many times companions seem sent, but by what there can be no understanding. And like them, their names are different and matter little, for the runeblade makes carrion of them all. Carrion, even those for whom there is more than love. Stormbringer rises clumsily to strike the dread Clown's throat, scoring the chest with another gash and flow of blood that is mocking, unnecessary for life.

Harlequin is the agent of change, called such by the Queen who says she is mother and aunt, artisan and mover. The Agent of Change, one of the two in this play of the worlds. And he who sold this event says change is something to be fought, and Chaos is not change but stagnation in all its forms in another guise. What is to be believed except the Clown steps in for another strike, dual-armed and fluid and there is little time for defense and none for thought?

Steps near the edge of the dueling square, forcing Stormbringer to give strength where there is little to receive. The automaton has no soul to devour, no life to steal. Half-black and half-white face surrounds eyes that are dead, cold, alive with taunts of life and flight. A quick glance reveals that the gallery looks on, and in that moment a thunderous crack is heard from afar, outside, perhaps the cry of war or perhaps Chaos themselves. A blade appears in the air and another follows, and money changes hands among the spectators amid their silence as a slash exposes more burning sinew to the air.

Where is the attack to be made, either in this life, the next, or merely in combat? Strategies ruling Melniboné are the fodder in this court, degrees even the aloof ruler of his sorcerous people does not fathom, for his pale flesh has scarcely seen these lands where machinations and automatons have contested for a time immortal. Merely to enter and expect elder skill and small experience to conquor is the dreams of fools that not even dragons portend to pass. More the fool thinks friends found among these citizens of politic provide a vaunted release, even the promised exchange of duties.

The fight. The fight! Would it be that it were not all important to all things as Stormbringer bites deep into an arm, the weight of its body drowning it in the waters of Harlequin's frame. Peace is all there is to seek, though the most cynical say that for peace there must be conflict, and conflict to maintain. The runeblade bursts free amid the shower of unneeded crimson and there is some small satisfaction when the automaton glances down with nothing and stares at less. And He the Man That Sold this mission said that there is naught important but what comes after, be it hope or truth or death. That is all, all the fight is for.

There is a soft bell behind, and the Clown stiffens and turns on limb-strings, lifting foot and frame in mockery of the river it has just been. As for the timbre of a near-dead Prince, his gait is unseemly and coarse, gross affront to all learned before the Ruby Throne where vengeful cousin plotted. The attendants do not step upon the field of honor, as the warriors must have the strength to leave themselves, as they were strong enough to enter the fray. He-Who-Sells offered that this is much as the lot of life, to leave the battle for another, again and again till there is nothing to fight, either for or against. For the reply there was little but grudging agreement and wondering why the man would offer such strange counsel. An intriguing custom, were it not that the pain of wounds chokes all thought, all mirth.

The rumble of thunder from beyond ancient, shrouding walls calls attention, but from all others in this congregation there is nothing. Concern or worry is not theirs to have, seemingly another calculation in their subtle plans that concern this pale, weak stranger and the machination which was built for a sole purpose. And where is the difference? The two are like mother and father, god and creation, bringing life to something that has none. Battle.

The attendant to the right speaks of the odds decreasing as the blood increases upon the marble, while the other points that the King has dropped a pearl in the queen's cup and bidden her drink. The heart beats louder than all this, and there is some doubt whether the fight alone is worth the struggle, or even if there is aught beyond. The sands of Chaos encompass all, grinding, drowning, misshaping; and when that occurs, even the singular thought of a thing will have no meaning, and the encroachment does not abate.

What matters is the state between Law and Chaos, the shifting balance of the footing on this blasted plain; marbled tile, black and white; though this in itself is not all. Thought may show two forces, one idiot, the other idol, both worshipped on their own ways. The fight so glibly put must have direction, a goal before black blade sweeps another flight, lending hell-strength to albino arm. And if what He-Who-Sells says bears truth, then battle upon the levels of which he speaks is merely pendulum swings toward the center, always missing, suffering and returning at every tracery arc. The attendant to the right points out that the Queen has drunk the wine in favor of the stranger. The attendant to the left says that the skills of a warrior are the most pure and fair, with but a single purpose that is Law, bringing Chaos, or Chaos to Law, his words are not sure.

The bell is struck again, and the battle starts anew, though this is not wholly true. There is still much blood lost, yet to lose, and there must come a point where the turnings of these machinations make the stranger-prince the final piece in whatever play is on the field of queen, warrior, He-Who-Sells, and those others with names numerous and varied. The gods themselves must look here, for by their very definition they look in all places; though by their own admittance, their power wanes and washes in each plane. The black blade comes up again and there is time to wonder how it is that the Sword Lords do not have more worshippers in this inconstant land of shrouded strife, or in any places their strengths are weak. If they see this struggle on the field of black and white, would that they lend some aid to their savior and soldier.

Harlequin's wounds continue to pour their fluids to the floor, viscous red like stained tears or rain running down arms to fall in drops. The blood of royals has clotted, but new motions make the slashes open again and begin the flow of life that only ends in darkness and death. There is no time for rest as the twin swords of a clown lock into the black guards of Stormbringer, who reaches down into the depths of its abyss and awards new strength to block the attack. Stepping over the mechanical's leg, a hard push sends it sprawling and a swift cut removes three fingers from the right hand, though what remains clings tenaciously to unbreakable metal.

The Queen clutches her throat and dies, face blue, drawn from pain. Her hands cling to the goblet as long as they dare before her spirit leaves this plain to bargain with whatever lords rule the lands of these dead. The King appears surprised as Harlequin continues, presses the advantage again. Three quick steps and there is blood in a pool where thigh meets armor; twin blades are lightning and there is thunder again from beyond the great walls of this keep.

Stormbringer howls. Loud, piercing, black and swift, new strength. Thunder again, sound mingles with black blade's. There is edge to the power, a knowledge that is denied to the wielder. Fate's Clown dances swifter, pirouettes and lances and slashes, twin blades, white against black, disappear and bite flesh.

No more pain. This thin frame bleeds and breathes its life to the air and ground, three-point clash sprays crimson onto the mute chorus. Stormbringer rises up from the riposte and lashes, baring a prince's teeth as shoulders heave and the edge cleaves an arm from the torso, the return driving deep, deeper, piercing the back.

Puppet body arches. Harlequin jerks his arm and his legs nearly give way. Black blade has found bones and tears, eating, devouring, unrelenting. Pale red eyes find death where life has been given and slowly taken away through battle. Resting and fighting on the edge of the sword, driving and forcing and asKing if this could be the time of rest, will there be release from this place?

The Clown can no longer laugh its silent song. It plays death. There should have been more of an elation, or perhaps a relief, but there is none to say the battle is complete. Peering down, Harlequin cranes forward and its lips part.

It says something in a language that flows with the blood foaming at its mouth.

There is no more strength from cursed blade, and the royal heart beats faster then falters. The herbs and potions that maintain princely life can no longer substitute for the life that took the life of its mother and the soul of its father. The weapon slides too easily from the automaton's flesh and legs collapse, rolling the body off the marble stage of black and white. The rush of thunder is not from lack of blood or injury, but bombards without; and still these people do nothing, know nothing about their fate to come, as it comes to the White Wolf. Servants attend, but their voices are silent.

The Queen is dead and the King stands before another, dying at the end of envenomed rapier, stage upon stage. There is a red mist before, and He-Who-Sells appears. And is triumphant.

"Who are you, that stands these halls and feels no play?"

"I am He-Who-Sells, who gives you freedom."

"Would that there be need of such, as the blood flows free and brings death."

"If that be your wish, then have it so. For oft have I spoke of that which follows."

"Do you say that there is choice?"

"Choice is yours, to a given point, though at a point might be truth to tell."

"Your cadence of speech is that of the Sword Lords themselves."

"Even they have need of such as I. For there is providence in the flight of an arrow. But now where will Prince Elric's needs lie? In the voice of the gods, or the auspices of man? Fortinbras is your humble servant."

"Servant, you say? You gave a promise which now cannot be collected."

"You may still leave, in any manner you wish. In either manner that you wish. Alive or dead, only Harlequin knows which is best."

Stormbringer rises unbidden to this man's chest, lifting hand and arm to strike as the thunder that once cracked these castle walls. That moment gives infinite understanding of this Fortinbras' life: he was that which came after, after the struggle, after the fight, after the life has given up the spirit. He plays dual roles to all men, all gods; being to some the force that plays clocks with the universe; artisans who machinate the likes of clowns and leave them to their own designs; or the being who forces all to action; that which forever comes after and is the purpose to which all fight and aspire. But his was a choice, and in one there was life.

The runesword drained the life from the man and he died in great agony; his soul screamed down the shaft of the blade into the abyss and gave up its strength so that the prince of Melniboné might live. The attendants shy away when they see crimson eyes flood with new life and know that their time has come again.

Struggling to stand, Harlequin gazes up with still, dead eyes, knowing the sadness of choice, and the weird of such as I.

THE GUARDIAN AT THE GATE

BY SCOTT CIENCIN

I

The albino did not look back to see if the wolves were gaining. He heard them crashing through the thicket he had vacated only moments earlier as he raced through the night. One of his boots sunk into a soft patch of earth and he nearly tumbled to the ground. His gloved hand reached out, caught a vine, and he pulled himself along, climbing the treacherous hillside as he ran. He heard movement on either side of him now, as well as from behind.

If he could reach the high ground before the creatures converged on him, he would have them at a disadvantage. Otherwise, he would unsheathe Stormbringer and make his stand wherever they trapped him. The black runesword hummed delightedly at the prospect of battle, for these were no ordinary wolves. They were sentient and he suspected they possessed souls.

His breath was labored and a bone weariness crept into his pale, broad-shouldered body. Ahead lay the plateau he had rested at earlier that day, on his way down to that accursed village where his troubles had begun. Only a few more steps, a final leap, and he would be ready to face his enemy.

One of the wolves darted from behind a bush off to his left. He had only a moment to turn and raise his arm in defense as a nightmarish vision of snapping jaws and blazing amber eyes overwhelmed him. The animal let out a cry of surprise and pain as its fangs clamped down tight on the steel bracelet he had purchased in the marketplace that afternoon. The albino stumbled back as the full weight of the wolf struck him. Together, they went down in a heap.

Where had this one come from? he wondered as the wolf rolled off him and he heard another leaping toward his exposed back. The albino twisted out of the way and scrambled to his feet. His hand settled on Stormbringer's hilt as the amber-eyed wolf bounded into the air, toward his throat. If any other weapon had resided in his sheath, the albino might have had no chance at all. Stormbringer moved with an unnatural speed. The albino maintained his grip on the weapon while allowing the blade to lead his arm. In a lightning-quick motion, the runesword freed itself from the sheath while yanking his arm up in an attempt to skewer the animal in midflight.

There was only one problem with Stormbringer's plan to feast on the soul of the amber-eyed wolf: The creature had somehow become frozen in midair, just out of the sword's reach. No, not frozen exactly, but *suspended* as it fought and hissed and spit in rage. A man had melted out of the darkness and had caught the wolf by the scruff of its neck, the way a bitch might gather up a stray member of its litter. The other wolves had broken off the attack and were silently gathering around Elric and the intruder. He saw that there were at least eight, perhaps as many as a dozen that had come after him. Stormbringer's wail of frustration caused the amber-eyed wolf to settle down and join its brethren in their eerie quiet.

"I'd wager you would prefer to leave this world alive and without a price on your head," the intruder said.

Elric could see him now. The man was greybearded and barrel-chested. A scar ran down one side of his face: three marks, certainly the work of the wolves. An old wound. He smiled warmly and seemed unafraid of the predators closing around him. His eyes were black and flecked with crimson.

"You're either a madman or a fool," said the albino.

The grey-bearded man winked. "I'll remember years from now that those were your first words to me. For now, though, do as I say and move your skinny little backside to the clearing up ahead. I'll try to reach some kind of accord with these curs on your behalf."

"I am Elric of Melniboné. No one speaks to me this way."

"Perhaps they should," the grey-bearded man growled. "Now get a move on."

Elric did not move. Stormbringer's wail had faded and been replaced by an angry buzz, like that of an insect horde.

The intruder released the amber-eyed wolf. The creature dropped to all fours, then lifted one leg and started to relieve itself on the boot of the barrel-chested warrior. He kicked its side and moved it off, ignoring a snapping chomp of its teeth that targeted the air next to his meaty calf.

"Your weapon isn't what's keeping these bastards at bay," the old warrior said with a sigh. "Put it away. I have no doubt that you could slaughter all of these and find your way back home. The question is, do you want more of their kind to follow and dog your steps for the rest of your days?"

Elric's ire had been raised, but he prided himself on his ability to focus past his anger and operate as a rational man, despite the Lords of Chaos' recent influence over him. But that was another story. For now, he chose to bow to the older man's judgment. Sheathing the blade was difficult, though not impossible. As a show of defiance he turned his back on the wolves long before it was necessary to do so and walked very slowly to the plateau ahead.

II

The wait for the greybearded warrior was mercifully brief. As Elric stood alone, he realized how the wolves had managed to ambush him. The majority of the pack had been trampling through the woods, making as much noise as possible in a bid to cover the sounds made by their advance party. The amber-eyed wolf and its companion were much closer and nearly silent. The albino heard a rustling and turned to see the grey-bearded warrior on the approach. The pack of wolves that had come after Elric was gone. He could hear the animals going back the way they came. One of them howled and the sound bit into him like the sudden wind that had risen with the approach of the old warrior.

"My name is Chatham," the grey-bearded man said with a wink, "of nowhere in particular, though this world itself is known as Autumn."

Elric nodded as if this had already been known to him.

"A few simple ground rules in this land. The wolves are the right hand of the Unseen, our God's avatars of justice. Commit a crime, the wolves are given dreams of your punishment. They will not rest until you are brought down."

"I killed a thief this morning," said Elric, not bothering to mention that he had meant only to wave Stormbringer in the criminal's face to warn him off. The runesword had been hungry, and so it had taken the bony man's head from his shoulders and swallowed his soul.

"A thief," Chatham said. "Well, there you go. If you had subdued him in any other fashion, the wolves may have left you alone. As it is, they wish to take your life as penance."

"This much I had guessed."

"What brings you to this world? Travelers such as yourself are very rare."

Elric shrugged. "There is a place I must find. I am told it resides not far from here. If the wolves hadn't come after me, I might have already been there."

"A place of power, one might assume."

"One might."

"Might one also assume that when you have found this place and taken what you are looking for, you have the means to leave Autumn and never return?"

"I have no choice. The magic I used has limits."

Chatham nodded. "The wolves now understand that you are not of this realm and were ignorant of our laws. They are willing to grant you amnesty provided you accomplish your business here and depart before morning. Can you achieve this goal?"

"I can."

"Of course, I will accompany you."

"I have no need of a guardian."

"No? Then perhaps you can perform that service on my behalf, as you are so clearly better versed in the ways of this land than myself."

Elric frowned. "Why have you chosen to help me?"

The old warrior laughed. "You've put in my hands the means to annoy those pompous curs. The least I can do in return is see that you get what you want and guarantee that they will be cheated of their prey."

Chatham reached out with his hand. Elric took it. The moment of contact made the albino realize that there was far more to this man than he might have guessed: The grey-bearded warrior wore the flesh of a man, but the power he radiated was much closer to that of this world's bloodthirsty protectors.

Earlier, in the village, Elric had procured a talisman that would help to lead the way: A small stone that tingled with life whenever he aimed it in the general direction of his destination. He set off to the east. Chatham followed dutifully, making annoying small talk on the way.

"Aren't you at all curious?" Elric finally asked as together they climbed higher into the mountains flanking the village.

"About what? Your purpose here?"

"Yes."

"So long as you have no intention of waking the Sleeping Gods, firstborn of the Unseen, and bringing about the destruction of our world — frankly, no."

"The destruction of the world," the albino said ruefully as his porcelain fingers grazed the hilt of his runesword. "Not this world. Not any time soon."

"Good, then!"

They walked on in silence. Elric's thoughts drifted back to the previous evening and the conversation that had started him on his current path.

III

The albino's table had resided in the deepest recesses of the filthiest tavern he could find in this strange city. He was disappointed on several counts. His outlandish clothing, usually an eyesore, blended in with that of the locals to the point of being passé; the tavern itself, though certainly the filthiest he had come across, was as close to pristine as one could ever want; and even his bone-white skin and glaring crimson eyes had, for the last ten minutes, drawn no attention. Even the serving wenches ignored him.

When an auburn-haired woman wearing a simple black gown finally approached, he was prepared to place an order. She sat down beside him and he quickly realized his mistake.

"If I gave you what you desire the most, would you do the same for me?" she asked in a silky voice.

"I seek no favors; nor do I grant them."

"You don't even know what I'm offering."

"I believe I have a fair idea."

The woman laughed. Her jade-green eyes sparkled. She was very beautiful. "Oblivion. Innocence. Trust. A release from your destiny. If, for even a single, shining moment, I could provide these for you, would you do my bidding?"

"I would not."

She smiled. "In that case, Elric of Melniboné, you are indeed the man I have been seeking. It is said of you that although you seem healthy enough to the naked eye, your vigor is an illusion perpetrated with drugs, magic and a sword that is an eater of souls."

"And you can change that."

"In a manner of speaking."

"You can take my thin blood and replace it with the robust liquid that coursed through the veins of my ancestors, the wine of dreamers and true kings? I cannot think of any but the gods who would have the power to complete such a task. Appearances are often deceiving, as you have said, but my every instinct warns me that you are not a god in human form, nor even one of their messengers."

"I am a woman who was once a withered hag, old before my time. A rare disease caused me to look and feel like an old woman on the brink of death before I was even ten. Miraculously, I survived until my sixteenth birthday, when I left my home and sought a place to lay my head and allow death to take me.

"In my grief, I wandered from this world to another, and ended up in a palace made of stone. I slept there for a night, determined to take my own life the next day if the gods did not spirit me away in my sleep. When I woke, I was as you see me now. Young and beautiful and strong.

"Before I departed, a voice whispered to me, carried by the wind that sometimes whistles through the drafty palace. It told me the price of my good fortune: Within a year of becoming reborn under the palace's auspices, I was commanded to find someone even more wretched than myself and send that one along to experience the wonders I enjoyed.

"There is only one warning I might give you before you embark. There is a guardian at the gate of this palace; one who will try to prevent you from gaining your heart's desire."

"A guardian? What does he look like?"

"That would be telling," she whispered, then hurriedly revealed the secrets he would need to find the other realm known as Autumn, and the woman in the market who would give him the talisman and direct him the rest of the way.

IV

Elric trudged on, occasionally falling behind the grey-bearded warrior. His companion seemed to know the route even without the indications Elric received from the stone.

"There is a legend in these parts," Chatham said abruptly. "Of a dilapidated palace hewn from a mountain. *This* mountain, as a matter of fact. If you see the place from enough of a distance, at just the right time of day, you can gather how the legend arose."

"Yes," Elric said, having witnessed earlier the exact sight Chatham described.

"A palace in which youth and vitality might be regained, and old scars finally healed."

Elric found his gaze drifting to the scar below the old warrior's eye. He stopped abruptly. "That is what draws you to this place? The promise of renewal?"

"I didn't say that. I was just making conversation."

"Of course." Elric felt a sudden pain in his hand, as if a blade had pierced his palm. He dropped the stone, then cursed as he bent low and tried to find where it had landed. The grey-bearded warrior was suddenly beside him, one heavy hand on the albino's shoulder.

"Look there," Chatham said, his crimson-flecked eyes appearing to sparkle in the moonlight. "A gate."

Raising his gaze, Elric saw a deeper patch of darkness directly ahead. Straining, he could make out an odd, jagged passage that might have been the stone maw of a hungry golem, or simply the entrance to a cave.

There was no guardian in sight.

The albino withdrew Stormbringer and held the runesword before him. Elric had not believed the woman's story for a moment. He had assumed that she was leading him into a trap or coercing him into aiding her under the pretense of serving his own needs. Nevertheless, he was bored, and this enterprise might have proved a release from the boredom. Over the course of the last day he had built up the image of the guardian in his mind until only the mortal incarnation of Arioch, the Duke of Hell, could have matched it as a worthy opponent.

The runesword hummed, ready for battle, but there was no one to fight. Disappointment burned through the albino, searing him with the power of damnation's flames.

"Shall we go in?" Chatham asked. "Or have we come to the wrong place?"

Elric considered turning back, then an odd notion came to him.

I have no need of a guardian.

He said those words to Chatham a scant hour earlier. Perhaps there was no guardian at the gate because the guardian was already with him.

Something else gnawed at him. Deep in the pit of his soul, he wondered what it might be like to be whole, to have the weak blood that coursed through his body replaced with that of his ancestors, to have his dependency on magic and Stormbringer's bloodlust brought to a crashing halt.

That was *not* within his grasp, of course. If such a thing were possible, Stormbringer would have found a way to put an end to it.

Elric thought of the runesword's attack on the thief and the near-fatal consequences. Had the blade sensed that there was something to the woman's tale? Was it attempting to force Elric away from this strange land before he could discover the truth?

"Perhaps you didn't hear me," Chatham said. "Shall we go in?"

"Yes," said Elric. "After you."

V

The palace, it seemed, was real enough. The walls were smooth and lit with some strange, inner fire. A greenish glow suffused each room.

He was not impressed.

Once, Elric of Melniboné had sat upon the ruby throne of the Dragon Isle. Compared to the mundane existence faced by most, he presided over miracles that defied the laws of men and gods on a routine basis. This "palace" had been carved from the building stones of nature and was quickly returning to its orignal state. There were no libraries here, no throne-rooms or places of judgment, no great feasting halls. Simply a wealth of empty rooms.

Chatham sat on the floor, his back to the wall. "It isn't much, I'll grant you that."

Elric joined him. "You're right."

"What were you expecting to find?"

"Don't you know?"

"Humor me."

"A little excitement, perhaps."

Chatham shook his head. "You took a man's life today and were nearly torn limb from limb by wolves. For most, that would be excitement enough."

"Perhaps, but I am not like most."

"That much is plain."

Elric closed his eyes and considered the course of his life if he could only be released from the grip of blood and magic.

No, this was the folly into which the woman had attempted to trick him.

Innocently believing that such a thing was possible, trusting that for once he would not be lied to, that he would not be used.

Oblivion, she had promised. Innocence. Trust. A release from his destiny. Pure folly!

He considered the grey-bearded warrior beside him. There was only one way to learn how much, if any, of what the woman had told him was true. He would have to sleep the night through in this place and see if he woke feeling any different.

Unfortunately, there was the issue of the guardian at the gate. If it were Chatham, the man might attack him in his sleep. How could he allow himself to be helpless, to be vulnerable in the company of the old warrior?

Stormbringer. He would have to rely on the runesword to watch over him, to remain in his hand and jerk him awake at the first hint of trouble. It had its own survival, its own destiny to consider.

What would he do? How would he decide?

An odd sound came to him. He looked over and saw that Chatham was snoring. The man had fallen sound asleep.

Elric stared at the old warrior, considering his options.

VI

Ten hours later, as the albino was scouring the empty rooms of the palace, looking for some clue that would address the mystery of the absent guardian, he noticed a stray beam of light piercing a crack in the ceiling. A single, thin beam fell before him, a blue-white finger that seemed to point accusingly toward the entrance to the reception hall where Elric had left his sleeping companion. The albino considered allowing Chatham to rest. After all, they were not friends. There was no fondness between them, no reason for a cordial farewell. The magic that would take him back to his own world would function just as easily in this place as any other.

He yawned and felt a weariness unlike any that he had suffered in years. The prospect of falling asleep while the guardian was still about, while it might very well have been Chatham only pretending to be asleep, had prevented the albino from even considering a decent night's rest. Besides, if he gave in to the lure of sleep and woke to find himself unchanged, he would unwork the magic the woman at the tavern had given him.

Her promises had led him on a quest that had not been of the usual sort, climaxing in some grandiose battle against a fiend or a god. She had, in truth, delivered much of what she had promised, if only for the brief hours when he found it impossible to consider anything other than the whereabouts of the mysterious guardian.

Oblivion. Innocence. Trust. A release from your destiny. If, for even a single, shining moment, I could provide these for you, would you do my bidding?

He had sworn that he would not, but, in fact, he had. Before she had appeared, he had been plagued by wolves of another kind —wolves of memory. They had been eating him alive slowly, seeking to devour his sanity. He had desperately needed a release, a few precious hours to concentrate on something other than brooding over the past.

The albino was about the enact the spell that would return him to the Young Kingdoms when he heard a growl from the other room, where he had left Chatham.

The wolves had returned. He debated leaving immediately. Chatham had said that the wolves could follow Elric to any land, but the albino was not certain this was true. Though he felt tired, he itched for the challenge of facing the wolf pack, of allowing Stormbringer to rip apart the snarling beasts and taste the souls of creatures that were touched by the right hand of an Unseen deity.

No, he thought. Better to leave now, while mysteries still existed. He opened the doorway and stepped through to his home. Just then, a moment before the doorway could vanish behind him, a howl came from the reception hall. He turned to hear the clicking of a wolf's nails against the stone floor and the excited panting of a creature on the hunt. The doorway he had started to open shimmered, the image it revealed already fading.

Elric drew his blade on the off chance that the wolf would leap for the doorway and come through to his world. He could see it now — black fur with grey streaks, gaping jaws that worked furiously as if their prey were already trapped within them, and nightmare-black eyes.

The beast came to the edge of the doorway and halted, whining piteously, as if to beckon the albino back to his death. Ah well, one mystery solved. The creatures did not have the power to come through to his world after all.

Then he saw it. A ragged scar just beneath the creature's eye, three marks, like the scratch a wolf might make — identical to the one marring Chatham's face. Elric took a step forward and Stormbringer jerked him back from the gate to Autumn.

The instant before the gateway vanished, Elric saw the wolf's eyes, black with flecks of crimson.

When he looked back, the gateway was gone. Elric looked down at his runesword, which hummed happily at the prospect of the near-endless river of souls it would devour.

He had spent the night that might have saved him looking for the guardian at the gate, never guessing that he had to look no farther than the scabbard at his hip.

CELEBRATION OF CELENE

BY GARY GYGAX

ONE

A lone and dust-covered rider paused on a low hill to look below him. Three roads met ahead, and all were thronged with travelers. The small man slouched in his saddle, grinning to himself as he contemplated what he saw. "There go companies of fellow libertines, Harvester, and soon we shall join them." As he thus addressed his mount, the horse blew loudly from its nostrils and flattened its ears. Wide mouth went from grin to laughter. "No need to curse me for your state. It was not my hand which made you gelding."

Nowhere below was there anyone like this small and travel-stained figure. At the rider's right hip was a small blade, which might be mistaken for a gentlemen's dress sword save that its hilt was of plain, worn bone, not some burnished material with gilt and gemstone decoration. So too the leather scabbard bespoke a weapon of war, not a meaningless bit of bravado worn as a badge of privilege and station. All doubt was torn away by the second sword whose brass pommel projected above the little man's left shoulder. That long and deadly sabre could be mistaken for nothing other that what it was: a tool of execution. There were indeed weapons aplenty amongst the many celebrants, but none which spoke so bluntly of purpose.

The rider guided his horse through tall grass towards the nearest of the ways leading to the city. The warm sun graced this land with a riot of growth, and its peoples echoed the diversity of nature. Verdant land, gorgeous flowers in profusion, and a fanciful place of spires and glittering buildings where the land met the end of this riot of growth. The stream of travelers approached in various ways. Most went afoot, were carried in palanquins, or mounted on horses; some went ahead in creaking carts or lumbering wagons; the richest were drawn in carriages; the mightiest looked down with hauteur from atop ponderous oliphants. Yet humbly or in state, all flocked east. The small man shook his head, grinned again, and urged his own mount ahead. "You have no vote in this matter, Harvester. We go to Eshraao — you to a safe stall, me to wherever the wine pours freely and the girls are friendly." In minutes the horse and rider became one with the throng.

It was a converging river of humanity, tall and lean, short and square. From all around they came, merrymakers who would soon be dressed in their finest costumes. Eshraao was the goal of all. Eshraao of the Silver Streets, City of Celebration, the capital of licentiousness on the eve of May. For a fortnight and more before the main festivities the pilgrims of pleasure flocked into Eshraao. Once within the city they would doff their ordinary apparel and become masquers. None could say from how far they came, but even a casual observer would note that folk from all of the Yon Eastlands seemed to intermingle on the roads leading to the city, merged into a mass of revelers therein. Where the sun rose from the sea lay the most exotic of the new Young Kingdoms. The Celebration of Celene might mark their arcane knowledge, an almost understood precognition of certain doom for all their civilization lurking just ahead. Did the revels of May deny the extinction of December? Moot.

He moved the big mount into a small space in the throng, fell in beside a pair of riders who were evidently from the north, Korillya by their felt cloaks and embroidered tunics. The nearer of the pair leaned close, eyed the newcomer, and sneered through his ash-blonde mustachios: "What have we here, a mannikin? Your head's afire, starveling!" His fellow laughed uproariously at the crude humor, then joined in: "There must be more of you to come, eh? What are you called, Half-a — "

The point of a sabre cut short the rest. It hovered a handspan from the angular man's neck. His companion was trying to get a grip on his own blade when the Korillyan noticed that a second point threatened to pierce his liver. "Hold there, Elwherner. Leave off! No need to take such offense, small sir. My friend and I meant naught but...."

"But bad jesting at the expense of your better. That is so, isn't it?" The two lengths of steel remained aimed.

"That's so."

"Small you said. Size is unimportant when it comes to being a man, yes?"

"That's a... err... very true statement."

The swords withdrew at that, and the wide mouth of their wielder split into a wicked smile which mocked the pallor of the pair. "Then make way for a bigger heart and a better man. Perhaps we'll meet again in the city, but for now I don't want your company."

Without protest, the two angular riders reined in and watched the red-headed swordsman move on ahead in a clear space made for him by those around who had been witness to the display.

"I'll show him something if he crosses our path again," grumbled the first, he who had instigated the trouble.

His comrade nearly shoved him from his saddle. "Are you crazed? We come for frolic and fun, not pain and death, you fool. If by chance we see that little one in Eshraao, I for one will head away." The expression he saw in the eyes of his countryman said that the fear of facing the little warrior was mutual. They left the road and headed cross-country to make their way to the city by the old northern road.

Because Eshraao lay beside the Eastern Sea, her beauty was enhanced by the shore and the dozen streams which wandered languidly from the west to merge with the greater water on whose verge the city was displayed. All of pale and lustrous stones was Eshraao built. The pellucid blocks which formed her streets shone brightly in sunlight, gleamed dove gray in moonlight, complimented the silver sheen of the rivers and cross-cut canals which formed the city's web of arteries serving the hundred thousand souls residing within the metropolis. Day or night, well-named was Eshraao of the Silver Streets, though cloud or dark might make argent seem leaden. Fair was the weather of the kingdom, rich its resources. No gloom ever served to darken this seaside jewel. Should cloud obscure light, a thousand torches and ten times that number of gay lanterns set ablaze the dark. Then silver street and flowing water were adorned by glittering streaks of bright jewels set in old but still-precious metal.

No guards stood at the great gates to the city. All portals in Eshraao's walls stood wide open to admit the revelers. None in all the Yon Eastlands would dream of assailing the city. Eshraao the Open was the neutral hub of the east, and no rival king would dare to attempt conquest. All others would then raise their hosts against such a one. Besides, warfare was at best a last resort hereabouts. In lands which provided easy living, there was little need to try to wrest anything from a neighbor. Especially true during the Celebration of Celene. There were, however, men, women too, standing near the mighty gates . As the small man atop the big gelding passed through, these folk shouted lewd greetings, laughed, and flung garlands at horse and rider with equal abandon. "Are you a pixie or a goblin?" shouted a buxom woman as she tossed her flowers to ring the small fellow's neck.

"Which would you prefer to bed?"

"Both!"

That brought ribald laughter from all, but the stream flowed ahead, and nothing more came of it. The rider with the flame-hued shock of hair was carried inward. The woman turned her attention to twins from Fadort who rode a three-wheeled cart.

Through a geometric maze of streets, over a dozen bridges spanning the streams filled with watercraft, and into the heart of old Eshraao he rode. At an inn whose sign displayed a jester with gold bells topping his cap, the small man with two deadly blades dismounted. A grubby lad came hastening to take the gelding by the bridle. "Here for a bit of refreshment, master? Or do you hope to find a room?"

"I plan to stay."

The stableboy laughed. "The inn has been filled for a week. You're in luck though, because I know of a private...." He let his sentence go unfinished as the gray-green eyes of the stranger bored into his own.

"Never mind that. Neither bumpkin nor fool am I. Take my horse to a stall, and see he's cared for properly — rub-down and then feed and fresh water. Do it right, and you get a coin; slack and lazy earns you something different, boy." Then without waiting to see the reaction, he turned and entered the establishment.

Early as it was there were already a score of drinkers in the public room. A long-faced, gray fellow stalked over to peer contemptuously down at the red-headed newcomer as if he were an intruder. "Is there something...?"

"Yes. That *something* is the best room you have."

"During Celebration? No such room exists." The flinty eyes in the saturnine face were more scornful than the tone, which was fairly dripping with derision. Noting the shabby garments but well-used weapons worn by the small fellow with too-long legs, the innkeeper added as if in solicitous afterthought, "There might be a place in the stable loft, and at a fair price." At the same time he raised a hand and a pair of burly porters came hastening. "Grodor and Tinz will show you the way, Elwherner."

"You will address me as Lord Glum," the red-head said, ignoring the pair of oafs who loomed ready for trouble. As he drawled those words, the small man produced a handful of thick gold coins, placed them on the reception table. "These should cover my initial expenses, and when I have used their value, my host, you may feel free to inform me. There are plenty more where those came from."

"Lord... Glum? Hmmmm. Yes, of course. I am reminded that we do indeed have a special suite which has just been vacated by a Daglernian merchant. Too costly even for such a wealthy man as he. Tinz. Grodor. Go to Yonish Vactir's rooms and assist him in removing to the kitchen loft." The two burly porters wore comic expressions of startlement, but hastened to obey. As they hurried off, conversing in low tones, the long-faced innkeeper inclined his narrow body. "Will m'lord be staying for more than two days?"

With a slight shrug the small man surveyed the premises. There was as much disdain in his gaze as had formerly resonated from the host's voice. "I can understand your misgivings, innkeeper. Seeing this place does give rise to certain qualms. However, as Eshraao *is* crowded during this amusing period, it seems your humble establishment will have to do for the whole of Celebration." As he concluded, the gray-green eyes of the small man met the flint-dark gaze of the lank proprietor. "Yet surely, my good man, you weren't suggesting that the daily cost of your best room, even during this time, exceeds five Negrilain Crowns?"

It seemed impossible, but the saturnine face grew gloomier still upon that query. "Well... no, Lord Glum. Though I did take into account the costs of meals, wine, and — "

"Done then! I have the suite, with all viands included, and such wine as I care to quaff at the sum of five crowns daily. I believe that you will find exactly twenty-one coins there on the table. Consider me your guest for no fewer than four days then, and keep the odd bit for yourself. Where do I go to find this suite?"

The innkeeper was torn between avarice and caution. The sum named was more than the usual inflated price he demanded during the festival time, but he had hoped for still more. Then there was the addition of the food and drink. Dare he try to exact more from this "lord"? A glance at the odd little man convinced him otherwise. "Thank you... m'lord," the innkeeper managed. To cover the hesitancy, he added, "Your pardon for the inconvenience, but it will be some short time before all is ready to accommodate your lordship. Perhaps you might take a wa — "

A commotion at the back of the big common room alerted the proprietor to impending trouble. Yonish Vactir, florid face now livid, was attempting to get to where the innkeeper stood, while the bumbling pair of porters did their best to intervene and prevent the scene he surely planned to make over his sudden eviction. "Please, m'lord," the host murmured as he gingerly took the small man's arm and steered him away. While groaning inwardly, the innkeeper managed, "Here is a private drinking room, a place reserved for quality only. It is stocked with rare vintages, and the sideboard bears all manner of cheeses, sausages, and dainties. Enter. All is yours."

"Perhaps I have underrated the quality of your establishment, host," Lord Glum said as he allowed himself to be ushered into the richly paneled private chamber. "I will test your wares as you urge."

Hastening to close the door, the innkeeper choked, "Enjoy, m'lord, enjoy."

The last word was punctuated by the bang of the door and the muted sound of shouting. Lord Glum laughed, knowing well what had happened and what was now occurring. "Indeed, host, indeed. I haven't eaten in a day, nor had so much as a glimpse of such vintages in weeks. Enjoy is the very least I shall do!"

TWO

Evening had passed and night had come before he awoke. Lord Glum stretched, luxuriating in the softness of the down before springing from the big bed and splashing himself with water. The act of dressing was accomplished in much the same strange mixture of dally and dash. A languid appraisal of his odd mask, then a flurry which ended in the small man's being attired in velvet so purple as to appear black in all but the most intense light. "Appropriate," he murmured to himself as he appraised the figure reflected in the somewhat cloudy but large mirror which graced the room.

The host's best suite was by no means royal, but it was posh enough. Any mirror in a lodging place was rare, and a full-length one bespoke accommodation for aristocratic clientele — or at least for those willing to pay dearly for such niceties. No noble would pay more than a single crown a night for these rooms The appointments given it were not quite right, so that petty nobles at best might find them satisfactory. Still, under the circumstances, he was pleased enough with the suite. It was, after all, the Celebration, all Eshraao was jammed with revelers, and the Jester with Three Bells happened to be located in the heart of the city. Perfect. The cellar here was good too. Thinking that reminded him of something, and Lord Glum grinned at himself. He turned away from the mirror, looked around, saw what he searched for. There was a bottle protruding from under the bed's dependent covers. He grabbed it casually, flipped its cork up and out with a thumb, and, as the movements were completed, expertly poured a stream of deep-red liquid from the narrow neck so that it arched through the air and entered his mouth from above his head. "Ahhh," he sighed after swallowing the last of it. "Imagine a thirty-year-old wine from the Purple Towns ending up in this place — and down my gullet!"

Tossing the empty bottle aside, Lord Glum picked up the mask, donned it, and paused again to see the result of the completion of his costuming. Knee-high boots of black hid the legs of the midnight-purple breeches adorning his long legs. The velvet doublet overly accentuated his short torso, but the cape's length discounted that flaw, so the overall effect was acceptable. The glittering sequins were indeed like stars when one swirled the long cape, and above their twinkling beamed the moon. That luminary was, of course, his mask. Lord Glum moved closer to the mirror, adjusting the fastenings of the hood with its roundish silver face-covering. The man in the moon looked serenely back at him, floating regally above the starry throng. No great sabre spoiled the line of the costume, only a straight little hanger which was quite in fashion, albeit the worn look of the sword was wrong; so with a twitch the offending bit disappeared under a fold of cloth.

The hood free and back to appear no more than a cowl of the mantled cape, the small man passed quickly through the inn's common room and into the night. Despite the fact that the hour neared the midpoint of the night, there was much activity. Celebration indeed. Even the stableboy was there. "Will you be wanting your horse, Lord Glum?" Word got around fast.

"Just continue to care for him well," the small man responded. There was a faint glittering in the air near the boy, the glint of lanternlight on metal. Quick as a bat swooping to gather in a fluttering insect, the boy caught the big coin and ran off. Nobody would want to ride tonight, as well he knew. "Clever lad, that," mused Lord Glum as he strolled off into the surrounding darkness.

Of course the whole city was ablaze with lights. Torch and cresset, lantern and candle made Eshraao like water beneath the midnight sky. Many were the bright pools of light, but between each lay the soft blackness of shadow. None of the alleys and few of the by-lanes were illuminated. Public buildings, warehouses, and certain other structures showed no light at all. It was a part of the Celebration, a planned contrast.

Walking with some purpose now, Lord Glum followed a narrow lane which crossed two broad and thronged thoroughfares of activity before it turned a little, then passed over a river branch by arching itself into a quaint, roofed bridge. As he neared that opening a pair of armed watchmen eyed him suspiciously. One spoke: "The High Isle is for gentry only!" The second, noting the richness of costume and the man's assured demeanor, intervened in haste: "Pass and revel long, honored sir!" Lord Glum ignored them both, walked past and crossed the span. He now was in the best quarter of the city, reserved for its leading, affluent citizens.

There were more lanterns here, but fewer celebrants abroad. Most of the folk coming here found their merriment in sumptuous mansions, not in street or public house. Yet in a short time he passed by no fewer than a score of masked people. Gallants wearing fanged bat-faces or prowling behind night-hunting tiger masks, damsels in dominoes of owl-form or winged fay. Here a wolf, there a radiant comet, stars too with her, a panoply of false faces and elaborate costumes to match. The full and smiling argent visage now covering Lord Glum's features provoked comment from such bypassers.

From a group of nearly a dozen came the first challenge. "A bold statement, sir," said one dandy clad as the sun in darkness. His bronze-rayed mask swung this way and that as he eyed the smaller man. The outline of the sword brought the appraisal to an abrupt halt. He walked on with a false laugh, adding to cover the retreat, "Too small a matter to bother with." Others simply japed as they observed him.

"A lunatic."

"The fullness of the face belies the waning proved by stature."

"Sink, pale and fireless one."

None of that surprised Lord Glum. The political rivalries of Eshraao were known to him as well as they were to the denizens of the High Isle of the city itself. The party of the sun, that of the starry constellations, and the moon faction too were indeed but laughable epithets, were it not for the vehemence of their followers and the blood shed on behalf of one or another faction. No riots would cloud Celebration, but there would be brawls below and possibly swordplay here on the High Isle.

Pondering thus he passed a tower and was in a small plaza almost without noting the change. At the far side were dark figures all in a swirl. The clash of steel sounded, a muffled oath, and a high-pitched voice cut short in a cry. With the grace of a cheetah Lord Glum sprang ahead, and as he sped across the square the sword went from scabbard to hand as if by magic. Almost soundlessly the small figure came, so that he was upon the group before any of its members realized another had joined. The short tongue of steel was sufficiently long enough to pierce the heart of a brawny fellow just finishing off a prone man. Only a slight groan escaped his mouth as his fingers loosed the cudgel they had so recently grasped, and he collapsed upon his lifeless victim, dark blood pouring from open mouth to commingle with that he had just spilled.

" 'Ware yer back, Nub!"

That warning came too late for the mugger going by that name. He was caught as had been the other, and Lord Glum's blade did like execution. Two down and four — no, five to go. One fellow was struggling to keep a cloaked woman restrained and silent. Two of the waylayers were engaged in combat with the last of the woman's companions. Two were already dead. Just a pair facing him. "More of an even score now, eh?" the small man said as he yanked his sword free and brought it around quickly to catch a blundering thug low in the belly.

The stroke sent the fellow reeling back, clutching himself, keening in a high voice, "Gutted. O Jatoon, I'm gutted!" He staggered off into the darkness, moaning and cursing.

"You stinking little pig!" This one was he who had first seen Lord Glum and tried to alert his fellows. He was average in size, lithe and economical in his movements, hard of voice. He advanced to meet the sword with a blade of his own, albeit a clumsy flachet. The heavy-bladed weapon he held before him on guard, the falchion-like blade ready to catch any thrust Lord Glum might make.

Gleaming darkly from its gory coating, Lord Glum's point went out as might a striking cobra. It was aimed at the mugger's eyes. The clash of thick steel ringing on thin was loud as the small sword was brushed aside, blood flying from it as the force of the parry sent it off and up. As that happened, the lithe attacker had the heavy-bladed weapon point upmost and moving out and down in a chopping stroke meant to cleave his opponent from crown to crotch. "Now I'll — "

He couldn't finish his threat, because a foot of steel through his neck silenced what he meant to say, ended all. The sword flew off, and his body fell to the paves to join the company already sprawled there. "You will die," Lord Glum concluded for him flatly. There was no pause in the small swordsman's activity for that, however. There was a stamp of booted feet and the plangent sound of blades crossing to remind him that assailants still remained.

Lord Glum turned in time to see the conclusion of the struggle between what must have been the noble young escort of the woman. He had fought well against a pair of attackers of status, for both used long and slender swords. One he had laid low, but the odds were too great. Weakened from wounds, the defender dropped his guard, and in a stroke he was run through the heart. The scuff of a boot alerted the fellow of danger, and he managed to free his rapier and turn in time to fend off Lord Glum's attack.

"A nasty little backbiting moon, is it?" the man grated behind his black leopard domino as he riposted and lunged.

Backing quickly and guarding, at a distinct disadvantage with the small sword, Lord Glum laughed and responded, "From one of a pack of lurking jackals, that statement is sheer whining. Your mask belies your nature, dog!"

His opponent stamped forward in a rush. This was surely a haughty aristocrat bent on revenge for the insult just given. Lord Glum kicked, and a discarded cap flew towards the cat-masked man. The rapier's point moved to intercept the soaring garment. The instinctive defense cost the man his life, for in an instant Lord Glum was close, and the shorter blade of his sword thrust home. "That was... unfair," the dying assailant gasped.

"As fair as your attack by seven on three men and a woman." He might have added more, but the man was dead. Lord Glum pushed him free with his left hand, and, as the corpse crumpled, looked to see what had become of the woman and her assailant. She must have noted what was happening, seen Lord Glum's sudden assault and slaughter of the band of muggers. Her attention then informed the one who held her prisoner. As Lord Glum advanced, the man hurled the woman down and dashed off into the darkness of a narrow walkway between buildings.

Ignoring the escape, Lord Glum hastened to the woman. As he picked her up he saw that she was barely older than a girl. Gossamer-costumed as a moth, crowned by crescent moons, she was lovely indeed. Her domino had come free, and he saw that she was as beautiful of face as she was shapely of form. "Vile indeed an assault on one so fair," he murmured.

"Never mind me," the young beauty said desperately. "Catch the man who flees. He has my necklace!"

"Too late. He is away in a maze he surely knows and with which I am quite unfamiliar."

At that she broke into tears. "Celene, aid me! It isn't so. *They* can't be allowed to have it!"

Lord Glum tried to comfort her. "Surely the loss of some bit of jewelry is better than being dead."

The gorgeous face turned and looked at him with incomprehension. Her eyes were silvery in the moonlight as they assessed him. Comprehension came. "You wear that mask accidentally. Your accent is not of Eshraao."

"More or less correct, my lady. I know the meaning of the face displayed, but I am from Elwher and have neither political nor devotional conviction with regard to matters which concern... you. Nonetheless, I am pleased to have been of some assistance to a devotee of Celene. I am Lord Glum, at your service."

This brought confusion to her. "I beg your pardon, Lord Glum. I am Lady Definee Adarothy — no ordinary servant of Celene but her high priestess in this city. I am in your debt, brave sir, and I shall repay you."

"No need for that. I consider it at best a poor service."

"What? Why so?"

"I failed to prevent the thief from making off with your necklace. From your reaction, it must be valuable indeed, Lady Definee."

She shook her head, sighed. "It is worth much gold, but that is not the measure of its real value. The necklace bears the True Moonstone."

"True or not, my lady, such a gem is not so precious as an opal, let alone a ruby or — "

"You prate of money, but fail to understand the significance of my words. The stone I speak of is a key to the Pathway to Order!"

"Your ladyship?"

With a second sigh the gorgeous young priestess looked away, then turned back. "Again I must ask your pardon, Lord Glum. Lord Glum.... What an odd name. Pray, remove that mask so that I may see the man behind it, the one to whom I owe so much."

"I fear the false face is far more handsome than my own, lady."

"Is that so? I shall be the judge. Come, doff the disguise and allow me the honor, sir. I will explain what I meant then."

"Very well." Without further words, Lord Glum pulled back his hood and stood with face revealed.

"Strange."

"Perhaps homely is more apropos, my lady."

That made her laugh despite herself. "No, gallant sir, I referred not to your looks but to some memory I have of seeing you before. I know. You have appeared in my dreams!"

The large mouth twisted into a wry grin. "This visage is not the stuff of ladies' dreams, high priestess."

"Yet I have seen it in mine," she countered. Definee Adarothy assessed the oddly colored eyes with her own even stranger ones, noted the upturned nose, wide mouth in the round face, wild mane of red hair — all of which set this small man apart from the average. "Unhandsome, certainly, but somehow compelling," she mused as if to herself. "You have a quality, Lord Glum, which is not of this earth, and I see terrible sadness in your eyes — great wisdom too."

"Thank you, my lady. I would be wiser still, would you but tell me the significance of the lost moonstone borne in the purloined necklace."

Lady Definee Adarothy tilted her head. "Are you really ignorant of it? I wonder. I'll take you at your word, though. Come. Let us get clear of this place. I am nearly as valuable to the foe as the gem is. The Master of Flames will send more of his assassins to this place soon. I must not be taken!"

Lord Glum shrugged and followed as she quickly led him out of the plaza, going on deeper into the heart of the High Isle. Soon the two came to a barred gate, and at a word from the priestess it opened, and they were inside.

THREE

"You have such strange new gods."

They were in a high chamber of the palace of the Adarothy family. Although there were no other members of the noble house there, the place swarmed with retainers and guards of the family. If there were safety for her anywhere in Eshraao, it was here. The words which her small rescuer spoke made Lady Definee straighten her spine and become very adamant. "That is near blasphemy, sir!

They are neither strange nor new, merely named differently than before. They are the Lords and Ladies of Law bearing new names to indicate their new and greater powers now. The time of Chaos is coming to a conclusion... forever!"

"Perhaps. Is the True Moonstone then fallen into the hands of the foes of this coming order?"

"Almost as bad," she said with a frown. "Law has its cruel minions too, you know. Not the demons of Chaos, surely, but violent and unpalatable nonetheless. The factions here in Eshraao are grouped around the White Ones. That of Celene is best, for we temper justice with mercy."

One fiery brow cocked at that. "Yes? And the others are less forgiving then?"

"Much less. So much so that I care not to contemplate their regimentation and execution of law. Factions are what the True Moonstone is all about, you see."

"Not clearly, but I think I have some better grasp of it now. The gem is a receptacle of power which makes a pathway for the White Ones."

Lady Definee's expression ran from pleasure to sorrow. "Yes, you have it. What *will* I do?! I have lost the stone, and now the Master of Flames will use it to bring the harsh and unbending gods to the forefront. It will be terrible."

After several pointed questions Lord Glum learned why the young high priestess had worn the necklace, exposing it and herself to the dangers which ended in the loss of the treasured, sacred True Moonstone. "So it is required that whoever possesses the talisman must bear it openly during the full of the moon in Celebration."

"Yes."

"You sought to pass unnoticed with a small party rather than risk a great confrontation between armed camps."

She smiled wanly, nodded. "We left by a secret way and would certainly have avoided trouble had not someone betrayed me — of that I am certain. It was generally thought that I would lead a throng of guards and followers from the temple to the grand square and back at the hour before moonset. By then I would have been back here, safe, but for some traitor!"

"Whoever was responsible will be ferreted out in due course, I assume. What seems to be paramount now is the necklace. Will the one you call the Master of Flames now complete the ritual and thus command the talisman's power?"

She collapsed on the low couch, covered her lovely face with her hands. "I am such a fool. They will pervert it completely — the True Moonstone will be held and defiled at the festival of the sun."

"Why so?"

"Then its gate will close to those gods of milder aspect, and the burning fury of the inflexible lords will come upon all."

After pondering that a moment, Lord Glum moved to a place beside her on the couch. He smiled reassuringly. "Time remains, my lady. The necklace can be recovered. Then there will be no terrible order imposed."

"Who can take it from the Master of Flames? You?"

He ignored incredulity in her voice, the look in her silvery eyes. "Perhaps I can, Lady Definee. Do you believe in a multitude of worlds?"

"If by that you mean endless numbers of earths with different futures, no. That is pap served out to placate those who suffer under the sole reality — that which we experience. Otherwise all striving is absolutely pointless."

"Only if there were a finite number of possibilities, and the struggle on each of those finite number of worlds, large as their number might be, affected an overall balance... retained the potential of the future thus. Perhaps the rigidity of Law leads to stasis even as the randomness of dominant Chaos brings total disorder and dissolution."

She drew back at that. "You speak to a high priestess thus? Chaos is vile and evil, Law good and right. The former must be destroyed, the latter exalted."

"Even if there is no mercy, as your foes would have it?"

"Even so. They are foes only in interpretation, not aim or spirit. If in order to have good we must sear the wicked into ash, so be it. Better than allowing the work of the demons of Chaos to continue." When she said that Definee Adarothy was looking hard at the red-haired man. Something in his expression alerted her. "You do not love Law!" she accused.

Lord Glum shook his head, but he assured her, "More than I do Chaos, dear lady. That you can be assured of. Tyranny is my foe."

"Law is not tyranny."

"If you say so."

"I do. How will you recover the True Moonstone?"

He was startled at that. "Have I suggested — "

"No, I have. Yet I can read much in you, and that I read. You plan to go after it. But never mind, you need not tell me. There is something of Chaos in you that I cannot approach. I recall the dreams in which you appeared to me more clearly now. You became the full moon, but then waned instantly to the dark. Does that signify you will die in regaining the talisman? Is that why you are named Glum?" As Definee asked those questions she drew close to him, slid her arms around to hold him. "I do not wish you to die, my lord."

It was not possible for him to resist her. "Once I was called Moonglum, dear lady. That was many... probabilities and long years gone and to come. Yet when you hold me thus I feel no moroseness. If it please you, then I will again take the first portion of my old name, Moon. How does Moonantic suit you?"

"Suit me? Not at all — but it seems apt for you, sir! If you recover the lost stone, then you shall be my dearest Moonantic, no lord at all but Prince Moonantic of Eshraao, consort of its queen, the high priestess of Celene."

He waved his hand weakly. "Far too grand for the likes of me."

"Is that so? Time to show you otherwise." With that Definee Adarothy kissed him passionately, then drew back. "Do not mistake this. I am neither a wanton as is typical of celebrants, not do I seek to bribe and bind you, Lord Glum — Moonantic. It is you who causes me to act thus. I am drawn to you."

"You are mistaken, Definee Adarothy. I am not what you think. My purpose, my fate, is different from yours."

She ignored his warning. "You love me, I see it in your eyes, even hear it behind your words. Yesterday is gone, and what comes tomorrow is shaped by now."

He thought to remonstrate further, to point out that time might not be so inflexible as those who placed faith in Law believed, that the emotions of two people or even two million were weak forces in a multiverse of savage powers. But her lips were upon his own, and the firm body pressed against him sent the thoughts scattering as dry leaves before an autumn gale.

His head was spinning when he awoke in late morning. Was he Moonglum, Lord Glum, or the newly made Moonantic? No, that wasn't correct. He was entirely different. Staring at the ceiling, the small man tried to avoid thinking about what that meant.

"Your thoughts are of me."

"That they are." As Moonantic he goggled his eyes and placed a lascivious expression on his face.

Definee slid across the silken bed to lie atop him, staring into his eyes. "Cease the clowning."

"You would have me Moonantic."

"I would have you love me."

He was very serious as he responded, "That I do."

Definee was not satisfied. She examined his face closely. "As I love you!"

"I love as I love, for I am me, not you. Yet I can say without fear of contradiction that I love you, Definee Adarothy, more than I have ever loved any woman — or dreamed myself capable of loving and being loved in return."

"That is acceptable. The love we share will make all other things right."

"Will it?"

She stopped her affectionate gestures, stiffened. "You will get the necklace?"

"I will try, as I promised."

"With my love you will succeed."

A feeling of whimsy seized him, one in which the moment was all. Leaping up, he cavorted, performed acrobatics there on the bed. His exertions tumbled Definee this way and than, ended with her lithe form pressed flat by his own. "That it will, as pledged now by your Lord Moonantic. But...."

Uncertain as to what had come over him, she asked suspiciously, "You have qualifications?"

"Certainly I do! If your love is to sustain me in the dangerous duty before me, then I must have sufficient stores of it in reserve to call upon when in peril."

At that she laughed and softened. "What a novel concept. Pray tell, my lord, just how do you propose to garner this trove?"

"How else but as we did last night, only in addition I wish to — "

"Hush! You are without shame."

"No shame in my love for you, sweet Definee, that is true."

She grew serious and stern for a moment. "Nothing which smacks of Chaos will be allowed. All else is yours."

"Spontaneity?"

"Don't be exasperating. No order is so complete that it denies chance within its bounds. You may surprise me."

He did.

Hunger drove them forth to enjoy a meal in a private salon adjacent to the garden at the center of the great mansion. The servants cast sidelong glances at both, especially Lord Glum, but betrayed nothing otherwise of their curiosity and suspicion. The pair laughed and ate and gazed at each other always.

"It is time for me to get ready."

Definee Adarothy observed the long shadows among the blossoms of jasmine and rose, and sighed. "Yes. There is but tonight to act. Tarry, and the talisman will surely be removed to some place where not even you could find it."

"Let us return to your chambers. I would have you explain the whole once again — and look again at the plans of the stronghold of the Master of Fire."

She arose, smiling with a gaiety which belied the heaviness in her heart, and, taking his arm said, "And you love me."

"Even more than a minute ago."

As the two left the room, a shadow moved and a figure stepped from behind an arras. The servitor came silently to the table, stared at the silver plates and crystal goblets, but touched nothing. Then he clapped his hands loudly, and other servants came hurrying in. "Clear this away immediately. When I return I expect all to be spotless and placed safely in the proper positions within the chamberlain's chests."

Above, Lord Glum and Definee Adarothy were doing what they could to assure the success of her plan.

The sun's scarlet orb sank below the distant mountains that marked the verge of the Yon Eastlands. Before it rose from the sea to mark a new day, there was much to do.

FOUR

"What do you want?" At that question, a hand was raised to the grillwork and a ring flashed. "Oh, I beg your pardon. Enter." The panel slid closed and the heavy door opened in quick succession. "Welcome to the House of Favorable Portents, master...."

"Lord Glum. I am an adept of sea-change. I am here to dispute the power of fire."

The doorkeeper was uncertain. "This is a matter of irregular sort."

"Not at all. Fetch your master."

In a few minutes a plump man of considerable height as well as girth came hastening up to where the newcomer waited. His expression was clearly that of a man uncertain of things but bound to manage with dispatch whatever arose. "See here, I — "

Again Lord Glum displayed the ring, a huge, faceted emerald into which was cut a strange sigil. "No. *You* see," he said flatly before the fellow could make his protest. "This is the place of association created by the followers of Law, is it not?"

"Of course."

"And who, sir, are you?"

The fat shoulders squared as the man drew himself up. "Tregaan of Inim'l'asty, steward of this hall and a master in my own right of haruspicy and of certain less-known divinatory practices."

The gesture and expression accompanying Lord Glum's reply spoke more directly than his words. "Pleasant diversions, I am sure, master Tregaan. Hardly of the caliber of what I contemplate." As the fellow deflated, and before he could think of a reply sufficiently guarded to avoid offense but strong enough to restore his prestige, the red-haired stranger pointed a finger, asking, "Does not the charter of this society contain a provision for the testing of supernatural command?"

"Of course, adept lord, but such trials are matters of formality which must be conducted after challenge and response... and elsewhere."

"Bah. That is nonsense. Perhaps the usual manner is as you have said, but it is not the only acceptable form. In fact, I know for a certainty that you have several rooms given over to games of chance."

Tregaan of Inim'l'asty actually blinked. "What has that to do with a challenge such as you would make?"

"Have made, my good fellow, have made. I have already sent a message to all members of this association. You see, the matter is simple, and gambling has everything to do with the testing. In a house of Law, randomness is at an ebb, no?"

Shocked, the steward stammered, "But of course, of course! It... it could not be otherwise."

"Exactly. So my challenge is this. I advocate the powers of the seas, champion the paramountcy of water above all natural elements. By means of its lords alone can we achieve order and reason."

"I am at a loss," Tregaan of Inim'l'asty said, wringing his hands. "How is this more than an assertion?"

"What? You would have me contest against fellow adepts with deadly wave and fell storm? Drown Eshraao? Harm servants of the White Lords? Chaotic. Unthinkable! Is that what your association supports?!"

Taken aback at such a suggestion of power, the steward barely whispered, "Well, no, certainly not that."

"I am, as you, being an augur, have undoubtedly noticed, not native to the Yon Eastlands but hail from the more westerly regions of the continent. There we neither engage in destructive battles nor bother with petty displays of semi-trickery and illusion."

"I see," Tregaan said without any comprehension.

Lord Glum waved him away. "Then you will prepare the table and inform all who enter that the challenge is to be conducted through the play of some simple and random game. Let it be yeeraht."

Several persons had gathered during this time, and when he named the ancient Melnibonéan divinatory device, now considered the most demanding of gambling games, there was a murmur. Was this little one such a fool? Eshraao was renowned everywhere for its expert gamblers, and masters of yeeraht were the greatest of the great. Not in decades had anyone from outside the city defeated one of its masters, although players from all parts of the east, the whole world, came. They left as sheared sheep, making Eshraao the wealthier for their visit.

Tregaan the steward of the House of Favorable Portents had to choke back his glee. "What you demand, adept Lord Glum, is a game against the best yeeraht players in all Eshraao, that is to say, the members of this society of magical evocation of Law."

"That is essentially correct, although the stakes are more than mere wealth. This is a matter of which force is most potent."

"I am corrected," Tregaan said politely. "However, regardless of the, ah, unusual nature of this challenge, and its higher nature, I must perforce inquire as to the stakes of mundane sort which will form the basis of play."

Lord Glum shrugged. "Let those who come to meet the challenge decide. I have some few talents of gold at hand and a letter of credit for a hundred more. I assume the former will suffice, but... have you a chamberlain?"

"Of course."

"Then he must take this draft to whatever banker this society uses, verify its authenticity, and thereafter you will provide me with markers equal to the sum indicated as I require."

Now the pudgy steward was beaming. The pretentious little man was nothing more than another of the birds who came to the city to be plucked and eaten. Adept of the water element possibly, but surely not a winner. "The matter will be rather difficult, adept lord," Tregaan of Inim'l'asty replied smoothly. "It is the height of Celebration...." His pause was theatrical and he timed the continuation of his words by cueing on the closely watched red-head. As Lord Glum reached for his purse, the steward supplied, "I will see to the matter personally — no need for any gratuity, adept lord." None was needed. His share from the members who stripped this mannikin clean would more than make up for the offenses and trouble.

"This way to the Pentacle Chamber, Lord Glum. We use such a place to assure that no acts — how shall I put it, violent reactions to loss? — other than those associated with the game are attempted."

The gray-green eyes fixed on the steward's. "Hold. How efficacious are the supernatural wardings of the Pentacle Chamber?"

The sly smile which crossed Tregaan's face lasted but an instant. "Oh, most potent, adept lord. In the decade I have served in my office not one evocation of any plane has been successful. Rest assured, the contestants are forced to rely only upon their own powers and skill."

"Then I am satisfied. Let the most potent and able of your members seek me out in the said chamber — and be sure they bring wherewithal as measure of the certainty they have in the potency of their professed mastery... and its overlord or -lady."

An hour later there were a dozen of the wealthiest and most powerful of Eshraao's citizens gathered in the Pentacle Chamber. Fully half were priests, the others individual practitioners of the white arts, the manipulation or evocation of Law. It would be difficult to have any other focus for magic, as the whole of the room was festooned with runes and symbols barring Chaos and the green magic of Balance. The major ban was, however, against the opening of any pathway to a higher plane, so that even the gods there were prevented from interfering. That of which the steward had informed Lord Glum was essentially true. Personal force of supernatural sort alone could be called upon herein, and that in but constrained form. What counted most was sheer ability to gamble, the skill at playing yeeraht.

The four who initially sat down at the pentagonal table were the least able of the group. If they succeeded in winning, then they gained much. However, the more skilled watched and took the measure of the strange little man who claimed to play for the supremacy of the forces of water. Be he a true adept of that element, or merely a professional gambler come to test the greatest, no matter. Should their associates be beaten, they would have a measure of their opponent, and the next four to pick up the gauntlet would be prepared.

No more than three hours later the last of the initial four was gone from the table. The second wave of players seemed to be faring no better. Before Lord Glum was arrayed a heap of valuables and stacks of golden talent bars, crowns and similar coins, which formed a veritable wall. He lost of course, but never large. He won more often, and that in quantity. In fact, Lord Glum now owned five slaves and a villa on the sea.

"This is d'alkkan, masters," said the thin adept who was flipping forth the bone tablets. "The arcana do not alter, only augment, the suits." The words were perfunctory, as all playing knew well the rules governing this form of yeeraht. After two rounds of betting the dealer had exhausted his funds and dropped out. His place was filled by Higmir Jeviil, chief priest of Daam-azage, Lord of Light.

By then Lord Glum had dropped from the hand and the pot went to one of the Eshraaoans. The second of the medial players left, then the third. Two hands later, there was a great stir as the small stranger won with with all elements under heaven, beating four knaves with fool and a court of wands. The two losing hands had staked all. Both departed play. One was the chief cleric who had just recently begun. Hisses from the darkness around the table indicated the consternation this caused.

"Is there aught amiss?" Lord Glum inquired innocently as he raked in his winnings. The amount very nearly doubled what was before him.

"Not at all," assured Duke Rin'nya as he took one of the two vacated seats. "What base stake do you name, Lord Glum? I trust it will not be so trifling as before...."

As the long fingers of his hands manipulated the wafers of pale bone, Lord Glum smiled. "At last, one truly assured of his discernment of random distributions and his command of order! Let it be a full talent, then, and nine-tablets spread — reversals counting so as to make it the more interesting." He paused before distribution. "I am impressed by your boldness. May I inquire as to your name?"

The man opposite was dark-eyed, tawny-haired, handsome, and arrogant in the extreme. His satin clothes were scarlet and saffron, ornamented with gold and rubies. "You may. I am Duke Rin'nya, the adept of empyreal essences."

"An odd name, quite unfamiliar to me."

"Perhaps you have heard of the Master of Flames?!"

The little sheets of bone were skidding across the baize cloth. "No. Let us play."

The scowling duke lost that hand to Lord Glum, won the next, then lost three straight. The high stakes soon drove all but the Master of Flames and the red-headed stranger from play however. Duke Rin'nya smiled, placed a carbuncle amulet upon the table. "Double the ante?"

"As you wish," came the laconic reply. Lord Glum lost the hand, placed the intaglio ring of emerald before him.

"Now you seek to test the potency of water, adept lord?"

"Let us say I counter amulet with luck charm."

The duke sneered as he dealt, but lost. Then he won, lost heavily, rallied and beat Lord Glum in five straight pots. Most of the winnings which had graced the small man's side of the table were now weighing down that portion at which the Master of Flames sat. "Heat evaporates puddles. Ten talents is the base, and it shall be your favorite game, nine-tablets, spread and reversals."

After three of the wafers of bone were turned, the duke bet and raised heavily behind juggernaut flanked by aces. "Let us make that one hundred," he grated, and then eyed the depleted reserve of Lord Glum. The raise was half of the total, but there was neither hesitation nor sign of uncertainty as the small man shoved forth the money. Three more of the little tablets gained the duke another ace, but a reversal countered his juggernaut. Three aces against a strange mixture of tablets before Lord Glum: Three were swords, the knight with nine and ten.

Duke Rin'nya did not press the matter until the last, when seven tablets were face up and the last round of betting was at hand. He tapped first the leftmost of his unturned tablets, then the other at his far right. "I have won."

"You haven't wagered."

"All before me, and these additional dozen talents from my reserve."

The gray-green eyes of Lord Glum opened wide. "You indeed play recklessly, Master of Flames. That is far more than I have here!"

"Match the stake or get out," the duke snapped without masking his contempt. "Where is the power you boasted of now?" He was reaching for the pot.

"A moment, good duke, a moment. What is before me is but a tithe. Here are markers to match your wager. I believe I shall up it by one thousand talents." The ruddy face of the Master of Flames paled, and it was now Lord Glum's turn to reach for the great heap of wealth there on the pentagonal playing surface.

Leaping to his feet, the duke shouted, "Not so fast, wretch!" He turned to his fellows, cried, "Which of you will prove your friendship and stand for me in this matter? It is but a thousand." No one spoke, eyes slipped from his, and the nobleman cursed. "Chaos' demons take you all! This stranger humiliates Eshraao and the White Gods while you niggle over gold."

"Most eloquent, but insufficiently moving, it seems, your grace," Lord Glum said in a voice which seemed to fill the chamber. "Then you fail to meet the stake, and the hand and game is mine."

"NO!" With a visible effort the Master of Flames controlled his fury, turned, and with a flourish set upon the table a necklace of diamonds and pearls. A great cabochon moonstone depended at its center. Indrawn breath marked the act as several of the onlookers saw it and registered their shock.

"What's this trifle? A pretty bit of jewelry, certainly, but even assessing the diamonds and pearls at full cost, the whole is hardly half the amount required."

The duke pointed at the opaline blue of the central stone. "If you are indeed an adept, and have the power you claim, then you will know that that single gem is worth far more than the gold in question!"

"A moonstone, large and fine, but only a semi-precious thing, unless...."

The Master of Flames smiled darkly. "Yes?"

"I sense a mighty supernatural emanation from it. Is this the Tr — "

"Say no further. It is."

Lord Glum picked up the necklace, peered at the moonstone, then inclined his head. "And you normally carry such a priceless talisman about on your person? Inconceivable!"

The arrogant scowl deepened. "Of course I would not normally have such a thing here with me, dolt! A spy has warned me that a thief and assassin stalks my palace. Thus I am safe here with this." As he said that the duke's scowl changed to a sneer of contempt for lessers, including Lord Glum.

"Understood. I accept this as meeting the stake."

"You LOSE!" Duke Rin'nya shouted, and fairly danced with glee as he turned up the two outer tablets. One was the ace of wands, the other the arcane flame wheel. His hand was all elemental power ruled by the empyreal plane. A virtually unbeatable hand. Shouts of wonder and triumph came from the onlookers. "Master of Flames, Rin'nya, wins!"

As Rin'nya leaned close to vaunt, Lord Glum ran him through with his sword.

"No.... You can't.... Not me..." the dying noble managed to utter as he collapsed.

"Can and did, you overweening bastard. And I cheated at the game too," Lord Glum hissed rapidly to the nobleman.

There was tumult at that instant as the onlookers realized what had happened. Two men-at-arms tried to get to the small stranger, but the confusion slowed their rush. Then gold bars, coins, and sundry valuables flew out into the chamber. Being no fools, the guards went clambering after the fortune as quickly as did the bankrupted gamblers. Lord Glum ran for the exit, not bothering to strike at anyone not attempting to impede his escape. Only two men tried. Both died.

As he raced out of the hall a dozen men followed on his heels raising a hue and cry. "Stop! Assassin!"

There were several cloaked figures there who moved to intercept the small man. As he raced towards them, they threw off their outer garments. Silvered cuirasses gleamed. Swords came forth, and their rank parted to allow the fugitive to pass. "Sun-serving snakes!" shouted one as he attacked the guards. "Too long have you burned us with your falsehoods!" A melee ensued, and both factions were reinforced.

"This way, Lord Moonantic," cried one of the two armored men who escorted him. "The House of Adarothy lies to the south."

The small man turned, nodded, and as the pair of stalwarts went ahead, he cut once, twice. Both fell with wounds in their legs. Without a pause, Lord Glum spun and raced off to the north.

"You filthy traitor!" called one of the men as Lord Glum made off. It was as if he heard nothing.

At the inn it took but a minute to have his horse brought to him. "Leaving so soon, m'lord?" queried the stableboy. "The best nights of Celebration are at hand!"

"I think not, lad," Lord Glum shot back as he mounted. "There's a riot on the High Isle, and before long the whole city will be engulfed in it. Get your ass inside, and stay out of trouble. You might survive it." He threw a handful of coins down, yanked on the bridle to turn the horse, and was away at a canter.

Purple dusk was long on the land when Harvester carried Lord Glum over the low ridge which hid Eshraao from view. Somewhere behind were a score of armed men, but they had no chance of catching the small man now. By morning he would be free of pursuit, free with a doublet full of gold coins surreptitiously removed from the table during play, free with the necklace which bore the True Moonstone. He was not laughing with pleasure, though, as one might expect. Lord Glum was weeping. He stifled his sobs, turned, and gazed in the direction of the city.

"Farewell, dear and foolish Definee Adarothy. No high priestess of Law will now use the stone to bring down the rule of even the most benign of the gods of order. This key to the opening of the planes of Law will be forever hidden away. You would have order and me, but neither shall be, for the scales must not tip here or elsewhere."

The wind heralding night played through the fronds and flowers. It bore a perfume like hers, and its sound seemed to be Definee's voice calling, "Come back to me, my Moonantic. Come back. I love you."

Slumped low, Lord Glum rode west. "No love can change Fate, lady of my heart. Some there are who are eternal heroes. Worse still are those cursed to be eternal rogues."

THE SONG OF SHAARILLA

BY JAMES S. DORR

One night, as Elric sat moodily drinking alone in a tavern, a wingless woman of Myyrrhn came gliding out of the storm and rested her lithe body against him.
— Opening to "While the Gods Laugh,"
Book II of *The Weird of the White Wolf*

Always the wind pursued,
mocking her trudging steps;
twenty days searching the paths of Filkhar as
long before then she had paced other continents.
Always the wind howled as, fearful,
foredoomed, she thought,
she quested onward,
a cripple,
an outcast.
And yet, she thought as she walked,
she was not without some touch of gracefulness —
some remnant, maybe, of that which should have been hers
by right of her Myyrrhnian birth —
some trace of beauty that might pique the interest of

one whom she sought now.
She laughed as she thought thus and,
under her breath, she sang.

⊕

She was afraid of the man she quested for —
she, Shaarilla,
the wingless child of a long-deceased sorcerer,
had never been a courageous woman —
and yet when she saw him, his face as white,
even whiter than her own,
his eyes red as her hair,
and when she knew all his reputation
as traitor and as a murderer of women
she still approached boldly.
She sought for the moment,
beseeching, offering herself for his pleasure, and
when even then he balked,
she seized his hand and dragged him out to the wind.
She knew then she was doomed,
and she was not a courageous woman
nor one she would think of as practical either.
And yet when the wind mocked, whistling louder,
pulling her cloak and tangling her long hair,
she knew it came back to hope —
trust in the moment —
ignoring the future although, as her kind did,
she did possess foresight,
however dimly.

⊕

She lived for the moment, as women like her did,
buffeted by the wind,
toyed with by love,

by fate,
yet always trusting that *this* time one might succeed, spiting all foresight
if one's hope were worthy.

⊕

Of Elric she was less sure.

⊕

She came to know him on their long journey,
by day speaking little but, by night, their love-play
made up for their silence.
The silken yellow walls of their tent billowed out like great wings to reflect
their motion,
soaring in cloud-light — the wings that should be *hers* yet which,
in the tragedy of her inception,
she had been born lacking.
And, yes, she felt sorry enough for herself when,
exhausted, they lay, side by side, touching softly,
and she heard him cry in his dreams the name "Cymoril" over and over,
that of his dead first love, his royal cousin,
while she, Shaarilla, named "of the Dancing Mist" —
mockingly of the wind —
wept and sang silently, always, her own song.
And it did not matter.

⊕

She lived for the moment
as women of her race did,
high on their mountain-tops,
fearing what she might find in the great Book they sought —
sometimes begging, even, that they might turn back from their doomed
quest —
yet other times hoping, insisting he hurry

as she led them onward.

The map she kept in her head. Part of her singing

concerned directions,

wind speeds and altitudes,

parts of the fog-bound Marsh they traversed where, despite the ground's softness,

the subsoil and rock might yet be firm for landing.

Sometimes she forgot herself, thinking for a moment she *saw* the land they passed through

not from a horse's back, but from above it,

borne by her own strong wings —

those wings *she* sought for despite Elric's musings —

and, thinking that, she was shamed:

Shamed for the grief her companion bore with him,

his own quest for knowledge that might quell his sorrow.

And then, when the wind howled,

when he was distant, conversing, perhaps, with the man who had joined them

during their fight with the hounds of the Dharzi,

ignoring her now as they rode the hard ground, the Marsh long behind them

as they climbed the foothills of mist-shrouded mountains,

she sang all the louder.

⊕

For was it unworthy, this thing she sought most of all?

Freedom to climb the sky?

Freedom of birthright?

She turned to the wind, her head back, her hair rippling crimson as dark flame —

whipped by the storm's blast —

and when the White Wolf, Elric, and his new comrade were lost in their own thoughts

she hurled her voice skyward.

⊕

To fly!
She sang the words, words she'd sung always, however much hidden beneath her breath.
Had sung since her infanthood.
To launch one's self up, up to the moon's sphere,
to feel the wind whistling, not as a mocker
but as a companion, a friend.
One's own lover.

⊕

She sang the words loudly now, fearing the courage her singing brought to her,
her balking at times, at times rushing toward danger:
The battle beneath the ground, fending off those creatures she knew as *clackers*;
the sea that sapped Elric's strength;
the castle guardian —
at that time her sense of doom grew overpowering and yet
she followed when even Moonglum shared in her demurral —
the climb to the Chamber.
The *Book's* final mocking.

⊕

Abandoned, she still sang,
facing back toward the gloom of their last passing,
the rock-cleft chimney.
She turned her face from the sky, yet she still sang, louder, of her lost birthright.
She sang of a dream, of a hope, of a moment:
Someday to lift on the dew of a morning,
the faintest dawn breeze to carry her upward, her wings beating rhythm,
to soar to the orange sun.
Circling, swooping, up, to embrace the clouds as the air, azure —
like swimming beneath the sea! —
hugged her in turn in its formless substance.
To seek the whirlwind, letting it grasp her, pushing her higher,

until the whole earth lay beneath her wingtips.
To seek out the lightning.
To roar with the thunder, diving through speckled skies,
snap-rolling, up again,
through black to blueness, to whiteness, to greyness,
to orange again of sun, now setting,
redness —
the red of her own hair, of a once-lover's eyes —
now black again, black of night, the air chilling.
Her wingtips fluttering. Quick! The sea's warmth now releasing its upcurrents,
sweeping her farther to kiss the brightness,
the sparkle of stars
far brighter than jewelry, even than magic....

And one jewel behind her, lost in the heather that covered the cliff's top,
brighter than *that* too —
that which *she* abandoned, despite Moonglum's last act of friendliness toward
her.
She lived, instead, for the moment before her,
as all of her kind did.
To sing —
TO FLY!

And, as Elric's slow feet descended the mountain
while Moonglum, his new comrade, bantered to cheer him,
her voice echoed after.

TOO FEW YEARS OF SOLITUDE

BY STEWART VON ALLMEN

They said he used silence well.

Elric of Melniboné, son of Sadric LXXXVI, who was the four hundred and twenty-seventh emperor of the most powerful kingdom of men (if indeed Melnibonéans could be called men), was a quiet child. He possessed an intensely brooding nature that was unknown and unthinkable for a Melnibonéan. Melniboné was in decline, that was certain, but the Bright Empire yet knew no threat that could be seen as even the seed of potential danger or alarm for the next two centuries to come. Adults, and especially adults of nobility, had no worries, so why should children, especially children of nobility?

Yet Elric was often deep in thought and there were concerns that plagued him. His father Sadric frequently heard of his son's unusual disposition. Myriads of instructors and tutors made pleas of dismay and consternation, and there was the gossip — gossip that the emperor, still grieving for his wife whom he lost as she gave birth to Elric, did not wish to notice, for he already heard too much about his albino son's physically weak condition in the whispers of the court. That his son also seemed distant and withdrawn spawned further and more troubled apprehensions concerning Elric's mental fitness for ruling the island kingdom after Sadric's death. Everyone in the court did agree on one thing — they didn't know for certain exactly *what* was going on in the mind of the prince. Those who thought Elric an idiot grudgingly gave him credit for a cunning that kept him silent. Because he didn't often speak, Elric could not be judged, and that kept others guessing. It was perhaps his only weapon against them.

Though his blood was thin and weak, though he suffered grave lethargy of spirit, mind and body, and though he was an albino who could not long stand the rigors of the outside elements without the special herbs that strengthened him, Elric was more fit to rule Melniboné than perhaps any of the last hundred or more emperors. His mind simply wandered, for he pondered too intently the ills of the world, the decline of his father's empire, and the forces of Law and Chaos that were greater than man or even Melnibonéans. On the last matter Elric brooded despite the millennia-long alliance between Melnibonéans and the gods of Chaos. Melniboné had not been visited by one of these supposed allies for centuries, unless such a greeting had taken place in quiet between the Chaos Lord and the bearer of the Actorios, the Ring of Kings worn only by the Melnibonéan emperor, so Elric was not inclined to put his faith even in Arioch, Lord of the Seven Darks, who was the patron of Melniboné. Perhaps gods such as Arioch were no longer even part of this world. Perhaps their time was fading just as Elric suspected the time of Melniboné was passing. Unless, that is, the denizens of the Dragon Isle found time to do more than talk of past glories and triumphs.

Matters such as this occupied Elric's morbidly meditative mind even whilst he sat silent witness to the grisly scene before him. He waited intently quiet, though at least one of those assembled with him could have disputed whether the use was an intentional ploy to shake the prisoner, or the result of an inattentive mind.

Doctor Jest, the emperor's Chief Interrogator, craned his slender neck toward Elric. He whispered, "Are you prepared to offer a suggestion, Prince?"

Doctor Jest was a youngish man, but one who had apparently never gained the full body and flush of maturity (though as a Melnibonéan he was certainly more lithe than most men), or who had lost the bulk of his frame many years too soon, perhaps as a result of disease or other supernatural affliction. His face was vigorous and his voice full of enthusiasm and passion for his duty, but his slightly hunched and very emaciated figure gave the appearance of a man debilitated by age. The result was diabolical, a trait that no doubt contributed to the terror of his subjects.

A scalpel danced in his sinuous fingers like a master's paintbrush, but Doctor Jest's only shade was red and the canvas before him had few strokes. A few very simple cuts were made in order to make sure the subject understood his situation, but they had to be placed in locations that would produce no lingering pain. A background of pain might only cause the subject to be less affronted by the little aches that would come later.

Doctor Jest had explained this to Elric and the other four Melnibonéan children assembled in the room far below Tower Monshanjik where the Chief Interrogator created his masterpieces. These other children were here for the same purpose as Elric — to see how the Bright Empire dealt with the pathetic threat posed by the Young Kingdoms: A threat represented by the dark-haired man who hung securely chained from the low ceiling of the chamber. A fierce fire burned in the man's eyes, and he had taken in the appearance of his tormentors as surely as they had his. What he saw must have chilled his bones. If demonic Doctor Jest were not enough, then the keen-eyed and cruel youths seated before him must have dealt his pride a great and terrible blow. His life was to be naught now but amusement for them.

But in one of the youths, the palest among them, the one who seemed to the prisoner to be set apart (though, and perhaps because, he sat in the largest chair), the man of the Young Kingdoms saw something else. It was the briefest of instants, but when Elric had first taken his seat the two had locked eyes. It was a mistake on both their parts. In such an exchange, a prisoner's defiance could only goad an enemy to greater heights of sadism, and a tormentor could only reveal a spark of pity in his eyes, which would grant the prisoner a glimmer of hope that, when not delivered upon, would make the punishment even more cruel and severe. But Elric was not the usual torturer and the man, whom Doctor Jest refused to name if indeed he even cared to know his name, was not the usual prisoner, for he exhibited a greater courage and pride than most. So in the moment that their gazes took one another in, each learned a bit of something that would be meaningful for the rest of his life, though the prisoner's life was bound to be the far shorter of the two. The prisoner saw that not all Melnibonéans were as cruel as the old stories indicated, and Elric resolved that there were among the men of the Young Kingdoms those of the sort he suspected might exist there — strong and noble.

Elric sat in the chair normally reserved for the emperor, his father. It was Doctor Jest who had recommended the seat and explained that Sadric would be unable to attend the performance. In lesser chairs, all to the left of Elric's seat, were the others. Two of Elric's cousins, Prince Yyrkoon and Dyvim Slorm, were among them. Classically Melnibonéan with his slender frame and golden-brown hair, Dyvim Slorm sat closest to Elric. Dyvim Slorm was the son of Dyvim Tvar, Lord of the Dragon Caves, and was among the few who would actually converse with Elric. This was doubtlessly due in no small part to the request of Dyvim Tvar, one of the rare true friends Elric could claim.

Elric knew little of the other two youths except that they too were sons of nobility, but Elric knew much of his cousin Yyrkoon. Elric had more than a little jealousy for this dark, cruel lad. Oh, he did not appreciate the qualities his cousin possessed, for they were Melnibonéan in the extreme, but Yyrkoon commanded respect and attention that Elric could not earn even had he wished them. There were times when Elric cursed his sensibilities and yearned to lose himself in ambition and passion as Yyrkoon did with such ease. Such thoughts sent chills down Elric's spine. How deplorable he was to find such behavior seductive! But it was a thought that occupied his racing mind from time to time.

"I was employing my technique, doctor," Elric replied flatly, finally snapping back to the situation at hand. "I thought to be silent myself, if he intended to do the same, so that each word I spoke later, each noise I made, no matter if it were the rattle of a chain or the sluice from a scalpel across flesh, would seem a thousand times more horrible. Besides, why torture him so when surely his imagination concocts far more heinous proceedings than I could ever devise?"

Doctor Jest slid his finger across the prisoner's chest as if to remind him that this aside for lessons would not long delay his fate. He said, "But men of the Young Kingdoms are but better than beasts, my Prince. Do not expect their meager intelligences to conjure images more horrible than the reality of my instruments across their hide."

"Remember, Chief Interrogator, my skills in this matter are little compared to yours, so perhaps my method is the only one that would work for me."

Yyrkoon scoffed, "Cousin, I think you simply lack the stomach for dealing with such dogs as this. Perhaps you are too frail for this event. You lack the constitution to survive any environment outside your bedchambers, and you certainly lack the fortitude to take the action that is required in situations such as this. This dog is an agent of our enemies and should be dealt with severely."

Turning to Doctor Jest, Yyrkoon continued, "Chief Interrogator, I should begin by spilling the man's guts. Confronted by his fleshly innards he will hear the words drip from his mouth just as will his blood from his core."

A thin line of a smile creased Doctor Jest's face. "Such a method can work at times, Prince Yyrkoon," he began, clearly appreciating this approach more than Elric's; but he suppressed his delight and continued in a manner more appropriate for relations with a potential future emperor, "but in this case I would not recommend it. The subject is too reticent. Confrontation with such imminent death, for every warrior knows that a blow to the abdomen signals unavoidable though lingering death, will irreversibly seal the lips of a subject like this."

"Can you not then simply remove his *stomach?*" Yyrkoon laughed and glanced at Elric as he emphasized the last word in mockery of his cousin's presumed lack of the same. "I understand that a Melnibonéan can continue to live without a stomach if the intestines and gullet are sewn together. Perhaps the same is true of these Young Kingdom dogs, and then perhaps not...." A sadistic chuckle escaped him then as it had many times already during the proceedings.

Elric was a bit incredulous, but knew it best to conceal it for the most part. "What good would that do then, Yyrkoon?"

Yyrkoon turned a heavy gaze to his future emperor. "What good? Good is not the question, cousin. If the subject will live...." He paused and glanced at Doctor Jest.

Doctor Jest said, "It's true, Prince, but again I think this method ineffective because a subject from the Young Kingdoms would certainly be unable to tell the difference between that method and the less specific one you first proposed."

Yyrkoon's smile was huge now. It threatened to snap his face. He turned back to Elric and said, "If the subject will live, then what the *harm?*"

Elric let a wry smile of his own slip. "You speak of this man as a dog, Yyrkoon, but I fear you would treat such beasts with more dignity than this man."

"You forget, cousin, that because of this *man's* plots against our great Empire he has become less than a dog."

"Aye, but behind the words I sense a broader, more general application of your theory." Elric fell silent again. He had been drawn out. Yyrkoon had this effect on Elric; he made Elric ignore his boundaries and participate in arguments where there was no hope of persuasion. He knew he was saying too much. He had already said enough to generate hours of gossip to entertain and satisfy those who would speak behind his father's back, but he was trying to divine what was really happening here. If this man were a spy, then yes, he should be treated harshly. Not crudely, but certainly with a sure hand; for what had Melniboné done to the developing nations known as the Young Kingdoms in the last century to continue to earn their ire? Just as the residents of the Dragon Isle had come to dwell on their past greatness, so too perhaps did the men of the Young Kingdoms still fear too much that waning power.

Still, he wondered, what could justify this drama? This man was no true prisoner, with no information of even passing importance. If he had been, then his father would have been required to attend — it was Melnibonéan custom. Perhaps this barbaric show was a practical demonstration of torture techniques and information retrieval. No, that couldn't be it. Yyrkoon obviously required additional tutelage in such practices, though he obviously relished the approach itself. The other three seemed attentive as well.

Dyvim Slorm acted appropriately Melnibonéan. He seemed interested in the event but disinterested in the result, no matter how awful it might be. Much like the time in the dragon caves, Elric recalled, when he and Dyvim Slorm had assisted the handlers in tying down food for the great winged beasts. The fare that day was horses too old to be of use even to a simple Young Kingdoms farmer. Elric and his cousin were both nearby when one of the dragons roused from its perhaps months-long slumber to take the food. However, in its only partially roused state it mistook the handler for the horse and swallowed the shrieking man whole before settling back to rest again. Elric felt remorse for not acting in some way to help the man — Elric felt certain he had noticed the dragon waking and might have alerted the handler. Dyvim Slorm, though, had been nonplussed. He had approached the now harmless dragon, untied the horse the handler left, and coolly led it toward another dragon, since it was no longer required by the first.

The other two youths (whom Elric now remembered to be Theryv Aarctos, a treasurer's son, and Eneasys, a cunning lad with twinkling dark eyes whose parents had died a few years ago) seemed Yyrkoon's compatriots in thought. Eneasys, now a charge of the emperor's court, had a particular sparkle in those dark eyes that Elric knew to be the fervored kind of loyalty that Yyrkoon seemed able to earn, though always, it seemed to Elric, at great cost to the one who gave that allegiance. Elric was the only lucky survivor, other than Yyrkoon himself, of one mad adventure in which he had participated. It had been a simple hunting foray. Elric, Yyrkoon and perhaps two or three others rode horses in pursuit of their dogs that in turn pursued wild pigs. A weary day of fruitless searching was passing until one of the dogs finally got wind of a fresh scent. The chase began. The Melnibonéans reached the dogs just in time to see the prey dash into a bundle of thickets. It was a pig, but it was tiny, perhaps only a few months old. Certainly it wasn't the kind of game the hunters sought. Elric recalled the dogs, and all but one responded. Yyrkoon's prized mastiff was ordered in pursuit of the piglet and Yyrkoon dismounted to pursue it as well. He demanded they all follow it to the mother. Of course they all did, even though the thicket looked impenetrable. One of the others bushwhacked a path but soon tired and another replaced him before the group reached a small clearing that was obviously the piglet's home, for the remainder of the litter was there as well. Yyrkoon's mastiff had cornered them all. Contemporaneously with the arrival of Elric, Yyrkoon and the others, though, and much to Yyrkoon's delight, was the return of the piglets' mother. It was a massive pig that barreled through the thicket. Trapped as they were by the tangled and thorny vines, the youths fell, bludgeoned and trampled by the pig. Only when the pig threatened Yyrkoon did the prince's mastiff interfere with the assault and kill the pig after a frantic battle. Only Elric and Yyrkoon remained alive. Even the dog died within moments of ending the threat. Yyrkoon killed every piglet before the two returned to the horses.

Elric found that he could not blame Dyvim Slorm for being what others expected of him; but the others, Yyrkoon and his understudy in particular, went too far when they began to enjoy the power they wielded. That, decided Elric, was the root of decadence — when power is enjoyed solely for its own sake. There had been no purpose in killing the piglets. It had been an act driven purely by cruelty.

The thoughts pounded through Elric's head too rapidly to be controlled, let alone tracked. Elric slowly massaged his forehead with two long, white fingers.

"Weary, Prince?" Doctor Jest asked.

Yyrkoon interjected, "As I suggested, Chief Interrogator, Elric does not have the constitution for such studies. Perhaps we should retire until he has rested."

Elric had to escape this insanity. The outside events were intruding too much. "Yes," he said and nodded his head, and the motion did indeed look weary. He was weary of all the words, ones implied as well as spoken.

Elric languidly stood and made to depart the subterranean chamber of Doctor Jest. Dyvim Slorm crossed his path, though, and asked, "May I assist you, Elric?"

"Thank you, cousin, but I prefer to help myself for a time now. I have had too much help thinking these last hours." He managed to look Dyvim Slorm in the eyes for a brief moment to impart at least a sense of gratitude for the offer.

"As you wish." Dyvim Slorm left the room and began to ascend the ramp that wound back to the surface. The other three youths lingered with Doctor Jest before the chained man, who now began to whimper slightly — it was the first noise he had made the entire time and it sent Elric's thoughts spinning again, for Yyrkoon had managed to break even that man's quiet courage, the last silence he would ever know.

Morbidly (for though many of the thoughts that echoed in Elric's head were unlike those of his countrymen he did share many of their ways), Elric reflected again on the performance that had taken place in the tower. Why did they bother him with such things at all? Why did they have to involve him in their pitiful dramas?

Then he suddenly realized the point of the entire episode. It had been entirely for his own benefit! They sought to harden him, to inure him to the heartless ways of his people, to make him Melnibonéan! It was an unspeakable cruelty not just to the man whose life had been carelessly tossed away as if he were but another puppet and the Melnibonéans were the Chaos gods they in turn bowed to, but also to Elric. So perhaps he deliberated more on how Melniboné should wield its vast power in the world and perhaps he would not be an emperor who would decisively move to put upstarts in their place — what right did others have to change this? There was strength inside of him that he would find, that he felt he needed to find in order to face his destiny, if he could but search long enough. Did any man have a right to seed motivations and ideas unbidden in his mind? Elric thought not. He knew from his studies that the gods probably had plans for every man, and if he were ever to stake his own destiny and plot the course of his own life, then he needed to start now. Without the time to prepare himself, to find this strength, then he would continue to be a pawn in the plots of his countrymen. Perhaps they all thought he would be a weak ruler and so sought to shape him to their needs now. But surely the games of Melnibonéans were petty compared to those of the gods and the Cosmic Balance. If he could not resist his fellows, then what hope had he against these?

He needed to use silence better, for who knew in what ways any of these others had already invaded his solitude?

WHITE WOLF'S AWAKENING

BY   PAUL   W.   CASHMAN

Being the tale of Elric of Melniboné at the time of his accession

I
AN EMPEROR DYING; AN ISLAND WAITING

The mist clung to the harbor's surface, a thick, silvery blanket oozing amongst the quays and poking tendrils into the lowermost sections of the city. Perhaps it was a harbinger of some greater calamity, for while the spring sun neared its zenith and the upper towers of Imrryr blazed in full daylight, yet the mist tenaciously shrouded the harbor and only grudgingly gave ground.

Normally the docks and quays of Melniboné's ten-millennia-old capital would have been abustle by this hour, but on this particular morning a curious feeling of gloom pervaded the waterfront. Captains and crew of Melnibonéan merchantmen glanced about uneasily in the unusual silence, wishing their ships were loaded and creeping out in the inner harbor under oars.

There was, indeed, not a breath of wind; on this eerie morning the entire world paused and awaited, trembling, an event of some importance.

For Sadric LXXXVI, four hundred and twenty-seventh Emperor of ancient Melniboné, lay gravely injured from, it was said, a hunting mishap that bespoke treachery.

Better to be beating about in a treacherous squall, those stolid sailors thought, than to be in Imrryr-port in tumultuous times like these!

⊕

The recalcitrant mist was of concern even to those who resided far above it in the upper towers of the imperial palace.

"My lord, the mist is lifting at last. You instructed me to keep you advised."

"Thank you, Terac." Dyvim Tvar's drawn, tense mien belied his easy words. The Lord of the Dragon Caves added, "I smelled sorcery on the winds last night, and 'tis most peculiar for such a fog to form over the inner harbor and linger until almost midday."

Terac nodded and stepped back to his guard detachment. His gold plate jingled lightly, proud symbol of his service in Melniboné's dragon-borne forces. Dyvim Tvar closed his eyes again and resumed his tired vigil outside his Emperor's door. Beyond lay the stricken Lord Sadric, attended now only by the royal physician Soru and his trusted servant, Eyin. The hallway outside, where Dyvim Tvar sprawled on a divan, was heavily guarded by a mixed force of regular palace guards, a detachment of the elite Silent Guard, and his own retinue of Dragon Cave forces; those last were there because he did not quite trust anyone else during the crisis.

The entire palace was crawling with troops, and curfew patrols in the city had been doubled. Units of Melniboné's navy, its small patrol triremes and even some of the great, unwieldy battle-barges, had been sent to cordon off the island by Fleet Admiral Magum Colim, who also suspected treachery and hoped to catch any smaller craft which dared the hazardous shoals ringing all of Melniboné.

A big, burly man was Dyvim Tvar, with long, well-kept, dark hair and a healthy beard. With his relaxed comportment he radiated a sense of stability not unlike a well-buttressed wall lashed by a rain-swept gale.

Dyvim Tvar was one of the few Lords of Imrryr still fiercely loyal to the succession; Admiral Colim was another. Sadric's son and only child Elric was a weak, sickly lad with disconcerting milk-white skin and hair — and even more disconcerting crimson eyes — as well as the scant stamina shared by all albinos. Most of Imrryr's bickering lords could not abide the thought of young Elric, just nearing his twentieth year, perched atop the Ruby Throne of Melniboné — although they couldn't agree on who was to sit in his place. Dyvim Tvar sighed.

If, gods forbid, Sadric did indeed die (and his hurts were nasty enough), there would be trouble aplenty.

Elric was the sole rightful heir, Dyvim Tvar reflected, but palace revolts were not unheard-of in Melniboné's long history. The "hereditary" nature of the Dragon Isle's royal lineage was more tenuous than most in the Young Kingdoms dared believe.

In contrast to Elric, the Emperor's nephew Yyrkoon was annoyingly healthy, Dyvim Tvar mused. The young lord was not stable, even by Melnibonéan standards. It was rumored that he had incestuous designs on his sister Cymoril, who was herself young Elric's favored paramour. Yyrkoon was widely known to covet the throne despite his few years.

Neither foible was unusual by Imrryr's jaded standards, but Yyrkoon bore close scrutiny. His father Yyrkahr had ever been a thorn in Sadric's side and two years ago he had been quietly removed through what was tactfully referred to as a "slight overindulgence" in the drugs for which Imrryr was named the Dreaming City.

Dyvim Tvar, who knew more of the story behind Yyrkahr's demise than he would admit, conceded now that the lord's removal had been a wise precaution on Sadric's part, as Yyrkahr would have proved a near-insurmountable challenge to the succession now.

All of Yyrkahr's hereditary possessions and much of his power had passed to his son when he died. Yyrkoon had studied the sorcerous arts just as Elric had. Dyvim Tvar wondered to himself about Yyrkoon's ability, for instance, to weatherweave a mist of contortion.

He roused himself and beckoned Terac over. "Go to Prince Elric. Double the Dragonforce around him and place yourself in command."

Terac nodded and sprang away, while Dyvim Tvar smiled slightly at the lad's excitement. He'd make a fine officer someday. His concern for Elric's safety now slightly assuaged, he returned to his idle wanderings.

And then there was Sadric's First Minister, Pent'arl. Dyvim Tvar knew him to be a highly capable lieutenant, clever and reasonably bright, but given to bouts of melancholia. During Sadric's infirmity Pent'arl commanded the Melnibonéan regular troops, and by custom he spoke as Regent for the ailing Emperor.

He had no reason to think Pent'arl was disloyal enough to attempt a revolt, but the Minister's high position and his lineage, distinguished even by Imrryr's inbred standards, doubtless made the prospect tempting. Pent'arl had also been with the Emperor's hunting party when Sadric was injured, whereas Yyrkoon had not. The Minister would bear watching also.

There were, indeed, any number of jealous lords and courtiers who could seize on the opportunity —

His musings were interrupted by the slow opening of the chamber door. Soru the physician emerged dolefully, followed by the aged Eyin, miserably wringing his hands. Dyvim Tvar slowly stood as Soru glanced up and down the corridor at the assembled soldiery and recognized Dyvim Tvar as a friend and as the senior officer present.

Drawing the Lord of the Dragon Caves aside, Soru whispered, "His end is very near, now. I have done all I can to prolong his time, but even I cannot deny him his fate. His Majesty bids his son and the First Minister attend him."

Dyvim Tvar nodded, noting the enormity of the doctor's news almost in passing. Later he would be astonished at his own detachment, but for now he simply strode over to a senior Watch captain and suggested meaningfully that the First Minister be summoned without delay. A messenger soon dashed off to the Audience Hall in the Tower of D'a'rputna.

Leaving his retinue behind to guard the Bright Emperor's final moments, he departed in haste to find Prince Elric, his two most trusted bodyguards falling in quick-step behind him.

11
A BOY-PRINCE: MEMORIES AND FAREWELL

The last of the mist had finally burned off and the sun now shone fully on the small roof-garden adjacent to the tallest tower of B'aal'nezbett, repository of Melniboné's arcane secrets. The unluckiest of the numerous guards were stationed in spots unsheltered from the glare, and they sweated profusely in their full-dress armor. The luckier ones had found or been assigned shadier spots.

Elric reflected that he had never seen the garden quite so crowded, with a pang of sadness when he considered the reason. His father was not an easy man to love, but young Elric loved no one more. And now, he thought, the gruff sorcerer-king lay dying.

"It's not easy, is it?" Avedis, who'd spoken, was his closest and virtually only friend. Not quite as tall as his companion, Avedis was, if anything, slightly narrower, which said much. He was two years younger than Elric. Melnibonéans tended to be somewhat pale in complexion, but Avedis was darker than most, and well-muscled. Prince Elric's milk-white hair matched a skin that was light even by Imrryr's standards, for he was an albino. His crimson eyes sometimes unsettled Avedis, especially when Elric was angry.

Elric stirred from his desultory examination of a grounded leaf and toyed with a fold of his bright-yellow silk cape. "Uncertainty increases the pain," he said.

He might have been discussing the weather, but Avedis heard the tension beneath Elric's calm words.

Avedis smiled suddenly, evoking a curious princely gaze. "I was recalling how we first met," he explained.

Elric managed, "I didn't think it was quite so funny at the time."

Avedis looked contrite, and Elric almost laughed at his friend's chagrin.

It had been on the occasion when Elric had received a thin leather breechcloth intended solely for swimming, an event which, at fifteen years, he considered to be the moment of his attaining adulthood, regardless of the "proper" court custom. He had gone swimming in the Oldest Ocean not far from Imrryr with some guards and his beloved servant, the withered Tanglebones, in attendance. Running was too strenuous for Elric's deficient blood, so he preferred to swim instead, since both water and climate were usually warm.

Avedis had been swimming well out from the beach, and, seeing the royal party arrive, decided to hide in the rocks of one of the coastal shoals for which the Dragon Isle was infamous among mariners. A strong swimmer even at thirteen, he was diving quietly in waters perhaps eight feet deep, dropping an Imperial coin and then recovering it amongst the stones at the bottom. In a rare mischievous mood, Elric, swimming along underwater, had come upon Avedis and grabbed the younger boy around the waist, intending only to surprise him. His plan had backfired. Avedis struggled fiercely in surprise, and, by chance, his ankle slammed into young Elric's groin.

Both boys broke the surface simultaneously, puffing and blowing; Avedis still startled and Elric in some considerable pain. After a few seconds — minutes in Elric's case — they were both chuckling over it. It was the first time Elric had ever encountered a child near his own age who was not a part of the court. They'd been close friends ever since, perhaps because they were miles apart in social station: Elric the heir of 'Melniboné and Avedis the youngest son of a minor subaltern in the city guard.

And perhaps because Avedis was like Elric in a crucial way. Unlike most Melnibonéans, both boys were tainted with unheard-of emotions like compassion.

"Remember I was so embarrassed about it? I thought I'd be executed for kicking the prince of the realm in the —"

"Aye, but I, in my great wisdom, decided not to mention it to anyone."

Avedis pretended to throw a dirt-clot at the Prince. "I think that was a wise decision," he said mock-seriously.

Then his smile thinned. "You'll be Lord of Melniboné soon," Avedis observed quietly. "There's bound to be trouble — I might not be allowed to see you anymore." The boy grinned ruefully, gesturing at the garden, occupied by more guards than insects this day. "Sometimes it's difficult now!"

Elric glanced wryly at his friend. "Oh, I expect trouble, but if I *am* to be Emperor, then I intend to choose my *own* companions, despite those who would have it otherwise!" He smiled weakly, and the change in his face was like the day's dawn. "I care not whether you are a soldier's son or a Great Old God. You are my friend."

Then his smile faded and, thinking of his father's demise, he whispered, "I hope it won't happen today."

But Avedis heard the doubt in his friend's words.

And so did Elric.

⊕

Moments later, Dyvim Tvar arrived with his summons. He inclined his head graciously to the heir apparent, whom he respected more than he did most adults. "My Lord Prince," he stated formally, "your father the Emperor bids you attend His Majesty at once."

"We see and hear you," Elric replied, just as formally, "and it pleases us to comply with your message." Aside he whispered to Avedis, "Wait here as long as you can; I'll try to sneak back later."

Avedis responded with a simple hand-signal in the silent code they'd developed, in the manner of many other boys before and since. *I will.*

Dyvim Tvar moved off with Elric, Terac, and a veritable brigade of troops in varied liveries. In a few moments the garden was empty, save for Avedis. Despite the warm spring sunshine the boy shivered slightly in his close-fitting leather breeks and tunic, a frisson of dread which passed as quickly as it came.

Afterward, he wondered if he'd felt it at all, and why.

⊕

Dyvim Tvar set a brisk pace back to Lord Sadric's bedside, not quite a full trot but much faster than a walk, hoping that Sadric would last long enough for his son to wish him well before — He shied away from that thought.

"Terac, stay here with the rest of the men." Dyvim Tvar selected a few of his guards and, without slowing, directed them to continue with him and the Prince. "The rest of you remain outside." He was mindful of the fact that the aggregate of troops would not only fill the hallway outside the Emperor's door but would also spill over onto adjacent floors.

He need not have worried; the Silent Guard had sealed off the Emperor's floor and the hallway was nearly deserted. He and the Prince were passed through, but they were politely relieved of their weapons as was the custom in the imperial presence. The remainder of their mixed escort was detained at the lower floor. He assumed First Minister Pent'arl had taken some initiative in clearing the area, but inwardly he fretted: Where had all those troops been deployed?

Prince Elric was ushered into his father's chamber, where physician Soru, servant Eyin, and the First Minister waited with the dying Bright Emperor. Dyvim Tvar settled again into his divan by the door to wait.

⊕

The Imperial chamber was dimmer than ever Elric remembered it by daylight, with heavy drapes over the windows. His eyes adjusted to the darkness slowly after the brilliance of the sun outside. Sadric lay motionless in his big, plain, warrior's bed; he seemed to have shrunk in stature from the wide-shouldered giant Elric remembered.

"He's said nothing yet," Pent'arl reported quietly, his patrician face gravely set. The First Minister was tall and thin, with intelligent brown eyes and a soft demeanor, but Elric knew it hid an iron-hard interior. An iron fist in a velvet glove.

"Your son is here, my Emperor."

Sadric's eyes fluttered open. He attempted to rise, but Soru slipped his hand behind the Emperor's head and lifted it, whilst pressing his body back into the pillows. "Now, now, my lord, you just talk and I'll hold you up," he scolded gently.

Sadric managed a thin, wry smile. "You don't fool anyone, doctor," he chided weakly. Then he focused on his son and the First Minister. "Elric will, of course, rule in my place," he began briskly, knowing that every word could be his last.

Pent'arl made as if to protest, and Sadric, misinterpreting his meaning, chuckled faintly. "Pent'arl, I know I'm dying. Spare me your reassurances that I'll live, that it is just a minor discommodation...." His voice trailed off weakly.

He coughed a little and Elric winced as he saw a little blood seep from between the royal lips; his father was clearly in great pain.

"I trust you'll show him the same devotion and service you've shown me," Sadric said after recovering.

A pause, then, "Aye, my lord," the minister replied. Elric glanced surreptitiously at him; he had barely caught that brief catch in Pent'arl's words.

"Please leave us then, good Pent'arl. I would speak to my son alone. You've been of great service to me, and I thank you deeply." This brought on another bout of coughing. When it had ended, Pent'arl had departed.

"Father...." Elric moved closer to the bedside.

"Elric, I've sometimes said that I longed for you never to have been born, for it was your birth which killed your mother —" Sadric coughed as Elric recoiled from other thoughts "— and I feared you were unfit to rule in the event of my demise." He spoke deliberately, knowing his end was close.

The Dragon Lord's words were faint, but Elric heard them, then and years later, as clearly as the stars shine in midwinter's chill sky.

"My son, I fear for you. I sense that you bring the possibility of Melniboné's greatest power— or its greatest apocalypse." He gasped briefly but continued, while physician Soru caught Elric's misty eyes. *Not much longer,* that shared glance said. "Place not your trust in Chaos; we serve it, but it need not obey us, and the Old Gods are fickle masters at best....

"You are so innocent in many ways. You'll need strength to rule the Empire, and cunning, and ruthlessness...." His voice trailed off and blood again trickled from between the regal lips.

Then, in barely more than a whisper: "Elric, know that I love you as much as any father of our race might love his son, and more. My harsh words before were said in haste; strive not to remember them.

"But I fear you will remember my despair more than you'll understand my love...."

Then Sadric, Lord of the Dragon Isle and descendent of Chaos' favored line, let his soul go free to be gathered by whatever Duke of Hell laid claim to it.

III
OF TREACHERY IS A WARRIOR BORN

For a few moments the chamber was soundless. Then, with a tiny sigh, Elric sank to his knees by the bedside and collapsed across his father's stilled chest. He could not remember when he had last wept freely. Old Eyin hung his head quietly. He had served Sadric for the Emperor's entire life, from infancy to death. Soru merely sat back on a nearby chair with a mien reserved for all physicians throughout Time who, strive as they might, are unsuccessful at the end of all things: a somber expression.

For several heartbeats there was a heavy silence. Then Soru reached past Elric's prone form and gently, reverently removed the Ring of Kings, Actorios, from Sadric's finger. He closed Sadric's eyes and slowly pulled the simple coverlet up and over the fallen Lord of Dragons. "This is yours now, Your Majesty," he murmured as he handed the Melnibonéan signet ring to the new emperor.

There came a commotion from outside the window. Soru pulled back one edge of the drapery, swirling dust-motes sharply and suddenly outlined in the sun-rays admitted to the room. A great flapping sound, and the sun was momentarily eclipsed by a fast-moving form.

It was the dragon Fleet-Raker, Sadric's favorite, named for his exploits in battle against the barbarian squadrons which sometimes foolishly dared the Dragon Isle's defenses. With a thunderous cry of grief — and perhaps outrage — the great form sped southwest away from Imrryr and the Dragon Isle in his final salute to his master, never to be seen again on that plane of the multiverse.

There was a stirring in the hall outside as the import of the dragon's actions sank home. Elric shook his head sadly and slipped the ruby-red Actorios on his own ring-finger, frowning as it slipped off again; Sadric's hands had been much larger than his son's. With a sigh, he transferred it to his index finger, where it stayed. Then he dried his dampened cheeks with a corner of his cloak. It wouldn't be proper to betray his grief to the troops.

Soru stepped slowly to the door and opened it slightly. The murmuring outside ceased. Elric rose to his feet. His legs were remarkably steady, he thought in surprise.

Eyin remained behind while Elric shuddered and walked slowly toward the bright doorway, his expression still carefully neutral. Soru had simply shaken his weary head sadly at Dyvim Tvar and the rest of the assembled guard and stumped off. The two Silent Guards always assigned to the Emperor's side snapped rigidly to attention, flanking the doorway as the new monarch stepped into the hallway. His lower lip trembled slightly at this overt reminder of his father's passing, and he restrained another sob.

Dyvim Tvar took young Elric in a sad embrace; for several moments he held the inwardly grieving lad — not quite a man yet, for all his nineteen years.

"There, now, my brave prince," he said gently, half-supporting Elric as they walked slowly away.

His life sheltered from the world outside by court protocol and seclusion, Elric had never confronted the death of someone close to him. His days were occupied mostly by combat practice with Tanglebones (a spry fighter despite his age), schooling in the sciences and history, some training in statecraft (despite his father's misgivings), and, when protocol and his schedule permitted, finally getting to meet with Avedis.

He spent his nights studying the ancient and arcane secrets of his ancestors, trying to recapture the herbal knowledge with which he could boost his stamina, and the sorcerous might of the Dragon Isle's violent and powerful past, when Imrryr's influence had covered every inch of the surface of the world.

He was ill-prepared by his upbringing to face the world beyond the gardens and palace which heretofore had comprised almost his entire existence. He was an innocent, adrift on a sea of intrigue.

"I can walk now, Lord of the Dragon Caves," Elric said wryly, with a shade of his normal good humor.

"My apologies, my liege," Dyvim Tvar said in the same slightly bantering tone. "And now we should make our way to the Audience Hall and make our formal appearance. I'd suggest you freshen yourself in you chambers, but —"

"— But Pent'arl is most conspicuously absent, with all of his troops. I see your meaning, Dragonlord. We must make haste."

The two retrieved their blades and strode briskly down the stairwell, Dyvim Tvar's dragon-cave troops and the detachment of Silent Guard following, out under the open sky and across one of the numerous connecting bridges between the palace towers, toward D'a'rputna rising in pastel blue and gold.

Now they were getting close to the tower — just one more bridge remaining....

Suddenly men appeared at the windows near the bridge access portal, and the heavy door itself slammed shut with a crash. Elric and Dyvim Tvar joined their escort in a retreat to the tower behind them, taking cover within as a few arrows clattered in their tracks. They exchanged a grim glance. Was it Yyrkoon attempting a coup, or Pent'arl, or someone else, or a coalition?

"Terac, take a detachment of our men back and make sure we have an escape route. I don't want to be trapped here! Who's the ranking officer here from the Silent Guard? You are —?"

"Phalanx Commander Vas'tris, Dragonlord."

"I need your opinion, Vas'tris. Will the Silent Guard stand with an usurper, or with Lord Elric?"

"With the rightful liege, I believe, sire," with a respectful nod to Elric. "We do have a corps loyalty, after all...."

"Very good. Take some men with you and contact your other commanders. Advise them of the situation and request assistance. If they can secure further points in Elric's name then have them do so; else we'll regroup here." Vas'tris nodded and departed at a run. A few tense minutes passed while their men scanned the nearby buildings, bridges and streets for other signs of the usurper's forces.

"If only we knew who the culprit is —"

"But we do." Elric nodded at the door into D'a'rputna, which was opening slowly.

Dyvim Tvar expected Yyrkoon's youthful, slightly addled countenance, but he was only mildly surprised by the sight of Pent'arl.

"It seems he wants to parley, my lord," he observed. "Surely he can't control so many troops that he expects to dicker with you for the throne!" He grinned absently. "They were foolish. If they'd waited a few more seconds we'd have been inside the Tower and easy prey for them." Neither of them was caparisoned for war.

Over the intervening space — half a bowshot or so — Pent'arl's voice cried out, "Lay down your arms, Elric, and step out into view, and you have my word you'll be well-treated!" His words echoed slightly against the multicolored rock comprising the palace complex.

As Terac returned with a few Dragon-troops, he and Dyvim Tvar conferred quietly while Elric retorted:

"You mean you'll shoot us on sight? You take us for fools indeed, First Minister. You may address us as 'My Lord' or 'My Liege' — or not at all."

"You are not my rightful lord, boy!" Pent'arl shouted. "You are an abomination, a white rat, to be expunged...."

While Pent'arl continued his ravings, Dyvim Tvar, Terac and Elric conferred. "Terac reports that Pent'arl commands his own house contingent and perhaps half of the regular Melnibonéan troops, which were under his command as Regent," Dyvim Tvar muttered. "My Dragon-troops — even without the aid of the dragons — plus the Silent Guard, plus the loyal army units, plus the City Watch, outnumber him easily two to one or more. Obviously he has some other plan, or reinforcements we don't know about. He has tight control over the Tower of D'a'rputna only, no evidence of his forces elsewhere."

"Perhaps he intends to take hostages?" A cold thought struck the fledgling Emperor. "Terac, any news of Cymoril?"

Normally young Terac would have been flustered to be addressed by the Bright Emperor himself, but in the excitement he forgot his awe. "Sire, I sent a squad to her apartments to see to her safety. Their leader signalled from a window that she was untouched."

"I'd have been surprised if he had molested her; her brother Yyrkoon would be a poor choice of ally to anger. Very well done, Terac."

Dyvim Tvar nodded approvingly as well. "Did you get word to the Caves?"

"Aye, sir. Your signalling plan worked well."

"Signalling plan?"

"Yes, Majesty. I had a feeling this might happen. I set up watch points with signal flags extending back to the Dragon Caves. We'll have reinforcements soon."

Elric muttered admiringly. Then his expression grew grim. "But what does he intend, I wonder?"

"Has Pent'arl some sort of supernatural aid? Does he have any arcane knowledge, my prince?"

"Little or none. Certainly he's never been known as a summoner of demons." The boy spoke with unaccustomed malice of those Melnibonéans who, ill-prepared, engaged in minor traffickings with the Higher Planes.

"He could have someone's aid in that." The two locked eyes. *Yyrkoon* had the necessary skills.

"Surely even Yyrkoon realizes I could probably defeat any sorcerous attempt of his...."

Pent'arl had run out of epithets, and now there was a new disturbance over in the Tower. Dyvim Tvar cautiously peered around a corner and sighed.

"Perhaps he's not *completely* wackoo...." His face was grave.

Elric stared across the abyss. What he saw froze his heart and steeled his resolve.

They had taken Avedis.

I V
OF STRATEGY IS A GENERAL BORN

He was disheveled, his long, dark hair tangled and his simple clothes in disarray. His hands were cruelly manacled behind his back with a bar inserted, twisting his torso forward. Elric was pleased that his friend had not been taken without a struggle. Avedis' father would have approved.

With a sinking feeling Elric realized that Avedis had been easily abducted from the garden, and that he himself had asked him to remain there. *It's my fault,* he thought harshly.

"This is quite unwise of you, Pent'arl," he spat grimly. "I had heretofore been inclined to show you some clemency, but you are rapidly wearing my patience thin...."

"Spare me your posturings, little lord," Pent'arl sneered. Elric was amazed that the person who'd sat at his father's councils and provided intellectual, rational analyses was the same Pent'arl he saw now, sniggering and raving like a madman. "You'll be loathe to assault my forces with my hostage's life in the balance." To underscore his point Pent'arl jerked his knee up into Avedis' crotch; the boy went down with a yelp and stayed down.

Elric winced at this reminder of his first encounter with Avedis. He felt a cold rage possessing him, that cruel battle-lust for which Melnibonéans were justly famous. He was on the verge of dashing out across the bridge, into the teeth of a dozen bowmen arrayed in the windows and parapet of D'a'rputna, to sudden death. Dyvim Tvar looked at him in alarm.

Then suddenly Elric had two ideas. His battle-rage cooled slightly, yet this vow he now made to himself: Whatever the day brought, the former First Minister would die by his hand and by his sword.

"Master, I've brought your armor, if you think you need it," a voice quavered behind him. Tanglebones stood there with the prince's fighting-leathers.

"My thanks, Tanglebones," Elric muttered gratefully. "Just leave it in a pile by the stairs — and go carefully." Tanglebones nodded knowingly and retreated down the stairway.

Elric put his first idea into operation immediately, hoping that many of Pent'arl's forces were within earshot. Visibly controlling his anger, he said loudly, "My friend Avedis is the son of a warrior under your very own command, Pent'arl. You were too much of a coward to abduct anyone closer to the royal line, I see. But I should have expected that. You prey on the easiest game."

This provoked another torrent of abuse from Pent'arl. A calculated risk on Elric's part, who'd gambled that the madman across the void would not hurt Avedis again in his fury.

The Emperor spoke to the Dragonlord quickly. "Have your troops below spread the word that Pent'arl has taken the son of one of his own troops hostage. That will not much please his men, and could sway some of the regular troops over to us."

"Good idea, sire. Terac, see to it."

Now Elric invoked his second idea. "Dyvim Tvar, do Pent'arl's men hold the catacombs?"

"Sire, I myself had forgotten them until now. I doubt he's thought of them."

Elric chuckled in a weak attempt at humor. "Even I was occasionally allowed to explore those old tunnels. They connect almost everything in the city. Our oldest scrolls say they were built for the city's defense. The passages beneath D'a'rputna and the palace I remember well. If he hasn't guarded them we can enter the Tower from below. Can you find us a stylus and paper?"

While Elric sketched the tunnel entrances and layout briefly, Pent'arl went silent. "Let him sweat for a while," Elric muttered. "I can't go with you; I'll have to keep that fool occupied. Leave me four squads plus the archers and go. You archers: to the windows and stay out of sight."

"Sire, even if we successfully storm the Tower we cannot guarantee the boy won't be killed. We surely won't be able to attack *completely* by surprise —"

"Anything's better than giving in to that imbecile! Besides," he murmured, "I think Avedis would want it this way."

"My Emperor, you are my law," Dyvim Tvar observed quietly. He departed at a run while Elric quickly outlined his plan to the remaining commanders.

V
IN COMBAT IS A WHITE WOLF BORN

For a few moments relative quiet prevailed around the bridge. Elric imagined he could see Pent'arl fuming and pacing, waiting. Then there came a shout: "Well, boy? Have you left in haste? Has the White Rat scampered off into his hole?"

Elric frowned, realizing that the man could not actually know of his plans. Still he waited.

"Show yourself," Pent'arl snarled. "Show yourself, Elric, or I'll kill the boy."

Elric stepped slightly out from the doorway. "I have gone nowhere, Pent'arl," he said. "I am considering your situation."

"Consider *your* situation, and consider your friend here, prince-that-was," the maddened minister said gleefully. "You have no choice but to surrender your birthright...."

A young messenger in Dyvim Tvar's livery had run up the stairs behind Elric and saluted him now, chest heaving. "My Emperor, the Lord of the Dragon Caves advises the tunnels were not guarded. He has begun his infiltration. About five candlemarks until he is in position in the basements, he said, sire."

"Well done," Elric acknowledged. "Go and rest below."

Elric again moved slightly out into view of the doorway across the bridge; he saw that Avedis had regained his footing, though he still looked shaky.

"Clearly, Pent'arl, you've planned this for some time," Elric said. "You were with Lord Sadric when he was injured. My father's accident was no doubt the result of your devious cowardice."

Pent'arl flushed, but replied evenly, "Oh, I'm proud of it. I also poisoned his canteen enough to disrupt his healing abilities. A strong Emperor rendered weak, like his weakling son."

"Hear that, men of Melniboné!?" Elric cried, directing his voice at D'a'rputna. "Your would-be leader murdered his rightful Emperor!"

"Shut up, rat, or your friend will face further pain."

"What are your demands, then, Pent'arl?" Elric asked, still gaining time. Avedis looked at him now, recognizing a nuance of tone which Elric used. With his left hand — the one in view — Elric signed in their secret, silent code, *attack — soon — rom — below*, casually and slowly to avoid arousing suspicion.

"You are to surrender your lineage and the throne to me. You are to order all armed forces to support my rule —"

"Oh, so you admit that I hold the throne, Minister? You admit that I *am* the emperor? Yet you just called me the 'prince-that-was'!"

Pent'arl flushed. "I meant nothing of the kind, upstart! I hold the throne, as I hold D'a'rputna!"

While Pent'arl was thus engaged, Avedis mouthed the words *What do I do?*, since his hands were shackled behind him.

"I grow weary of this," Pent'arl continued. "All forces must be relinquished to my control...."

Stay —out —of — the —way, Elric signed with a trace of his old smile. *Keep — your — head — down. Don't — get — kicked — again!* Avedis grimaced so comically Elric had to smother a grin despite the situation.

"...Certain military commanders are to be handed over to me for later disposition —"

"Execution, you mean. Does this include, perchance, the commanders of your own troops, after you've gained all you require?" Elric's rejoinder apparently hit home. "Such capricious men — who, after all, just today deposed their rightful liege — might take it into their heads to depose *you*, eh?" Elric's voice was silky.

"Mind your words, whelp!" Pent'arl cried.

Elric saw one of Pent'arl's guards at the base of D'a'rputna disappear suddenly, jerked silently back from behind. He smiled and slipped surreptitiously into the shadows by the stairway, quickly donning the leather breastplate and a vambrace left by Tanglebones. No time for the rest of it....

After a few moments: "And what of me, Your Eminence?" he asked, sardonically.

"You will be executed, White Rat, as befits you. Exile would be far too dangerous."

"Pent'arl, why should I surrender to you, if my only reward is to be killed? To save Avedis? Even if you let him go, we would be separated by my death." Elric raised his right arm and balled his fist, out of view from the Tower.

"No, former Minister, I think you offer too little in recompense for my abdication."

"Exile, then?"

Elric laughed aloud. The man was practically pleading with him. "Now there's a true bargain...."

Distantly Elric heard the first clangs of swordplay; unlike his eyesight, his hearing was keen.

"Pent'arl, I fear I'll have to disappoint you this day. My firm answer is: No!"

On the final syllable he jerked his arm down. Ten arrows whirred from nearby windows, eight of them burying themselves in Pent'arl's own archers across the abyss. The sounds of battle echoed much closer now within great D'a'rputna. "Spare the Minister; he's mine!"

Together with his own squads he dashed across the bridge. Pent'arl's three remaining archers loosed a volley. One man on Elric's right went down with a brief cry, writhing. A solid *chunk* from his breastpiece; Elric looked down and saw the arrow. *Thank you, Tanglebones, my old friend.* He heard the other arrow skitter across the marble arch.

They were too close to D'a'rputna's walls for Pent'arl's archers to shoot without leaning out and making themselves even better targets for Elric's crack bowmen, who aimed instead toward the doorway, riddling the soldier attempting to close the door.

They were at the threshold. Three of Pent'arl's hidden men leaped out. Despite his battle-lust Elric let his men engage them until one, evading his attacker, sprang toward the albino, who skewered him on his longsword with a sigh. *I fight my own people,* he thought. *What madness this is.*

The sounds of combat from within were closer now. Looking around, Elric saw some of Pent'arl's troops being driven back into the large entry foyer by Dyvim Tvar's larger force. Off in a corner Pent'arl held tightly to Avedis' bonds, three of his men warding him.

Elric's squads divided, some to check the other adjoining rooms and flush out the archers, some to take Pent'arl's defenders from the rear. Five remained with Elric, who advanced upon the cowering minister with murder in his crimson eyes.

"Pent'arl, it is now I who ask for *your* surrender. I might offer you exile —"

With an almost animal snarl Pent'arl snatched a sword from one of his guards, while Elric and his forces rushed them.

The next few seconds were forever etched in Elric's memory: how the three guards were swiftly dealt with; how Pent'arl raised his sword and plunged it into Avedis' slender abdomen; how Elric cried in grief but still managed to order his men to hold the feverish-eyed minister and not kill him outright; how Dyvim Tvar's men disarmed the remaining defenders —

How he held Avedis' head to his breast as he died, crying openly as they whispered final, sad words to each other. How he lay near Avedis, his only true friend taken swiftly from him, wishing there were some way he could trade places with him — and realizing eventually that he could never do so, that destiny called him elsewhere, and that life would have to continue —

How he then regarded Pent'arl in grief and cold fury, cleaning his sword of the blood already on it, saying, "I would not mingle this braver man's blood with yours. He deserves better." —

How he motioned to his men to release the gibbering First Minister. How he cried, "Observe how a white rat becomes a wolf, treacherous lord!" How he took his sword and rammed it into Pent'arl's vitals —

How he then collapsed on the floor next to Avedis' prone form, and knew no more that day.

VI
AFTERMATH: PHOENIX OF THE WOLF

He awakened in his own bed, seeing at first a dark blur which coalesced into the gravely concerned face of his beloved.

"Cymoril...." he whispered.

"Oh, Elric, I'm so sorry," she murmured sadly, her long black hair contrasting sharply with her pale face. "I know what Avedis meant to you...."

Elric blanched now at the memory. Cymoril grasped his hand lightly in hers; he seemed to draw strength from her contact.

"Rest well, my liege," Dyvim Tvar said quietly. "We have secured the city. You are the uncontested Emperor now."

After a few seconds, Elric struggled upright, his curiosity for the moment overshadowing his grief and pain. "What of Yyrkoon?"

"We found Yyrkoon cloistered in B'aal'nezbett. He was exhausted by some sorcery, but he swears he knew nothing of Pent'arl's attempt upon the Throne, and nothing of your father's passing until we found him."

"Weather-weaving, eh?"

"Aye, milord. 'Twas he who wove that mist of contortion two mornings ago."

"Two?!"

"My Emperor, you've slept for over a day," said Dyvim Tvar.

"Then it's time I rose." He spoke with a trace of his former lightness.

"Rest if you will, Elric. Your coronation must be soon, though, if you're to consolidate your victory."

"Did we lose many?"

"Not as many as we might have, thanks to your strategy, my lord. Most of Pent'arl's men simply surrendered, when they heard how Pent'arl murdered your father and took Avedis captive. We tried to incapacitate Pent'arl's men rather than kill them. Perhaps another five dead and others wounded. Terac was slightly injured." He paused. "And Avedis, of course."

"He was about to join his father's detachment." Elric sighed. "This is an ill omen for my reign, eh, Dragonlord?"

"My Prince," Dyvim Tvar was unconscious of his mistake, "you have already proven yourself fit to rule Melniboné well."

Elric gave him an odd look. "What do you mean?"

"You changed, my lord, in the very course of our struggle. You took command readily. You were economical with the lives of your troops. You displayed cunning, and —" He glanced meaningfully at Cymoril.

Elric was amused. "What's this? The great Dyvim Tvar embarrassed? Cymoril, wait outside for a moment. Please don't go far!"

Dyvim Tvar spoke rapidly after the door closed. "Elric, you proved yourself appropriately ruthless, especially when Avedis died. Forgive me, but, put bluntly, you have become a man and a true Melnibonéan leader. Two days ago you were a boy. Today you are a man and my Emperor. I am proud to serve you."

"So, in a way, Pent'arl was the architect of my transformation, eh?"

"If you like, though he took your best friend from you. But eventually someone would have sought to test your power and skill.... What was it you called yourself? The White Wolf? Aye, we have a wolf now."

"Merely a boyish choice of words, made in the heat of battle."

"Perhaps, my lord." But Dyvim Tvar seemed pensive.

Elric struggled free from the bedding and tried to stand upright. He spoke quietly. "The boy that was me died when Avedis was slain. I feel you speak the truth. I am a man now, Dyvim Tvar."

"Cymoril! You may enter!" Dyvim Tvar called. "Your Emperor bids you help him to the window, that he may survey his new realm!"

Thus ends the tale of Elric's accession.

THE DRAGON'S HEART

BY NANCY A. COLLINS

The white prince pulled his cloak tighter, trying to block the icy wind sawing against his flesh. His horse nickered its discomfort; it knew it was too cold to be standing motionless atop an exposed hill, even if its rider did not.

The white prince stared down into the valley laid out before him like a rumpled blanket. It would be warmer in the valley. And more dangerous. He frowned as he fumbled with the vial in the pouch fastened to his belt. The elixir that helped fire his weak blood was so cold it burned his lips. His ruby-red eyes dilated as the herbs and drugs did their work.

Elric of Melniboné, last of a royal line that stretched beyond the dawn of Human memory, sank his spurs into the flanks of his trembling mount and descended into the Valley of Dragons.

⊕

"We need dragons."

This came from Yaris, the young, upstart king. More than once he had made his distrust of Elric known. Of the seven Sea-Lords who'd entered into the conspiracy with the exiled Melnibonéan to raid ancient Imrryr, the fabled Dreaming City, he was the one who complained the most.

Count Smiorgan Baldhead frowned over his horn of ale. He was the closest to a friend the albino prince could claim amongst the seven, and the chief co-conspirator.

"You're speaking nonsense, Yaris! Next you'll be wanting the moon on a string! Where would we get dragons?"

"Ask *him*." Yaris pointed a finger at Elric, seated at the end of the table. "His people have used them for centuries! That's how they founded the Bright Empire! If we are going to raid the Dragon Isle, I'd rest easier knowing we have dragons of our own to call upon."

"The boy has a point," muttered Naclon of Vilmir, the most patrician and respected of the Sea-Lords. "The Melnibonéans did not become known as Dragon Princes for naught."

Elric shook his head. "The dragons of Imrryr are all but extinct. The ferocity has been bred from them, rendering them sterile. Your men and their ships have little to fear from them."

It was a lie, but he did not want his human co-conspirators backing out now that his dream of avenging himself on his scheming cousin Yyrkoon and rescuing his ensorcelled lover Cymoril, was finally within his reach.

Naclon stroked his beard pensively. "Still, your people tamed the beasts and bent them to their will enough to build an empire. Surely you could use your knowledge to our advantage."

Elric shrugged. "But where could I obtain dragons — and trained ones, at that, capable of responding to a rider's goads and directions? The beasts require a human lifetime to break them until they're docile enough to accommodate a rider."

No sooner than he'd spoken, Elric envisioned himself astride a flying dragon, caparisoned in the bat-winged helm and black armor of his ancestors, Stormbringer held aloft in one hand as he waved his band of mercenaries onward toward the Dreaming City. The idea of the last of the royal line leading the final assault on the heart of the ancient, decadent Bright Empire astride one of the beasts that had made that dynasty possible appealed to his vanity. And, as with all Melnibonéans, vanity was Elric's greatest weakness

He stood up and fastened his cloak about his broad shoulders. "Gentlemen, I must take my leave of you. The raid that we are planning will require a great deal of mental and spiritual strength on my part. I must go forth and prepare myself. You will not see me for some time, I fear. I will return when the tides are right and the hundred ships promised for this venture are gathered in the fjord."

Count Smiorgan Baldhead left the table and hurried after his friend. While he had grown used to the high-handed manner in which the Melnibonéan excused himself from matters he considered boring, the same could not be said of the other Sea-Lords. Each was, in his way, a king and master, used to being heard and to having his words acted upon. Granted, their kingdoms were little more than barbaric tribes compared to a lineage as old and powerful as Elric's, but that didn't mean they enjoyed having their noses rubbed in it.

"Elric! Is this wise?" Smiorgan hissed as he grabbed the Melnibonéan by the elbow. "For you to take an indefinite leave while the combine is at such an early — and precarious — stage risks disaster! What if Yaris should decide to pull out his support? Fadan of Lormyr would not be far behind in joining him — then where would we be? Elric, you're leaving me to tend a house of cards!"

Elric stiffened at the grip on his elbow but, in deference to his friend, did not yank his arm free of the heavier man's grasp. He turned his crimson eyes toward Smiorgan and spoke in a cold, iron-edged voice.

"Your only hope of successfully navigating the Sea Maze that protects Imrryr's harbor is through me. With me, you have an alliance amongst your fellow raider-kings, forged by greed and a deep-seated hatred for my people. Without me, you are seven reaver-kings, constantly battling one another for the meager loot offered by the coastal villages of the Young Kingdoms. We will attack Imrryr when the tides and time are right. My being on display for your fellow Sea-Lords will neither hurry nor delay what will come. But if I do not prepare myself in the prescribed manner, there will be no raid. Is that clear?"

Smiorgan's frown deepened, but he let go of Elric's arm.

"We shall await your return."

Elric nodded a farewell to his companion and left the room, pulling his cloak's hood over his head. *And when I return I shall be astride a flying dragon.*

⊕

Elric's schooling in preparation to ascend the Ruby Throne of Imrryr had given him knowledge of things and places unknown to the Human races. One such piece of arcana concerned the beings known only as the Eldren.

Once the Melnibonéans had worshipped the Eldren as gods, although by the time of Elric's birth they had devolved into half-remembered legend. As heir to the magicks and lore of the sorcerer-emperors who had ruled the Bright Empire for ten millennia, Elric knew more about them than anyone else, with the possible exception of his demented cousin, Yyrkoon.

It was said that the Eldren had emerged from the swirling, formless mass of raw Chaos that stretches beyond the Cliffs of Kaneloon at the place called World's Edge twenty-five thousand years ago. An Ordered race born from Chaos, the Eldren were rumored to serve neither aspect, while mastering both forces. They, and they alone, were successful in harnessing the dual natures of stasis and entropy.

As a youth, Elric had found a series of scrolls written by one of his ancestors — Yrik XVI, also known as the Wandering One — that detailed how, twelve thousand years earlier, the Eldren had created a race of beings like themselves, yet baser and more "animalistic," not unlike the apish nomads that infested what would later be known as the Young Kingdoms. This degenerate offshoot-race became the Melnibonéans.

If the story were true, Elric could understand why it had been allowed to fall into disuse. The Melnibonéans had long prided themselves on their superiority to the lowly Human race, which it had terrorized and enslaved before the first man had had wits enough strike flint against rock.

The scrolls also went on to describe how, after a virus had decimated the dragon caves, Yrik had gone forth to the Valley of the Dragons where the Eldren made their home, and had successfully bargained for a breeding pair of winged serpents with Tanoch, Lord of Dragons, ruler of the Eldren.

Somewhere along the line Yrik lost his reason — or at least the ability to concentrate on one thing for more than five minutes at a time, judging from the meandering passages in his journal after his return from his meeting with the Lord of Dragons. This had occurred three thousand years ago.

Whoever — whatever — the Lord of Dragons might be, the Eldren were not beings to trifle with.

And until Yaris planted the seeds in Elric's milk-white skull, the Eldren and their dragon cavalry had been just another piece of occult trivia cluttering his back-brain. Now he was leagues away from his marshalling naval force, coercing his weary mount to trudge through harsh northern weather in search of a lost race sheltered from the roar and press of lesser civilizations by a magically maintained valley. It was a fool's quest. But when had knowing his actions were folly ever stopped him?

During his journey northward he had caught tantalizing hints that what he sought actually existed. He'd heard blue-skinned barbarians invoking their fearsome, comfortless northern deities, and one they spoke of in the most reverent of whispers was called Tanoch. Tanoch the Storm-Giver. Tanoch the Sky Lord. Tanoch the Night-Bringer. He'd even glimpsed a crude graven image: a winged man with a beard and breasts, the fingers crooked into punishing claws. Could this horrific hermaphroditic sky-god be the same being his ancestor had petitioned centuries ago?

These thoughts ran through Elric's mind as he goaded his horse down the narrow mountain pass into the mist-shrouded valley. He had no doubts that he had located the legendary Valley of Dragons. The lush hothouse foliage and steaming jungle below reeked of sorcery. The surrounding mountains were harsh, cold, granite giants sheathed in snow and black ice; such a place could not exist without the aid of powerful magicks.

His weary mount nickered nervously as they went deeper into the valley's dense greenery. The trail they'd been following was now little more than a pig-path and Elric was forced to dismount and lead his horse as he hacked back branches and vines with his short sword.

Suddenly the horse pulled against its reins, yanking them free of his hands. The beast reared onto its hind legs, its wildly rolling eyes showing their whites as it impotently clawed at the air with its forelegs. There was not enough room along the trail for it to turn and bolt, and all it succeeded in doing was to tangle its bridle in the underbrush. Elric swore as he tried to calm the frightened animal. He grabbed at the flailing reins, but he feared one of the beast's madly stamping hooves would connect with his head.

As he wondered what could have thrown the stallion into such a sudden frenzy, he caught the scent of dragon.

It was a rank, reptilian stink, reminding him of the boyhood he'd spent playing with his best friend, Dyvim Tvar, in the Dragon Caves below the gleaming spires of the Dreaming City. Then there was the sound of tree trunks snapping like kindling and the sibilant hiss of a thousand angry serpents, and the dragon was upon them.

Elric spun, snatching Stormbringer from its sheath, to face the monster that shouldered its way through the forest.

The dragon towering over him was unlike any he'd seen in the husbandry charts of his ancestors. The dragons of Melniboné were winged serpents, their snake-like bodies narrow-snouted and equipped with powerful, whip-like tails. This beast, however, stood on two thickly muscled hindlegs, the forelegs dangling in front of its chest resembling more the withered arms of an old woman than grasping claws. Its head was massive, the jaws capable of snapping a fully-armored battle-horse in two with one quick, dreadful bite. The monster's mouth was full of teeth the size of dirks — and just as sharp.

With a speed surprising for its bulk, the dragon seized the terrified horse in its massive jaws. The horse screamed like a girl as the monster's razor-sharp teeth pierced its vitals. The dragon shook its head back and forth, spraying its dying victim's blood in all directions. The horse's hindquarters fell to the ground, severed completely from the still-struggling head and forelegs.

Even armed with Stormbringer, Elric could see there was no point in pitting himself against such an engine of destruction. Leaving the dragon to feed in peace, he hurried on his way lest another, even more fearsome beast be attracted by the smell of blood.

⊕

Night came to the Valley of the Dragons. He had walked for hours along the narrow trail winding its way through the jungle floor, suffering the hot, muggy weather and the bites of numerous blood-drinking insects without finding any sign of civilization, Eldren or otherwise. He had, however, narrowly skirted confrontations with the terrible two-legged dragon — or its nest-mates — and spotted a few lumbering, well-armored four-legged dragons sporting unicorn-like horns. Much to his relief, these seemed more interested in feeding on the lush vegetation than in molesting him.

Now he sat watch in front of a meager fire, his sword ready at hand should the surrounding jungle present him with an unwanted visitor. He anxiously fingered the vial of elixir that kept his thin albino's blood enriched. He had enough for two, perhaps three days, assuming he did not have to call upon sorcery. Working magick always depleted him more than simple physical exertion, which was why he was loathe to call upon the arcane arts except in the direst of situations. In any case, if he did not find the Eldren within the span of three days, he would soon weaken and fall victim to the ravenous giant reptiles that roamed the valley floor.

He scowled at the tiny fire and reflected on how, once again, his willfulness had led him into a dire predicament. His refusal to accept the mantle of emperor had led to his ousting by his cousin Yyrkoon, and the endangerment of the one woman who had ever held any meaning for him, Yyrkoon's own sister, the lovely Cymoril. He had turned his back on power and love in exchange for the freedom to wander the world and know life as something other than a noble-born scholar. Now he was plotting with the ancestral enemies of his people to overthrow the kingdom that was, by rights, his own. And even that plan was in danger, now that he was leagues away from his friends and comrades, none of whom he'd dared tell where he was going or for what reason.

Should he die in this lost, enchanted valley it would all be for naught; Yyrkoon would continue to rule Imrryr and, in time, he would marry his own sister, Elric's beloved, and their offspring would inherit the Ruby Throne. The thought made Elric's guts roil.

His light-sensitive eyes ached from staring so hard into the fire. As he blinked back his tears of outrage, he lifted his gaze from the flames and saw that he was no longer alone.

They stood before him in a rough semi-circle, their armor gleaming like snakeskin. There were six of them, caparisoned in tight-fitting greaves and breastplates made of an iridescent material that looked like leather but shone like metal. Their faces were all but obscured by ornate, winged helmets, and they held tridents in their hands.

One of the strangely-garbed warriors stepped forward, removing his helmet in a single fluid gesture. A thick rope of violet hair, plaited into a single braid, dropped onto the warrior's shoulders. Elric could not keep from gasping at the sight of the Eldren's eerily familiar features.

The Melnibonéan race had always prided itself on the delicacy of its features, especially when compared to the brutishness of the Human species. The being standing before Elric made even the finest-bred Melnibonéan courtier look like a scullery slave.

The Eldren's cheeks were high, tilted to give the eyes a cat-like slant. The eyebrows were upswept, the ears coming to a slight point. There was an androgynous beauty to the warrior's finely chiseled features that defied gender classification. The most disturbing element, however, was the Eldren's eyes: they were of a solid color, lacking both iris and whites. The warrior's eyes were the same shade as its hair. It was like looking into the painted eyes of a marble statue.

The Eldren warrior held up a narrow, slender hand with six fingers and made a ritual gesture that Elric did not understand.

As Elric got to his feet he felt a sharp pain in the back of his brain, as if it'd been pricked with a pin. His hand closed about the hilt of Stormbringer, which pulsed in his grip.

"I wish to see the Lord of Dragons." He tried to make his voice sound as authoritative as possible.

The purple warrior did not smile, or frown, or show any signs of having understood anything he'd said.

"I have come to see the Lord of Dragons."

The purple warrior turned to look at one of his fellows. The second warrior removed his helmet, revealing hair the color of seafoam braided into two heavy plaits. The green warrior twisted the six fingers of his left hand into an arcane symbol and twitched his head in a strange, bird-like manner. The purple warrior nodded and turned back to face Elric.

The Eldren warrior's thin lips opened and an oddly clipped, almost mechanical voice issued forth. "Kalki informs me your race is Mute. So I shall communicate with you in the manner to which you are accustomed."

"I am Elric of Melniboné...."

"We know who you are. What you are. Your coming was foretold. The Lord of Dragons sent us to gather you, lest one of the Eaters accidentally harm you." The purple warrior made another arcane gesture with his long, oddly jointed fingers. "I am Euryth, First General of the Dragon Cavalry. Please come with us."

The silent, blank-eyed Dragon Generals lead Elric from his rough campsite to a nearby clearing, where their flying dragons were tethered. While winged, these dragons were vastly different from their Melnibonéan cousins. The Eldren's mounts resembled monstrous featherless, birds with peaked crowns and cruel beaks that clattered like clashing swords. Their huge, leathery wings stretched thirty feet from tip to tip and the Eldren rode astride their backs on ornately tooled saddles.

General Euryth motioned for Elric to climb behind him and, without a single look or visual signal exchanged between them, the Dragon Cavalry took to the air as one.

It had been years since Elric had last ridden the great beasts his people had made their tools of war and empire. Now, looking down at the jungle from astride the Eldren's mount, the thunder of its wings and the rushing of the wind in his ears, he realized how much he'd missed such simple pleasures.

As dawn broke, they came within sight of the Eldren's walled city, the legendary Dragon Arum.

The sight of its towering spires and shimmering, glass-smooth walls reminded Elric of the place of his birth. No other city in the whole of the world could claim the knowledge and craftsmanship to create such delicate architecture. The Young Kingdoms were centuries, if not millennia, away from discovering how to build anything except brooding castles and thick-set keeps. And, the truth to be told, the Melnibonéans themselves had long lost the incentive to continue creating such wondrous architectural confections. Imrryr itself was little more than a distant reflection of this wondrous city, glimpsed in a looking glass warped by time and neglect.

The squadron sailed across the lightening sky, circling downward like raptors descending the thermals. Their destination seemed to be the tallest of the ornate shimmering towers, its pinnacle open to the elements. One by one the dragons swooped down, landing in the aerie with incredible precision.

The Dragon Masters of Melniboné manipulated their serpentine mounts by way of sharpened goads and the use of special pitch-pipes that "charmed" the great beasts, but Elric had been unable to determine how the Eldren kept their breed of dragon under control. The Dragon Generals and their beasts performed as one.

Servants dressed in their masters' livery hurried forward to take possession of the squawking dragons as the Generals dismounted. Euryth removed his helmet and twitched the thumb and sixth finger of his right hand at a young Eldren dressed in violet jerkin and breeches. The youth lifted an open palm in response and Euryth nodded. He turned to fix Elric with his blank gaze.

"The Lord of Dragons awaits you."

Euryth handed the reins of his dragon to the youth and motioned for Elric to follow him into the heart of the tower.

Elric had seem many things on his travels, but nothing compared to the halls of the Dragon Palace of the Eldren. What had at first glance appeared to be walls of colored glass proved to be actual Chaos-stuff trapped between twin layers of Order. As Elric passed through the tortured arches and passageways of the palace, the walls became a giant's kaleidoscope as the Chaos surged and shifted its way through the colors of the universe.

For all their vaunted reputation as servants of the Chaos Lords, the Melnibonéans had never been able to turn the raw stuff of entropy to their will. Elric was duly impressed.

They came to a set of doors fashioned from metal, into the face of which was worked the image of a grimacing dragon. The door silently opened inward and Elric was ushered into the presence of the Lord of Dragons, ruler of the Eldren.

The throne-room's ceiling stretched into infinity, its walls hung with silken tapestries and lit by braziers that gave off light but no heat. On a raised dais sat a massive throne chiseled from a single piece of obsidian. The throne crawled with carved serpent-dragons, but was otherwise empty.

Euryth arched his long-fingered hands as if they cupped an invisible egg, the fingertips straining but not quite touching.

There was a rustling sound from deep within the darkness above their heads and a shadow spread itself across the floor.

Elric started as he realized there was a someone kneeling in front of them. At first Elric mistook the black leather spread about the crouching figure to be a cloak of some kind. Then the Dragon Lord of the Eldren raised her head and smiled at the pale warrior-prince.

She was taller than him by a full head, her hair silver, her eyes solid black. She wore black suede riding breeches cinched at her narrow waist by a thick leather belt fixed with the silver-plated skull of a feral dog. At first he thought she was wearing a ram's-head helmet; then he realized the luxuriantly curled horns were actually growing from her own forehead.

She was nude from the waist up, her chest corded with heavy muscle that connected to the bat-like wings folded against her back like a peaked cape. She lifted a six-fingered hand in greeting.

"Welcome, cousin."

As Elric spied the scabbard hanging from her hip, Stormbringer twitched within its own sheath, emitting a low-pitched cry, like a beast calling to its mate. He rested his hand on the pommel of the black sword and stroked it, silencing its plaintive moan.

Euryth took a warning step toward Elric, the tines of his trident suddenly glowing with a purplish witch-fire.

"That will be all, Euryth," said the winged woman, making a complex gesture with her right hand. "We do not wish to offend our guest."

The crackling aura surrounding the trident disappeared and the Dragon General bowed curtly before retiring from the throne-room.

The Eldren ruler stepped forward, her wings twitching like those of a restless bird.

"Elric of Melniboné, Agent of Chaos, Master-Slave of Stormbringer, Eternal Champion.... Your coming was foreseen by our Oracle." She gestured to the slender, fair-haired Eldren youth crouching beside the ornate obsidian throne, his empty eyes hidden by a golden cloth.

"Then you know why I have come to petition you."

"You wish dragons. Why else would you venture into Eldren territory?"

"I was not certain if the legends were true. I had read of an ancestor's journey to your land on a similar quest three thousand years ago... but I had no way of knowing if his directions were correct or if your people were extinct."

The Lord of Dragons smiled gently and gestured with one of her wings. "As you can see, the Eldren continue. As we shall always continue. Here or elsewhere, if need be. Yes, we remember your forefather Yrik very well."

"You — you are that Tanoch?"

Her smile widened. "Eldren are a long-lived race. And the Lords longest-lived of all. We were a youth of three centuries when Yrik came before us. But, yes, we are Tanoch." She reached out with her left wing, touching him lightly on one shoulder. "Come, you must be tired after such a long journey. Our servants shall see that you are rested and properly cared for."

A pair of androgynous attendants dressed in silver and black livery appeared as if from nowhere.

"We shall see you come the evening, Child of Chaos," smiled Tanoch. "Until then." And with a single beat of her huge, bat-like wings she shot upward into the dusky shadows of the throne-room's vast atrium.

⊕

After he had slept, bathed and changed into fresh clothes, Elric was once more escorted into the throne-room by the silent, blank-eyed Eldren servants. There he found a large banquet table set for three. The blind Oracle sat at the right-hand seat next to the head of the table.

Elric glanced about, but could see no one else. "Where is Tanoch?"

The Oracle did not answer, but instead angled his sightless face so it looked as if he were staring into the shadows above their heads.

There was the sound of wings and Tanoch Night-Bringer dropped down to land behind the chair at the head of the table.

"Forgive us. We were delayed by affairs of state."

She gestured for Elric to seat himself at the foot of the table. "How have you found Arum?"

"Wondrous and mystifying. Yrik did not do it justice in his journals."

Tanoch nodded as she carefully folded her wings against her back and took her place at the head of the table. "We have often wondered about what happened to him."

"He went mad shortly upon returning to Imrryr."

Something unreadable crossed the Lord of Dragons' finely chiseled features, then was gone. "We feared as much." A servant emerged from the darkness and filled the goblets with a wine the color of turquoise. "He was a man of great measure. There is much in you that reminds us of Yrik."

Elric grunted, fumbling with the tableware. The fork and knife were weighted for a six-fingered hand and felt alien in his grasp.

"We have given thought to your request for dragons. We have decided to help you."

"Then you will give me dragons?"

"More than that. We are prepared to turn our generals and their cavalry over to you for the raid on Imrryr."

Elric tried to hide his surprise but was not entirely successful. "You know? You know that I plan to raid the Dreaming City?"

Tanoch regarded him with her blank, black eyes. "Of course. There is nothing of which we are not aware."

The Oracle twitched his head and Tanoch shrugged, making a dismissive gesture. "Don't be a fool, Auberon. We know what we're doing." She smiled at Elric. "Please forgive our Oracle. He feels we are being — injudicious."

Elric's initial wariness quickly gave way to elation as he realized what this meant. With the Dragon Cavalry at his side, Imrryr would fall in a matter of hours! Yyrkoon's still-beating heart would be offered as a sweet morsel on Lord

Arioch's unhallowed altar before evening's shadow! How sweet an irony that the Bright Empire would be reduced to rubble by the races that had once begotten it and been enslaved by it! Surely beings as powerful and wise as the Eldren would have no trouble breaking the magicks that held his beloved Cymoril in stasis.

"Before you proclaim your victory over your usurping cousin, perhaps we should discuss the terms of payment." Tanoch's voice was tinged with both amusement and seriousness. Elric's chalk-white complexion colored as he realized the Dragon Lord had been privy to his fantasies of conquest.

The Oracle shook his head violently. Although his hands were narrow and delicate, almost feminine in appearance, there was unmistakable anger in the blinded man's gestures. Tanoch's fingers clamped tightly onto the arms of her chair as she lowered her horned brow.

Elric massaged his own forehead. It felt as if a bladder full of poisoned water were expanding behind his eyes. Tanoch slapped her left hand flat against the tabletop and emitted a weird, high-pitched noise that resembled the ultra-sonic piping of bats. Elric felt something warm and salty trickle from his nostrils. He touched his upper lip and stared at the smear of crimson on his bone-white fingertips.

The Oracle made an unmistakably obscene gesture in the Melnibonéan's direction and left the table, moving with surprising surety for someone without eyes.

Tanoch picked up her cutlery and resumed eating. "Do not mind Auberon. He's just jealous. Here, have some minted jelly with your rump of Grazer. We recommend it highly."

⊕

After the meal, Tanoch brought Elric into a room hung with black velvet draperies and dominated by a huge latticework of finely braided silken ropes that hung suspended from rings sunk into the walls like a vast spider's web.

"What is this place?"

"It is our bedchamber."

"You sleep in *that?*" Elric motioned to the web-like net.

"Sleep?" Her smile was tired.

Elric frowned. "You still haven't asked me what you expect from me in payment for the dragons...."

Tanoch laughed without opening her mouth, making Elric's brain flex and tremble inside its cage of bone. He took a step away from her, his vision swimming.

208

He flinched as she touched his shoulder with one of her wings.

"Forgive us. We meant you no harm, neither here nor at dinner."

"I believe you."

"To answer your question, princeling.... What we ask in the way of payment from you is the same we asked of your ancestor, Yrik, three thousand years ago. If you wish our aid, then you must spend a night with us in the web."

He thought of Cymoril, his one true love, kept from him by her brother's sorcery, and shook his head. "My love belongs to another."

"Did we ask for your love?"

Elric fell silent, contemplating his next move. Tanoch watched him with her bottomless eyes.

"Before you make your decision, it is only fair that we warn you of the consequences. You have noticed that the Eldren communicate using thoughts and emotions. But there must be dividing lines between individuals, lest more powerful personalities subsume and consume lesser ones.

"That is where we fit into the Scheme. The Lord of Dragons exists to keep the peace amongst the Eldren. To insure the sanctity of Self is maintained without falling into the extremes of selflessness or selfishness."

"You bear this burden alone?"

"Not exactly. I have my consort — the Oracle. He alone of the Eldren can embrace me without fear of death. And there is Mind."

"Mind?"

She smiled and rested her hand on the sword hanging from her hip. The pommel was designed to resemble trysting dragons. "You are not the only one whose well-being is tied to a sword of arcane manufacture. Mind belonged to our predecessor. Mind *is* our predecessor and all the Dragon Lords that went before, just as, in time, we shall become Mind. But we digress.

"To mate with a Dragon Lord is a dangerous thing, Child of Chaos. We are telepathic, and to join with the body is to join with the mind. And our mind is that of all Eldren. We are the Heart of the Dragon. Are you willing to risk madness, my white prince? Are you willing to risk the loss of your sanity — your very self — to win our favor? You could emerge from our lovemaking dead or, worse, an idiot. Like Yrik before you."

Elric unhooked Stormbringer's scabbard from his belt and held it before him in his pale hands. "I have carried this cursed weapon in the service of Arioch; I have slaughtered innocents to keep my master fed with blood and souls. And you ask me if I fear madness? Lady, I would look upon it as a gift!"

She reached for him with her wings, encircling him with their elongated fingers. The light from the braziers illuminated the capillaries of the skin stretched between the vanes and for a brief moment Elric recalled what it had been like inside his mother's womb.

"Take us, Child of Chaos," she whispered, her twelve fingers slowly working on the lacings of his shirt. "We are damned, little prince. Chained by fate and biology to roles we would rather not play. There will be time enough in what remains of our lifespans for remorse and pain and grief. Let us enjoy what little pleasure and warmth our liege lords will allow us. Do you understand what we're trying to say, Melnibonéan?"

Elric looked into Tanoch's face, but her eyes were unreadable.

Her kisses were long and deep, as if she were weighing his soul with each taste of his lips. She took his manhood in her hands, using the extra fingers to tease him to erection in ways he'd never before imagined.

As he penetrated her body she penetrated his mind, plunging him into the vast, alien machinery of her Self.

A rush of sensation and memory filled his skull, blossoming behind his eyes like a flower made of fire and ice. It was as if he were standing naked and alone on a sandy beach and had been taken unawares by a massive tidal wave. All that ever was and ever would be Tanoch surrounded him. Past, present and future lay before him, jumbled together like so much abandoned knitting.

The warmth of the sun on her wings as she swoops through the clouds....

The churning sea of Chaos at Land's End spits forth a winged humanoid clad in chitinous armor that reflects the infant moon's cold rays....

Gently stroking her blind consort's penis with a six-fingered grasp....

A winged woman with sky-blue hair and slender , gazelle-like horns draws from her scabbard a sword with a hilt fashioned to resemble tyrsting dragons... .

The flash of light from the laser as it severs her umbilical cord....

The coppery taste of human blood as she feeds on the ritually butchered sacrificial victim offered to her by the terrified, blue-daubed barbarians....

The winged woman with blue hair takes the sword and falls on it; the gleaming tip punctures her sternum and exits between her pinions.... Mother.... Mother....

The delicious, erotic prickling of skin as she swoops in and out of the gathering thunderclouds....

Mother....

She holds the sword called Mind for the first time and hears the voices of her ancestors, crooning and cajoling her into triggering her clairvoyance. Feels her mother's love... is her mother's love....

A roiling cloud of Chaos obscures the sun. She spreads her wings, signalling the others to follow her. And the Eldren, astride their dragons, cross the threshold from this world to some new and unknown universe....

The warmth of Yrik the Melnibonéan's semen on her thigh as he withdraws from her womb, screaming... screaming....

The ground convulses and the sky cracks, spilling Chaos across the land. Elric stands alone at its heart, the unwilling epicenter of mass destruction, screaming and waving Stormbringer like an angry child. Stormbringer leaps from its master's hands of its own volition and...

Elric cried out, forcing himself back into his body at the very moment his seed exited him. The sensation of being both penetrated and penetrator remained, and for a brief moment he saw himself through Tanoch's bottomless eyes: a pale demon with mad, unfocused eyes, teeth bared in a rictus grin. He tried to push himself off her in disgust, but was too weak. Instead, he lapsed into sleep.

⊕

He awoke to find himself curled under one of Tanoch's wings. The leather was soft like moleskin, but tough, and it radiated body heat, making it a serviceable blanket. He lay still for a long moment, studying the Lord of Dragons' sleeping features. Her eyes jerked rapidly back and forth behind their closed lids and occasionally a muscle in her face twitched, but she was otherwise motionless.

Elric eased himself out from under her wing and nimbly descended the web, careful not to disturb the sleeping Eldren. His head still ached from the torrent of sensory images and snatches of racial memory that had sluiced through it, but he no longer felt drained as he had earlier.

One borrowed memory had particularly intrigued him.... And it had to do with the sword Tanoch called "Mind."

The Lord of Dragons' scabbard lay amidst her discarded clothes, the sword's ornate handle gleaming softly in the muted light of the bedchamber. Elric's own weapon, Stormbringer, stood propped against a nearby table. As the albino reached for the Eldren blade, Stormbringer began to moan to itself like a mistreated pup.

"Damn you, be quiet!" he whispered. "If I didn't know better, I'd say you're jealous! I have no intention of casting you aside. Yet. I'm merely curious as to the manner of sorcery used in creating this sword."

Apparently mollified, the black sword lapsed back into silence.

Elric returned his attention to Tanoch's sword. From what little he was able to glean from their shared memories, Mind was similar to Stormbringer in that it incorporated and stored souls. At least, that was *his* understanding of its function.

He awkwardly wrapped his fingers around the sword's hilt, acutely aware that it was designed for a six-fingered grip. Mind's scabbard felt strangely warm, almost hot, to the touch. Dismissing the tingling in his fingertips as simple anxiety, Elric freed Mind from its sheath.

A dozen voices, male and female alike, swarmed and yammered inside his head like a cloud of angry hornets.

(*who?who?who? stranger! not one of us! access denied! Tanoch!Tanoch!Tanoch! access denied! Tanoch!Tanoch!Tanoch! purge!purge!purge!*)

The pain that travelled up his arm and into his head and chest was so immense that there was no way he could scream loud enough or long enough to give it proper voice. In the brief moment before his brain and nervous system shut down, he glimpsed Mind's naked length: a roiling tendril of Chaos preserved between two gleaming slivers of Order. Somewhere he could hear Stormbringer keening like a widow.

There were strange hands with too many fingers touching his body, probing muscle and tissue with peculiar instruments made from metal and horn. Something was squeezed between his clenched teeth and forced down his throat, billowing his collapsed lungs.

Elric reflexively gagged and struggled to sit up. Tanoch squatted over him, studying him with her polished onyx eyes. When she spoke, there was a great sadness in her voice.

"We saw this happen before you ever agreed to lie with us. We knew you would do this. Yet we had hoped there could be a way around Fate, just as we had hoped Yrik would find a way to escape the madness that was his destiny."

Elric shook his head and coughed, spraying the back of his hand with blood. "I bleed inside...."

"Not for long. We have fixed what was harmed. You are not to die here and now, Elric of Melniboné. This I know. Now get dressed."

Elric got to his feet. "The dragons...?"

"There will be no dragons. You forfeited them the moment you touched Mind. It's a miracle you're alive at all! None but a Lord of Dragons can wield Mind. Had Chaos not put its stamp on you from birth, every cell in your body would have imploded! We will give you another gift in place of the dragons."

"You can foresee the future. Let that be your gift."

Tanoch shook her head. "You don't want to know what we see, Melnibonéan. Choose another gift, princeling, we beg you...."

"No. Tell me my future. Will I succeed with the raid on Imrryr?"

"Elric — please — "

"Tell me!"

"Yes. Imrryr will fall before your marshalled forces. The Dreaming City shall burn and the Bright Empire will be no more."

"And what of Yyrkoon, my traitorous cousin? Will he die by my hand?"

"Yyrkoon shall die."

"And Cymoril? Will I be reunited with my one true love?"

Tanoch closed her eyes and her wings flinched.

"Answer me!" he barked.

"You will be reunited. But your time together will be brief before she dies, impaled on Stormbringer's blade."

"That can't be true!"

"We cannot lie. That is our curse."

"Damn you, tell me the truth!"

"We have, Elric Woman-Killer."

"No! You're lying! By my Lord Arioch, I'll *make* you tell me the truth!" Elric reached for Stormbringer, intent on hacking the empty-eyed demoness to bits, if that's what it took to negate the future she had scryed for him. Stormbringer growled like an angry dog, eager to taste blood. Tanoch did not move to defend herself.

"My people learned to shape and sculpt Chaos and Order when the stars were little more than clouds of cosmic dust. Do not think to threaten me with Stormbringer, sweet Champion Eternal."

Elric's shoulders slumped as he met and held Tanoch's black gaze. "Then it's all for naught. If I sail against Imrryr, Cymoril will die. But if I stand idle, Yyrkoon will make her his wife. Either way, all that is mine is denied me. But I would rather Cymoril live in incestuous wedlock than spend my days knowing I am guilty of her murder."

"I fear it is not so easy. The die has already been cast, Elric of Melniboné. Your doom began the moment of your conception. Mortal things were not meant to see beyond the now; such knowledge would paralyze even the bravest and boldest of your kind." She reached out and brushed his milk white brow with her long, weirdly jointed fingers. "Let this be my final gift to you: None of this ever happened."

⊕

Elric awoke suddenly from his dream, sitting upright in his narrow bed. Something — he wasn't certain exactly what — had disturbed his troubled slumber. He scanned the shadows pooled in the corners of his rented room, but they held neither assassins or demons. He swung his legs over the side of the bed, instinctively reaching for Stormbringer as he did so.

He had leased the attic room a fortnight earlier in order to prepare himself for the coming raid on Imrryr. He had spent the last few days fasting and meditating, secluded from all human company.

There had been a dream of a woman — a woman with the head and wings of a dragon. In his dream Elric had battled the dragon-woman, skewering her heart with Stormbringer. Dreams meant things. Every sorcerer's apprentice knew that. Perhaps it was a favorable omen, foretelling the fall of Imrryr and the destruction of his evil cousin, Yyrkoon. Yes, that sounded right.

There was the sound of something moving outside the attic window. Elric threw the shutters back, but the eaves were empty of spies. He stared up at the moon's cold, dead eye and thought of Cymoril, his beloved, held captive by her brother's sorcery.

Soon she would be free and his once more. In a few days' time the tides would be in their favor and the Sea Lords' hundred warships would set sail for the Dreaming City. And then Yyrkoon's jeering head would look on from high atop a pike as Elric reclaimed both his throne and his betrothed.

"It won't be long, my love," Elric promised the moon.

But that's another story.

⊕

Twelve months and thirteen days from the day she took the Melnibonéan into her arms, Tanoch was delivered of a male child. It was the first and only time she had become pregnant during her thirty-three hundred years.

The boy-child was pale like his father, with pointed ears, garnet eyes, upswept eyebrows, and five fingers and toes. From his mother he inherited wings. And while they were still little more than crib-buds, his horns promised one day to become a handsome, curling rack.

She named him Lucifer.

But that's another story.

A WOMAN'S POWER

BY DOUG MURRAY

The sword howled, a great mourning sound that filled the air, swirling like demonic bagpipes.

The attackers hesitated for a moment, unsure of what it was they were fighting. Surely this was not a man. Men didn't have faces that shone corpse-white in the early sun — or eyes of pure, hellish red.

The red of blood. The red of death.

The soldiers, shocked, froze in position, their eyes caught and held by those glowing orbs, fascinated, entranced....

And then the dead face that surrounded those incredible eyes turned fully toward them — and smiled.

It was not a human smile. No, this was a smile of bitterness, a smile of contempt and hatred and blood.

A promise of death to every one of them.

They would have broken then. Broken and run. But they were stopped by their leader. A big man, mounted. He was among them in seconds, screaming curses, flailing around him with the flat of his sword. Pushing them away, back toward the albino.

Toward that gleaming-white face of death.

They wavered for a moment, but their panic passed. They were soldiers, and this was only a man.

Whatever else he might be, he *was* a man.

The soldiers took a new grip on their weapons, wiped the sweat of fear out of their eyes, and moved back into the fight.

The hellish black blade rose to meet them, moaning louder as it waited for their blood.

Waited for their souls.

⊕

Elric of Melniboné jerked his head quickly to one side, forcing a stray hair out of his eye, dashing a few drops of sweat from his brow. He had almost won just then, almost forced the dogs to run. It had been a near thing. If their leader hadn't moved into the fray just when he did, hadn't given them time to stop, to realize they were running from just one man....

No use thinking about that now — the men had rallied, and there was nothing to do but go on fighting. Elric muttered a little prayer to Arioch, his patron lord and took a firmer grip on Stormbringer, feeling the rush of power as the ebon runesword forced more strength into his body.

The first of his attackers was within swordstroke now, and Stormbringer moved even before Elric thought about it, the black blade's keen edge slicing through the man's meager armor of leather and studs as if it were so much gossamer. Elric looked full into the soldier's face, seeing the paralyzing fear as the man realized that it was his soul as well as his life that was being sucked from his ruined body.

The man screamed in helpless horror as Elric pulled Stormbringer free and turned to the next attacker.

The runeblade struck again and, with a fresh rush of strength, Elric began chanting a song of his own — a song of death and destruction — a perfect counterpoint to Stormbringer's shrill howl of savage triumph.

The albino's mouth moved, baring his teeth in a grim smile — a smile that promised death to those around him. He dropped into the berserker fighting rage of his forefathers, letting the huge black blade dip and swirl and kill all those within reach of his arm.

⊕

Aubic, Count of Agincoure, moved restlessly on his saddle, his horse pacing to and fro, trying to get a better look at the continuing fight. This Elric was amazing! He was slaughtering the Count's best troops! *Hell, if I hadn't been here to rally them, they'd be running for their lives right now!*

Aubic knew then that his spies had been right. With the sort of power that black sword held fighting on his side....

Of course, to gain that power he had to understand it — and that meant capturing the sword *and* its albino master — something his men were having a great deal of trouble doing.

Aubic frowned — and made a decision. "Balfont!" he cried. "I have need of your talents!"

⊕

Elric fought on, Stormbringer feeding him incredible amounts of energy. It was as if the huge black runesword were a mere feather in his hand — one that moved of its own will. Elric felt like a giant striking at a horde of insects worrying at his boots. He was laughing now, a titan's laugh, full of the power of the dead and dying.

Another wave of men came at him, and Stormbringer moved and sliced, falling again and again. Its shrieking song was a paean to death and destruction. So loud that the skies seemed to fill with its cry.

The whole world seemed to be moving at half-speed now, allowing Elric to pick the point at which he would strike, taking a head here, an arm there — and always, Stormbringer would pause in the wound and drink the dying man's soul....

Suddenly, still esconced in that magical, crawling world, Elric saw the stone. It was almost upon him, inching through the air, turning very slightly as it moved. Elric examined it as it grew closer and closer. It was perfectly round, sharp edges smoothed by the action of water and wind. White it was, with veining of some golden quartz material....

Elric watched as it came closer and closer, his own reactions paralyzed, unable to move or react or do anything but wonder at the thing's wormlike approach....

That it struck, shattering the noseguard of Elric's dragon helm with its force.

There was a dull explosion in Elric's head, a thunderclap of sound and light like the warning of some angry storm giant.

Elric stood stock still for a second, the whole world frozen around him. He could see the stone, falling now, accompanied by the remains of his helmet and a few drops of bright red blood.

He could see the sling it had come from, and the face of the slinger, still frozen in concentration.

Next to that slinger was his enemy, the man who had ordered this whole attack.

Elric started to move toward that man, started to lift Stormbringer for a final meal, a final soul....

And then the ground filled his vision — a patch of earth stained with blood and gore and bits of dead men. Elric fell, the world reverting to normal speed around him, men racing toward him....

Then it all went black, and Stormbringer moaned one last time, as if in lament.

⊕

Aubic looked down on the still form of Elric of Melniboné. The sword lay under his hand, still moaning a low, chilling note. *Amazing weapon!* he thought. *Could it actually be alive?*

The Count reached down for Stormbringer, his hand closing gingerly on the plain, black leather hilt.

Immediately the moaning started again.

Incredible! Aubic thought. *And the hilt, so warm! Almost as if....*

"My Lord Agincoure!"

The Count turned, surprised at the nearness of the voice. Hadn't he told Balfont to keep away? Stormbringer turned with him, seeming to twist in his hand. Its moaning went up another octave, growing louder, more demanding.

Balfont gasped as the ebon blade touched him — then blanched as its point slipped into his unprotected stomach.

"My... Lord...."

Aubic watched, stunned, as blood dripped down the black sword, filling the runes until they seemed to glow in the fading sunlight.

"Balfont! I didn't mean...."

The older man screamed then. "It's eating me! Taking my... my soul!"

Balfont struggled, tried to pull away, but the sword stayed seated, seeming to claw its way deeper into the man's chest.

And all the while, Aubic felt strength run into his body — the strength of a giant — the strength of....

Balfont dropped to the ground, dead, drained of whatever it was that had made him a man.

Aubic stared at the body for a moment, seeing the face distended by horror. Then he looked at the shrieking banshee of a sword in his hand.

And dropped it to the ground, almost throwing it in his eagerness to separate himself from the hellish thing.

There must be a way to control it! There must be!

He unfastened his cloak — thick with wool and fur — and wrapped it around the blade. He picked it up gingerly, feeling an odd sort of vibration under his hands. *Amazing! The albino* must *know how to control it. I must learn from him!*

Aubic motioned to several of his troopers, directing them to lift the unconscious Elric and set him lightly across one of their own horses. Aubic watched them carefully — he knew they would love to kill the man who had accounted for so many of their comrades, and yet he couldn't let that happen just yet. He had things to learn about this White Wolf. Questions that had to be answered.

After that, though....

⊕

Time seemed to stand still for Elric of Melniboné. He lay in a deadly sleep, dreaming of his past.

He dreamed of the Dragon Isle and the Ruby Throne — a throne that should have been his, but which had been stolen by his cousin, Yyrkoon. He dreamt of Cymoril, the girl he had loved — the girl he had wanted to marry — the girl he had killed.

The black sword raced through his dreams then. Stormbringer, the Stealer of Souls, the demon that he carried the length and breadth of the Young Kingdoms.

Stormbringer. He felt its presence nearby, but somehow moving further and further away. The blade called to him, promising him new strength, new power.

But Elric was helpless to follow, unable to grasp the runesword's hilt.

And as that hilt moved away, Elric's strength went with it.

He stirred in his sleep....

⊕

And came suddenly awake. His ruby eyes stared wildly for a moment, then focused, hard and bright, on the girl kneeling in front of him.

"Cymoril? It cannot be you! You are dead!"

The girl started for a moment, unprepared for such an outburst. She'd been told that the Albino was a prince, but this...

"My Lord?" She knelt more deeply, bowing her head before this strange and powerful man.

Elric came fully awake now, his hand moving to his side, searching for the hilt of Stormbringer.

And finding nothing.

"Where is it?" he demanded of the cowering girl. "Where is Stormbringer?!"

The girl gasped, her forehead touching the floor now, long, golden hair fanning out around her. "I know nothing about anyone named Stormbringer, Lord. I am here to serve you."

Elric looked at the girl, crimson eyes gleaming as they weighed and measured the quivering flesh before him.

"Who are you?"

The girl brought her head up at that, stealing a glance at the albino, but unable to read anything in his impassive face.

"I am called Jenna, my Lord. Slave to the Count of Agincoure."

"Agincoure. He was the one then." Eyes darkening, tiny hell-storms in that still, white face.

"You are in Castle Agincoure, in the North Tower."

Elric strained to his feet at that, feeling the weakness pulsing through his veins. *Already!* He looked around himself, anxious to see the extent of his prison.

The tower room was a good-sized one, well furnished with a large, canopied bed and several chairs of ebony wood. A table stood against one wall, holding a wine decanter and several goblets.

Elric ignored these marks of comfort and made for the door.

It was locked.

"So, I am prisoner to Count Agincoure." He turned to the girl. "And you are his spy?"

The girl dropped to the floor once again, shivering. "I am no spy, my Lord. I am here to do your bidding. Please."

Elric watched her grovel and turned away in disgust. "Only a slave, then." He headed for the room's sole window, barred and buried deep in the heavy wall. "And what am *I* now? I wonder...."

⊕

Some distance away, in a much larger, much more comfortable room, the Count of Agincoure pulled his cloak away from a sword, carefully laying the black runeblade down onto his study table.

Such a plain thing, he thought, looking down at the undecorated hilt of black leather. *So ordinary. And yet....*

Aubic's hand went out, a finger moving to touch the leather of the hilt.

Instantly he felt a tingle through his entire body and a low moaning filled the room.

Do I dare lift it again? Will I ever dare to use it? Aubic looked down at the sword. It seemed to squirm in his grip, fighting for release, demanding blood and souls and....

The Count of Agincoure pulled his hand away as if it had been burned, staring at the still-moaning weapon on the table. *So powerful still....*

Aubic again threw his cloak around the black sword, tucking the edges so that the thing was completely encircled. He heard a last, low moan as the runes were completely covered.

"Truvian!" He called, and in seconds a bent man appeared, hands held before him, ready to serve. "Truvian, I want this... thing taken to the strongroom and locked away. No one is to touch it. No one is to look at it. Is that understood?"

Truvian had been the seneschal at Agincoure for nearly twenty years. He knew better than to gainsay its master. "Of course, my Lord! No one will see or touch the... item."

Aubic picked up the wrapped weapon, gingerly. He thought he could still hear *something* through the thick cloth, and his hands seemed to tingle with new strength. Unbidden, his mind began to picture taking the sword out, the runes glowing in the light of the room, glowing brighter and brighter until they suddenly filled with red blood as Aubic plunged the weapon into the helpless, screaming Truvian....

Aubic shook his head violently, breathing hard as the room cleared around him. He noted that Truvian had backed away from him, the smaller man's eyes wide with fear or wonder. Aubic smiled — yes, this was *power!* Better to keep it out of sight until he could determine how best to use it.

The albino would help him with that — or face the consequences.

⊕

The feasting hall at Agincoure was one of the finest Elric had seen in the Young Kingdoms. It was large, the vaulted ceiling three or four man-heights tall, and well appointed. The fireplaces were even ventilated so that hardly any smoke backed into the room. And the dining table! Even in fabled Imrryr, such a work would have been given a place of honor.

Carved from some fine-grained, dark wood, the table stretched across the big room, spacious enough for twenty or thirty men to sit comfortably, feasting and talking.

Of course, on this occasion there were only two — Elric and the large, dark man whom the albino took to be Aubic, Count of Agincoure. Elric studied his host carefully. This man had Stormbringer, and unless Elric could find a way to retrieve the runesword....

"So, Prince Elric. You are recovered from yesterday's exertions?" Aubic's greeting was jovial — that of one equal to another.

Elric stared at the other man from hooded eyes, a touch of fire in their depths. "Do you mean yesterday's attack, my Lord Agincoure? The attack you ordered?"

Aubic smiled at the albino, taking a sip from his wine chalice. "I, order an attack on the Emperor of Melniboné!? Never! My men and I merely found you engaged with a bandit band and brought you here where you could safely recover!"

"Then I am your guest?" Elric's eyebrows lifted wryly as he asked the question, already knowing the answer.

"Of course," Aubic looked hurt. "What else would such a noble be?"

Elric lifted his own chalice of wine then, taking a sip of the fine vintage within. "Perhaps, then, you would be so kind as to return the rest of my possessions. My horse. My saddlebags, my sword...."

"Of course." Aubic stared hard at the albino. "We have all of your things carefully safeguarded. As soon as you are fully recovered, we will be happy to return them to you."

Aubic took another sip of his wine. "That sword of yours! Never have I seen such a weapon! Would you be so kind as to answer a question or two about it?"

Elric smiled, a thin parting of the lips that had nothing of humor or amusement in it. *So! He finally comes to the point.* "And what questions might you have about your...*guest's* sword?"

Aubic looked Elric full in the eyes then — and saw something there that disquieted him, something... inhuman. He swallowed his question, a deep shiver going through him. He hurried to take another sip from his wine cup, playing for time to recover. "They can wait, Prince of Melniboné." Aubic lifted his hands, marveling at their steadiness, and clapped once. "For now, though, rest and regain your strength. We will talk again at break of fast."

Elric stood as Aubic's seneschal appeared, noting that the old servant seemed tense and ill at ease around the albino.

"As you say, Count Aubic. We will talk again on the morrow."

⊕

Elric had spent much of his life fighting his own churning thoughts and

222

emotions. His whole past had been one of pain and trouble, his background too morbid for him to see the world clearly.

He had become a slave to melancholy, letting the world swirl around him, never a part of it, never belonging to any group or person.

Even while he sat on the Ruby Throne, Emperor of the Dragon Isle, he had not been free — his white skin and weakness had seen to that.

Later, after he had betrayed his own people and watched the Young Kingdoms fall on Melniboné and snarl over its bones, he realized that the only way to gain some control over his own life was to find some meaning in it — or to come to terms with its chaos.

But he had failed even at this. His life seemed nothing more than a succession of events, some good, some ill, and try as he might, he could impose no order, find no pattern in any of it.

So time after time, when difficulties arose, he had merely withdrawn into himself, content to float on the seas of fate, letting the winds of conflict blow him where they might.

After all, it was through that conflict — and his black runesword — that he retained the strength to live, the power to keep trying to find some meaning to his own existence.

But now, captured, held in the Castle of the Count of Agincoure, he fell back into melancholy, lying in his bed, his clouding red eyes staring at the ceiling.

Staring at nothing.

Nearby, at the foot of his bed, Jenna stared at the albino's wan face. There was something about this man, something tragic. She would like to be able to help him, to give him whatever he needed to make him better.

But there was nothing she could do for him. She was only a slave — part of the furniture.

She knelt more deeply and began to weep bitter tears that dripped onto the floor, disappearing into the thick rugs laid there.

⊕

Aubic of Agincoure looked at the albino sitting across the table from him. He couldn't understand the change that had come over this strange man. He'd seen Elric in battle, had watched as the man had single-handedly slaughtered a dozen of his best troops! Aubic knew that Elric's crimson eyes — demon's eyes, his men called them — had been a weapon in their own right, nearly forcing his men into flight. Only Aubic's own intervention — and Balfont's expertly thrown stone — had saved the day.

Why then was this fell fighter, this living legend, sitting at table like some sickly woman? Aubic glared at the albino, willing some sign of rebellion, some signal that there was life under that deathly pale exterior.

But there was nothing. For all practical purposes, the Elric Aubic had seen the day before was gone, replaced by... what?

Aubic took another look at the slack-faced man before him. This was the master of the hell-sword? This was the sorcerer-prince that the whole world feared?

The Count gulped down some more wine. Was the albino acting? Was he playing the harmless oaf, waiting for the moment to leap upon Aubic and take his vengeance?

Or was the legend of Elric of Melniboné more in the sword than in the man?

Aubic drank and wondered. He had to find out for certain. Another few days should tell.

⊕

Back in the tower, Elric fell bonelessly onto his couch. The albino knew that he couldn't survive long this way. His strength was draining away and it would not be long before he did not even have the power to breathe. He had to have the black sword back — and soon.

Elric tensed himself, gathering what strength he had left. "Stormbringer" He whispered. "Come to me, Stormbringer. Come and bring me strength, my brother. Come...."

But even as he made the call, Elric knew it was useless. Stormbringer was too far away, held too closely to reach him. He must think of another way.

Another way.

⊕

Jenna watched as the Prince concentrated — and saw his despair as he failed in whatever it was he was trying to do. She knew all about despair — had felt it herself when she was first made a slave, first made to serve men.

Still, there was something different about Elric's despair — it was as if his heart were gone — pulled out of his body — taken prisoner.

She looked at the albino's face as pain flashed through him. He was getting weaker by the day, she could see that — but why? He had no wasting disease that she could detect, no weakness of the body.

She knew that it must be a weakness of the soul.

He's already given up, she thought. *Lost all hope of ever getting out of here, ever being free.*

Such a foolish idea. As if freedom was automatically a good thing. Had *she* had been better off when *she* was free, at liberty to endure days of starvation punctuated by nights of pain when her father beat her for her *weakness?* That was what freedom was like.

At least for her.

Perhaps it was different for this Elric. Perhaps *his* freedom was something sweeter, stronger.

She looked at his face, saw his eyes close in new pain, long lines of weakness and despair marring his elegant features, and wondered. Could there be such a freedom? One that was strong and good and sweet? One that would give her peace?

She would have to think about that.

⊕

In his study, Count Aubic started as he heard a noise behind him — an impossible noise coming from where nothing could be. Nevertheless, Aubic drew his dagger and whirled, ready for anything.

He saw nothing at all, as it should be. After all, there was nothing behind the Count except the wall of his study, less then six feet away. Nothing there could have made a sound — and beyond that wall....

Aubic's mind began to race.

The sword! Could it be?

Aubic raced out of his study, brushing past an astonished guard as he used his master key to open the strong room. *It's impossible, but....*

The door snapped open and Aubic stepped inside — and stopped dead at what he saw. A few feet away, point touching the wall, lay the black blade, uncovered, its runes shining in the light of the guard's torch.

Aubic looked to the other side of the room. To the table upon which the weapon was supposed to be. To the torn and tattered remains of his cloak.

It moved! The sword moved! Aubic noted the direction in which the blade had traveled. It was moving to the north — toward the tower its master was in! *Did Elric call it somehow? Is there some magic at work here that I don't understand?*

Aubic knew one thing. He had to find out the secret of this black sword.

Had to know how he could possess, how he could master it. If the secret were his....

The Count's eyes closed for a moment and he saw himself, the black sword held high, as King of the Young Kingdoms — master of the known world.

Stormbringer moaned — louder this time — a sound almost like human laughter.

⊕

Elric came awake in an instant. Something was wrong! Someone had....

Then he felt the soft flesh against him, and knew whose it was.

"Do not be afraid, Prince." It was the slave — Jenna, he thought her name was. "Let me help you. Let me give you strength."

Elric laughed inside. *She* was going to give him strength? Only Stormbringer could do that! Stormbringer or some of the rare herbs in Elric's pack.

Still, it wouldn't do to offend the only friend he might find in this place. It wouldn't do at all.

⊕

Aubic looked at his 'guest' with surprise. For days the albino had steadily grown weaker, his eyes showing naught but pain and despair.

But that had changed.

Elric was definitely stronger today, crimson eyes glaring at the Count, as if daring him to make a mistake — any mistake.

Aubic sipped at his mulled ale and thought. He knew that the Prince of Melniboné hadn't gotten to his sword. Something else had happened, something that had increased the albino's store of strength. He wondered....

Then his eyes fell on Jenna, the slave kneeling at Elric's side. He saw something on her face — a look of satisfaction — a look almost of... freedom?

Could it be the girl? He wondered. *And if it was, can I use that to find out what I need to know?*

Aubic took another sip of his wine and leaned back to think things over. Perhaps there was a way.

⊕

That night, Elric of Melniboné wondered at what was happening to him. All his life he had thought of women as the weaker sex, fit for nothing but childbirth, cooking and cleaning. But now....

Jenna had not lied when she promised to give him strength. It seemed to flow into him when he held her in his arms. It was odd, for it was not the sort of power Elric drew from Stormbringer. No. This was not the wild inpouring of a dying spirit. It was something subtler, much more powerful.

It was as if the little slave girl were able to *give* Elric bits of her own soul — sharing her own strength, her own life with the albino.

Elric felt the joining, and he felt something else — hope. The hope that he might not, despite everything, die here in this castle.

And he owed that hope to Jenna, the piece of furniture who had given him a chance.

He looked down at the sleeping girl in his arms, a softness in his eyes that his enemies would not have believed possible.

He would not forget what she had done for him.

⊕

Aubic looked again at the bit of parchment in his hand. Were they mad? For months he had made his plans, building up his army, training them, procuring weapons.

And now this.

Yosrian dares attack me?! The Count crumpled up the message and tossed it towards the fire. *He knows he cannot win — and yet....*

Aubic started to pace. If Yosrian was working with the Count of Potian, attacking to gain time, forcing Aubic to shift forces from one border to the other....

They're working together! The conclusion was unmistakable. *Yosrian will bleed me on one border while Shallic arms his peasantry. They'll force me to fight on two fronts, wear me down....*

Aubic shivered. It might work. They might defeat a divided Agincourean force. And if they did....

I must learn the secret of that damned sword! Aubic signaled for a guard. *Perhaps I can start with the girl....*

⊕

Elric lay in his bed, worrying. Jenna had been taken away by guards that afternoon and Elric had not seen her since. The albino felt his strength draining from him by the second, and with it his vitality and urge to live. *She must come,* he thought. *I don't know if I can survive without her.*

The moon rose higher, and still Elric lay there, alone, wondering if he would die that way.

⊕

Deep in the bowels of the castle, Aubic turned away from the girl Jenna. He hated this kind of thing, but, he told himself, it had to be done. It was necessary to save the realm — and if one woman had to be hurt....

He looked back at Jenna, hanging limp in her bonds. He hadn't hurt her all *that* badly — at least, not yet.

She didn't seem to know anything of importance, and yet there was something....

Aubic sighed and turned back to the helpless girl. He had to know.

⊕

Elric forced himself out of his bed as soon as the sun came up, finding just enough strength to get onto his feet and pull on his clothes. He fought against his accustomed melancholy state, knowing that if he allowed it to strike him down now, he would never rise again.

The albino prince couldn't let that happen. He had debts to pay. Debts to the slave girl who had kept him alive, and debts to the Count who had brought him here.

Elric moved to the door, ready to pay those debts.

⊕

"I *need* the magic of your sword!" Aubic paced in front of the great hall's fireplace, nervous and uncomfortable with the situation he faced. "I need it to conquer those around me — before they conquer me!"

Elric sat in one of the great chairs in the room, his crimson eyes mere slits, his features composed and settled. "And you think that all you have to do is wave Stormbringer and your foes will surrender? Fool!"

Aubic whirled on the albino. "Watch your tongue, demonspawn! I am master here!"

Elric's head came up at that, his eyes, still hooded, seemed to glow for a second. "For how long, my lord Agincoure? For how long?"

"So," Aubic whirled toward his own chair. "You refuse to tell me what I must know."

Elric sighed. "It would do you no good."

Aubic threw himself into his seat, leaning toward the motionless albino. "I will give you one last chance. Go back to your room and see what happens to those who gainsay the Count of Agincoure."

Elric came to his feet, fighting the weakness that was racing through him. He bowed almost imperceptibly toward the Count's chair. "Threats mean nothing to the Prince of Melniboné."

Aubic watched as Elric stumbled out of the room. *So. Threats mean nothing to you? We will see. We will most definitely see.*

⊕

Elric turned as the door to his chamber opened, and pulled himself out of bed as Jenna was thrown in.

"Look at her, demonspawn!" the guard spat in. "It'll be your turn next!"

She had been brutally beaten, the marks of dozens of lashes marring her body — but her eyes still shone with hope and caring for the albino who knelt to support her body.

"He wanted your secrets." She coughed for a moment, closing her eyes to gain some strength. "I had nothing to tell him — nothing...."

Elric held her as she labored for breath. He felt her soul's grip on her body grow looser. He had to do something! *Something.*

He closed his own eyes, concentrating as he never had before, calling out to Stormbringer with a force and vitality he had never known he possessed.

Stormbringer! Come to me, Stormbringer! Come to me....

⊕

Count Aubic sat in his study sipping a chalice of wine, trying to plan his next move. He had to get the secret out of the albino. *Perhaps he'll see reason. After all, he cannot want me to do to him what I did to that girl.*

229

Aubic took another sip of his wine. *Elric's a sensible man, he'll tell me what I want to know.*

Suddenly a tremendous howl came from the closet behind him — a noise like the very hounds of hell. Aubic started to his feet, whirling to see where the noise had come from.

And then he saw it. *It's the damn demon sword! It's moving again!*

Stormbringer was free, a ragged hole in the door of his closet showing where it had broken through. The sword was questing through the air, point forward, runes glowing, almost as if it were a living thing. It moved closer to Aubic, the runes growing brighter, brighter still.

⊕

Elric came back to himself as the girl moaned. He looked down on her face, wiping the sweat from her brow. Then he shut his eyes once more, and withdrew into a near-trance state. *Stormbringer! Stealer of Souls! To me, my friend. to me!*

⊕

Aubic relaxed when the sword dropped to the floor, the runes growing fainter as it lay there, moaning softly. He pulled the cord to call his seneschal and yanked down a drape to serve as a proper covering. *I'll have to get the answer now!* he thought. *I can't chance this happening again!*

Truvian opened the door just as Stormbringer lifted itself from the floor again. Aubic tried to grab the weapon as it sped toward the opening, but was just a moment too late. "Quickly!" he cried. "Follow the damned blade! We can't let it get into the hands of that albino demon!"

⊕

Jenna's heart was weakening with each beat. Elric knew that he would have to act soon if she were to be saved — and if he were to act at all, he would have to have...

Stormbringer! To me, Stealer of Souls! To me!

And then, quite suddenly, Stormbringer was there, howling, in Elric's hand. But the blade delivered no power, no vitality. *It's been drained!* Elric thought. *There's nothing there! I've been cheated.* He looked down at the girl. *She's been cheated!*

230

⊕

Jenna's eyes fluttered open. She'd been somewhere else for some time now, someplace where pain didn't exist, where men didn't demand answers she didn't have — and didn't hurt her for not having them. She looked up, letting her eyes clear for a moment and saw Elric. He looked so different now, so angry.

Then she saw the sword.

And she knew what must be done.

⊕

Aubic and his men hurried to the North Tower, the Count yelling at them to move as quickly as they could. If Elric regained his sword and his strength....

⊕

Elric looked down at Jenna and saw that her eyes were open and aware. He smiled at her, his own crimson eyes tearing as he realized that there wasn't much time. The girl reached out to him, her hand touching the edge of Stormbringer's blade.

The sword moaned, lower, more hungrily than he had ever heard it speak before.

"You must use this." She coughed, frothy blood coming to her lips. "Use it on me — take my strength."

Elric bowed his head, looking down at her. "I cannot. It will take more than your strength. It will take your soul."

Jenna smiled then, looking the albino full in the eye. "I will stay with you, then. Always."

Elric's head came up, grief filling his mind. Was this his destiny? Must those he loved always die at his hand?

Almost of its own accord, Stormbringer lifted, the point turning toward the naked breast of Jenna....

Elric was shocked at the depth of the girl's vitality — and by the strength that now coursed into *his* body — strength greater than that of whole bands of men. *There is more to women than I'll ever understand,* Elric thought as Jenna's eyes closed for the last time. The albino picked up her body and arranged it carefully on his bed, then hefted Stormbringer and headed for the tower door.

There were debts to be paid.

⊕

Aubic pulled out the great brass keys as he reached the door to the North Tower. He looked back at the two-score men who had followed him, some half-dressed, but all carrying sword or ax. *I only hope we're in time!*

He jammed the key into the lock and turned, pulling the door open to reveal....

⊕

Elric of Melniboné, standing ready, the great black sword in front of him, his ruby eyes glaring toward the door, his face set into a gargoyle mask of bitterness and hatred.

"Gods help us!" Aubic gasped.

"Too late for that," the albino snarled, and Stormbringer licked out for the first of Aubic's men, shrieking with the wildness of its battle call. A great mourning sound filled the air and the hearts of the men who heard it. They hesitated for a moment, backing off just a handsbreadth from the sword and the thing which wielded it.

For surely this was no man — but rather some demon out of hell. White he was. The white of death. All except for his eyes. They were red. Red as blood. Red as death.

Red as the fires of hell.

The men stood for a second, watching as that white face twisted in a bitter smile — a smile that promised death to them all.

Then their leader, the Count of Agincoure, stepped forward, knowing that the day was lost if his men broke now. Aubic brought his sword up, trying to parry the demon blade, trying to slow it down long enough for one of his men to get in a fatal blow.

Elric's eyes almost glowed then, and, light as a wand, Stormbringer licked out over the Count's blade and buried itself in his heart, shrieking louder still as the Count screamed.

Elric laughed then, a dry laugh like that of a corpse, and the rest of the men broke, running for their lives.

Running for their souls.

Aubic saw them go. Watched them as his blood trickled onto the tower floor and his soul rushed into the black blade that transfixed him. He shrieked one last time as his world turned black.

Forever.

⊕

Stormbringer shrieked louder still in final victory. And as his sword howled, Elric of Melniboné laughed, a loud, wild laugh. The laugh of a man on the edge of sanity. And as he laughed, ruby tears cascaded from his crimson eyes.

While the soul of a slave girl filled the heart of the Prince of Melniboné.

ANDREW MITCHELL

THE GOTHIC TOUCH

BY KARL EDWARD WAGNER

Night was gathering too rapidly. Lightning was flickering across a leaden sky. Sounds of distant thunder were no longer so distant. Dark-winged birds were streaking across the sky for cover. Elric sniffed the air, pushed the white hair from his face. His horse was restless beneath his thigh.

Moonglum watched the horizon unhappily. They had been riding all day. Thus far they had eluded human pursuit, but the storm was quickly overtaking them. "We'll have to find some sort of shelter soon."

"*They* won't seek shelter." Elric searched his memory. He was uncertain of landmarks in this part of the land they fled across, but he remembered talk of a ruined castle, supposedly haunted. That sort of legend might hold off interlopers, and if it came down to it, better to make a stand behind walls than to be hunted down like a fox.

Thunder drew closer. Neither Elric nor Moonglum heard the blast as lightning tore apart the earth close behind them. It was enough to hold saddle as their panic-stricken horses plunged headlong through the sudden torrent.

"There!" shouted Elric. The lightning-blasted sky revealed stone walls ahead. He and Moonglum fought to control their horses, somehow galloping into the walled enclosure through its breached gate.

"There's a light!" Moonglum pointed as they crossed the courtyard. Elric smelled smoke through the drenched wind. Most of the interior structure was still standing, albeit gutted. What appeared to have been the castle itself had retained some of its roof. A fire could be seen through its open doorway.

Lightning crashed again. Elric and Moonglum rode their horses through the castle doorway, caring not who might challenge them. The interior was reasonably dry, if fusty from long disuse. There was a good fire burning on the massive hearth. There was a broken table set with food and wine. There was no one present.

"Isn't this castle supposed to be haunted?" Moonglum was searching the shadows of the cavernous room. Little remained except ruin, rotted tapestries, crumbling furnishings. Whoever had overthrown the castle had not stayed to loot it.

"All ruined castles are haunted," said Elric, dismounting. "At least to the popular mind. Now tether our horses. Someone abides here, and we'll share this fire."

As Moonglum saw to their mounts, Elric shook off his cloak and warmed himself at the fire. The thin albino had little tolerance for the drenching, cold night. He considered the food and drink upon the table. Three settings. Cheese, bread, cold fowl, some apples, wine and — Elric delicately sniffed the bottle — brandy. He poured some of the brandy into a chalice of ruby glass. He could not identify its place of origin, but it was of excellent quality, and it warmed him.

Moonglum returned from the horses and almost struck away the chalice. "There might be poison!"

"Who knew that I would be here?" Elric was exhausted after almost two days on the run. He broke off a bit of bread. "Try the fowl, Moonglum, and tell me if it's poisoned."

"Three places are set," Moonglum pointed out. "Yet no one is here. And where do you find fresh apples at this season? I tell you, this castle is haunted."

"That fire is freshly laid," said Elric. "Our hosts are other travellers seeking shelter for the night. As the storm struck, they dashed away to see to their horses and goods. I'm certain they will join us soon."

The storm winds were moaning so furiously through the broken apertures of the castle that at first Elric did not notice the faint moan of Stormbringer.

Elric glanced toward the empty doorway, laying his hand upon the hilt of the runesword.

Lightning set fire to the night. The doorway was no longer empty.

It was a man, almost too large for a man, clad in mail, leather breeks and high boots, and a flapping black cloak. His long red hair was torn by the wind despite the rain. His eyes seemed to glow with cold blue fire in the burst of lightning. In his left hand he carried a long sword; in his right hand he held a human head.

Lightning faded.

Elric drew Stormbringer.

The man was already beside the fire.

"We both like dramatic entrances," said the man. He held the severed head to the light. "Know him?"

Elric looked carefully. "That's Duke Breidnor. He and his men are hunting me."

"Well, now he's not." The man wiped his sword free of remaining blood and sheathed it behind his shoulder. "And you can put away Stormbringer. What's left of Breidnor's henchmen are fleeing homeward. I left a few of their bodies outside the walls. Doubt the rest will try it again. In fact, I know they won't. I hope you haven't finished that brandy. We have a long night."

He poured a chalice of brandy for himself as Elric regarded him uncertainly. His hair and beard were red, his features somewhat brutal, and there was something very disturbing about his blue eyes. Elric judged his height at about six feet, and his weight had to be enormous for that mass of muscle — yet he moved like a cat. Elric sheathed Stormbringer.

"Good decision," said the stranger, sipping the brandy. "And now, Moonglum, please put away your sword and do something with that head. Just don't lob it into the fire. I've already set out a cold dinner."

He dropped down onto one of the remaining chairs. It creaked, but held his weight. "About as solid as the Ruby Throne, don't you think, Elric?"

Elric found another chair and some brandy. He was tired, and things were happening too fast. "Who are you, and where are you from?"

"I'm Kane, and I'm not from around here."

"Where are your men?"

"I'm alone."

"How did you manage to kill Duke Breidnor and his soldiers if you were alone?"

"I kill things. That's what I was created to do. I'm rather good at it."

"Are you from Arioch?"

"Only a nodding acquaintance."

Elric lowered his chalice in annoyance. The man was either mad or playing with words; his accent was not one Elric could place. Nonetheless, this Kane had brought him the head of his enemy.

Elric turned his pink eyes full into Kane's cold blue gaze. He felt a sudden chill throughout his body. "Are you a demon?" Elric had not meant to speak the thought aloud.

"Something far worse," said Kane.

"How do you know me?"

Kane tore off a wing and began to eat it with some show of appetite. "By Stormbringer. Not to say that you do have certain distinctive features. Moonglum, stop pacing about and join us."

Elric closed his eyes and concentrated. There was an aura about this man which he could not penetrate. And yet....

"You are neither of Law nor Chaos."

"Correct. Slice of breast?"

"You are not of this world."

"I've already told you that. More brandy?"

"You raised a storm and drew us here. Then you killed my enemy."

"And just in time. Don't forget the dinner."

Elric angrily leapt to his feet, drawing Stormbringer. "Friend or not, I won't be trifled with — and I'm tired of your riddles!"

Moonglum slid away, circling.

Kane remained seated. His left hand was hidden as he sipped some wine. "Pray be seated, both of you. We have a long night. All shall be made clear."

Elric nodded to Moonglum, then sheathed the runesword. They sat down, and Kane quietly replaced the throwing stars he had held.

Moonglum gnawed on an apple. "Where is your horse?"

"Somewhere else."

"And these apples? Whence?"

"Same place."

Elric was growing angry again, but poured more brandy to keep his temper under control. The stranger was mad, but meant him no harm. Tomorrow he and Moonglum would continue their journey without pursuit, thanks to Kane, if he were to be believed. Obviously the man was dangerous, but not an enemy. Elric wasn't certain as to what else he might be. He ate another piece of bread and decided to put up with the situation. Outside it was raining heavily, and Moonglum had just thrown more bits of wood onto the fire.

"I noticed your sword as you were cleaning it," Elric said. Conversation would soothe his anger. "I haven't seen its style before, nor the odd sheen of its steel. Is it from the Young Kingdoms?"

"It's from Carsultyal. Very old." For an instant there was a touch of pain in Kane's voice that only Elric could have discerned.

"And has it magical powers?"

"Only that it cuts well. I never worked out the actual alloy. Ran out of star ships to melt down."

Elric assumed that Kane meant falling stars. He had seen blades forged from such iron. "Where is Carsultyal?"

"Long ago and far away." Kane was punishing the brandy. "Elric, let's stop fencing. We are both sorcerers. We know that other worlds and other universes exist, sometimes side by side."

Elric paused, wondering. "Granted."

"And that there can be gateways between these other worlds."

"Yes, that's true." Elric had begun to get ahead of Kane's line of reasoning. No, Kane wasn't mad. Not in that way.

Kane considered his brandy. "Well, Elric. We three are sitting on the threshold of one of those gateways, and I crossed over with a hamper full of goodies to nibble on. And other fun stuff. Sorry about the storm, but there always are these atmospheric disturbances. Call it the gothic touch. So you got wet, but now you're warm and well-fed, and I took care of your immediate difficulty. Where's that head, Moonglum?"

Elric wasn't certain he'd caught every word of that, but he had understood enough. "How do you know of me?"

"You'll understand later. You and your various incarnations leap through time and universe more than I do. It was merely a matter of intersecting you, Stormbringer, and this gateway. My being here is a feat any sorcerer could carry out." Elric suspected the man was lying, but let it go for the moment.

Stormbringer seemed to moan to him. Elric felt his own forehead. Either his hands were cold or he was feverish from the thunderstorm. "Overlooking the *how* of it — then tell me *why*."

Kane was having some cheese. "Oh, that. Well, I did just save your life. Don't forget the dinner."

"You created this situation, didn't you?"

"Well, I wasn't the one who was being chased down by a mercenary duke and fifty soldiers. But to be truthful, I may have used the situation to my advantage. Some."

"What do you want of me, Kane?" Elric considered riding away into the night. It was a stormy night. He thought about killing the man, but Kane did not seem inclined to do him harm —rather the opposite. Elric sighed and massaged his temples. He wasn't at all sure he could take Kane. Something in the man's eyes suggested he couldn't.

"Stormbringer," said Kane.

"What!"

"Just the use of it."

"You're mad."

"Oh, yes. I'll need you to wield the runesword. I didn't mean to imply that I wanted to take it from your possession. The thing is dangerous. Nor does it like me."

Elric decided that he and Moonglum would take watches beside the fire and leave at first light.

"Let me tell you a story," offered Kane.

"You are our host," said Elric wearily.

"What do you know about this castle?"

"Nothing. I just remembered that it was in this vicinity. Abandoned for a century. Supposedly haunted. All ruins have their ghosts."

"Some much worse than ghosts."

Kane examined the empty brandy bottle and said something unpleasant, or so it seemed to Elric's ears. It was in no language he had ever heard. He watched as Kane vanished into the darkness beyond the firelight, moving surely, then returned with a wicker basket. He *had* brought a hamper... from wherever.

As Kane brought forth a last bottle, Elric observed: "You can see in the dark."

"Can't we all, to some extent," said Kane. "Excellent Moonglum, please open this and pour for the three of us. We'll have need soon."

Once chalices were filled: "As I was saying." Kane sniffed the brandy and shrugged. "There are physical gateways to other worlds. This castle is one of them. Elric, you should know more about this than I do. I only know what I have learned from my side of the portal. Our time channels run very close. Too close. Virtually this same castle exists in both of our worlds."

Lightning continued to flicker past the empty windows. Rain seeped down from the failing roof. The wind kicked at the rotting tapestries. Kane cursed, rose, and threw a broken section of sideboard into the fire. He did this without apparent effort; Elric judged that the wooden construction must weigh over a hundred pounds.

The great fireplace caught up the ruined sideboard. The firelight flared, illuminating the three of them as they sat at the table. Kane studied the remains of the fowl, tore off the other wing. "Wants more salt," he apologized, eating carefully.

Elric was growing impatient. "I've told you that I know little about his castle. Get on with it."

Kane sucked the last flesh from the wing bones and tossed them into the fire as easily as he had thrown the broken sideboard. He licked his fingers and reached for the brandy.

"Some years ago — I'm not certain how many in your time frame —a certain object fell to earth near here. The lord of the castle rode out with his men to determine what had happened. They discovered a torn and burnt expanse of field where a star had fallen. The star was encrusted with fabulous jewels beyond their imagination. The lord had his men bring up carts and oxen to carry away this treasure. They did so, securing it within secret vaults deep beneath the castle.

"Of course, word of this treasure spread. Clever thieves tried to find it. Other powerful lords tried to demand their share. In the end, a demon was summoned from the outer depths to guard the treasure. The demon guarded the treasure, but not the castle. When the walls were finally breached and the defenders massacred, the victors did not live to enjoy their spoils. No one left the final battle, and this castle has been cursed ever since."

Elric vaguely remembered such a tale, or one similar: this was an isolated province and of little notice to him. He toyed with his chalice, not drinking. "And where does all this lead us?"

"I can find the treasure room," said Kane. "All that I want would fit into this hamper. The rest is yours. Enough to raise a mercenary army, sit upon the Ruby Throne, whatever you desire. Yours for the taking."

"And why are you my benefactor?"

Kane swirled his brandy. "The demon is still there. On guard. I can't kill it alone. I need you. And Stormbringer."

"You're a sorcerer. Exorcise it."

"Not this one."

Moonglum drew Elric aside. "Don't trust him."

"I won't," said Elric. "But he has some oblique scheme in mind and hasn't harmed us. I'll play his game and seek for the advantage."

To Kane, Elric said, "We'll follow you. Only first explain to me why this castle is a gateway to your world."

Kane paused. "Crystal. A magic crystal from the fallen star. That's all I want to take with me."

Kane carried the hamper off into the darkness, returned with it and a pair of lanterns. "Light these, Moonglum, and we'll be off."

Moonglum made a taper from the fire and lit the lanterns. In passing, he started to lift the hamper. Kane quickly took it from him.

Moonglum whispered to Elric: "The hamper must be filled with lead. I nearly sprained my wrist."

"Kane is carrying it," said Elric. He held aloft his lantern. "Keep your wits about you."

"Let's just take to our horses," Moonglum whispered.

"I want to see what game Kane plays. Kane knows too much about me, and I know far too little about him."

Moonglum shook his head. "A man who sets out food and drink, then goes off to destroy a demon."

"Can't fight a demon on an empty stomach," Kane called back from the perimeter of darkness. "And you two were done in."

Either he had excellent hearing, or Kane could read their thoughts. Elric wondered if he should heed Moonglum's advice.

Kane led them down a stone stairway, slippery with mouldering debris. Water had penetrated here from the torrent outside and ran in rivulets down the steps. Elric thought of the warm fire above and wondered why he shouldn't leave Kane to prowl about these cellars on his own.

The stairway descended to a cellar of cavernous size, seemingly far out of proportion to the castle above. At the fringes of their lantern light, Elric could discern vast heaps of wreckage, festooned with cobwebs and grotesque traceries of fungi. Probably the castle had been provisioned to withstand a long siege, he judged.

Kane strode confidently past it all, further increasing Elric's suspicions, and led them to another stone stairway which descended into a dank subcellar. A rusted iron gate had been battered apart, and their lanterns revealed mouldering instruments of torture. Broken remnants of human skeletons huddled beneath the chains that had pinioned them, some with bony wrists still captive in their manacles. Upon the ruins of the rack a desiccated corpse had long ago broken apart. Suspended overhead, leathery arms still reached pleadingly from an iron cage. No rats, Elric observed; but then there was no longer anything here for them.

At the far end of the dungeon stood a massive door. Its hinges set well into the stone wall, it was forged of a black iron, strangely unrusted, and not unlike the appearance of the runesword. It was constructed to withstand a siege engine, and it bore an equally massive lock.

"And do you have the key?" Elric asked. His tone was sarcastic, but he wasn't at all certain that Kane might not.

Kane set down the hamper. "I think I can work this."

Moonglum whispered to Elric: "That is *not* the hamper he was using to carry our dinner. It's solid metal."

"I know," said Elric. "But I can't quite guess the nature of his game. Be on your guard."

Kane pressed his hand against the massive lock. There was a loud snap as the bolt broke away, and then the entire mechanism rotted into dust. Kane pushed, and the huge door fell open. Foul darkness bellowed from within.

"Impressive," Elric remarked.

Kane stepped back quickly and drew his sword, watching the opened doorway.

"What now, Kane?" Elric had already drawn Stormbringer.

"There's something I neglected to mention." Kane retrieved the metal hamper. "Not everyone in the castle died in the final battle. Quite a number of them sought refuge here and were shut away for at least a century — I said I'm not certain of your time frame. Their descendants are likely to be unpleasant."

"What could they have eaten?" Moonglum asked.

"What do you think?" answered Kane.

"Mushrooms and fungi?"

"For starters. Let's have a look."

Elric examined the ruined lock as he passed by. He knew of magic that could open any lock, but not by the simple touch of a hand. If Kane's powers were that great, why was this stranger requiring his help in whatever mad expedition Kane was leading him into? Elric cursed himself for allowing Kane to sweep him along on this scheme, but his curiosity urged him to follow. It would be one short diversion from too many nights of painful unrest.

Beyond the doorway their lanterns shone weakly into an indeterminate length of vaulted stone passageways. They were deep within the earth, and water trickled from everywhere —masking the sound of their footsteps as would dripping leaves in a dense forest after a drenching rainfall. The stones of the arches were rimmed with nitre and dripping loops of fungus, creating an almost palpable glow. The air stank of the tomb and hurt Elric's chest, but a faint wind shuddered the flame of his lantern. Elric thought about the source of that wind, then pushed the thought from his mind.

The tunnel broke into numerous intersections, yet Kane seemed confident of his direction. Slight scuttling sounds scurried from black corridors. Elric glimpsed the glow of rats' eyes and the slither of a large salamander. Grotesque white toads shuffled away from their advance. Pale spiders as large as his hand clung to the stones, watching for prey. Elric began to feel a certain kinship: this was a netherworld of albinos.

Elric guessed that they had been walking beneath the earth for perhaps half a mile. "Kane, do you know who dug this maze — and why? There are easier means to protect a treasure."

"They must have followed the descent path," Kane said helpfully. "They reinforced the chasm with walls and arches, following blind rifts as well."

"*Who* did?" demanded Elric.

Kane's sword moved faster than Elric thought possible. At one instant the barely glimpsed creature was leaping at Kane from the darkness of a side tunnel. In that same instant Kane's blade had cut through its neck and shoulder, flinging it to the tunnel floor. The two pieces writhed for a moment. Elric had never seen a swordsman strike such a blow one-handed. He made a mental note and wondered how many of Duke Breidnor's henchmen were still alive.

Moonglum brought his lantern close. The creature was naked, male, and vaguely human. His flesh was as pallid as Elric's, but there was some dirty grey color to the brain that hung in filthy tatters from a scabrous scalp. The limbs were shortened and misshapen, covered with pustulated sores. The face was bestial, less apish than wolfish, with a protruding muzzle. A second head, no larger than a doll's, snapped at them from the center of his chest. Kane casually sliced it away with his sword tip.

"Pretty," Kane said. "Unless they pause to feed on this one, we'll soon be up against far worse."

"You said there were survivors imprisoned within here." Elric stepped past the dead thing. "By what sorcery was this created?"

"Residual radiation." In response to Elric's blank look, Kane amended: "The power of the guardian demon. That's why I need you and Stormbringer. We must kill it quickly."

Moonglum hadn't understood some of Kane's words. "This demon. How does it feed?"

Kane pointed back to the misshapen corpse. "Lot of these about. Sacrifices locked here in this maze."

"You said they were survivors of the last battle." Elric's tone was suspicious.

"Both," said Kane. "Look out!"

The creatures rushed them from the darkness, from everywhere. *Creatures.* Elric could not see them as anything human. Most of them were naked; those with a few tatters of filthy clothing were even more obscene. Some few carried rusted weapons. Most seemed not to know the use of weapons beyond rotted teeth and talon-length nails.

They were monstrous, misshapen mockeries of humanity, parodies created from the drug-induced nightmares of some deranged artist. Men, women, children — they flung themselves upon the three from out of the darkness. Elric had no coherent impression of their numbers. They were boiling out of the blackness like an eruption of vampire bats from a putrid cave.

"Guard your lantern!" Elric had already set his aside — he needed both hands to wield Stormbringer — and Moonglum did the same. Kane was somewhere in the darkness beyond. He could fend for himself after leading them into this.

Something with three arms clawed at Elric. The runesword swept it away as Elric turned to cut both heads from the thing that had crept up behind him. A woman with six breasts flung herself upon his sword even as she flung her child into his face. Elric felt the brush of teeth across his scalp, stepped away to disembowel a mewing thing whose ribs grew out of its skin. His lantern overturned and went out.

Elric leapt back toward Moonglum. "Guard your lantern! We're dead without it!"

"Where's Kane?"

"Dead, I hope."

Strength was surging through Elric as Stormbringer struck lethally again and again. Moonglum fought gamely at his back. They were normally overmatched against these odds, but these were demented beasts rather than skilled warriors. Nonetheless, Elric knew that numbers of mindless killers with no thought of self-preservation could not be held at bay for very much longer.

A giant with three eyes across his forehead lurched toward Elric, raising a massive club as the albino tried to wrest Stormbringer free of the ribs and dying four-handed grasp of something that still clutched and screamed. Elric tried to twist away. The giant fell to his knees. His lower legs fell elsewhere. Elric freed his runesword and split the giant's skull down through the third eye. The club flew off into the darkness. Kane stepped over the corpse.

"Nice piece of work," said Kane. "I knew we could work well together." He peered through the darkness. "I think that's about all they can manage for now. Still, we'll have to keep close watch. Moonglum, see if you can light the other lantern."

"I don't take commands from you."

"Moonglum, see if you can light the other lantern," said Elric. He felt tired and cross. Whatever strength Stormbringer had stolen from these creatures of the dark, it wasn't sufficient for his needs.

"Kane, you led us into this ambush."

"I warned you there might be difficulties. Let's be going before they regroup."

Moonglum relit Elric's lantern. Elric held it aloft. "How many are left to regroup?"

Revealed now, from the darkness in which Kane had fought, was a slaughterhouse of broken and dismembered and vaguely human bodies. Elric remembered Kane's words: "I kill things. That's what I was created to do. I'm rather good at it." Before, Elric had assumed it was no more than a morbid jest. It was not a jest.

"I doubt they'll attack again," Kane called back. "Those who fled will leave us to their demon guardian. Besides, they'll have plenty to feast upon now."

Behind them, from the fringes of their lantern light, Elric could see misshapen bodies being dragged away into the maze of tunnels. Kane had recovered his metal hamper and was moving along confidently.

"Keep close to him," Elric murmured to Moonglum.

"Why don't we just go back?"

"Do you know the way?"

"It's worth trying."

True enough, Elric told himself, but the scant strength from Stormbringer made him reckless. He said: "Just stay close."

The tunnel abruptly fanned out into a vast cavern whose limits were well beyond the reach of their lanterns. A dull blue glow — seemingly from the cavern walls — provided murky light. Elric thought that this might well be the abode of Arioch, or at least an antechamber. The cavern must stretch on for hundreds of yards.

It wasn't a cavern.

Elric touched his hand to one wall. Not stone. Torn metal. Cold. He pounded the hilt of Stormbringer against its surface. It pealed like a sunken bell. What he had first assumed were stalactites and stalagmites were wrenched metal girders. Elric touched them, trying to imagine who had created this broken palace.

"Primarily that's a titanium and iridium alloy," Kane said, watching Elric closely. "I'm not certain what else. Likely osmium as well, but that's just a guess from the fact that the ship is relatively intact. As you will have observed, it hit rather hard."

Elric strained his eyes to look about. He might have been in the belly of a gigantic whale. Water dripped from the metallic ribs above, formed pools of slime upon the floor. Great masses of corroded mechanisms lay smashed and shrouded in layers of fungi. Gaping holes revealed black depths to decks below. It *was* a ship. But what sort of ship? And from whence?

"I don't see any great heaps of treasure." Moonglum was awed, but remained practical. "Nor do I see any guardian demons."

"All in good course," Kane assured him.

Elric's fascination with the ruin overpowered his initial anger and suspicion. He thrust Stormbringer into a mass of webby fungus beside one of the smashed machines. A skeleton fell apart as the shroud tore open. The skull that rolled away had a jaw bone not unlike that of a crocodile. One of the huge, pallid spiders scurried for new shelter.

"Kane, what is this place? And no more lies."

Elric looked for an answer, but Kane was no longer there.

Moonglum gaped. "He was just...."

Kane reappeared some thirty feet away. Under the soft blue effulgence Elric was certain that Kane hadn't simply dashed away before their eyes.

For once Kane seemed somewhat shaken. "Time slip. We're balanced on an uncertain flux between our worlds. I'm not at all sure how long I can maintain this. We'll need to work fast."

Elric sat down on a mouldering pile of rubble, the runesword clenched in his fists. "First you will tell me where we are and why this metal cavern was built. Then you may speak about treasures from the stars."

Kane forced the anger from his voice as he started to speak. It was obvious that he needed Elric, and that matters were swiftly getting beyond his control. He glanced at the lead-lined hamper and sighed.

"Right. You have some understanding of the heavens. Perhaps then, you are aware that the stars are distant suns, some with other worlds revolving about them, some with advanced life forms."

"I have heard such hypotheses."

"Right. Assume that there are also parallel universes to your own world. Invisible and unknown to you, but only a rift in time and space away."

"For the sake of the argument." Elric was intrigued, but he kept his fists clenched upon Stormbringer.

Kane nudged the metal carrier with his boot. "Ships sail across the seas. This is a ship that sailed across the stars. It crashed here, tearing into the earth. Most on board were killed. The rest were worshipped. A cult was born, and a fortress was built to preserve the wreckage. They fed on human sacrifices, mutating over the generations. Finally the people rose up, stormed and destroyed the castle. They feared the demons beneath and put their captives away in this maze. Then fled the region."

"Assuming I believed you," said Elric, remembering the story about the jewel-encrusted falling star, "just why have you lured me into this deadly puzzle?"

"You cut a deal with Arioch, and you're questioning *my* motives?"

"I am."

"Yes. Well." Kane kept his eye on Moonglum, who was carefully circling to get behind him. If Kane had to kill him, his brittle alliance with Elric would be ended.

Kane continued: "First of all, you and Stormbringer are very good. Sit down somewhere, Moonglum. You've seen the mutations of the former humans who infest this place. Imagine what may have mutated from the survivors of this ship. I need help."

Elric wished he were asleep and dreaming. He knew he wasn't. "Why should I help you?"

"Because that last time slip landed you firmly in my world. You won't like it. I can send you back to Melniboné. We're tottering on the edge of a major trans-dimensional warp. I have to block it."

"Such unexpected altruism."

"I mentioned the jewels."

"A lie. I ought to kill you now."

Kane unexpectedly grasped the runesword by its blade. Elric jerked it away. Kane opened his hand. There was no wound. Elric felt a sudden pain in his chest. The runesword felt icy cold. His heart seemed to falter. Elric stepped away, gathering his strength for whatever might follow.

"Don't make casual threats," said Kane. He had not drawn his sword.

"Next time I won't be so casual," Elric promised.

"Save your anger for the demon." Kane examined his hand, then vanished.

He reappeared some twenty feet away, behind them. "It's breaking apart." Any anger he had shown toward Elric was forgotten. "Where's my case?"

"Just where you left it," said Moonglum, pointing.

Kane snatched it up. "Continuum is close to breaking up. We have to move fast." He stared at Elric, as if seeing him for the first time. "Corum?"

"What?" Elric was still looking for Kane's blood upon the runesword.

"No. Of course not." Kane took a deep breath and glanced all about. Elric was reminded of a sleeper awakening from some deep dream. Kane had vanished for only a few seconds.

"We have to kill it first," Kane said. He seemed to be fully recovered from whatever had happened to him. "We'll take it from two sides, Elric. Moonglum can wait for a chance to strike."

"Strike at what?" Elric asked patiently. He had decided that Kane was completely mad. A mad, dangerous, out-of-control sorcerer.

"Whatever is lurking in the control room."

"The demon?"

"Well, it's probably lurking amidst the power units. We might be lucky. I just need the control room."

"No heaps of treasure?" asked Moonglum, expecting the answer to be no.

"There might be heaps upon heaps," said Kane. He didn't sound wholly sincere.

"Elric, let's leave this place," begged Moonglum.

Elric was stirred beyond his deep mood of brooding depression for the first time that he cared to recall. "I want to see this to the end."

Kane led them forward through the gigantic wreckage. Elric wondered again how Kane seemed to know his way through it all. Despite the bleak despair that had claimed his soul, he began to experience the rush of discovering things he had only known in partially remembered dreams.

"This is it," said Kane. "Be on your guard."

"What is *it?*" Elric demanded.

Kane was dismantling a control panel, using his sword and long fingers to rip away metal surfaces. "Should be about here...."

Kane vanished. Elric and Moonglum stood staring at one another. A large tentacle thrust out of a rift in the deck and sought for them. Elric hewed it away with the black sword. The tentacle severed. There was an inhuman scream. Stormbringer shuddered in Elric's grasp. Another tentacle thrust forward from the darkness below.

Kane slashed it apart. Elric had not seen him reappear. The tentacle twisted away, to be replaced by another.

"Time surge is mounting," Kane said. "I'm losing time phase. Keep that thing at bay. I only need a few minutes."

Elric was too occupied to tell Kane what he thought of him. Moonglum darted in and about, as Stormbringer cut cleanly through another grasping tentacle. Elric felt no increase in strength, but then he was only wounding the creature below. Or were there many such creatures?

Elric felt a sudden blow to his chest, and then he and Moonglum were sprawled across opposite sides of the chamber. Neither had a wound. Kane suddenly appeared next to Moonglum. He was dazed, but instantly on his feet.

"Elric! Now!" Kane shouted.

From the pit beneath the control desk a massive shape was rising. Its face was a mass of writhing tentacles surrounding an elephantine head. Crab-like jaws were clicking at them; eyes glowered from stubby stalks. Membranous wings hung from its shoulders, as webbed talons reached out. The last, mutated survivor of the star ship had entered the bridge.

Kane threw all of his strength into a blow at the creature's neck, or where its neck should be. A tentacle sent him crashing against the control room wall.

Elric saw his chance in that instant and brought Stormbringer slashing down upon the tentacled skull. Its head was as large as Kane himself, but the black blade split it apart, sending the monster sliding back into the pit from whence it had arisen.

Elric felt sickened.

Kane regained his feet. He was stunned and in pain, but he had taken far worse. His genetically altered body had once again held together, as it had been intended to do. "I think you killed it. Good work. I knew I could count on you when there were demons to be slain."

"This treasure you spoke of," reminded Moonglum.

"Kane was lying," said Elric, still weakened.

"Well, not as such." Kane removed the remaining section of control panel where he had worked earlier and lifted out a box-like instrument. It was as large as a man's chest and seemed to be a heavy burden even for Kane. "It's a transducer. Crucial for what I have in mind."

Elric stood up angrily. "You engineered this entire interlude just so you could acquire an armload of rubbish."

"I *did* need your help. And it's not rubbish. Sorry about all the jewels. I owe you."

Kane opened the leaden case he had dragged along throughout their journey. Elric heard some faint clicking sounds. Kane closed the hamper.

He cradled the transducer. "Well, I hope this still works, after all this. Oh, in about an hour ten pounds of bomb-grade plutonium will explode here, closing the gate to certain forces who wish me no good. I stole this lead picnic basket from them. This portal opens to other worlds as well, and I'm not the only one seeking a transducer. There will be a *very* large explosion, but it will close the gate — *this gate* — between our worlds. There are others.

"Come on, I'll lead you back to your world. Then you have to make a run for it. Elric, we will meet again."

⊕

Soon Elric and Moonglum were astride their horses, galloping madly into the night, with only confused memories of their adventure. Daylight seemed close at hand.

Miles behind them, the ruined castle blossomed into a mushroom of fire, ejecting itself from the earth like a rising star, bursting into the night sky. The blast caused their horses to stumble, but they kept racing through the rain and darkness.

"Where did Kane go?" Moonglum wondered.

"I hope we never find out," said Elric.

THE SOUL OF AN OLD MACHINE

BY THOMAS E. FULLER

In which Elric makes a wager with Mercurios
of the Cold Laughter that there is no one
more afflicted than he.

The conflicts rage around me, constant and eternal. The ground groans and splits beneath my steps as it bleeds in the frenzy of my dance. The very skies rupture with the passions of my kind, bursting asunder with fiery streamers. I hear their screams and roars, their triumphs and defeats tangible as taste to me, as we ravage and rage.

The conflicts roar around me, constant and eternal. As they should. As they always have.

As they always will.

⊕

Winter had come to Menii, the Island of the Purple Towns. It had come as it had always come, from the north, prowling in from the Sighing Desert and the Weeping Waste, pausing only to rim Old Hrolmar with frost. Then the thick flotillas of fog had sailed across the Straits of Vilmir, the fanciful "ghost sails" of Meniian legend, until cold mists blanketed the robust Purple Towns and their harbors.

Winter had come to Menii, and the Merchant Princes had retired to their villas and counting houses to plan next spring's sailings and to divide among them the twin concerns of trade and raid. Lately, trade was steadily replacing raid, the Princes having discovered that with trade one could visit a port annually instead of having to wait until everything was rebuilt. And a great deal of respect and prestige went with trade, although the more tradition-bound held that piracy was more honest.

Winter had come to Menii, and to the Inn of High Winds and Full Sails, a reasonably charming establishment in the Purple Town of Semeniomous. The Inn of High Winds and Full Sails catered to a higher class of sea-going rogue and a lower class of entrepreneur, men who *might* be pirates but *could* be merchants, depending on how well-armed their potential customers proved to be. Still and all, it was a cosy enough place, with low beamed ceilings, two great roaring fireplaces, and a majestic view of the city harbor.

When there wasn't any fog, of course.

This day the Inn was fairly filled with the captains and mates of a number of highly suspect ships currently being bedded down for the winter. The Inn's owner, one Zemous Vintermina, was justly famous for his roast beef, his nut-brown ales, and his excellent — but over-priced — wines. He was also famous for his extremely saucy serving wenches, buxom little brunettes who, for some reason, were never over five feet tall. All in all, an excellent place to greet friends, swap tales, compare profits and check up on the going price of everything from Ilmirian silk to Eshmirian slaves.

Zemous Vintermina, his gaunt, vulpine body so different from what was usually expected of an innkeeper, looked around his common room with some consternation. Yet the roasts sizzled over the fires, the girls bounced back and forth with their tankards and goblets, and his guests were drinking and lying. It was shaping up to be a good afternoon shading into an excellent night. Or would if he could do something about the source of his concern, the party in the Harbor corner. He glanced furtively in that direction. Yes, they were still there. Both of them. Damn.

The ghostly albino and his diminutive companion had drifted in with the fog two days before. Their gold was good — their gold was *very* good — but their presence had an inhibiting effect on his regular clientele. The Inn of High Winds and Full Sails had a reputation for respectable rakishness — these new guests brought winter in with them. The albino especially drained the warmth from Zemous' great fireplaces. The little one was amusing and would have fit in nicely — perhaps a bit too nicely, since the innkeeper had noticed at least two of the girls staring at the small man covetously as they avoided his pale companion. Still, the gold was good.

And no guest stayed forever.

⊕

Elric of Melniboné slouched in the high-backed leather chair and stared moodily out into the swirling fog. Just the other side of Zemous Vintermina's prized glass windows it billowed and boiled. And in its soft grey mists he fancied he saw — things.

Elric raised his blown-glass goblet and drained the last of the shimmering emerald wine. It was called Memory's Tears and was imported at great cost from vineyards north of Hwamgaarl, the City of Screaming Statues, on the mysterious island of Pan Tang. It was reputed to excite the memory. It worked well enough for Elric to have purchased the Inn of High Winds and Full Sails' entire stock for his own consumption.

He pushed his white hair back with one languid hand and concentrated on the fog. Yes, if he stared long enough into the clouds, *they* would appear, mist-made, before his eyes. The greyness billowed and the towers of Imrryr, the Dreaming City, rose glistening, only to dissolve back into the fog. That would be the first, now the faces would come. Yes, let the faces come. Dyvim Tvar, Lord of the Dragon Caves, a man who once had called Elric both Emperor and friend. Tanglebones, who had taught him archery and fencing. The vague shifting face of his father, Sadric LXXXVI. Elric concentrated his wine-enhanced stare. Only one image more between him and what he wanted most to see. Outside the fog formed the face of a man, a man with darkly handsome features and raven-black hair, his eyes bright with intelligence and madness.

"Leave me, Yyrkoon," Elric whispered at the saturnine face. "Leave me, cursed cousin, and return to whatever hell you harrow now."

With a smirk, Yyrkoon's face drifted apart into grey streamers, coiling back into the void. Like transparent silk snakes, they writhed back, twisting and turning until a final face formed in the fog. The languid face of a beautiful woman, her eyes closed in sleep. Elric gripped the twisted stem of the empty goblet, his red eyes staring, haunted, at the apparition.

"Cymoril."

No words of endearment escaped his pale lips, only the name, the name of the woman he would have made both his wife and the Mistress of Imrryr, the Dreaming City. Now both woman and city alike had perished, destroyed by the same hand. His.

"Cymoril."

The sleeping woman seemed to stir at her name, as if she were about to waken. Elric felt the goblet's stem shatter in his hand as he leaned forward, knowing that it was useless even as he moved. Just as it seemed that this time he might actually succeed, Elric felt something drag him back, something heavy and dark and malignantly intelligent. He did not even have to look down to know what it was.

The great black sword that men called Stormbringer throbbed dully at his side, shattering his concentration and dispelling the effects of Memory's Tears. Outside, the beloved face faded and the fog became, once again, merely fog.

"An interesting game, Master Elric, but you really don't seem to enjoy it."

Elric glanced over at the concerned face of his companion. Moonglum stared back at him, his hands cradling a prosaic mug of Fall's Breath ale. Elric looked down at the broken glass in his hand.

"No, I don't seem to, do I? Still, it is the only game I have at the moment. I shall continue to play."

Moonglum sighed and jauntily waved his hand towards the other end of the common room.

"Ho, my sweetling! More of your fine master's most excellent wine for Master Elric!"

One of the serving girls reluctantly approached them with another bottle of Memory's Tears and another of Zemous Vintermina's carefully hoarded glass goblets. She set them in front of Elric, her head bowed both out of respect and to avoid having to look at him. She then shot a much warmer glance at Moonglum and finally, her courage exhausted, she fled back to the fireplaces. Moonglum sighed again.

"My friend, isn't it bad enough that your melancholy must rob you of female companionship; must it rob me also?"

Elric looked over at the girl, who was busily dodging the romantic attentions of a very drunk first mate and shrugged.

"She is rather short, Moonglum."

"Might I remind my Lord Elric that I am also rather short? Her height is part of her charm."

"While I seem to have none." Elric poured the heavy green wine into his fresh goblet and stared into it. "I grow tired, Moonglum, I truly do. I have seen too much, I have lost too much, and what little I have gained has gained me little. I don't know what it is to be happy anymore. I don't think I ever have."

"Happiness is not the normal state of human affairs, Elric. We must treasure what little bits we can hoard."

Elric drank the wine. It was like liquid emeralds sliding down his throat. The fog moved again.

"Still, there are times like this when I would wager that no one in all the great sweep between Chaos and Law has ever been as afflicted as I."

The fog convulsed and something spoke out of it.

"A wager. How delightful."

Both Elric and Moonglum turned towards the window, their hands instinctly moving to their swords. The albino felt Stormbringer's hilt throb beneath his hand and that throb seemed to whisper, "Blood and souls, blood and souls for my Lord Arioch! Blood and souls! Blood and souls!" He fought down the whisper and focused on the figure in front of him.

Who bowed.

"Mercurios of the Cold Laughter, at your service. Please forgive the descriptive, it wasn't my idea. But then so few descriptives are, are they?"

Mercurios of the Cold Laughter was a small, slight man dressed in the white-and-grey travel silks of the Mystikers of Rignariom. His hair was pale gold, as was his neatly- trimmed beard. The only other color he displayed was a bright band of blood-red silk that covered his eyes. It didn't seem to affect him.

"It is customary for strangers to announce themselves before interjecting themselves into private conversations," said Moonglum with cold dignity. It annoyed him that Mercurios could have appeared before them without his noticing it. That hurt his professional pride.

"But I have done so, have I not, Master Moonglum? You have my name and me before you. In places such as these, that constitutes a friendship of lifetimes." Mercurios spread his arms and smiled, displaying a mouth full of small white teeth. "And wagers are of a particular interest to me. Chance and fate are so fascinating, don't you think?"

"Sit, Mercurios," Elric gestured to one of the chairs. "I do not remember mentioning anything about wagers."

"Ah, but you did, Master Elric," the little man said as he hopped into one of the high-backed leather chairs, looking for all the world like an elderly child angling for a treat. "You wagered that no one in all the great sweep of History has ever been more afflicted than you. I am merely the one who is accepting your wager."

"I do not know you, Friend Mercurios."

"But I know you, Master Elric. Oh, I know you very well!" Mercurios smiled again and Elric seemed to feel hungry eyes staring at him from behind their mask of blank red silk. "You are the albino warrior-wizard, Elric of Melniboné, who was once an Emperor and is now a wanderer. You are called Womanslayer because you killed the woman you loved. You are called Kinslayer because you slew your cousin Yyrkroon; Destroyer because you obliterated Imrryr the Dreaming City from the Isle of the Dragon; and Traitor because you abandoned to the golden barges of Melniboné the Sea Lords who aided you in that obliteration. You are a Sorrow on the World, bonded to the greatest of the Lords of Chaos, fed by and feeding the black runesword Stormbringer that even now hangs by your side."

Mercurios' voice came forth as a joyous whisper, each damning word a caress. Moonglum glanced quickly at his friend. All they needed now was for this lunatic to set Elric off — the man must be mad! He obviously knew who they were, but he wore no weapons that Moonglum could see. What did he think he was doing?

Elric's eyes burned red in his bone-white face but they were not looking at the smiling Mystiker. He was staring past him into the fog. Memory's Tears was affecting him, joining him with the joyous voice that still rang in his ears. The mists convulsed as if something gigantic and alien were looming up behind them, something so huge it dwarfed the Inn of High Winds and Full Sails as a castle dwarfed a hut. Unlike his own memories, this one was indistinct. He swung his gaze back to Mercurios. It's not *my* memory, he thought.

It's his.

"It is not a very pretty picture you paint of me, Friend Mercurios."

"But accurate, Friend Elric?"

"But accurate, Friend Mercurios."

The small man leaned forward across the table. "Your wager is that you are the most afflicted of men, that your weird is greater than any who have lived before or since you. You make a very good case. My wager is that there is one more miserable, more doomed than you can ever imagine. My wager is also on the table." His hand moved across the fine wood and as it moved large golden coins appeared, like miniature suns.

Elric picked up one of the coins. Across its face writhed two twisting dragons. Melnibonéan coins, Melnibonéan gold. How appropriate, he thought as he stared across the table into a band of sanguinary silk. He reached into his pouch and removed a large purple gem, the souvenir of an adventure he preferred not to think about, and laid it down next to the glistening coins.

"I accept your acceptance of my `wager' and your description of myself. Now, how do you propose to win it?"

"With proof, of course. Proof enough to satisfy even you."

"And where will you find this proof?"

"Oh, friend Elric, I will not find it. You will."

And the fog poured into the Inn of High Winds and Full Sails.

My shadow swords slash at the horizon and rake their light-stained blades across the bleeding skies. The broken carapaces of my brothers slide disemboweled past me as I advance, vengeance primed. The ground is a morass of dirt and tainted water and wasted life fluids. In places it burns, sending clouds of greasy black smoke to mask the vision. It does not mask ours. It does not mask mine.

I advance.

Elric staggered down into the mud as the Inn of High Winds and Full Sails vanished, to be replaced by a nightmare landscape painted by a mad god. He heard Moonglum gasp next to him.

"Oh, Lords of Law and Chaos! What mad hell is this?" the little man yelled as he fought to hold his balance on the slippery sludge.

"The hell where we are to meet the one more doomed than I, I suppose," Elric yelled back. "It seems Friend Mercurios takes his wagers very seriously."

"I don't remember making any wager! I resent this disruption of my life!" The ground next to Moonglum suddenly exploded, erupting upward like a solid geyser, knocking him flat. He stared in annoyance up at Elric, his red hair plastered to his head. "Almost as much as I resent its termination."

Elric ignored his companion's discomfort, just as he ignored his own. He stood, a gaunt figure, all dead-white skin and hair, all black leather and silk, and stared across the tumult into which idle self-pity had thrust him .

The air screamed and raged about him, alive with thunders and explosions. In the distance the horizon burned as if a thousand cities blazed along its tormented edge. Smoke oozed across the ground, denying its nature, as if afraid to rise. Streaks scarred the skies, made by silver... things that twisted and turned around themselves. Occasionally there would be a flash and one of the streaks would end, but there were always others to take its place. Elric felt Stormbringer reaching hungrily out from his side and through it felt the awesome throb of life forces around him. Lives were being ended and souls released everywhere and Stormbringer yearned to join in the harvest. Blood and souls for my Lord Arioch. Blood and souls.

"It's a war, Moonglum, some kind of monstrous war! The very earth and air join into it! I have seen nothing like this in all my travels!"

"'Ware the armies, Elric!" Moonglum called pointing to what seemed to be the east. "They pass!"

The two stood on a small hill. In the distance a vast horde of soldiers marched forward under enormous banners of yellow and white. Moonglum stood with his mouth agape and even Elric felt his imagination stagger. It was as if all the folk of the Young Kingdoms had formed themselves into battalions and gone off to war. There was no counting the millions that streamed by and yet he somehow knew that this was only one of the great forces that contended in this monstrous conflict. He could sense others, perhaps even greater. And in the midst of the army things moved, things like mobile castles that churned their ways forward.

"This is Chaos made real, Moonglum — surely we are at the last great War Between Chaos and Law. The Balance is gone and the world is mad!"

"That is not all that is mad, Elric! Look behind you!" And Elric whirled, Stormbringer finally in his hand.

They must have been outriders, soldiers moving along the fringe of the march. They came over the edge of the hill, clad in muddy yellow and white, their strange weapons at the ready. Elric lashed out at the first one, felt Stormbringer slice through cloth and bone and exult as it drew a soul into its black-etched runes. Moonglum drew his own sword, blessedly free of any magic or intelligence, and joined his friend.

Elric heard death sizzle past his ear and brought Stormbringer crashing down before his foe could aim his deadly weapon again. The runesword seemed to scream with hunger as it ate yet again. The two stood back to back as the silent yellow and white soldiers closed, clubbing and firing. They slashed and fought and the soldiers died. And died. And died.

Elric wiped the blood off his forehead, not knowing or even caring if it were his. The mysterious warriors lay in the mud where they had fallen. Moonglum was bandaging a nasty gash in his left arm.

"We are not popular here, Friend Elric. We are not popular at all."

Elric did not respond. Instead he looked around at the fallen and felt his body start to tremble with rage. "He is not here!" He turned screaming at a shocked Moonglum. "He is not here! These are just men, ordinary men, nothing more, nothing less! Where is the afflicted one?" Elric shook Stormbringer at the smoke-blasted sky and its streaks and scars. "Where is the proof of your wager, Mercurios? Where is the one more miserable than Elric of Melniboné? Where in the Seven Hells is he?"

I advance.

Elric looked up to the crest of the hill, and half the sky disappeared.

I advance.

The cold voice rang in his head as a blunt metal edge like the prow of some lunatic ship thrust itself into the air above him. Colossal belts and wheels at its sides churned it forward, mud and broken bones caked into their treads. Great tubes jabbed out from its sides, smoke and vapor drifting from their cavernous bores. It hung there for a moment, balanced on the lip of the hill, then it slowly started to tip downwards.

Elric stared up at the descending mass. He could feel the life force that radiated from the living metal like the blaze from a colossal fireplace. It would blot him and his sword from the face of this hellish plane and there was nothing he could do to stop it.

Moonglum barreled into Elric, sending them both sprawling in the oily mud as the mighty machine smashed down next to them and slid uncontrollably down the slope. Its great treads missed them by inches, plowing up the wounded land in their passing and burying the dead who had so recently escorted it.

"Arise, Friend Elric! The metal beast is only momentarily confounded! We must get away before it can recover!"

I sense you, little enemies.

The cold metal voice rang in Elric's ears again as he fought his way to his feet, mud fouling him from head to foot. The armored thing was swinging itself around, bringing its multiple tubes and nozzles to bear on him and Moonglum.

I would sense you no more.

The tubes belched fire and smoke and the top part of the hill vanished in an eruption of filth. Moonglum ducked back down, but Elric found himself still standing, held erect by the power that flowed into him from Stormbringer. It's a fortress, he thought, a fortress of moving — no, of living — metal. The cyclopean thing seemed to stare at him from multiple spheres of quicksilver that circled its upper works. It began to churn its way back up what was left of the hill.

I will sense you no more.

Elric could now see that the fortress had suffered in the great battle that raged around them. The top part of the prow had been blown apart, exposing incomprehensible tangles of wires and glowing vials. His sorcery-trained senses could feel the sharp surge of its life force, all crystalline bright and knife-edge-metal cold. Stormbringer felt it also and hungered for it. Strength in waves blasted through his body.

"I am Elric of Melniboné! I am not some vagrant dog to be ground into the dirt by you or anything else! Come forward, thing of metal and magic, come forward to Elric and your doom!"

I come.

The tubes erupted again, sending more death and destruction screaming up the hill. Moonglum dove back into the mud to escape, but Elric was past escape. He charged down the slope, Stormbringer thrust out before him. Moonglum dug the dirt out of his eyes and could not tell if Elric ran or if the black runesword dragged him along behind it.

Elric leaped, and his free hand grasped the ragged lip of the prow. The jagged metal dug into his hand and he felt his own hot blood run streaming down his sleeve. He swung up to the broken deck just in time to be nearly brained by one of the great tubes as it cranked by, trying to bring itself to bear on the little figure that scrambled over it.

Stormbringer throbbed and the quicksilver eyes swirled around to confront it. Elric stood knee-deep in the twisted wires and glowing glass that spilled from the guts of the beast. Here he knew it could not reach him. Here at his feet was the source of the monster's life force and its soul.

"Blood and souls," Elric howled, swinging the great sword over his head. "Blood and souls for my Lord Arioch!" And he brought Stormbringer hurling down into the raging alien life force coiled beneath him.

Stormbringer cut greedily into the wires, prepared to drink and feed.

And nothing happened. Nothing happened at all.

Elric stood confounded. Where was the soul? He somehow knew that he had struck true. If the monster had a heart, Stormbringer had pierced it. Sword and bearer should be vibrating with the sorrowful, hated screams of a living soul being sucked into the sword that was both his life and his curse. There was nothing. Stormbringer jerked him forward, thrusting and thrusting again and again, independent of Elric's will. Then, to his horror, he felt his own life, so recently replenished by the defeated soldiers in yellow and white, flowing back into Stormbringer as the sword sought frantically for the soul that it should have tasted. Elric hurled himself backwards, desperately trying to disengage Stormbringer from its frustrated slashing. As he did so, his frantic red eyes looked up into the multiple spheres of quicksilver that lined the fortress' upper works. The spheres stared back at him, powerful, cold.

And soulless.

"Lord Arioch protect me!" he screamed. "It has no soul!"

As he screamed, Stormbringer's frenzied slashing shattered one of the quicksilver spheres and lightning surged along Stormbringer's black length, sending both sword and wielder flying from the ravaged deck.

Blind! I am blind!

Elric sprawled in the oozing mud, still holding his blade, now strangely quiet. The fortress slowly began to slide further back down the slope and as Elric stared, the sundered wires and the shattered quicksilver sphere began to reform and rejoin, to knit and heal themselves.

You have hurt me, little enemy. The cold voice sounded fainter as it throbbed through Elric's aching head. *They Who Command summon me and I must advance. But I will remember you, little enemy,. I will remember.* And with a rumbling, grinding noise, the fortress laboriously turned and moved to join the vast army that still flowed by in the distance.

Moonglum cautiously raised himself up out of the muck and looked around. The metal beast was leaving, limping away to the west. Elric sat upon a broken rock, his shoulders slumped. In his arms he cradled Stormbringer, almost as if he were comforting his dreadful sword. As Moonglum approached, he carefully wiped the blade clean with the edge of his cape and slid it uncomplaining back into its scabbard.

"Are you well, Elric?" Moonglum started to say, but stopped when the albino turned his haunted eyes to him.

"It had no soul, Moonglum. Stormbringer sought to take it and there was nothing there. For all that strange, alien life force, there was no soul at the center of it. I bargained my soul away to the Lords of Chaos, but at least I had a soul to bargain with, to keep or give as I chose. There was nothing there, Moonglum. There never was and never will be. Help me up. I am drained beyond any weariness I have ever known."

Moonglum helped his friend to his feet. As he did, Elric turned his eyes to the scarred and bleeding sky where things he did not comprehend — nor did he want to — fought and died. "You have won our wager, Mercurios. There is indeed one more afflicted than Elric of Melniboné. More afflicted than I could ever have imagined possible. You have won."

Fog began to boil up around their feet, and Moonglum suddenly realized that he did not care where the fog took them , as long as it was away from this tortured land and as long as Mercurios of the Cold Laughter did not wait for them at the end.

⊕

Everything was going quite well at the Inn of High Winds and Full Sails when Zemous Vintermina glanced over and discovered that his two high-paying but unwanted guests had finally departed. In their place was a small man dressed in outlandish white and grey. Zemous stalked over to his prized Harbor corner, indignation radiating from his crane-like body. They still owed for the redhead's ale.

The small man was hunched over a small pile of large coins, intently observing a brilliantly shimmering purple gem with his hooded eyes. A band of bright-red silk lay casually coiled on the varnished table top.

"Where are the two rogues who were at this table?" Zemous demanded in his best indignant-innkeeper voice.

"Oh, they had to leave," the little man replied, still intent on his gem. "But they asked that you accept this small token for your goods and services and hope that you find it adequate." He pushed one of the large coins across the table.

Zemous picked the coin up and felt his eyes bulge at the weight of it. *Lords of the Sea, if this thing is real it will cover my expenses for the next sixmonth!* "It will suffice, barely," he sniffed. He turned to go, but something made him turn back.

"Um, you wouldn't happen to know where they went, would you?"

"Oh yes, they went to visit family."

"Family! Theirs?"

"Oh no, good innkeeper, they did not go to visit *their* families." And Zemous found himself staring into the upturned eyes of Mercurios of the Cold Laughter. Eyes that held no whites or irises or pupils, but were merely shimmering globes of liquid quicksilver set in his sharp-featured face.

"They went to visit *mine*."

And Zemous Vintermina fled from his own inn, pursued by the soft, cold laughter that sparkled soullessly behind him.

⊕

I drive forward, ripping the wounded land beneath me, scarring it anew as others of my kind have scarred it before me. I reach out and sense the presence of Those Who ComImand. Their orders fill me with purpose and serve to blot out the minor engagement from which I have just emerged. I arm and reload and repair. I search my circuits and wires for the source of the malfunction that disquiets me, the sense that something should be functional that is not. I discontinue and drive forward, for the conflicts roar around me, constant and eternal. As they should. As they always have.

As they always will.

THE WHITE CHILD

BY JODY LYNN NYE

Elric sat upright, blinking at the red sun on the horizon, surprised at its color. Sleep had fled. The vision had returned again, stronger than ever.

As it had night after night for nearly a month, the white child stared at him in his dreams. Its wide, red eyes, so like his own, beseeched him. The ragged cloud of white hair framed and barely concealed the hollow cheekbones. The child was so thin: too thin. Its frail body wore a baggy garment of no particular color whose hems were shaggy and torn. A three-cornered rip near the waist revealed a palm-sized expanse of spare, white flesh. And yet the child had nobility of carriage, a pale desperation of dignity. Was the dream a hell-sent vision of his own youth? He could see every detail, yet could not remember ever having gone in tatters quite like those. No, though without love, his childhood had been spent in the presence of wealth. Melniboné was not kind, but it allowed its kin to save face. Unless the dream was a warning of some kind, sent to Elric by the Gods of Chaos: That, he did not know.

Stormbringer muttered greedily in its sleep beside him. If it had been a man and not a sword, it would have rolled over, taking most of the blanket-like cloak with it. Could the staring face in the dream belong to a byblow he'd strewn behind him at some point, the mother having flung it out to live among street beggars when she discovered its body was weak and pale and that its face bore features of a ghostly cast? Elric nodded grimly. If Stormbringer craved its soul, the dream-child must be real and human, though it could not be of Melnibonéan stock. He sensed nothing of the power about the small figure. But why was it calling to him? Before Elric had awakened this morning, the white child's mouth had formed the word, "Come."

Elric made a hasty breakfast and saddled his horse. The beast wheezed uncomfortably to itself as he mounted to the saddle. Both of them were tired. They'd endured days of hard riding since Elric had left the side of now-Queen Yishana. He'd had to deliver to her the bad news that her brother was dead, partly through Elric's fault. She was a fierce woman, as well-constructed for the arts of war as for those of love. She had not been as angry as Elric had feared, and had let him leave fairly soon thereafter. When the dream of the white child first came to him, he'd thought it was because he had lately been with her. The depletion of Melnibonéan stock on the face of the earth troubled him. In the presence of a vital woman, perhaps such hopes of replenishing his dying line had awoken. But now he was certain it had nothing to do with Yishana. The feeling of the child's reality became stronger as he rode farther south, away from the queen, and toward the source of the dream. He had been riding so for more than a month.

He glanced around. The terrain had risen and fallen three times since he left the central plains behind. Green, deciduous forests had given way to mountain scrub as they traveled high, craggy mountains, the likes of which he had never seen before. Now they were riding downhill among sea pines and cypress. His horse picked its way cautiously through high, wiry grass until it chanced upon a road which led, Elric sensed, in the correct direction. He let his steed follow the well-worn trail down the south face of the mountain range. Trading towns nestled in the high passes behind him, and he had wondered who came from the south along those tough, nearly inaccessible paths. He'd never heard of any commodity worth having which came from the peninsula of Solaidignia.

The headlands knelt before him, broad backs bowed to the sky. White gulls wheeled in the air and screamed to one another. A taste of salt touched Elric's lips with the next gust of wind that came over the rounded hill. He had to be very near the sea. Impatiently, Elric spurred his horse to a canter, suddenly possessed by an urge to see what lay on the other side.

If he was disappointed he refused to let himself feel it. The island town below looked like any other fortified trading village. The headlands continued climbing upward to his right, ending in a steep cliff overhanging the sea. The town abutted the mountain face, with piers lined with ships and boats nestled in its shelter. Signs of prosperity were everywhere, from the bustling warehouses to the pennants flying from the towers of the small castle at the south end of the island. All seemed ordinary, except for the sensation of urgent summons deep in his soul which told him that hidden amid the bustle and busyness below was the white child.

By land the town was accessible only by a causeway that looped down from the headlands to the left. The road cut sharply away from the cliff at the shore, and followed a land bridge just high enough to remain above the line of high tide. A portcullis and guard towers to either side of the wide gate at the road's end were nearly unnecessary afterfittings. The town had admirable natural defenses.

Elric hammered down the sea road toward the tossing, iron-gray waves. Explosions of water in the crags threw jets of spume high into the air around him, making the horse dance and show the whites of its eyes. With knees and hands he made it concentrate on its path. The waves churned in a surly fashion, slapping impatiently at the causeway sides. He was afraid they would reach up over the edges of the road and yank them both in. Elric had seen this mood before. It was the sea at play — like a cat with a mouse. The Sea King was toying with his prey, though what the prey was Elric had no idea. He was not concerned. His only interest lay ahead of him, beckoning to his very blood.

A hundred yards from the town walls the road narrowed to a mere tongue of stone. A company of men or horses could only go single file onto the island beyond. Well-constructed, Elric thought. A force could be held off by a single sure archer. A crack of thunder and a brilliant flash of lightning reminded him that the biggest threat to this town was of no mortal origin. The wrong wind, the wrong current, and those ships riding at anchor in the lee of the cliff could easily be dashed into splinters against it. Were he a trader he'd think twice about risking his ships to this port, no matter what commodities could be had here. As he got closer, he saw that the gay show of color and wealth was on the surface only. Walls had been painted with bright murals to hide the patching of their surface. The fluttering pennants had once been flags.

The steel-banded gates opened. Elric pulled up the horse as a force of men marched forth and spread out on the apron of rock before the walls. The grim look on their faces showed they knew they were facing the scion of their ancient overlords, and they were wary. By contrast, the man who rode behind them on a noble white horse, the equal of Elric's own, bore a broad smile.

"Welcome, my lord Elric!" he called. "I am Nereis, Sea Lord of Solaidignia. We've been expecting you."

Elric sat up straight in the saddle and addressed the Sea Lord. "Where is the child?" he asked.

⊕

"We have been expecting you a month or more," Nereis said, seating himself amidst the cushions in the great chair at one end of the gloomy, gray stone reception hall. He was a tall man, with most of his height in his torso. His black hair was clipped short to an olive-skinned skull. An old scar etched a white line between the clusters of sun wrinkles at the corner of his right eye. "One didn't know where you'd be faring, so there was no way to tell how long a journey it'd be. Thank all gods you're here at last." Tapestries, thick and good though old, hung against the walls, keeping out the chill of the winds outside, but not their howls. Nereis gestured Elric toward another seat. Elric ignored it, continuing to stand stiffly in the middle of the room and to stare at the Sea Lord, poising one hand on his sword hilt. The guards had withdrawn to the end of the chamber, except for the few flanking Nereis.

"You are responsible for the dreams?" Elric asked, holding his temper with difficulty. "I am not accustomed to being summoned."

"I performed the summoning," said a short, stocky man standing in the shadows just behind the high seat. He stepped forward, and Elric noted that his eyes were sharp in a face that was otherwise rounded and pudgy. "I am Tabisian. I assure you we didn't make such a calling lightly, but we need your aid, Lord Elric."

Elric looked to Nereis for clarification. The Sea Lord nodded his head. "We are in danger here, Lord Elric," he said. "You must have noticed the face of the sea."

"It looked angry," Elric said, nodding.

"It is more than merely angry," Nereis said. "I have lived near the sea all of my life. I don't fear her natural phases, but this — this is beyond anything we've known in living memory. We've been hammered by storms again and again, months out of season. Though it's high summer, ice forms on the sheets and lines of every vessel. Not one sailing leaves port that does not return missing one or more of the crew. We've lost men to waves crashing across bows and monsters rising from the depths in the night. We rely upon the sea for our living. More than that, we require its protection. The auguries have shown that Solaidignia has given some offense to the Elementals of Water."

"What offense?"

"My lord, if I knew that, we'd have placated them in any way possible!" Nereis exclaimed, sitting upright and banging his palm on the arm of his chair. "I know from legend that you have the ear of the Sea King, Straasha, Lord of Water Elementals. You have even had his cooperation at times."

"Aye," Elric admitted. Straasha was a friend to him, and had predicted that one day he and Elric would meet again. Nereis must know of the legend.

"Will you summon him, my lord Elric?" Nereis asked. The Sea Lord's face was hopeful. Elric could tell that he was a proud man, not accustomed to asking favors. "Tell him we are under your protection. I beg your assistance. Save my town."

"And why should I do this?"

"If you do not," Tabisian answered instead, "we will throw the child to the waves."

"*What* child?" Elric asked.

"You should know that, my lord," said the wizard, who had remained behind the throne in the shadows. He stepped forward, leading a small figure by the hand. "You've seen her image in your dreams this past month and more. I knew the sending would draw you. Here she is."

Tabisian returned to his post behind the Sea Lord's throne. One of the guards took the girl forward to within ten paces of Elric. A frail little thing, dressed in the rags Elric remembered, she looked up at him with almond-shaped red eyes rimmed with thick white lashes. She could be no more than four or five years old. Among the dark people of Solaidignia she was a white cloud in a stormy sky. The guard's hand on the child's arm seemed like a block of wood overlying a fragile slip of paper. Stormbringer's impulses were correct as ever: she was a human pawn used to draw him to this island. Elric knew at once he'd been wrong about her origins. She would one day be as strong a wizard as he. She was of the blood of Melniboné. But whose?

"This child," the wizard said with a certain amount of satisfaction as he watched Elric. "I see you recognize her. Indeed, you should."

That last puzzled the Melnibonéan. Should the cast of her features remind him of someone?

"What is her name?" Elric asked, attempting to sound unconcerned.

"She has no name. She was never given one," the wizard said, hooding his eyes with amusement. "Such things are not important. If you help us, you may name her if you wish."

Elric was suddenly disgusted with the lord and his vassals.

"I am not involved in your quarrel with the sea," he said angrily, spinning on his heel to stride away. His heart ached for the child, but to have these barbarians assume he would call upon the sea demons for such a trivial matter infuriated him. The wizard's voice called him back.

"Do you not care for your own flesh and blood?" Elric stopped, turning about to stare at the grinning enchanter. "Yes. She is formed from a single drop of your own blood that fell on the blade of a sword which pricked its way through your defense in battle. Its owner, one of my lord's men-at-arms, managed to escape your demonblade Stormbringer and carry it home to me. Such a prize! I set the drop in the womb of a woman six years ago. It matured and was born. Here she is: your daughter. Do you deny your inner knowledge of her?"

Elric swallowed.

"I... I do not believe you." But he knew in his heart that the wizard's words were true. He remembered the battle, though it was undistinguished in most ways from others he had fought in his long life. His arm ached when he looked at the little girl, in the same place where the blade of a Southern warrior had wounded him.

No wonder he could not sense any magic in her in his dreams. She was himself, spell for spell, fiber for fiber, and any echo he would have heard would be absorbed in the likeness of his own being — until he saw her in the flesh. Yes. He could tell that she had recognized in the same moment what he was, and that she welcomed him.

"Why don't you do something yourselves?" he asked, returning to the matter at hand. "You have power enough to create life. Use it to save yourselves."

Nereis shook his head. "Chaos hammers at us. The sea would swallow us. The Chaos Ships are coming, Lord Elric! Tabisian has seen them in visions. We have offended the Sea King in some way, and our lives are forfeit. We need you."

Elric shook his head. "Evacuate. You still have your lives. Your ships ride at anchor. There must be enough to carry every man, woman, and child away from this place."

Lord Nereis paused perceptibly. "We cannot leave. This island contains our destiny, our birthright! Would you see an entire city made homeless? Who would give us land again, a favorable placement on a harbor? You have the trust of the Sea. As a descendant of the Bright Lords you have also a relationship with Chaos, which holds sway in the great deeps. Save us!"

Elric became impatient. "I have no reason to fight your battles."

"Then the child will die," Tabisian said. He appeared to be more ruthless than his master.

"She was only a drop of my blood before," Elric said, with difficulty. "I have shed many since. I have no right to dictate her life or death."

For the first time the child looked terrified. Trembling, she stepped forward. She raised a hand and touched his wrist above the mailed gauntlet that rested on the hilt of Stormbringer. Her fingers were warm. "Please."

He wanted to lash out and strike her hand away. He nearly did. Then he saw in his memory the image of his own father, who never failed to show his disappointment in the sorry albino thing that he'd begotten. At least Elric could spare the child that much rejection. He took her small fingers in his other hand, patted them, and put them away from him. Flawed she was, yet still of the blood of Melniboné. His blood, when he thought that he had no offspring, could never have any. She gave him and his people a future. She was a princess, yet clad in rags, half-starved by her masters. It was a deliberate insult to him. She ought to have warm, pretty clothes; toys; good food; the respect of her peers; even love.

"You shall leave here with me," he said, with a smile for her alone. The child's thin face lightened.

"Oh, no, my friend," the wizard said. "She belongs to me."

For answer, Elric swept Stormbringer out of its scabbard. He reached for the child with his free hand, but she had backed away in fear from the keening blade and was just out of reach. He leaned over to recapture her hand.

"Guards, to me!" Nereis shouted. Elric was suddenly surrounded. Stormbringer cut gleefully through the shafts of pikes and the blades of puny swords, hacked deep into armor, sliced away limbs and fingers. Elric felt the disgusting satisfaction of the demon blade sucking the soul from one of the men-at-arms. The man died screaming. Elric concentrated on defending himself by wounding only, avoiding kills if possible.

Two more corpses had joined the first by the time Nereis called off his guard. Elric, panting, looked around him for the child. She was gone, and Tabisian with her.

"Now, my lord, perhaps, we can talk about your aid," Nereis said, elbows propped on his chair arms, fingers tented. He no longer looked soft or frightened. Archers had flooded into the chamber and knelt, lining the walls, their bows nocked to the ear. "If you attempt to attack Tabisian or me again you will die, no matter how badly we need you."

Elric was splashed with blood, though none of it was his own. Exhausted, he let a little vitality from Stormbringer flood his veins. "If anything has happened to that child, *you* will die, and nothing can prevent it."

"A spell only," Nereis said, spreading his palms in appeal. "That's all it needs. Send to Lord Straasha and bid him calm his seas to spare my town. Then you and the child can be on your way. This is a trading port, my lord. True, we are not as wealthy as our neighbors. They won't chide us forever for our poverty, but to make them stop, we must survive!"

Elric wasn't listening. He was sensing a wave of fear. The white child broadcast terror as she was carried away. She was unused to such treatment. Evidently the wizard who had bred her had had no idea what to do with her beyond the experiment until the seas had begun to rage around the island. Now she was truly a pawn in a gods' game: prize or sacrifice, depending upon who won. In a way, Elric was grateful to Straasha for his fury with Solaidignia; else he might never have seen the girl. Now she needed his aid.

Stormbringer hummed its displeasure as Elric turned away from Lord Nereis. So many souls willing to die — the blade desired them. Elric felt distaste for the sword's frank hungers even as he knew he would probably soon require an infusion of the strength Stormbringer garnered from its victims.

"Come back!" Nereis called to him as Elric pushed his way out into the passageway. "My lord, you'll only get her alive in one way. Cooperation is all we ask."

Elric strode out into daylight. The sky had darkened alarmingly in the short time he had been inside. The gulls were gleaming specks of white on the metallic canvas of iron gray, riding the gusts of wind like bits of cork bobbing on the water's surface. If the howl of the wind was loud inside, it resounded deafeningly outside. Women hurried past from the docks with only a glance at the white-haired warrior. They kept looking back over their shoulders at the sea. One lass with long black hair in plaits had her fingers stuck in her ears as she ran. She glanced up at Elric. Her eyes widened as she realized what he was, and she stumbled away, disappearing into a narrow alley that led between two houses.

Elric listened more deeply than sound. Inside him, he heard the wail of the frightened girl as he tried to place her location spatially. He could only do as he had in coming to Solaidignia. He followed the sensation of her reality in the direction in which it was strongest. That led straight across the seaward side of the town.

His horse was nowhere in sight. The grooms had fled, probably when the call went out for archers and men-at-arms. He didn't dare to waste precious moments seeking a substitute. Time was fleeing before him.

He pushed his way into the narrow maze of streets that led through the dock district. None of the pathways led straight toward the feeling of the child's woe. At every intersection four or five narrow, stinking alleys offered themselves. Elric cast about for the one which would lead him the most directly. The blaze of his red eyes and the gleam of his sword frightened away any of the district's inhabitants who might have led him.

One of his pathways dead-ended in a blind alley filled with baskets of refuse. A small cat, disturbed from its meal of rotting fish, hunched its back and hissed defiance. Elric almost smiled, though he was frustrated. The longer he was separated from the child, the greater the chance that the wizard could spirit her forever out of his reach. Already he knew they must have flown from Nereis's castle, using some eldritch aid. But where to? And how much farther would they go? Elric ran up and down the streets, crossing and recrossing his own path. His boots slipped on the muddy cobbles as he cursed the unsteady footing. Drying nets slung between the buildings impeded him. He slashed through them with Stormbringer, seeing the threads shrivel up like burning spider's webs as he strode through.

And everywhere people were running; running away from the sea, running for their possessions and children, running from the strange man with the huge demon sword. He thrust them aside with careless strength, caring only for the sensation that led him onward.

He emerged from the tangle of alleys on the waterfront, halfway from the castle to the cliff-face. The sea roiled and rumbled dangerously only yards from his feet, and Elric wondered exactly what the rune had shown. Had the people of Solaidignia offended the Elementals to such a degree that the Sea King was determined to destroy them? To disturb Straasha to ask such a question was to play precisely into the hands of Nereis and his wizard.

A clattering on the stones alerted him. Elric looked up to see a young man on horseback riding along the waterfront from the castle. He wore Nereis's livery. This must be a messenger, probably sent to tell Tabisian that the Melnibonéan had escaped.

Elric deliberately put himself in the horse's path. The metallic song of his sword blade stopped the animal in mid-gallop. Whinnying, the animal reared. Expertly, the rider brought the animal under control. Elric grabbed for the reins. The rider made as if to strike out with his crop at the man obstructing his way, then focused his vision. He blanched, and his jaw dropped. Elric seized the leads under the horse's jaw with one hand, and leveled Stormbringer with the other. The blazing fury in his eyes caused the rider to dismount without further demur. He turned and fled as Elric vaulted up onto the horse's back. He sheathed Stormbringer and kicked the beast to a gallop.

So the wizard's fastness was this way! And there must be a road wide enough to allow a horse to pass. Elric kicked the horse to a canter, guiding its direction through his knees as the sense of the child guided his mind.

So much had happened in the last hour that Elric felt befuddled. Which God of Chaos could have aided Tabisian in bringing to birth a natural child from a drop of blood? Elric was furious that it was *his* blood with which the wizard had chosen to toy. He sensed the hand of his patron god, Arioch, who must have decided to punish Elric by splitting his vitality between two bodies.

There was a strong imbalance of power in this place. Elric could fell the wrongness, tasting it in the air like a sour, metallic tang. Between the Sea Lord and his wizard there existed some unholy pact to grasp power. But whose? And with what weapons?

The sea's rage worsened. Boats only half-full of fish slammed into the harbor. The crew tied off the lines and fell onto the wooden dock, all but kissing the filthy boards in gratitude to have made it ashore alive. If it got worse, there wouldn't be a square yard of dry land on the island within a day. Elric wondered if the Sea Elementals heard the girl's cries for help. Since the child's aura was so much like Elric's, Straasha might have thought it was the prince who was in danger, and done his best to respond. There was little they could do on land, and the creatures of Air were not as kindly disposed toward Elric as those of Water. Formless things starting to throw themselves up on the piers, causing screaming sailors and dock workers to flee inland. One man dashed hysterically into the street, ending up under the hooves of Elric's steed. He lay still on the cobblestones, bleeding from a scalp wound, the whites of his eyes rolled up. Elric was sorry for the man, but had no time to stop and see if he was dead or only wounded. The child had first call on his aid.

The winds blew nets and small boats across in front of him. Drying fish strung on lines narrowly missed him as they tore loose from ranged poles at the waterside. Tossing waves threw the moored ships into the air like toys.

With a snap like a thousand bones breaking, the keel of a ship broke as two waves heaved it back and forth between them. Lazily, the sea tossed one half of the ship onto the dock and swallowed the other. Indeed, these people were in danger. Elric couldn't understand Lord Nereis's stubbornness in refusing to abandon the island.

All around him, people were bundling up their few possessions and heading for the land bridge. Elric had to urge the horse through the large crowds moving in the opposite direction to follow the child's trail. Where the way was clear, he kicked the horse to a trot.

He turned a corner, which opened up into a wide road leading uphill. It was strangely empty of inhabitants. A few paces ahead of him the road was obscured by a fume of yellow-brown. The smell of salt air, dead fish and old timber became abruptly polluted with another smell that Elric recognized at once: dark sorcery. He pulled up the horse's rein, but not soon enough. As soon as the beast's nose touched the ochre haze, Elric was thrown off its back by a huge burst of magic flame that consumed the screaming horse. Elric ended up in the angle of a wall covered in cobwebs, plaster dust and salt. He realized grimly that the messenger had returned to Nereis in time to send word in some other way that Elric was coming: Time enough to set a trap like this.

Elric rose slowly to his feet, drawing his sword. The fume was gone. Evidently the trap was made to take the first being that wandered into it. Tabisian was interested only in gimmickry and power. A rat could have tripped the spell, leaving the wizard's defenses open to whoever came next. No wonder he had made a magic child and waited six years to make use of her. Tabisian lacked foresight.

As Elric had guessed, the rest of the road up to the fortified house at the top of the hill was unguarded. The Melnibonéan kicked open the great door, brandishing his sword in an arc until his eyes grew accustomed to the gloom within.

What wealth there was in Solaidignia was divided between Nereis's castle and this place. Gold and gems were inlaid in wooden wall panels. The best work of the last five hundred years: decorated furniture, book boxes, windows, and floors. Tapestries of fine silk and woven leather displayed magic pictures that shifted and flowed like dreams. Such had not been seen since the days of the Bright Emperors. Elric wondered how this man had laid hands upon them. Tabisian had many questions to answer.

His sense told him the child was below the level where he stood. Her fear was a palpable trail that led through the fortress to a stone staircase. Tabisian's servants never challenged him. They gave him a single glance and took to their heels. He heard doors slam in the distance.

The stairs bore a film of water that made the stone slippery. Elric walked with great care ten, twenty, a hundred steps, all the time spiralling downward. His sensitive nose detected the salt of the sea and the occasional freshening of a breeze. Somewhere below him the caverns must be open to the sky.

The ticking of his heels on the stone beat out a hypnotic rhythm. Combined with the endless downward loop, the tapping dulled his mind so much he nearly missed the quiet hiss of something sliding onto the steps above and behind him. Elric turned at bay.

Looming over him was a horror which could only have come from the remotest depths of the sea. Its formless, dark-purple body was scaled here and there in patches of ultramarine, green, turquoise, and blue. The monster let out a roar and rolled down the few steps toward him. Eight — no, ten — no, six pseudopods reached for him. Stormbringer flew upward and passed through a waving arm of purple and green, severing it. The arm slipped to the floor and rejoined the mass. The creature wailed its agony. The mass split into three identical but smaller beings and tried to surround him. The flashing sword kept them at arm's length. The creatures keened, seeking to strike at him. They exuded pseudopods over and under the arc of steel until Elric failed to parry one. The contact burned through his left sleeve and into his flesh like salt rubbed into an open wound. He gasped, bringing up Stormbringer, which chopped the undulating mass once, twice, and again, until the monster backed away, keening.

Elric slipped between the triple beings and fled down the stairs, wincing at the pain in his left arm. He did not recognize their kind but he knew to whom they belonged. These were creatures of the Elementals of Water. No wonder the sea wished to swallow this place!

Toothy monsters with bony exoskeletons like sea horses undulated upward on snaky tails to meet him. The outlines of their bodies glowed with green ghostlight. Without arms or legs, they were defenseless against Stormbringer. Elric killed as many as he could and hurried onward, down into the darkness. The child's summons were becoming urgent.

Dried sea wrack and strands of kelp matted the floor of the great cavern Elric found at the foot of the stairs. What little light there was glimmered from hand-sized globes of green dotting the walls at eye-level. At last he saw Tabisian and the girl. They stood against the wall opposite, only a couple of dozen paces away across a pool of darkness. Elric lunged for the magician, then realized that at his feet a ravine yawned. He stopped himself falling into it just in time, and looked for a way around to the girl.

"Have you made your mind to help us, Lord Elric?" Tabisian called. He pushed the child out a small way. The sensation of panic lessened as soon as the child saw him. She was glad to see him! Elric became more determined to free her from the man who had made her.

"You are the one doing all this!" Elric shouted across at him. "You offend the Elementals of Water by enslaving their minions, then expect others to intercede for you? Cease, and you may live."

"I cannot!" Tabisian cried, throwing out his hand. "I am stretched to the limit, helping my lord. Too much depends upon my maintaining all the spells which I have laid. Help us! Call on the Elemental: tell him we are under your protection, and you shall have her. You owe me something for bringing her to birth, my lord Elric. Summon the Sea King. I will give you any tools you need for the spell."

"Give her to me and I will spare your life." Elric said tightly. "That is all I owe you. I will not bargain. She is of Melnibonéan blood, and must come with me. You have no right to her. Straasha is entitled to his revenge for your interference in his domain. The town is forfeit. You may escape if you can before Straasha causes it to be swallowed up if you leave now."

"No!" Tabisian shouted.

The child raised her hands out to Elric in mute appeal. Elric cast to one side, then the other. The lip of stone upon which he stood extended only a few feet to either side. He could not walk all the way around. Nor could he jump. Tabisian must have used a spell or an artifact to allow him to fly over there. Elric at last conceded that only diplomacy would save the girl. Her wide, red eyes, just as he had seen them in his dream, pleaded with him.

"If you give me the child, I will aid you," Elric said slowly.

"No!" Tabisian said. "The spell first, my lord. Should I give you the child, what other hold have I over you?"

"My word of honor!" Elric shouted.

But Tabisian wouldn't trust him. With one hand, he clutched the girl by her skinny neck and held her out over the void. Her small bare hands and feet dangled over empty air. She looked like a frightened white kitten.

"Call the Sea God, Lord Elric. Summon him *now*. If you do not recall the rune, I do. I will recite it for you, but you must summon Straasha now. Do it, or she dies!"

The wave of panic the child broadcast nearly knocked Elric off his feet. He could throw his sword like a spear across the gap, pinning Tabisian to the wall, but there was no guarantee the girl would fall on the ledge. Elric could still walk away and let the wizard do as he pleased, but he knew he would never be at peace if he let the girl die.

"Let me go," the child whimpered in a meek, little voice, turning her face toward Tabisian. "Master, don't hurt me."

"Do not hurt her any more," Elric said, swallowing the anger he felt. He kept his voice level, trying to keep from alarming the girl. "I will perform the spell. Draw her back."

Tabisian beamed, creases appearing in his broad, swarthy face. "Well! Reason at last, my lord. You will not regret this, I swear. She is yours."

He drew the girl back toward him. But her weight had caused him to lower his arm slightly, and her heel caught on a protruding rock at the edge of the ravine. As Elric watched helplessly, the little body jerked loose from Tabisian's grasp and slipped down the rock face. The wizard grabbed for her, but he wasn't quick enough. The child, desperate red eyes upturned to Elric, screamed for his help as she fell. Elric flattened himself on his ledge, reaching out with his scabbard, extending to the uttermost length of his body. The girl's head snapped back as she hit a protruding boulder, and her eyes closed. The body tumbled down and down until it landed in a crumpled heap like a discarded rag of white linen. Her disordered hair hid her face, but Elric had her last, desperate appeal imprinted on his eyes forever. The magical aura that had drawn him hundreds of miles over more than thirty days thinned and vanished. The intelligence, the soul he'd felt when he met her, was gone.

Elric drew himself to his knees and screamed his grief to the heavens. Cheated of the future he had only just begun to grasp, he snarled with fury. "No one will be spared! I, Elric, swear this! No one!"

Tabisian, stupefied by the accident, snapped out of his own shock. Elric was likely to begin fulfilling the vow of vengeance on his own person. Muttering incantations to himself, Tabisian began to rise from the stone ledge, hovering upward toward another cavelike opening in the wall some thirty feet above their heads.

The murderer must not be allowed to escape! Elric, mad with grief, leaped across the void. Only moments ago he would have considered such an attempt suicidal, but now he did not care.

He missed his footing only by inches, and clutched with his fingertips at the stone ledge. The least weakness in his fingers and he would fall. To survive now to kill the murderer would take the utmost concentration. Elric flattened his other forearm on the level ground above, trying to pull himself upward. Maliciously, Tabisian dropped from the air to stamp on Elric's wrist and kick away his handhold. Clinging to the rockface, Elric called upon the superhuman vitality in Stormbringer, and pulled himself up, painful inch by inch. The sorcerer's glee changed to alarm as Elric crawled, panting, up onto the cliff. Tabisian turned to fly away, but could not outpace the swiftness of the demon blade. He threw a protective spell around himself that enveloped him like a golden globe. Stormbringer hacked easily through the bubble and sliced through the muscles of his leg. Pain broke the wizard's concentration, and he fell to the stone ledge, screaming. Elric stood over him, drawing Stormbringer back for the fatal blow.

"Spare my soul!" Tabisian cried, choking in fear. Elric, knowing neither mercy nor pity as he gazed down at the small, crumpled form at the bottom of the pit, struck hard, cleaving the sorcerer's body from collar to sternum.

He wiped the corpse's blood from Stormbringer on the man's own robe, and sheathed it. An ominous rumble, subterranean or possibly submarine, issued from deep within the void. Elric realized that with Tabisian dead his sorceries would disintegrate. This entire complex which he had constructed was falling apart. Elric heard a rushing as the sea, long denied its caverns and secret places, hurried in. Within moments, the void would be full of water, and churning, angry elementals.

Elric would have taken the child's body and given her a princess's funeral, but he dared not take the time to pick her up, nor did he dare encumber himself. He might not be able to escape to take vengeance on the other author of the child's doom.

He ran along corridors already losing their magical gilding. Precious stones faded to bits of colored glass, and the handsome woodwork rotted away to splintered fragments.

Sea creatures of horrific description pushed past him as he ran up the hundreds of stone stairs. Freed of the spells keeping them on dry land, they hastened to return to the welcoming depths.

The rumbling was all around Elric now, shaking the walls and ceilings, dropping beams and plaster and stone into the corridors. A huge stalactite broke off with a crack and plummeted to the ground just moments before Elric would have run underneath it. Two of Tabisian's human servants were less lucky, crushed to death by the hail of small building stones that followed. Elric heard no cries for help from the rubble as he clambered over, running for sunlight.

Outside the wizard's fastness, Nereis and his men were waiting for him. Grim-faced, Elric brought Stormbringer on guard. The blade, appetite whetted by the soul of the wizard, keened a song inaudible but certainly perceived by Elric's mortal opponents. They rolled the whites of their eyes at him as Nereis shouted to him.

"Fool!" Nereis blazed, shouting over the rumbling of the earth. "You have but to cooperate, not kill, and we could share power, *wealth* here! The child would be yours."

"The child is dead," Elric said flatly, without raising his voice. "So is Tabisian. Flee for your lives. I shall. That is all I have to say to you."

"You shall not leave," Nereis growled. He drew his sword and spurred his white horse. "At him!"

Even with Stormbringer's eldritch aid Elric hadn't a hope of standing against such a large force. Surprising Nereis's men, and even himself, he thrust into the crowd, swinging the sword, hacking at limbs and heads, feeling the sword's unholy joy as it devoured soul after soul.

He cleaved through other blades and pikestaffs, and eventually found he had broken through to the other side of Nereis's guard. This time the narrowness of the streets and the byways of the town was on his side. With corpses piled upon one another, it was difficult for the men who remained living to pursue him. Nereis screamed orders from his horse's back. Men sprang forward to remove the obstructions, but Elric had a head start.

He must not go toward the castle. More men, probably including archers, would be following. Elric took the first left turning, and found himself again on the waterfront, very close to the cliff face. His ribs and legs ached from his effort, and warm wetness flowed down both sides of his face. He dashed a hand over his cheek and looked at it. The liquid was not blood, but tears. He mourned for the death of the child, and for what could have been. It was the end of any hopes he might have had for his line. He wished the child had stayed a dream. Her all-too-brief reality had opened a wound in his soul that would never heal.

Shouting erupted behind him. If the line of Melniboné was not to end right there, Elric must make his escape. He drew further upon the hated power in Stormbringer. Ignoring the pain in his side and his heart, he ran. Pushing puzzled sea folk to one side, he dashed over the boardwalk, judging each fishing boat in turn. Could one of these take sail quickly enough to carry him safely away? Could one be used to pursue him? None should have the opportunity to try.

A dozen yards ahead of him women in salt-stained skirts were weaving rope with bubbling pitch in a cauldron. Using the magical strength to bolster him, Elric yanked up a driftwood piling and plunged it into the pitchpot, then set it ablaze at the fire beneath. He ran from pier to pier, setting fire to the tar-soaked mooring ropes of each boat, letting the rough sea carry each away from the town.

The guards were closing in behind him. Elric leaped over stinking carcasses of fish, broken baskets, tangling piles of net, knowing that these obstructions would also hamper his pursuers. With Stormbringer in one hand and the burning brand dripping pitch in the other, he looked like some Chaotic fury as he set fire to lines and ships. As each blazed up, destroying all hope of escape for hundreds of Solaidignians, he thought: This is for the child.

None of the ships or boats he saw looked as though they would be capable of a turn of speed. He was nearly to the cliff. In a moment, he would be trapped. Which way to turn? Then he saw the door.

Cut into the rock of the cliff face, invisible from sea or land until one was almost on top of it, was an opening twice the height of a man. Elric leaped down the long ramp and dashed through the archway. Behind him, the guard came over the rise and pursued him into the darkness. Underfoot, the wooden floor echoed the rhythm of his footsteps. Arrows whisked past him. He realized the torch he held made him a perfect target. He made to throw it away, then stared around him at what its light fell upon.

Concealed within this cave was a vast fleet of warships at anchor, already tossing dangerously on the rising waves. So that was why they wouldn't evacuate the island! Lord Nereis refused to give up his fleet, even at the cost of the lives of his people. Probably he had had ideas of attacking his neighbors and conquering more sheltered harbors and more profitable trading ports, until the sea took offense at Tabisian's overreaching into its realms. Nereis was a man who planned long for the future. Elric would have admired such a mind if it hadn't attempted to make a pawn of him.

Shipwrights and dockhands already in the cavern flattened themselves against the walls as the men-at-arms flooded in. Elric braced himself as the guardsmen rushed him. Nereis's voice, a noise of screamed commands garbled by hoofbeats, footsteps, and the clash of steel, echoed off the cavern ceiling. With superhuman strength, Elric parried the first man's thrust, gutted him with Stormbringer, and flung the corpse back into the throng of guards. Elric took the momentary confusion as an opportunity to jump for the first ship.

With the torch, he set the fine, painted, brass-fitted craft aflame. The wood was newly varnished and oiled, and caught fire readily. The fire provided a handy delay to the men behind him as he leaped from ship to ship, turning each one into a burning brand. The cavern began to fill with pitch-smoke. Elric sheathed Stormbringer and drew a fold of cloth across his mouth and nose.

He jumped from ship to ship, thrusting the flame into the sails lashed tightly to the booms. Cries and wails went up from the shipwrights huddled together in the innermost lip of the cave among the burning hulls. Men-at-arms, slipping and swearing, bounded along behind him. Lacking his eldritch strength, many of them fell into the water between tossing ships. Elric heard the screams as the ships bobbed together, crushing the unlucky. He came to the last vessel. Two men, more determined than the rest, had kept up with him. They sprawled on the deck of the final ship just as Elric slashed loose the mooring lines. The Melnibonéan called upon Stormbringer's evil strength to help him shove off singlehandedly from the pier.

The two men, seeing that no help would reach them over the steadily widening gap between ship and dock, attacked Elric. Stormbringer had taken an unlimited supply of soul-strength, and the prince made short work of them. One man fell with a single gasp, the other died begging for his life. The men he left behind could be doing no better. It was no longer possible to see Nereis or his men. If they hadn't fled they must be dying of suffocation in the smoke-filled cavern.

His ship drifted out under the low stone arch facing the sea. Elric flattened himself on deck, watching a ribbon of light widen into a full, silver sky. The gunwales bumped heavily again and again, splintering the beautiful carved rails into firewood, but at least most of the ship made it intact. Once it was in the open air, Elric sheathed his sword and dragged up sail. This was an admirable craft. Every line was greased, responding to the first pull. A cunning series of blocks and tackles helped him raise and swiftly seat the main mast in a socket set on the main deck for the purpose. The ropes, supple as leather, he tied down in strong knots. Elric tacked, using the wind blowing straight inland to bring him around the rough harbor's edge and thence out to sea.

Nereis's plans were clever and well laid, with only a single exception. Such a man would have been a good general, but his plans were either too small or too grandiose. A pirate fleet such as Elric had left burning behind him could have ruled all the southern seas, let alone two or three small and ill-defended peninsulae. Or Nereis could have made a fortune selling the services of his shipwrights all around the civilized world. His only error had been not keeping a closer watch on his wizard. Sharing power was dangerous. It was better to be alone. Elric knew that from long experience.

Yes, alone. He was alone; alone again. It was better that Tabisian was dead. To have a man living who knew the secret of raising true life from a single drop of blood was too dangerous. He could have created demons instead of kings. In any case, all his skill had bought him was his doom. Elric hated him and Nereis for the death of hope. He hated them for compelling him to ride southward for an endless month on the weary heels of battle, and all for nothing. Most of all, he hated them for making him drink so deeply of other men's souls.

Risking the rocks in the outer harbor, Elric abandoned the sail sheets and strode to the prow. He concentrated on a rune he dredged from memory. Putting his mind in the correct frame of reference, he called to Straasha, the Sea King. This was not the rune for which Tabisian had hoped, to summon him, but merely a spell for communication. In his mind's eye he saw the turquoise hair and green skin of the Sea Elemental. Lips over fishlike teeth spread in a mirthless grin as Straasha recognized his one-time comrade's call.

"Straasha, they're yours!" Elric cried. "Take them! There's nothing for me here. There never was," he said sadly, allowing contact to fade. With heavy feet, he stepped back to the tiller, steering a true course for the northeast.

The dark ship heeled silently, like a funeral barge, flowing sedately against the wind. Behind her, the seas rose up and concealed the island of Solaidignia from view. When the waves parted again, Elric saw no one alive.

TEMPTATIONS OF IRON

BY COLIN GREENLAND

"A Sword, gentlemen, a Sword!"

"The devil you say so!" cried Sinden Creache, starting forward. His other two opponents, long eliminated from the battle, gave a simultaneous groan and curse from the bench against the wall.

With a flashing white smile, the slender traveler showed his hand.

"The Three, to be precise," he said.

And with a mocking bow he tossed the rectangle of pasteboard into the center of the table.

Sinden Creache exhaled noisily. He looked distempered. He twisted his mouth in a sour expression, looking the victor full in the face as he had done but rarely that evening. He confronted the weak crimson eyes, the bone-white skin, the hair no less white. He seemed on the verge of making an accusation, a denial of some kind.

The traveler was unperturbed. He was used to animosity from the human race, unreasoning hostility being a characteristic humor of that upstart kind. His smile merely became a degree or two bleaker.

"The girl is mine," said Elric of Melniboné.

From his seat in the corner, where he could watch both doors of the bar, Moonglum of Elwher whistled silently between his teeth. There'd be trouble now, one way or another. Then he grinned, his ugly mouth stretching broadly across his weatherbrowned face. Traveling with Elric, what else had he ever had but trouble? Better a quarrel with a would-be welsher who didn't know who it was that had beaten him at tarocco than the ruined prince's displeasure. If Elric had lost the game it would have meant tedious hours of orations about doom and the malevolent gods. Let the stupid merchant try to talk Elric out of his slave. Moonglum's hand slipped to his belt, fingering the pommel of his dirk.

Then the vanquisher had the satisfaction of seeing the recalcitrant Creache turn to snap his fingers at the brown figure crouching patiently by the hearth.

As the slave stood up, looking nowhere but at the floor in front of her, Creache said loudly, loud enough for the whole company to hear, "Stiis, this is your new master. Go with him and obey him. And may you bring him half the bad luck you've brought me." Then he swept his cloak about him and strode rudely from the room, his friends hurrying after him.

Prince Elric, too amused by his victory to notice the discourtesy, reached out his long, white fingers and touched the young woman under the chin, lifting her face to his.

She was sixteen, perhaps, of about Moonglum's height, and slim beneath her homespun dress. She was dark, her skin brown as fumed oak, her thick hair stained the same deep, burnt red as the palms of her hands. The skin was darkest, Moonglum noted, around her heavy lips and her eyes, which were large, and brown too. They stared suspiciously, sullenly, into Elric's red ones, and did not flinch. She had not favored her departing master with so much as a glance.

There was no way to know whether she had understood his final order or not. She had made no sound all evening, nor given any sign of comprehension. She was completely mute, Creache had said.

"Stiis," said Elric. "Welcome into the royal household of the Bright Empire." And he grinned mirthlessly.

Moonglum swilled the dregs of mucky ale doubtfully around in his pot before lifting it and downing them in a swallow. He grimaced. "I remember you decrying the slavers' trade," he observed.

Elric's eyes never left the face of the slave. Lightly he ran a fingertip along the line of her jaw from the brass ring in her ear to the corner of her chin. "What is any of us," he asked softly, "but a slave? Back and forth across this blighted land we toil under the accursed whips of Law and Chaos, seeking only a little respite, a little place to rest our heads...."

Moonglum yawned hugely and deliberately, stretching out his arms and curtailing the monologue. "Yes, well, that's where I'm going right now, Elric," he said. "Are you coming up?"

Moonglum was hoping he wasn't. He was hoping Elric would sit up half the night filling himself with the strongest wine, as he had done last night and the night before. Lodgings in Karluyk were so scarce he and his traveling companion had been obliged to take a single room, and sleep for Prince Elric was not a restful state for anyone else. For Prince Elric, the strongest wines were rarely strong enough.

Elric was gazing into the wide brown eyes of his prize. "Yes, Moonglum," he said. "Yes, I think we shall."

Moonglum glanced at him uneasily, and at the girl, who stared intently, fearlessly at her new master's alarming face.

The room was on the first floor, at the end of a crooked low corridor. Shadows bounded around as Moonglum entered. The only light was the ailing candle he himself had carried up from below. He looked in the corners and up among the rafters and under the beds before setting the light on a dusty three-legged stool that stood beside his bed.

He supposed there would be less work now if they had a slave. Still, certain basic tasks of housekeeping he would always prefer to do himself. He checked that the windows were latched, and wished as usual that there were locks to them. Then, unfastening his belt, he removed the dirk from it and slipped it as delicately under his limp pillow as any pilgrim his amulet.

The young woman stood watching while Elric unbuckled the great sword from his back and laid it under his bed. Then, while her new master pulled off his boots, Stiis curled up to sleep on the foot of his bed, for all the world like a favored hound.

Moonglum shook his head. He scratched his heavy mop of hair and, raising one eyebrow at Elric in inquiry, blew out the candle end. The room filled with the darkness of midnight and a new moon.

"Pleasant dreams to you, Master Moonglum," said Elric lightly.

Moonglum dreamed he was riding high in a blood-streaked sky on the back of a metal bird. His perch felt highly insecure. Someone was shouting to him from the ground, and he felt an urgent need to hear whatever it was they were trying to say.

He woke. It was the voice of a man, crying out sharply. Moonglum was half-sitting up in bed with his knife in his hand before he recognized the voice and remembered where they were. It was only Elric, with his customary nightmares.

He relaxed; until another cry, a different voice, startled him.

She was not completely dumb, then.

Moonglum lay still and listened to the unmistakable sounds of sexual congress.

He was amused, and a little surprised. Since Myshella Elric had refrained from women, preferring to get drunk and declaim gloomy poetry instead. The little slavegirl had obviously raised his spirits.

Moonglum grinned to himself in the dark. For all her skin was so dusky, this Stiis reminded him of Shaarilla of the Dancing Mist, the wingless Myyrrhnian who had been Elric's companion when they met. Moonglum had been rather fond of Shaarilla, and often wished Elric hadn't dumped her. Elric had been in a bad mood after Shaarilla. He had tormented Moonglum with it for days.

As the Melnibonéan accomplished his climax, Moonglum sighed silently. He turned his face to the wall and tried to pull the scanty covers over his ears. It was uncomfortable to have to listen to another man's pleasure while you yourself lay friendless. Perhaps they would be quiet now, he hoped. Elric was not a strong man, except when the evil force of the hellblade flooded his deficient arteries. No doubt he would fall asleep instantly.

The voice, when it came, struck ice into Moonglum's abbreviated bones.

It was low, every consonant soft-edged and every vowel deep and drawled. There was music in it, and yet it was subdued, as if disease or disuse compelled it to speak in a monotone.

"Melnibonéan, I charge you. I charge you. I charge you. I am your mistress now as you are my master."

Moonglum cursed and sat bolt upright. He groped for his tinderbox.

The couple ignored him and his candlelight. Prince Elric leaned back on his elbows, more at his ease than Moonglum had seen him in many a day. The slave straddled his midriff, her heavy hair hanging down over his face, and both her hands pressing together on his narrow chest. But for her nakedness she looked more like a child playing a game with a favorite uncle than any kind of enchantress. Beneath the bed Stormbringer lay inert as a slug of pig-iron. That was the most reassuring thing Moonglum had seen since he lit the candle. Still he kept hold of his knife.

Elric's voice was nonchalant. "What charge is this of which you speak?"

"I am a princess in my land," she said. "I swore to find a champion to lift the curse that is upon Chlu-Melnoth, and never to speak until I had laid that charge upon him and sealed it. On the barren coast of Samarianth I and all my companions were seized by raiders and sold into slavery. Since then I have watched and waited. Tonight the gods have smiled on me. They told me you were the one, Melnibonéan; and they told Sinden Creache to wager me on a last hand of cards.

"This is your task, champion. There is a demon abroad in Chlu-Melnoth. It cannot be defeated by iron, nor by cunning, but only by the dark arts. It will tempt you to use iron, but if you draw sword it will eat you."

She shifted on his stomach, arching her back. This had the effect of thrusting her bottom more prominently in Moonglum's direction. He winced. He preferred women with more meat on them, and he didn't care for all this stuff about demons and dark arts. Still, flesh was flesh. He lay back on his pillow, breathing slowly and staring deliberately up into the cobwebbed rafters.

"Fail me," said the slave princess, "and every hand in Chlu Melnoth will be turned against you. Prevail, and you shall rule at my side. We are not a rich people, but you shall want for nothing."

Elric spoke drowsily, as though her revelation had failed to make the slightest impression on him. "It has been many a day since any man presumed to command Elric of Melniboné," he remarked, "or any woman either."

His name seemed to mean nothing to her. "I knew you for a man of the Dragon Isle by your features and your accent. The gods marked you out to me. Melnibonéans have the ancient dark knowledge. Melnibonéans have no fear."

Wonderful, thought Moonglum as he lay listening to the hypnotic voice continue in the candlelight.

"And if I choose not to go?" asked Elric, as though she had invited him to a party.

"You will, champion. You must." An element of languid selfsatisfaction entered Stiis's tone. "Since you lay between my thighs you have been dedicated to the task. The royal blood of Chlu-Melnoth has this power."

"Then I shall follow you to the ends of the earth," said Elric equably, "and disembowel each demon at which you snap your fingers."

Moonglum grinned to himself. Elric was in a good mood. As for the girl's power of compulsion, Moonglum doubted very much it would outlast the night. Elric was humouring his new pet. Let him enjoy himself while he could. Gods knew it happened rarely enough.

Moonglum closed his eyes and left them talking as he slipped back into the merciful, warm, black waters of sleep.

Next time he woke it was what he had been expecting. They were good, quick and silent. Two of them were already in the room, a third climbing over the sill, his shape a dim blot against the stars.

Seizing his dirk, the hardy little outlander rolled sideways out of bed, trying to land lightly on the floor.

They heard him. One of them came for him while he was still crouching beside the bed, drawing his sabre from its sheath. The advantage of surprise lost, Moonglum yelled as he swiped at the intruder with his knife. "Elric, wake for your life!"

Moonglum's attacker was armed with a short sword. As he swung, Moonglum ducked under his arm, diving across the room towards the other bed. There was a cry — the girl — one of them had seized her, hauling her out of the way while the third sought to dispatch the Prince of Melniboné with a single swing, grunting, "Here's your three swords!"

Moonglum's assailant blocked his way. Moonglum feinted high with the dirk and cut low with the sabre. The man chopped downward with his blade — a butchery must have been these northerners' sword-school. He missed completely. Starlight gleamed faintly on their blades.

Elric was awake, Moonglum could hear that. Moving swift as a snake, he had rolled aside as the sword came down. The girl cried something in an unknown tongue. There was the sound of a sharp blow on a skull and she fell silent. Her captor began to haul her towards the door.

Elric and his attacker were tangling hand to hand. The man must have lost his sword. Moonglum ducked another savage cut — there was an advantage in the dark, men often underestimated his size — he thrust up with the dirk and felt it strike home. His assailant shouted out and lost his footing. The man went down, his head striking the floor, and lay still.

Elric shouted, landing a kick on the chin of his man and pulling free. "Stiis!" he shouted. There was no reply, save for the dragging of her feet on the bare boards. Elric flung himself back against the wall at the head of the bed, drawing up his feet. Why did he not reach for Stormbringer?

As Moonglum reached the bed there was a flurry of witchlight in the swarming air. Elric's attacker began to whinny and choke. He clawed desperately at something invisible in front of his eyes. Elric had caught him full in the face with some occult glamour.

Two down, one still fighting. Moonglum grabbed at the blinded man, who struggled violently, eluding his hands. Pausing only to pull the man's sword out of the mattress, Elric leapt across the unconscious form of Stiis, his naked body a white blur in the black air, white as the light of the all-seeing stars. The renegade prince menaced the thief with his own comrade's blade.

"Leave her, dog, and face me!"

They were made of something stern, these assassins, though they had underestimated their quarry badly. The last man was not giving up. Backing into the doorway, he held the lolling woman up in front of him, forcing Elric to thrust awkwardly from the side. He parried the thrust ably with a flick of his short blade.

Moonglum could hear Elric panting hard. Passion and fury were a fine fuel, but they would not last the frail albino long. Why did he not take up Stormbringer?

The mage-maddened man was still whimpering and clawing at the darkness. Moonglum caught his arm and twisted it up hard behind his back. Levering the man off-balance, he reached up with his knife. He could see dimly the sinews of the neck, standing out like wire in the man's panic. He could see the artery, pulsing like a worm beneath the skin. The dirk went up, in and across. The man jerked like a cut pig, flinging blood across the window, and fell to the floor, coughing and kicking.

Stiis was also on the floor. Elric had cut the man's hand, forcing him to let go of her. Still he was fighting back, and Elric was hard beset. Moonglum could tell exhaustion was close. "Elric!" he shouted. "I am here!" He flung himself into the battle, slicing at the man with his sabre, ready to take his cut arm off altogether.

Then the sky fell on his head.

Elric saw Moonglum crumple, saw the first man Moonglum had felled standing over him, the stool in his hands. Gasping now, the thin blood pounding in his temples, the Melnibonéan flung the dead man's sword clumsily at him and threw himself to the floor, grasping beneath the bed.

The men closed in. Both of them had swords now. They lifted them up in the starlight like a triumphal arch.

The hilt of Stormbringer fitted itself neatly into Elric's clutching hand.

At once he was filled with a violent energy, like white fire coursing through his veins. His lean frame unfolded. He stood on tiptoe, brandishing the black blade, his white hair crackling, floating in a wild aureole around his head.

The room was filled with moaning, sobbing, a low, ululant cry of longing and despair.

And Elric laughed.

"Do you weep now, you mercenary creatures, you pond-scum, you beetles, you less-than-worthless things? Do you cry for your misspent lives and your paltry misgotten pelf? Do you moan for mercy from Elric of Melniboné, White Wolf of the Sighing Sea?"

But it was the runesword which was groaning.

They knew him then. The raised blades fell clattering to the floor. The man who had taken Stiis turned and bolted for the door. The other, trapped by Elric in the angle between bed and wall, dropped to his knees. "Mercy, Lord Elric! If we had known it was you —"

The keening rose to a high clamor, the song of a desperate, vile appetite about to be sated.

Then in black lightning the black sword fell. Elric slew both, dispatching in a trice the mewling man at his feet, then turning with superhuman speed and leaping over the unconscious Stiis towards the man who was scampering down the corridor, clutching his wounded hand and crying out in terror.

Like a javelin Stormbringer flew, pulling Elric along behind it in its very eagerness. It lunged into the back of the fleeing man. The bedroom filled with his screams. An unearthly crimson light blazed in from the corridor, bathing the three forms that lay motionless on the floor, and the fourth, Moonglum's victim, still slowly writhing. A hideous sucking sound came through the doorway.

Stormbringer was feeding.

Elric, brandishing the hellsword as though the room still contained an enemy, an army of enemies, came stalking back in. The blade twitched towards the sprawling Stiis and he shouted. "No, Arioch, no!"

And the Chaos Lord was in sufficiently lenient or inattentive humor to allow his vassal to wrest the humming sword away from the slim form of the slave princess and plunge it into the breast of the man with the slashed throat.

Moonglum, rousing, his head throbbing, saw the room filled with the sick glow of the drinking sword and turned away in disgust. On hands and knees he crawled over to see if Stiis were still alive. She was breathing. She was unconscious, but not in danger from her abductors, from her hurt, or from her rescuer. Moonglum found himself feeling grateful she had seen nothing of her new champion's eternal shame.

Moonglum lifted her and eased her back into Elric's bed. The room fell silent. It would be a moment or two before the landlord would dare venture out to see what screaming demons had invaded his inn. He would find three dead robbers, two sleeping guests, a manic albino sitting on a stool and blood everywhere.

"Take good care of my princess."

It was Elric, sardonic, breathing hard. His eyes glowed like red needles in the darkness. It was obvious to Moonglum that whatever power of enchantment the slave claimed, Elric's hands were already at the disposal of a higher — lower — possession.

Elric righted the stool and sat on it, watching the last traces of gore as they vanished into the gleaming surface of the black blade. Moonglum's head was spinning. He patted his friend on the shoulder and stumbled back to bed, back into unconsciousness.

In the morning they sat in the yard on three of the shaggy local horses, watching them bringing out the bodies. A small crowd stared at the cloaked and hooded albino with a mixture of awe and detestation. Elric ignored them. The morning smelt of dung and sour beer.

Moonglum's head ached. "Will you not kill the merchant who sent these?" he asked.

"Let him live," Elric said, "for my greater glory." And he smiled wintrily around, acknowledging the crowd with ironic majesty.

Moonglum looked askance at Elric's slave, not letting her see him looking. The princess appeared to have suffered no ill effects from her attack: not even a bruise, Elric said. It was as if she did indeed have gods who protected her. She had found a jerkin of deep-green worsted to throw on over her slave's dress and had tied a silk kerchief of Elric's own, green too, about her neck. Sparing barely a glance for the sack-draped heap of drained bodies, she shortened the rein and turned her face to the north-east.

"Come, Elric."

"Your Highness."

Moonglum looked concernedly at his friend's face as he rode past. It was unlike Elric to carry a jest so long; or at all, really.

They rode up to the high plains country. The ground was stony, the roads negligible. Flocks of drab brown birds rose from the meadows as they passed, sweeping up into the air like a thrown cloak and settling again immediately after. On the skyline, yellow and black barns slid gradually into dilapidation while crippled windmills signalled forlornly into the sky.

They rested in a shed at an abandoned stockade. Moonglum lit a small fire for Elric's potion. While it was brewing, Stiis sat on Elric's lap. She kissed his mouth and murmured into his translucent, pointed ear. Endearments or incantations, Moonglum was not allowed to hear.

They rode on again shortly after noon. Down in a gully a man was digging with a heavy spade. He looked suspiciously at the travelers as they rode by above him, then bent again to his unprofitable labor, not even sparing them a greeting.

They slept at lonely inns, at farms, once in a barracks of shepherds. Hospitality in these parts was given grudgingly, and reckoned down to the last farthing. Stiis had, if anything, less tolerance even than Elric for such dealings. Moonglum thought she would have had her tame wolf skewer any who impeded her mission by so much as hesitating over the porridge. Impatiently, she urged them always onwards. Elric recited interminable epic poems in the Old High Tongue of Melniboné. It was all one to her, as long as he kept following.

Moonglum grew disgruntled. He had gone right off Stiis as soon as he knew she was not what she appeared to be. He got Elric on his own. "I do not know what you see in her," he said.

"She does not want me for my sword," said Elric.

"Well, yes, but — "

Elric interrupted, gesturing delicately to his own breast. "She does not know who I am," he said with pride. "I think you cannot imagine what that means to me, Moonglum. Where should I find another such?"

Everywhere, Moonglum thought. Not everyone was as preoccupied with the doomed lord of the Dragon Isle as he was himself. There were other legends. Instead of saying this, he hitched up his breeches and scanned the desolate terrain: broken fences and cabbage fields. "Lucky if you can find anyone out here," he said.

They rode over a bridge guarded by a stone carving of a troll, or perhaps a real troll turned to stone.

"Tell me of this demon," Elric said.

"It lives in the earth and is conversant with the dead," said Stiis obscurely. "Its shape is loathsome, its arms grip like the devil-fish. When it moves, it moves very suddenly, like a spider. It will devour several people at once."

Elric merely nodded. Probably he had heard of its kind. Probably he knew some elemental that ate them for breakfast.

Moonglum reckoned he himself was having the worst of it on this trek. He was bored. His feet itched for city streets, his ears for human voices. When anything moved he grabbed Elric's arm and pointed excitedly. "Look! A coyote! Look at that!"

Stiis ignored him, while Elric gazed dreamily. Gods knew what he could see out there. He was sustaining himself by herbs and chipped roots, pinches of powder from a small pewter box. Stormbringer he had swaddled like a newborn infant, binding the sword into its sheath with strips of woven stuff, then wrapping the whole thing in sack and binding it again. He slept with Stiis in his slender arms, and for once his sleep was quiet.

Moonglum scratched beneath his cap. He disbelieved in all of it: demon, princess and kingdom, all in one parcel together. He had never heard of any of the names. What was more, there was something devious about the route she was leading them. She consulted the stars more often than the ground. Yet though he mistrusted the cause and feared the outcome, because the tortured prince seemed to be at peace for once, or thereabouts, Moonglum kept his own counsel.

"Tell me again of Far Chlu-Melnoth," Elric bade her, mildly. His face was gaunt in the mornings, and he gasped sometimes while riding, as though plagued by old wounds; but still the runesword stayed wrapped on the packhorse, like a piece of baggage.

"Far?" echoed Moonglum, aghast. They sat on a high bluff with bleak grey downs beyond, eating roadbread and dried apples. There had been no sign of habitation for days.

"Not very far, little man," said Stiis patronizingly. She considered him Elric's manservant, and it annoyed Moonglum every time he failed to convince her he was a free agent.

"*How* far," he asked, adding for Elric's sake as much as her own, "Your Highness?"

Stiis lifted her brown face to the sky. "Soon we shall be there," she said confidently. "Can you not smell it in the wind?"

Moonglum sniffed obligingly. He could smell grass and horses and themselves. The wind was as cold as ever, and as uncommunicative.

Elric touched Stiis's hand. He often seemed to be suing for her attention these days, as if he felt he depended on her in some way. To her he never spoke impatiently, let alone imperiously. Moonglum thought he had never seen him so passive. It was somehow unpleasant, like the moment between a bad cut and the pain.

"Stiis? Will you speak?"

Stiis shifted in place, drawing herself a fraction away from his tremulous white hand. She looked away across the downs and spoke at random. "The horses of Inaurim are fleeter than the sharks in the sea. In Samarianth a woman once put her hand to the ground and picked up a diamond as big as a vulture's egg. My tent is large enough to race three horses around inside."

Horses featured prominently in these descriptions, Moonglum had noticed. He had also begun to feel the absence of palaces, cities, houses of pleasure, buildings of any kind whatsoever, apparently. If he got one more inkling they were traveling as aimlessly as a fly on a windowpane, he would challenge her. Damn Elric's tranquility.

Then they were compelled to make a detour to find a particular ingredient for the albino's increasingly elaborate infusions.

Stiis was displeased. There was nothing of the slave about her now, nor of the infatuated lover. "Have I found Melniboné's only weakling?" she demanded in a temper.

Haltingly and distantly, Elric explained these simples were feeding his magical powers. "When he gets like this," Moonglum interjected quickly, "it means he's getting stronger and stronger. On another plane." He paused then, wondering whether there was any truth in what he had said, and why he was defending him to her. He was sure the pair of them were no longer making love, though they shared a bed. Waking one foggy midnight, and drawn from his blankets by an eerie noise, Moonglum had come upon her standing naked on a knoll and laughing at nothing visible. Perhaps she had been sleep-walking. Perhaps that was it.

Another day, at no particular point, Stiis suddenly kicked up her mount and rode ahead at speed, around a clump of black trees and out of sight. When they caught up with her she had the horse at a stand facing back down the track towards them. She was smiling, beaming. "This is my land."

Moonglum eased himself in the saddle and surveyed the waste all about them. Low gorse and raw rock, gritty yellow dust that clung to fetlock and mane, a pale hillside topped with duncolored trees — he saw no people, no tents, no horses; in short, no kingdom. He would have laid money they'd never left Ilmiora. He signalled to Elric with his eyes; but Elric was gone. His face looked starved as a shoulderblade, the skin taut from his cheekbones down to his long white teeth. His slanted eyes stared myopically over Moonglum's shoulder. "There's nothing here," said Moonglum loudly. They both ignored him.

They rode on, seeing no one, no sign of life all day.

Somewhere about mid-afternoon the princess led them down an escarpment to a black gash in the hillside. Moonglum understood it was the mouth of a cave. There was no smell, no spoor, but perhaps for a demon there would not be. In Elric's company Moonglum had seen demons enough to last him several lifetimes and still he felt he knew nothing.

Stiis told them both to dismount. Elric roused himself. With vague but steady hands he unstrapped the sacking bundle from the packhorse and thrust it into Moonglum's arms. He did it as if it were an action he had been rehearsing long in his mind.

Gingerly Moonglum received it. He was more than reluctant: he hated handling the evil thing. Elric had once told him, "Be wary of this devil-blade, Moonglum. It kills the foe — but savors the blood of friends and kin-folk most."

It felt like a sword tied up in a sack. It did not crawl or burn or start to sing. Still, it gave him the creeps. "What am I supposed to do with this?" he asked, his voice jerky and high.

"Keep it for me," said Elric, and his voice was low. For a moment Moonglum felt a flush of relief — Elric had some plan, some secret purpose — but then the albino added, "No matter how I beg."

The princess signalled to Moonglum. "Make fire," she said.

Moonglum started to get angry. "I beg your pardon?" he said, warningly.

"He will need a torch," said Stiis.

Moonglum exhaled noisily. He set the unwelcome bundle down on the ground and groped for his box.

No sound came from beneath the earth, though it was a while before he had enough fire to light a brand. More than enough time for Moonglum to make up his mind.

Stiis held the torch and led Elric into the darkness. She looked glad to think her kingdom's pain would soon be over.

Moonglum waited a minute. Then he picked up Stormbringer and followed.

The ground went down steeply inside the cave, the tunnel following a fault between two kinds of rock. It was low, and twisted, but did not branch. It was not hard to keep track of the torch, or to stay out of sight. When the princess stopped suddenly by a large boulder, Moonglum drew back and flattened himself against the wall.

"Within is the demon's lair," he heard her say. She sounded tense, excited. He looked. They had their backs to him. Stiis was ushering Elric before her through a natural doorway in the rock. She followed him in. Moonglum ran quickly to the boulder and ducked down behind it. He set his long bundle on the ground before him. Then, holding his breath, he peered round the boulder.

The doorway led into a cave several paces across and taller than a man. There were bones, strewn bones; accumulations of dirt and withered vegetation and rags that had been clothes; some metal that glinted among the rubbish, coins and jewelry, it might be, whose owners were no longer in a position to use them. Here there was at last a smell, the smell of something that was brutal, if not exactly a brute; but it was faint and stale, as though the creature had not been here for a long time.

Maybe some other champion had seen to it. Maybe it had gotten tired of waiting and died of old age.

Maybe it was lurking.

Elric stood in the center of the cave with his arms spread, as though about to begin an incantation. He turned to look around him. Moonglum ducked back out of sight. He heard Elric say, "Where is your demon, princess?"

And he heard the princess say, "Here, prince!"

Then the light changed. A fierce glow of no true fire flared up around the boulder. Moonglum grabbed the hilt of his sword, then let go of it. He stood up, gazing into the cave.

There was a demon in there. It was pale, and wet, and tall, its blunt head leering down over the unarmed Melnibonéan. It had large, hooved feet, but no legs to speak of, and great flat fins for hands. But even as Moonglum watched the fins folded moistly in against its flanks and were no more. Horrified, he watched as it changed shape, growing a beak and a spray of fat tentacles. They shot out and gripped Elric tight, drawing him into its body. Absentmindedly or parodically, it sprouted a pair of breasts.

Then it spoke. Her voice was pinched, coming from the rigid mouth. "At last I can shed that feeble form!"

Stiis was nowhere to be seen.

Glistening mandibles extruded suddenly from either side of the beak, sluicing Elric's white head with smoking drool. The tentacles were crushing the Melnibonéan's face into the soft, scaly body. Whatever spell he had been about to utter would never be spoken; nor, in a second or two, would anything else. His head was sinking into the demon's flesh. It had legs too now, lots and lots of legs.

Moonglum swore, his gorge rising. He clutched his sword, his knife. In agony, he hesitated. The creature had woven a maze of lies as tortuous as the passage to this cavern. How was he to know the right thing to do?

His hesitation lasted no more than a heartbeat. He had no magic, no power but the power of steel. He drew sabre and dirk together. If the curse was true, let it be proved on his own body. Let the thing eat him, if there were a chance it would let go of Elric of Melniboné.

Even as he started around the boulder, something rose up from the floor and hit Moonglum painfully across the knees. While he was hesitating, Stormbringer had taken its own decision. With a screeching sound of ripped leather and sack, it sliced straight through sheath, swaddling and all, and flew into the inner cave, into the pinioned hand of Elric.

At that the demon crowed with great glee.

Stepping inside after the flying sword, Moonglum looked up and saw the girl's head and torso reappear, green now instead of brown, larger than life, naked and glistening. "Now you are doomed, Lord Elric!" it squealed. "Touch but one limb with that blade — " Its legs telescoped out rapidly, flailing slimily against Elric's back and legs. Moonglum dodged as one came slicing past, missing him by inches. "— and you are mine throughout eternity!"

Elric dragged his face clear of her enveloping stomach. It came away with a sticky, squelching sound. "This is no ordinary blade, foul creature! This is Stormbringer," he screamed, his voice breaking, "the Stealer of Souls! Blood and souls for Lord Arioch!"

Moonglum winced as the cavern filled with blinding red light and the stench of sizzling ectoplasm. The keening of the hungry sword was ten times louder in the confines of the cave.

And the demon laughed on. "I know your sword, Prince of Ruins, as I know you! Destroyer of your own kind! Your own darling cousin!" it taunted him. "Stormbringer cannot harm me, my soul is long gone. Gone in fee for my invulnerability!"

The laugh grew higher, harsher, like the cry of a mad, giant seabird.

But Elric replied, and for all his frenzy there was pity in his tone. "Is that what he told you, Stiis? Is that what Theleb Kaarna wished you to believe? Then laugh at *this!*"

And with a clumsy, powerful jerk of his arm, he drew back the black blade and plunged it up between the writhing breasts.

The demon screamed. "It burns! It burns! Help me, Lord Kaarna! Help me — "

But there was no response to her prayer.

Moonglum averted his face from the flashing, flailing, screeching wreck. When he heard the grating, gurgling sound of Stormbringer starting to feed, he decided he truly was going to be sick, and bolted for daylight.

Afterwards, while Elric lay resting in the cave mouth beside a small and cheerful blaze, Moonglum turned over the stuff he had picked out of the rubbish down inside. "She was no demon," Elric said drowsily.

"Was she not," said Moonglum automatically. Problems of classification he left to Elric.

Elric picked up a pebble and turned it idly between his long white fingers. "She was human as you, once, when he took her." He tossed the pebble into the darkness. It fell feebly, a couple of feet away.

Moonglum, squatting over his finds, turned and looked suspiciously at his friend, his hands cupped on his knees. "How did you know she was a puppet of Theleb Kaarna?"

"Her eyes, Moonglum. What the Sorceror of Pan Tang took, he marked. Quite visibly, to one who has the witch-sight." Moonglum threw down the fistful of coins, careless how they scattered on the ground. He half-rose, crouching as though to leap on Elric and throttle him.

"And we followed her all the way up here? You slept with her, knowing that?"

Elric was not angered, or distressed, or apologetic. His voice creaked like a gate in the wind.

"I felt sorry for her, wandering in the world, not knowing that her master is dead and food for worms."

The old familiar mocking tone was back in his voice, and he smiled; but his companion saw how he shivered, despite the fire, and how pale his pale lips had grown. Moonglum's rage turned suddenly cold as fear, a fear he had not even felt in that hellish cave. He wondered what manner of man this was, this bleached, driven scarecrow to whom he had linked his fate.

"She pleased me, Moonglum."

THE OTHER SWORD

BY ROBERT WEINBERG

It was in Karlaak by the Weeping Waste, the farthest outpost of the Western lands, that Elric, last prince of Melniboné, found peace. The use of certain esoteric drugs he unearthed in Troos had provided him enough strength to be free of his cursed blade, Stormbringer. Years of bloody toil and destruction had burned from him any further desire to wander. And the love of beautiful, black-haired Zarozinia, daughter of the Chief Senator of Karlaak, had finally given him the happiness he had long sought.

Thus it was with some trepidation that Moonglum, Elric's truest friend and long-time companion, answered the midnight summons of Zarozinia little more than a month after the three of them had arrived in Karlaak. It was several weeks since the happy pair had wed in a magnificent ceremony. Moonglum, feeling somewhat underfoot in the palace afforded the two, had spent most of his time drinking and gambling in the local taverns. Recently he had begun contemplating a visit to his own home, the fabled city of Elwher, which he had not seen in many a year. If Elric could at last find contentment, the red-haired Eastlander reasoned, could not he as well? Now Moonglum worried that his companion rested not as well as he had believed.

Zarozinia's first words when her retainers brought Moonglum before her did nothing to reassure him. "Elric cannot sleep," she said, her eyes filled with sorrow, and more than a touch of dread. "It has been two days now since he last rested. He barely touches his food. Day and night, he sits in the garden staring at nothingness, his eyes focused on things unseen. When I ask him what is wrong, he shakes his head but does not speak."

Tears filled the princess' eyes. "He seemed so happy, so carefree this past week. Then, suddenly, without any warning, came this change." Bewildered, she stared at Moonglum in anguish. "I don't know what I have done wrong."

"Have you no clue, no clue at all," asked the Eastlander, "as to what troubles him? Elric carries within him many sorrows, more than any normal mortal could bear and still stay sane. But he is no mere human: He is a prince of Melniboné. He shrugs off his grief like a duck sheds water."

The princess shook her head. It grieved Moonglum to see the normally light-hearted Zarozinia cry. Impulsively, he reached out and took one of the princess' hands in his own. "Be assured, whatever troubles Elric is none of your doing. For the first time in our many years of adventuring, I have seen my companion happy, truly happy. There is nothing you could do, nothing you could say, that would alter the love he feels for you. The despair enveloping him has another source. One that I will discover and vanquish. I swear it."

Releasing Zarozinia's hand, the red-haired man rose to his feet. Beyond them were the palace gardens. In the moonlight he could just make out the silhouette of his friend. "I will talk to him now. Some things he cannot tell you, he might reveal to me."

"There is one thing," said the princess thoughtfully. "Earlier this evening as I came up to my lord, before he was aware of my presence, I thought I heard him murmur, 'The other sword.' Yet when I repeated those words to him, he remained silent."

"The other sword?" repeated Moonglum, wondering what the phrase might mean. A cold chill swept through his body as a possible answer came to him. The one blade, the little man knew, had to be the runesword Stormbringer. But there had been a second sword, a mate to the first. A black runesword named Mournblade. Its haunted name rang through the Eastlander's mind as he made his way through rows of blood-red flowers to his motionless friend.

⊕

Elric looked up as Moonglum approached and, for a bare instant, a flicker of a smile crossed the albino's face. Then, as quickly as it had appeared, the expression was gone, leaving the prince's features wreathed in a look that Moonglum knew all too well. The sunken red eyes; the gaunt, drawn flesh; the distant gaze focusing on everything and nothing: Moonglum had seen it many times before. And had hoped with this marriage never to see it again on his friend's visage. Elric was lost in the past, caught up once again in the tragedy of his youth.

"This brooding ill becomes a bridegroom," said Moonglum to Elric, settling into a chair across from his friend. The Eastlander had never been one to hide his innermost feelings. "Your new wife blames herself for your heartache. Bad enough that you punish yourself with these depressing memories, but making Zarozinia suffer as well is cruel and unjust."

Moonglum expected no reply and he was not disappointed. It would take more than a little guilt to break through Elric's wall of melancholy. However, more than any other man, Moonglum knew the secrets of his companion's past. And he was prepared to use them as a knife to slice open the cancer that gnawed at Elric's brain.

"The other sword," said the Eastlander softly but clearly. Instantly, Elric was alert, his red eyes glaring in astonishment at Moonglum. "Only one blade could bear that title. Your thoughts are on Mournblade, and the last time you saw it."

Elric's long thin fingers curled into fists. "Yyrkoon wielded the runesword against me," the prince murmured in a voice as cold as the darkest night, "when we fought in the Tower of B'aal'nezbett. He held it the night Stormbringer took his soul and that of my cousin Cymoril as well."

"True," said Moonglum quietly. "You have repeated the tale to me many times before. Still, it happened years ago. And while time cannot destroy the memory, it can mute its pain. Cymoril is long dead. She needs you no longer. But your wife Zarozinia does."

With a fluid grace that spoke of his ancient, inhuman lineage, Elric rose from his chair. His face was a mask of terrible anguish. Only once before could Moonglum recall his friend in the grip of such torment. That was when the legendary Dead Gods' Book had dissolved in the prince's hands. Whatever horrors plagued Elric's thoughts, they possessed the power to drive him mad if they were not controlled.

"As I walked through this garden a few days past," said the albino, his voice crackling with emotion, "my gaze touched upon the blood-red flowers. Once again I remembered the blood of Cymoril staining my blade that night years ago in Imrryr. This time, though, the pain was not so great; for, as you stated, Zarozinia filled my thoughts. And thus, for the first time ever, my recollections turned to my foolish, mad cousin, Yyrkoon, and how his insane ambition brought about my ruin."

Elric paused, drawing in a deep breath. "It was then that I thought of Mournblade, the other sword." The albino's red eyes burned in despair. "The second runesword, the blade Yyrkoon had tried to use against me in the Pulsing Cavern. It vanished into the cave walls when I defeated my cousin. When we returned from Ameeron, beyond the Shade Gate, Mournblade was left behind. But when Yyrkoon fought me a year later, he once again held the other runesword."

"How did he regain the blade?" asked Moonglum, afraid to ask but afraid not to. "I thought you told me that your cousin was terrified of the Pulsing Cavern."

"Exactly," said Elric, reaching out with both hands and taking Moonglum by the shoulders. "There was no way Yyrkoon could have returned there. Someone else, for only a mortal could handle the sword, must have retrieved the blade and given it to my mad relative." Elric's fingers tightened until they dug like needles into the Eastlander's skin. "That is what gnaws at my vitals, Moonglum. The mystery howls through my thoughts. I cannot rest until I learn the identity of Yyrkoon's secret ally."

"What does it matter?" asked Moonglum, drawing away from his friend. "Yyrkoon is dead. He is the one who stole your throne and brought about Cymoril's death."

Elric shook his head. "Yyrkoon was a fool. A weak, ambitious fool. He wanted power but had not the strength to hold it. I left him as ruler of Melniboné during my absence because I knew he lacked the necessary will to usurp the Dragon Throne. I was right, Moonglum. But I never counted on Yyrkoon gaining possession of Mournblade."

"The sword..." began the Eastlander.

"...Twisted his mind and provided him with unholy energy," continued the albino. "Many times you saw the effect Stormbringer had on me. And my will was a hundred times greater than that of my demented cousin. Mournblade filled Yyrkoon with a berserk rage. Without the sword, he would never have had the courage to defy me, to disobey my commands. In truth, _it was the other sword that killed Cymoril and made me an outcast._ My destiny was twisted and cursed the moment Mournblade was returned to Yyrkoon's hands."

Elric collapsed back onto his chair. "Now do you understand why I cannot rest, why I cannot sleep? I have to discover who gave Mournblade to Yyrkoon. Blood calls out for blood. Whoever returned the blade to my cousin must die. Only then will my soul know peace. Only then."

"You set yourself an impossible task," said the Eastlander unhappily. He knew Elric too well to try and argue. Once the albino set his mind on a course of action, he was unshakable in his resolve. Unfortunately, Moonglum could see no way for Elric to locate an enemy about whom he had not a clue. "The past is a closed book. It cannot be opened, even by the last prince of Melniboné."

An odd expression crossed Elric's features. He rubbed his eyes with one hand, as if trying to recall a long-lost memory. "A closed book," he murmured. "So it seems. But there is a spell...."

Slowly the albino raised his head until his red eyes stared directly into Moonglum's. "It can be done," he declared, "but not alone. I need your help."

"Given gladly," said the Eastlander, wondering only for a second what he was letting himself in for.

⊕

"When I was a child," said Elric an hour later, after all the preparations had been made, "my father used this spell to show me the greatness of our vanished empire. Fortunately, he instructed me in the preparations, so that I could someday do the same for my children."

Zarozinia, the only other person in the chamber, stared anxiously at the two men lying side by side on the large bed. Next to it stood a small wooden table on which rested two cups of a dark brown fluid. Her voice was cool and steady when she spoke.

"There is no danger?"

"None," Elric assured her and Moonglum both. "The spell is called *Focused Return*. The user and a companion both take the concoction I have prepared and fall into a deep trance. In that state, the sorcerer concentrates all of his mental powers on a particular instance or happening in the past. While his mind, acting as the catapult, remains in place, the ego of his companion is hurtled back through time to the envisioned moment. In such a manner my father enabled me to see the conquest of the Hamish empire by the dragon riders of Melniboné. And by my efforts, Moonglum will spy on my cousin, Yyrkoon, when he receives the runesword, Mournblade."

"You're sure my mind will not be trapped in the past?" asked the Eastlander, licking his lips nervously. Moonglum had nothing against sorcery, as long as it did not involve him personally. Like right now. He had a terrible vision of his soulless body lying helplessly on this bed for years without number.

"You have my word," said Elric. Taking a goblet, he handed the other to his companion. "Once we drink, the spell will begin."

The albino raised the cup to his lips, then hesitated for an instant. "No matter who it is," he declared softly, his gaunt stark features a death's head mask, "I must know the truth. After all these years, only the truth will let me rest."

"Even if it is one you trust?" asked Moonglum.

"Even so," replied Elric.

"Even if it is... Cymoril?"

Elric shuddered, then nodded. "Even Cymoril."

They drank.

⊕

At first Moonglum thought the spell had failed. Groggily he shook the sleep from his eyes. He was still in bed, though the chamber was now dark. Nearby lay Elric, still unconscious. It took a few seconds for Moonglum to realize that his friend appeared quite different than he had only minutes before. Nor was the chamber the same one in which he had swallowed the potion. Only then did he think to look down at his own body. And to discover that he possessed none.

"I'm obviously a spirit," the Eastlander declared aloud, quite sure no one could hear his voice. "But what is Elric doing here? More to the point, where is here? And when?"

A few minutes looking about the room answered Moonglum's first question. There was no question, based on the description fed to him in bits and pieces over the years, that he was in Elric's own bedroom, in the Royal Palace of Melniboné. Which, along with the apparent youthfulness of his friend's features, gave him an approximate feel for *when*. But neither solution provided a clue to *why* he was here. That came a few minutes later.

"Elric," whispered a voice from nowhere, a voice like that of a child. "Arise, oh prince, for I need to speak with you."

If it had been possible, Moonglum would have broken out into a cold sweat. He recognized that evil voice, had heard it too many times over the past few years to mistake it for any other. It was Arioch, Lord of Chaos, calling to Elric.

"Yes, my lord," replied the young prince, sitting up in his bed. With a shiver of apprehension Moonglum noted that the albino's eyes were still tightly shut. Elric was fast asleep; nevertheless he responded to Arioch's command.

"Tomorrow you leave for the mainland to spend a year among the peoples of the Young Kingdoms. Is that not so?"

"Yes, my lord," said Elric, and the first beginnings of panic gripped Moonglum and would not let go.

"And you leave your cousin Yyrkoon to rule as emperor in your place?"

"Yes, my lord," replied Elric, his breathing slow and shallow as he slept but spoke.

"But Yyrkoon is weak and a fool," said Arioch in his child-like voice. "He does not possess the strength to control the nobles of Melniboné. His rule will collapse in ruin and civil war. As your chosen empress, Cymoril will be cast in deadly peril."

Elric frowned, though his eyes remained shut. "Yes, my lord. But I gave my word, my lord."

"Then lend Yyrkoon the necessary assistance before you go, my favorite pupil," said the Lord of Chaos. "Deliver to him the one thing that will enable him to rule in peace and harmony while you are gone."

"No!" screamed Moonglum, but, ghost-like, went unheard. "No!" He knew full well what the Chaos Lord was about to say.

"Bring him Mournblade," said Arioch.

"Yes, my lord," replied Elric.

Moonglum groaned, watching helplessly, as Elric rose from his bed. From a darkness deeper than the night stepped Arioch, Lord of Chaos and Elric's patron. As always, he assumed the shape of a beautiful youth, his immortality betrayed only by his ancient eyes.

"I will open a doorway into the Pulsing Cavern," said the God, "so that you can retrieve the blade without anyone being the wiser. For all intents, no one will ever suspect that you left this room tonight."

"As you command, Lord Arioch," said Elric, putting on his clothes. His eyes were open but without the spark of reason. The prince of Melniboné was walking in his sleep.

"Only a mortal can wield the runeswords," said Arioch. "Not that I ever desired to handle the blades. They are part of your destiny." For an instant the Lord of Chaos seemed to stare directly at Moonglum. The Eastlander shivered, wondering if the God sensed his spirit in the chamber. "Your fate is bound to that of Stormbringer and Mournblade. It cannot be changed."

"Yes, my lord," said Elric, drawing forth the black blade Stormbringer from its scabbard. The runesword glowed with an eerie light and its shrill howling filled the room.

Instinctively Arioch stepped away from his disciple and, for a bare instant, a look of apprehension crossed the Chaos Lord's face. It was then that Moonglum understood that even the Gods were not immune to the terrible power of the runeswords. And, with that knowledge, the Eastlander guessed that his friend's peace in Karlaak would not last very long. A mortal possessing the power to slay the Gods was not destined to die in bed.

"Sheath your sword," commanded Arioch. "You won't need its power in the Pulsing Cavern." The God waved one hand and a gray bubble the size of a man appeared in the center of the bedroom. "Step into the gate. It will take you to your destination."

Wordlessly, Elric did as he was bidden. And Moonglum followed.

Prince of Melniboné and accompanying spirit spent only a few minutes in the Pulsing Cavern. A round chamber with spongy walls that throbbed with life, it was a place of madness. Even Moonglum, though immaterial and ghost-like, was troubled by the constant, never-ceasing pulsations that hinted at a mind-searing sentience.

Nor was the sleeping albino unaffected by the cavern's spell. Elric's breath came in deep, ragged gasps as his eyes, glazed with sleep, quickly scanned the cave searching for Mournblade. They stopped at the center of the room, where the sword hung suspended in the middle of the air.

As if struggling through thick paste, Elric reached out and grabbed the runeblade with both hands. Like a flare, the albino's features blazed with unholy power, then dimmed as he thrust the sword into a black scabbard that appeared magically at his belt.

"Arioch," cried Elric, his voice muffled in the strange atmosphere of the cave, "I have the blade. Open the door so that I may return."

This time, however, the gray bubble led not to Elric's chamber, but to another bedroom in the palace. A figure stirred sleepily in the sheets, then sprang awake in sudden shock when he spotted Elric at his bedside.

"My prince," said Yyrkoon, his voice trembling with fear, "why are you here? The hour is late."

"I bring you a gift, cousin," said Elric, his voice toneless and remote. Carefully the albino unbuckled the scabbard holding Mournblade and tossed blade and sheath onto the bed next to the astonished Yyrkoon. "Use it well in my absence."

"Oh, I will, my prince," said Yyrkoon, reaching out hesitantly to touch the black blade. Only Moonglum caught the barest trace of mockery — and madness — in Yyrkoon's voice. "I will put the blade to good use."

Then they were back in Elric's bedchamber and the prince was settling down beneath the sheets. It was as if nothing had actually taken place. But Moonglum knew that the events he had witnessed were all too true.

"Sleep well, my favorite one," said Arioch in his sweet, child-like voice. "Sleep and forget. You sought to alter your future by rescuing Cymoril and letting Yyrkoon live. But tonight's venture has set you once more on the correct path." Arioch giggled, a sound incredibly evil. "None can escape their destiny, my foolish puppet. Not even a prince of Melniboné."

Then, for the second time that evening, Moonglum awoke in a bedchamber with Elric nearby. But this prince was older, with lines of grief and suffering etched into his chalk-white features. Standing close by his side was Zarozinia, her dark eyes wide with concern. And thus Moonglum knew he had returned to the present.

"Well?" said Elric, his voice anxious as he helped Moonglum sit up and held a cup of warmed wine to his lips. "Did you learn the truth? Did you see who gave the blade to Yyrkoon?"

Moonglum nodded, knowing that if he said otherwise Elric would only try again, with another as his confederate. Try again and again until he learned the answer. The answer which would drive him mad.

For Moonglum realized that, despite Arioch's intervention, his friend would blame himself for giving the runesword to Yyrkoon. Elric had always accepted the responsibility for all of his actions, even when controlled by the will of another. This time, though, Moonglum suspected the truth would be too much for the albino. Not only had he slain Cymoril with his cursed blade, but he was also the one directly responsible for the events leading up to her death. No mortal could shoulder that monstrous burden of guilt and remain sane.

"I witnessed everything," said Moonglum, staring directly in his friend's eyes. "After your departure from Imrryr, Yyrkoon brewed a potion made from the leaves of the black lotus. The drink gave him the courage to brave once again the perils of the Pulsing Cavern. He retrieved the sword himself. And, as you suspected, it gradually drove him mad."

Moonglum shook his head. "It is over. The last mystery is explained. Let go of the bitter memories, my friend. There is nothing more to be done."

Slowly, ever so slowly, Elric's red eyes closed. The lines of tension in his face eased and a heavy sigh escaped his lips. Zarozinia grasped her lover tightly around the shoulders as she sobbed with relief. With a wan smile, the albino rose to his feet.

"My thanks, Moonglum," Elric whispered. "Now, perhaps, I can finally find peace."

And Moonglum, though he had lied to his friend and betrayed a great trust, knew that he had done the right thing.

ARIOCH'S GIFT

BY CHARLES PARTINGTON

Many are the songs sung of the fall of the dragon isle.

Each account varies wildly or subtly, according to tradition and custom. Always, the music of history is discordant, complex, difficult to understand; but the ear can be trained and eventually the simple, underlying theme can be unravelled.

Stag, Heir Presumptive of Melniboné, strode angry and unconsoled in the ruins of vast, echoing marble halls, armor clanking, the head of his great war axe stained with drying blood. "Where is the sword?" was his only demand, his only reply to repeated entreaties that his people were waiting to see him enthroned. "No warrior can legitimately call himself king here without one of the runeswords in his scabbard. Can you find no one who knows?" he demanded. And Stag's demands invited attention.

The Isle of Newly Dead Dragons was scoured from its bottommost, foulest dungeons, where unimaginable living carcasses still crawled in a tragic semblance of life, to the fire-wrecked glittering gold minarets where the decadent Lords of Melniboné had amused themselves in savage delights and cruel arts. Eventually, an old, weak man was found. He was brought in fear and chains before Stag.

"What is this?" Stag grumbled.

"This creature, indeed doubly fortunate to be in your divine presence, is Moonglum, once confidant of Lord Elric."

"Does he know where Stormbringer sleeps?"

"No, sire."

"Where the Mournblade waits?"

"I fear not."

"Then kill him."

"Yet he has significant knowledge, Sire...." This was a risk. The death sentence need not only be applied to prisoners.

"Of what?"

"There is a legend that both runeswords were cast from a lump of miraculous metal which fell to earth somewhere in the Weeping Waste, a gift from the demon Arioch."

"Then it is lost forever. Kill him."

Another chance was taken. "His current concubine was eventually persuaded to reveal that old Moonglum knows the exact location of Arioch's Gift."

Stag grinned, leaning forward hungrily. "Then he will lead us to it."

"Never!" Moonglum spat out blood.

Stag leered at his henchman. "Would anyone care to place a wager on that? What is the name of this metal?"

Moonglum mumbled and mumbled. Even *with* teeth, the name was unpronounceable. Weakly, he lifted a trembling finger, pointing to a distant, brass-studded door. They dragged him through the door to the hall beyond.

It was empty of furnishings. Empty of hangings. Empty. War is expensive for the loser. A single rune was carved in the base of a central pillar of jade so wide ten men could not join hands around it. Stag ordered his ministers to translate the rune. They tried seven languages. It was unpronounceable in every variant. Written down, it read, "*yunjgbhguvbfhbfgcbpibabafeeweaf.*"

A stone goblet containing honey had been dropped during the sacking. In a sticky, drying pool, Moonglum wrote, "Only the Lords of Melniboné could pronounce the rune. Lesser beings entrusted with such knowledge called the iron after the first letter of its name, y."

Stag called for a caravan to be assembled and provisioned for a long journey. His best warriors were entrusted to guard it. To the horror of his people, all of whom, it is alleged, loved him dearly, Stag insisted on personally leading the march into the Weeping Waste. Moonglum rode a horse on his right. On Stag's left rode Hoot, his most gifted blacksmith and weaponmaker.

There was no doubting that Moonglum knew the location of Arioch's Gift. And equally no doubt that he was desperate to find it as quickly as possible. Persuasion was constantly applied. He was given no opportunity to attempt suicide: Stag was methodical and determined. But the Weeping Waste had few constant features. It was landscape of living geography, of mutable geology; around them stretched an eternal horizon of illusion. Change was the only constant.

Stag grew morose. Stag grew impatient. Stag grew angry. Moonglum suffered and grew weaker.

"Are we close yet?" Stag thundered. "Where is Arioch's Gift? Where is the iron called y?"

Along the Ghost Rocks they traveled, past the Caves of the Drunken Blind, over the Ten Bruises. For a strong, fit man, such traveling was difficult; for an aged and damaged Moonglum, there could be only one outcome.

On their fifth day's journey into the Weeping Waste, he died. According to tradition, Moonglum's frail corpse was subjected to ritual mutilation, yet nothing could assuage Stag's frenzied disappointment.

As the sun edged towards the massive outcropping known as Three Bent Thumbs, Stag roared his spleen at Arioch. "Damn you," he screamed, "where is your gift?" No answer came. But Stag was a leader of men. He tried one last time. "Where is it? Where is the iron y?"

In the distance, geodynamic change occurred, rebounding from the surface of the Thumbs the word *iron* and the initial letter of Arioch's Gift. And the echo closed the space.

And all around the Weeping Waste laughed....

THE TREMBLER ON THE AXIS

BY PETER CROWTHER AND JAMES LOVEGROVE

I

Resolve can be a wondrous thing and, for Elric at least, it proved to be almost as intoxicating as a fine wine or potion. Indeed, there were times when he felt its overwhelming and constant presence to be virtually indistinguishable from the effects of any drug he had ever encountered. And it was without the inevitable, often painful descent back into a normal state. But, as the days wore on, the very determination he had nurtured in order to complete his task proved, somewhat paradoxically, to be in equal part a burden of some magnitude. For resolve without resolution or accomplishment is the stony road towards madness and, in truth, Elric felt locked onto this road with nary a single sign nor waypost to offer him respite.

In the five months since he had bid farewell to Rackhir the Red Archer amidst the soft hues of the purple stones of Menii, Elric had continued his travels. After crossing the Straits of Vilmir — during which voyage he had scanned the azure depths for some sign of the Ship Which Sails Over Land and Sea, then so recently reclaimed by King Straasha — he had circumnavigated the Weeping Waste and moved deep into the Unknown Kingdoms, always reminding himself as each day dawned, bringing with it a fresh start, new hopes, and new opportunities, that he would return to Melniboné by the fading light of the final day in the year. On these occasions Elric would make a silent pledge to the gods that this day would, if not see his mission completed, at least carry him forward markedly. But, deep inside, he feared nothing heard his words save the accursed black blade by his side, constantly sighing and soughing, moving both with and against his own

313

motions, seeking resolutions all of its own... resolutions which he had no mind to discover.

Between the gods of light and darkness, of Order and Chaos, Elric knew there was little to choose. The capricious nature of immortality and omniscience played little part in the way of character-building. Too much time — and too little with which to fill it — made the Great Ones no less obstreperous and objectionable than a spoiled tavern brat with a belly-full of cheap ale and an itchy sword-hand. Thus, just as he would strive to avert his gaze from the local folk in the numerous hostelries he came upon during his travels, so, too, did he rarely look into the sky, the distant plateaus beyond which the gods lazed, their milky eyes scouring the land below for any potential amusements.

And there was another reason to avoid the sunlight.

Elric's skin was as white as alabaster. Even the slightest exposure to the sun's rays would cause him discomfort at least and, if prolonged, even sickness. For all he knew, it could even lead to his death. Such a fate he could not countenance. His course was set: to explore the outer ranges of the world there to see if mankind could ever run its own affairs. At the end of one year, he would return to the once-Bright Empire of Melniboné, there to rebuild his kingdom and take his rightful place as ruler, and, in so doing, become husband to the beautiful Cymoril. It was an honest goal and one which frequently gave him solace when he felt his determination weaken. But on many a windswept desert night, when the sand rose in thin veils on the distant horizon and stretched across the land, burying all in sight with a billion singing, gritty spicules, he thought of Cymoril, sometimes wishing she could have steeled herself to accompany him... sometimes wishing he could have steeled himself to stay. But there is little gain to be had from wishes, the last attempt at a solution for the weak and the lazy. The Albino Prince of Melniboné had made his decision and so he would stand by it.

Thus, many miles from his true home and often days without other human company, Elric would spend his days truly alone. In the shadow of the mighty dunes of the desert of Hy-Napir he walked, and along the whispering, twisting woodland paths of Tamaela Dom. And each night he nestled beneath rough blankets to watch another day set in the distance. Nearby on some of these occasions a temporary mount endured a troubled sleep while, by the prince's side, the black shape of Stormbringer, his magic and, perhaps, accursed blade, twitched and moaned. Sometimes — and more often than not — his only company was the sword. It fast became a deep concern for him that Stormbringer's constant and anxious litany quickly ceased to have any effect. But though his sleep was deep and undisturbed, his dreams were sorely troubled.

Sometimes these dreams would concern the Dragon Isle itself: Melniboné, which for ten thousand years had ruled the world but whose control had ceased some five centuries ago. Sometimes the dreams would include his mother, whom he had never seen and whose life he had taken through the simple act of being born. Each time she entered these dreams her appearance was different. Sometimes she would be dark-haired and warm-cheeked; other times she would be fair, both of hair and skin; and still others she was different again, sometimes older, sometimes younger. But always she was his mother. And always she looked upon him with a sad yearning that bemoaned not merely her premature passing from the plains of life but also her failure to be there with him.

His cousin Yyrkoon also put in frequent visits in these elaborate dreamscapes. Yyrkoon the malevolent, whose life Elric had spared even against the advice of Arioch, the primary Lord of Chaos. What did he do now, Yyrkoon? In Elric's dreams his cousin was ever laughing, though at what Elric had no inkling. Nor did he wish to know, curled beneath an uncaring moon half-a-world away from all that he held dear.

But the worst dreams of all were those populated by people and cities that not only did he not know but which, in some inexplicable way, he recognized, though they were, he knew, people and places he had never consciously visited. In these dreams he would be called by a seeming multitude of names. But always, he knew, he was the same person, though perhaps inhabiting a different body and even, he was sure, entirely different planes of existence.

And each time he awoke he would carry fragments of the dreams with him into the morning light, and he would strive to hold on to these fragments for all he was worth. But all too quickly the dream remnants lost their substance and evaporated, slipping back deep into his head like half-remembered tastes of interesting dishes from long ago or far ahead.

Each morning he would rise and clean himself before beginning the day's travel, always thinking of what lay behind him, always questioning what he was doing and where he was going. These questions would persist throughout the day, hovering like troublesome insects about his person as he walked or rode to a destination of which he had no knowledge.

His quest encountered, as does any quest, all manner of diversions.

Some of these he would pass by. Others he would embrace.

And so it was, on the afternoon of the fourth day of the twenty-first week since he left Menii, Elric came to the town of Tomesk, its battered gates standing proud but weathered in the heat.

It was behind these gates that Elric was to encounter a diversion that would almost prevent him from ever seeing Melniboné or his beloved Cymoril again.

II

Night was drawing in, the setting sun's last fury draining from the sky as Elric trudged wearily through the dusty streets of Tomesk in search of board and lodging. Many a curious eye was cast in his direction, and many a word was whispered behind his back when he had passed, usually with reference to the whiteness of the hand that clasped the folds of his cowl together at his throat and to the blackness of the sword that hung by his hip.

Tomesk was situated at the edge of a vast desert plain known as the Grey Lands, not least by virtue of the color of its constantly shifting sands — though there were other reasons, too. The town itself was frequently used by travelers as a last staging-post before they entered that barren and seemingly endless waste. Thus the townsfolk were accustomed to all manner of eremites, ascetics and seekers after enlightenment in their midst; for the Grey Lands were reputed to bestow the gift of self-knowledge upon any who ventured into them with an open mind — though there were inevitably prices to be paid for all advantages gained and, generally, for any sought. However, the slender limbs and pallid skin of the albino prince excited much speculation among the usually phlegmatic Tomeskians, most of whom recognized him for a Melnibonéan, though by the cut and richness of his robes rather than by any close familiarity with that fabled and famously cruel race.

So it was that when Elric came upon a tavern by the name of the Silver Hand, such was the swiftness with which rumour spread in Tomesk that his appearance at the door caused less of a stir than might have been expected. Indeed, the innkeeper, Janquil, scarcely batted an eyelid when Elric drew back his hood and let it fall around his neck to reveal his skull-like head with its ruby eyes and hair like wisps of tapering cloud. Rather, Janquil's most pressing concern was whether the Melnibonéan was going to pay in advance for his room; a concern which Elric was easily able to allay by the production of a solid gold coin from his purse.

"Would you like to see the room?" Janquil enquired.

"I would rather be shown to a table and given meat and drink," said Elric in a voice as faint and pale as his skin, "for today I have walked far and I am footsore and hungry. And I fear," he added, indicating with a nod of his head an unoccupied table by the window, "I will provide little in the way of good companionship or idle banter. I merely wish to see the world going by without, for a few moments at least, me traveling with it."

Janquil, the gold coin now tucked firmly in the pocket of his apron, led Elric to the table he had requested and shortly thereafter set before him a mug of ale, a loaf of bread, and a plate of steaming viands.

For all his hunger, Elric hardly touched his food but sat with his elbows resting on the tabletop and his chin sunk into his hands, gazing out of the tavern window at the night-dimmed street along which vague figures flitted like moths, shapes glimmering briefly in the gloom and then gone. His thoughts, if they were anywhere, were on Imrryr and his sweet Cymoril and on the cares which any emperor-to-be, even one in self-imposed exile, must feel.

By and by the tavern, though hardly crowded, emptied, leaving just three other patrons seated at a table by the hearth, eating heartily and talking quietly among themselves. The first of these was a broad-shouldered giant of a man whose pine-green eyes and flaming hair marked him out as a member of the Klöef, that mountain race whose aggressiveness and ferocity in battle was matched only by their generosity of spirit and their love of song, wine and the tender caresses of a buxom maiden. Opposite him sat an almond-eyed, wizened-face character of indeterminate age, his sharp gaze suggesting he might just as easily have seen only forty of the eighty summers of which his hunched and withered frame spoke so volubly. On his left index finger the man sported a ring of gold in which was set an amethyst of unusual size and remarkable depth of color, a great, glittering gull's-egg of a stone which caught the firelight and flashed all shades of purple and violet and mauve as its owner gestured and gesticulated to make a point or correct a contrary opinion. The third member of this band, and the quietest of the three, was a youth in the first flush of adulthood who listened eagerly to his companions' conversation, nodding when he agreed (which seemed to be most of the time). He occasionally interjected a remark of his own, offering it tentatively as if uncertain how it would be received.

Elric, in his habitual self-obsessed gloom, was oblivious to the presence of these others, although the impression he gave was of ignoring them with the aloof, aristocratic disdain which Melnibonéans were wont to affect in their dealings with the upstart races of the Young Kingdoms. The three were, however, not oblivious to him and, when there came a lull in their discourse, the giant Klöef turned towards Elric and addressed him loudly. "Ho, pale stranger! Would you not sit with us awhile and share your thoughts? For profound thoughts they must be, if the furrow of your brow is anything to go by."

An invitation so genially put is hard to refuse and, loath as he was to exchange his solitude for the company of strangers, Elric nonetheless felt obliged to cross the room and take a seat at their table.

"I am Gaarek," the Klöef announced proudly. "Men call me Gaarek the Overbold, and women sometimes, too." He guffawed lustily. "This sly-looking devil," he said, pointing to the ageless creature with the amethyst ring, "goes by the name of Trypaz, and is clearly a sorcerer of some sort though he denies that questionable honor."

"Most vehemently," said Trypaz with a small, reptilian grin that did little to endear him to Elric.

"And this enviably youthful fellow, who has clearly barely begun to grow whiskers with which to blunt his knife of a morning," Gaarek continued, amiably clapping the young man on the shoulder and making him blush, "calls himself Kyval Kesh."

"Pleased to share table with you," said Kyval Kesh, extending a moist-palmed hand to Elric.

"And I am Elric, a humble traveler," said the Dragon Prince of Imrryr, with a slight inclination of the head.

"And a Melnibonéan, if I'm any judge," said Gaarek.

"I am of that race," Elric confessed, "though there are times when that inheritance is a burden I would rather were not mine."

"Honorably spoken, friend Elric," said Gaarek. "But we are all humble travelers here, and we shall drink together as such. The road has no prejudices and the rain falls equally on us all. Janquil! Where is that damned — Ah, Janquil, another glass and a fresh flagon of wine, if you will."

The innkeeper quickly returned and filled the travelers' glasses with blue fishbone wine, a potent local brew. Gaarek proposed a toast — "To travelers, whatever their road and whatever their mission!" — and the rest of the evening passed in an exchange of travelers' tales, with Gaarek recounting more than his fair share of outlandish adventures and amorous escapades, which amused the impressionable Kyval Kesh greatly but managed, too, to raise a smile now and then on the stern faces of Trypaz and even Elric himself.

Listening to Gaarek, Elric was reminded of his liking for his erstwhile companion Rackhir, whose light-hearted, easy-going nature had been so at odds with his own dark demeanor. It was as if he were drawn to such men by the very attraction of opposites, their openness and abundant love of life contrasting with but also somehow compensating for his reticence and deep-rooted sense of futility. Their warmth was as intoxicating as the strong-tasting wine and, it seemed, equally successful in pushing back his despair as a brazier pushes back the night.

Their talk continued into the small hours of morning, until Janquil the innkeeper began giving small signs that he would rather be abed than waiting on his guests' apparently inexhaustible pleasure. His extravagant yawns and elaborate sighs at last had the desired effect on the travelers.

"Perhaps we should repair to our rooms," said Gaarek, draining his glass and returning it to the table noisily. "I for one wish to make an early start come morning, for I have heard that the Grey Lands are at their most illusory — and their most dangerous — in the heat of the day, when the sun makes a liar of the landscape. Many a man is said to have fallen to his doom wandering over a precipice which he thought merely a crack in the parched ground. I may be the Overbold but I am not the Foolish. During the middle of the day we shall rest, and make the best of the morning and evening to travel."

"You are venturing into the Grey Lands?" Elric asked.

"Venturing? We intend to cross them, friend Melnibonéan."

"I thought then impassable. My own intention was to skirt them by a more traditional route."

"Our friend Trypaz here believes he has discovered a way through."

Elric turned to the wizened man with the almond eyes, who smiled back at him enigmatically. "Few men enter the Grey Lands unless it is to seek the solace of solitude and the enlightenment that desolation can bring," he said. "The Grey Lands hold up a mirror to the soul and, in their emptiness, the wise man finds Truth. I, however, sought more than that when first I crossed their boundaries and, in return, was accorded knowledge of a route that could see one swiftly and safely from one side to the other."

"And have you yet explored this route for yourself?"

"The opportunity has not arisen until now, friend Elric. And with such boon traveling companions as Gaarek and Kyval Kesh —and perhaps even yourself, Melnibonéan — the journey will certainly be easier and considerably less hazardous for one so frail as me."

"For my own part," Gaarek interjected, "the challenge of crossing the uncrossable is reason enough to undertake this journey. As for young Kyval Kesh here—"

"I must reach my homeland, Zalonikad," said Kyval Kesh, "which, as you may know, lies due west of the Grey Lands. It is a journey of some thirty days or more by the traditional routes but which, if friend Trypaz is correct, need only take me a little over seven or eight. I have had word that my mother is unwell, you see, and I would wish to be by her side should the worst happen."

Elric looked at each of them in turn. Though his ruby eyes gave nothing away, something in each man's statement of his reasons for crossing the Grey Lands filled him with suspicion. He had no cause to distrust any of them; equally, none of them had yet proven himself wholly trustworthy. It was a moot point. However, setting his doubt aside for a moment, Elric was seized with a curiosity to visit the fabled Grey Lands himself. Something the alleged sorcerer Trypaz had said had aroused his interest: something about the Grey Lands holding up a mirror to the soul. Elric had, after all, embarked on his wanderings in order to learn more about himself and to discover whether he was right — and, indeed, deserving — to take his seat on the Ruby Throne of Imrryr. What better way could there be than to enter the Grey Lands and see if Trypaz's words held true? And if they did not, the journey would amount to little more than a week of his time.

"I can see by your expression, friend Elric, that you are inwardly debating whether to join us on our voyage of exploration," said Gaarek.

"And we would be more than delighted to have you with us," Kyval Kesh added, though something in the timbre of his words suggested otherwise.

Trypaz nodded. "And that sword by your side looks as if it demands a good arm to wield it," he said with a wry smile. "And often, unless my intuition deceives me. I should feel much safer in the company of *two* good swordsmen," he added with a nod at Gaarek, who bowed back graciously.

"I don't know, though I confess the prospect intrigues me," said Elric. "I shall think further on the matter overnight and let you know my decision in the morning."

"Very well, friend Elric, but don't think too hard," said Gaarek with a raucous laugh. "We leave at dawn and, should you decide to accompany us, you will need your rest for the journey ahead."

When the innkeeper had shown them to their rooms, the four men bade one another a good night and retired. For Elric, as perhaps for the other three, sleep was a long time in coming.

III

Though Elric was by nature an early riser, needing little sleep to replenish his slight frame, he was nevertheless the second of the four travelers out on the street. "Ah, friend Elric," said Trypaz, interrupting the tying of a leather strap beneath the last of the four horses lined up against the tethering-rail by the door of the Silver Hand. "I trust you rested well and long."

"I did indeed, friend Trypaz. And you, too, I hope."

Trypaz nodded. "Quite so," the wizened man said, "though, for me at least, sleep and its benefits are perhaps overrated."

Elric smiled agreement.

"Do I take your presence here to indicate that you will, after all, be joining us on our 'adventure'?" His tone at the last word suggested a faint mockery.

"I think I shall accompany you, yes, if that still has your approval."

"Nothing has transpired during the night to make me think otherwise," Trypaz said. "As I said last evening, I consider your involvement to be only good tidings," he added, returning his attention to the leather strap.

Elric stretched, setting his mystic black blade to shuddering by his side, and breathed deep of the morning air.

Overhead, two dawn-treaders were chasing each other on the wing, chirping frantically while, in the faraway distance, the first red tendrils of sunlight streaked the last remnants of muted night-greyness like veins on a corpse's skin.

"Ho, friend Elric!" bellowed Gaarek.

Elric turned and smiled at the big Klöef who stood, flanked by a seemingly sheepish-looking Kyval Kesh, in the doorway.

"I fear I spoke before my turn last evening," Gaarek grunted. "It would seem that my reminder as to our time of departure, while it was not intended to be indelicate, could be likened to my telling my own father which was the most satisfying of a female's many entrances." He laughed loudly and bent forward to allow air to escape noisily from his backside. "Ah, much better," he said. "I've a mind I quaffed perhaps a little too much of that blue wine for my own good. I'd suggest, in all of your interests, that I take the rear this morning."

Kyval Kesh moved out from behind Gaarek and threw a patched leather valise across the smallest of the horses' flanks.

"Did you rest well, friend Kyval Kesh?" Elric enquired.

"Very well," came the reply.

"Very well, then" boomed Gaarek, "if we're all fully prepared, I've a mind that we be off before the day gets too long in the beard. Friend Trypaz, perhaps you will lead the way?"

Trypaz nodded his head once, slowly, with an almost imperceptible closing of his eyes. This man, Elric thought, was one neither used to — nor comfortable with — being given orders, no matter of how little consequence they were.

Elric waited as the others moved to their mounts, discerning that the remaining horse was intended for his own use. "I believe I owe something for the horse?" he said.

"Ah, fear not, friend Elric," Gaarek said dismissively. "I'll not bid you a fare-thee-well without we settle up. I suggest we concentrate what little brains we have left from last evening's excesses on the journey ahead and leave matters of money-changing for one of our many respites."

"Your confidence in my honesty is matched only by that in your memory, friend Gaarek," said Elric, reaching into his tunic for his purse. "Even so, I pay as I go and would as soon settle outstanding debts before they become too outstanding."

"As you will," Gaarek said, and he held out his hand. Elric dropped three small gold coins onto the Klöef's palm and watched them cover a small, hairy wart growing in its center. "You are most generous, friend Elric," said Gaarek, pulling his hand back sharply and examining the coins. "I fear you need —"

"I need no return on that," said Elric. "Let us say that we are now neither of us in the other's debt."

For just a second Gaarek looked sternly at Elric, his eyes slightly hooded, and then he smiled, his face opening like a flower's. "As you will," he said with a chuckle, "as you will."

Trypaz was already on his horse and had watched the exchange with undisguised interest. Elric saw the faintest glimmer of a smile in the man's eyes as he mounted his horse, but it faded immediately.

"On your lead, then, sorcerer," shouted Gaarek.

"What of our host?" Trypaz enquired, only his glower acknowledging the Klöef's address.

"Our host?"

Trypaz nodded. "Aye, did he not say he would see us depart?"

"Ah, indeed he did," Gaarek agreed. "Indeed he did." He looked aside at Kyval Kesh and then to Elric. "Perhaps he has better things to be occupying his time at this hour," he said with a shrug and a wink of his eye to anyone who had a mind to see. "I'll wager he's sleeping off the effects of that hellish concoction he dished out so liberally last evening," he added, smiling and rubbing his stomach at the same time.

"Yes," Kyval Kesh agreed, though Elric thought his comment lacked any real conviction.

Trypaz reined his mount, spun around and, with a muttered instruction into the horse's ear — which twitched as though it had been stung — galloped down the street.

"Hmmph, if it's a race he's after," Gaarek muttered loudly, "he'd do well to bear in mind my own advantage of a windy backside." He turned to laugh at his own remark with Elric but the albino prince only nodded and, with a sharp slap of the reins, galloped after Trypaz. First Kyval Kesh and then Gaarek followed on.

As they sped through the battered gates of Tomesk, the sun showed the top of its head behind the distant mountains of Mendaala. Not for the first time in his life did Elric begin to wish he had perhaps had just a little more sleep.

IV

The sun hung in the sky and cast opaque half-images along the grey dunes: strange swirling mounds of sand that seemed to lack both life and energy and behind which occasional whispering sighs could be heard. For the most part, the four riders ignored these visual and aural intrusions, concentrating instead on making time and putting distance between them and the old town of Tomesk. There was little in the way of conversation.

For Trypaz, who retained his lead all morning until they broke for rest just a half-day's ride to the east from the ghost town of the Insect King C'byrt Yrk, by the stagnant waters of Lake Shemeel, the disturbances seemed to pose no distraction. Atop his mount, the old man — for surely, Elric thought to himself, he had seen more than eighty summers — belied his ancient appearance, riding stiff-backed and prompting his horse firmly with knotted reins every few minutes.

The young Kyval Kesh had passed Elric while Tomesk was still a fresh memory, falling in behind Trypaz and keeping pace effortlessly. Elric marvelled at the boy's apparent horsemanship and wondered more than once if Gaarek had been a little premature in writing him off as a novice. He, too, Elric noted, seemed singularly unimpressed by the constant movements and sounds along their sides: movements and sounds which increased in occasion and intensity with the leagues.

Gaarek himself kept back, dogging Elric's mount's hoofprints as though he were tethered to the Melnibonéan with taut twine. Twice the Dragon Prince reined up and fell back slightly only to find that Gaarek, too, had slowed his pace. On each of these occasions he moved on almost immediately, hearing the same soft, animal grunts behind him, though whether they were from the man or his mount, Elric had no idea.

Only Elric seemed to be disturbed by the fluttering shapes and the soft sighs of the Grey Lands. They dogged the periphery of his vision and his hearing, sometimes appearing as thin, gossamer veils wafting behind a dune, sometimes as secret callings of his name, pledging, beckoning, promising, threatening. All of them he ignored, although by the time the leaden smell of Lake Shemeel held the wind all to itself, his concentration had seen fit to paste his hair to his forehead.

Their mounts tethered to a grove of spindly, long-dead slingfang bushes, upwind and out of range of the glistening, still waters of Lake Shemeel, the travelers lay on old blankets atop the grey sand and rested. The mutterings and insinuations of the desert around them seemed to have increased as the sun drew higher in the sky to become a snarling, keening chorus that fairly hammered the ears. It was hard to ignore the sound, yet all knew they must if they were to retain their sanity and their lives.

Gaarek sat against the legs of his horse and removed from his tunic a circular pouch with a gold-chain drawstring of such ornate design that Elric could not help but stare. "Idle hands make good helpers if the Lord Arioch would but have his way," he said gustily as he shook a gritty, pungent-smelling hemp into equal piles upon his stretched tunic front. "I may just as well prepare some welcome distractions now as later for our bedrolls this night," he added with an almost conspiratorial nod. "It's my wager we'll be little placed for anything requiring but the slightest strength when we rest for the day." Having completed the task to his satisfaction, Gaarek lifted the pouch to his face and buried his nose in the neck. "Ah," he groaned, removing the pouch and drawing the chain tight again. "That makes a welcome relief from the noxious fumes I've been producing of late."

Trypaz sniffed and turned over noisily.

Gaarek made a pouting face at the old man's back and dropped the pouch back into his tunic. From the same pocket he then produced a small roll of parchment from which he tore four square strips. Then this, too, was returned to the pocket. By the time Gaarek had finished the entire operation, four neat but somewhat lumpy rolls lying on his tunic, Trypaz was on his feet staring at the sky. "It's time," he said simply.

Kyval Kesh, who had apparently been asleep since they had stopped, sat bolt upright and yawned.

Gaarek turned to the boy and frowned, then turned to face Elric. "Never knew a youngster as did not need his rest," he said, stifling a chuckle.

Elric said nothing. He got to his feet and walked across to his horse. After they had emptied themselves of excess water — all but Trypaz, who appeared not to require many of the same privileges as the others — they were on their way again.

V

They rode hard for most of the afternoon, sparing neither time nor thought to matters of conversation. The constant distraction of the apparitions and calls that surrounded them every step of the way — coupled with the almost insufferable heat exacerbated by his thick, woven cowl — took their toll on the albino, and he all but stumbled from his horse when they arrived at a small, unmarked oasis around which dust devils of grey sand danced in outlandish shapes and movements.

Trypaz and Gaarek helped the Melnibonéan to the shade of a huge caphenaic tree, from where, as he was drifting off to sleep, Elric heard the Klöef offer his hemp-sticks around. Kyval Kesh took one immediately but Trypaz declined graciously. An exchange of heated words followed, the depth of which Elric did not fully understand, and the old man finally if reluctantly accepted Gaarek's generosity. Sleep came more quickly then, with the sweet smell of hemp wafting around and mingling with the desert wind.

The snatches of conversation sounded strange to the Dragon Prince, but he had neither the inclination nor the strength to become involved. They quickly gave way to a deep sleep, blank and dreamless, as though the Grey Lands were infecting Elric's deepest subconscious.

When he opened his eyes, feeling considerably stronger than he had earlier, Elric immediately sensed something was wrong. By his side, Stormbringer jerked anxiously, the blade's mournful hum vibrating in his hand though he had no recollection of taking hold of it.

The night was dark but, in the dim glow of the settled fire which someone had apparently built while he had been asleep, Elric could see the hunched shape of Gaarek, his back to the Melnibonéan. He thought he could hear the Klöef whispering — it sounded like *Easy, boy, easy...* — but the sound might have been the wind blowing through the branches of the caphenaic tree. He sat up silently and leaned over to one side so that he might see what Gaarek was watching.

It was Kyval Kesh. And Trypaz too.

The young man was kneeling by Trypaz's side, holding one of the old man's hands in his own. Trypaz was clearly deeply asleep, probably as a result of Gaarek's hemp, but he was troubled, shifting from side to side and moaning quietly.

As Elric watched, Kyval Kesh appeared to be heaving, arching his back and constricting his stomach while he lifted Trypaz's hand nearer to his own mouth. Then, suddenly, the boy retched and a steaming spittle rained onto the old man's hand and arm.

Now Elric *did* hear Gaarek. "Easy, now," he said. "Gently does it. Remember what I told you...."

Kyval Kesh wiped his mouth and then smoothed the thick substance around the old man's outstetched palm, building a small pool in its center. Then he seemed to constrict his head onto his neck and, opening his mouth wide, out snaked what could only be the boy's tongue, though its length and its diameter seemed entirely at odds with that appendage.

Elric shook his head and looked again.

Kyval Kesh's tongue had now balled at the end, making what appeared to be a fist. Then Elric saw two eyes open on the fist and a second mouth open at its snout. In that mouth, the clear gleam of teeth sparkled like hidden jewels. As the mouth descended onto the old man's palm, burying itself into the carefully prepared pool, Elric heard a sucking noise. Then he was on his feet.

"Ho, Trypaz," he shouted. "Wake up, old man."

Gaarek spun around and stared at Elric. For the briefest of moments, his hatred burned into the Melnibonéan and then, his expression changing into one of surprised concern, the Klöef, too, jumped up.

"Step back, lad, and look sharp about it," Gaarek snapped, pulling his own blade from his waistband.

Kyval Kesh turned and stared in shock. "Wha—" His voice around the thick stem which protruded from his mouth sounded as though he were speaking beneath water.

Trypaz opened his eyes and jerked back his hand, rubbing the palm ferociously and trying to take in all that was happening about him.

Kyval Kesh leapt to his feet and, as he did so, the long tongue closed its eyes and recoiled into his dripping mouth.

"Gaa—" Kyval Kesh gagged and appeared to choke on the words before trying again. "Gaarek?" he said at last.

"Don't Gaarek me, boy," the Klöef said, "Step back."

The boy shook his head in horror but did as he was told.

Elric moved around Gaarek and Kyval Kesh so that he was beside Trypaz. "How go you, old man?" he asked.

Trypez, still rubbing his hand — upon which a huge swelling had started to sprout — nodded, though his eyes were filled with pain.

"You have some explaining to do, friend Kyval Kesh," said Elric, "and I fear it will not lead to our calling you friend thereafter."

Kyval Kesh was terrified. He looked down at Trypaz, then at Elric and finally at Gaarek.

Gaarek looked across at Elric and shook his head.

"Gaa—"

"The time for explaining is done, lad," he said, stepping quickly across the empty space between them, "you go to meet Lord Arioch. May his hearth have a space for you." The Klöef's sword sang as it swept through the night air and then through the boy's neck. The body stood for a moment or two while Kyval Kesh's head bounced across the ground. Then the stump of his neck erupted in a stream of flesh and blood as a long snake leapt into the air and fell in slack coils upon the ground. Behind it the boy's body sank in upon itself and collapsed into what appeared to be little more than a pile of clothes and rotting flesh.

Gaarek seemed as astonished to see the thing as Elric and Trypaz, and the three men watched as the beast twisted and writhed in the dust, clearly distressed and in great agonies. Then Gaarek stepped resolutely forward and brought his blade neatly down on the thing's head, splitting it eye from eye.

A silence fell upon them.

Trypaz shuffled from his blanket and reached gingerly into the pile that had been Kyval Kesh, pulling from the tangle an arm that appeared to have no substance within it. The old man turned over the boy's hand and exposed a small wart, festooned with hairs and crusted over with some kind of carapace. "Temoraal," he said.

"Who?" said Elric.

"Not *who* but *where*," Trypaz replied. "The Isle of Temoraal. I've long heard stories about the things that dwell there and how they may only gain exit from the accursed island by means of a carrier to transport them."

Elric turned to look at Gaarek and, seeing that the Klöef's blade — now dripping with gore — remained at the ready, he stayed returning Stormbringer to its scabbard. Gaarek caught the albino's gaze and reflected no recognition in his own stare.

"I have not heard of such an Isle," Elric said, turning to Trypaz.

The old man shook his head. He was removing the amethyst ring from about his finger, effecting the maneuver with obvious difficulty. The wart on the palm of his hand seemed to grow bigger as Elric watched. "Nor should you have, friend Elric," Trypaz announced at last. Holding the ring in his blighted hand he lifted the stone and then, carefully dipping thumb and forefinger into the exposed casing, removed a pinch of dust. "It all happened many years past, so many that I barely recall it myself.

"There was a war, just one in a long line of wars, fought for beliefs and principles as all wars have ever been fought and will ever be in days to come. Little was achieved, nothing was gained. Lives were taken and pain was inflicted. The real reasons are lost in the mists." He paused and, grimacing, rubbed the dust onto the wart, muttering some kind of oath the language of which Elric did not recognize. It seemed that a wind had risen — Elric could hear its soughing moan all around them, though there was no trace of its passing in the flames of the fire before him. Then, suddenly, Trypaz hunched over and vomited onto the sand. The Melnibonéan was somehow little surprised to see a small version of the worm creature lying amidst the bile, flexing its still undeveloped length once and then becoming death-still.

"Suffice for it to be said," Trypaz continued, wiping his mouth, "that none of those who visited the island returned. Not at first, anyway." He sat back, clearly fatigued, and clapped his hands together. The wart dislodged itself and dropped beside the worm-thing. "And then, or so it is said by campfire and inn-table, the warriors returned. This was after the passage of many years, though, strangely, none of them had grown any greyer nor did they bear the symptoms of deprivation one might associate with a great ordeal. They returned to loved ones and friends and all seemed as though it might continue as it once had been. But then the deaths began."

Gaarek cleared his throat.

"I fear you have me at a great disadvantage, my friends," Gaarek said. "There being two of you, I must draw my second blade, for I am not so skilled with one sword to be able to dispatch you both with a single swing, suspicious as you clearly are — and not without reason, I agree."

"Gaarek?"

The Klöef nodded to Elric. "Aye, it's true. I visited the accursed Isle and, as the sorcerer says, I returned carrying a special cargo." He shrugged. "She asks for little and keeps me healthy and young. All she requires is to feed every once in a while... and to reproduce," he added with a side-glance at the worm-thing. Was that the faintest trace of sadness and pity he saw in the big man's eyes?

"And Kyval Kesh?" Elric asked. "Did he accompany you to this Temoraal?"

Gaarek shook his head and hefted a short-sword in his spare hand. "I met young Kyval Kesh on the road but three days ago. I sat with him through the night — a long night, I might add — until her child was in place. I am not a cruel man."

"And his mother?"

Gaarek nodded. "That part is true, friend Elric though I agree it sounds a falsehood. He came to terms with his passenger slowly and not without bitterness." The Klöef turned to face Trypaz and forced a smile. "You would have been but his second meal."

"Let us get on with it, friend Gaarek," said Elric. "The time for banter is done."

"Aye," Gaarek agreed, not without sadness. He crouched down between the men, each hand at the ready, and each bearing a blade that gleamed in the light of the fire.

"Hold," said Trypaz. "You do not deserve the honor of combat, even if its outcome were to be to our advantage."

Gaarek looked questioningly at Trypaz as the old man raised his ring-hand and waved the fingers before his eyes.

Immediately Elric noted a stiffening of Gaarek's stance, almost imperceptible at first but, as the seconds passed and Gaarek moved not a muscle, it became more noticeable.

Trypaz waved his fingers again and the Klöef's two blades disengaged themselves from his hands and set about hacking and swiping at their erstwhile owner. In a frenzy of blood-spray and the soft thuds of dropping flesh — interspersed with Gaarek's cries and the cracking and splintering of his bones — the mighty warrior was thus reduced to a steaming mound of body-parts. Amidst the final few shards, Elric noted, there could be seen the unmistakable sections of a black snake, its eyes forever closed, its belly now forever empty.

Trypaz closed his eyes and muttered a few words that Elric could not hear. Then he looked up again. "I fear I am spent for an hour or two, friend Elric. But it will be that long at least before the sun once more graces us with its presence."

Elric returned Stormbringer to its scabbard and nodded.

"I am indebted to you for my life, friend Melnibonéan," Trypaz said as he lay back on his blanket. "Rest assured it is an obligation I do not take lightly." The old man seemed visibly to sink into himself. "If you've a mind for one more act," he said, throwing a well-aimed snatch of dust into the fire, "then you'd do well to burn that meat before the day gets older." And then his eyelids dropped and he was asleep.

It was some time before the Dragon Prince had consigned the Klöef's remains and those of Kyval Kesh to the cleansing conflagration, which burned mercilessly until there was no trace left, though there was no discomfort to Elric as he tended the pyre. When it was done, and the flames had settled and the embers glowed less fiercely, Elric lay down and looked up at the jewelled sky to await the morning light. He felt a long way indeed from his homeland and from those who waited for him there.

VI

Through the sighing, shifting wilderness the albino prince and the wizened sorcerer rode on, leading their companions' horses behind them.

The experiences of the previous night — though they had forged a bond between the two travelers — had not completely dispelled Elric's mistrust of Trypaz. An accomplished magician himself, Elric looked askance at other practitioners of the dark arts, for he knew how magic could eat away at a man from the inside; how magic was a parasite, not unlike the worm-creatures of Temoraal, which could dwell within its host and render him outwardly sane and normal while inwardly he would be quite mad. If the ever-altering landscape of the Grey Lands had taught him anything so far, it was that the more innocuous the exterior, the more one should be wary of what lay beneath. Thus, while glad of Trypaz's company, Elric was careful to keep him within swinging distance of Stormbringer. And, indeed, the black runesword — denied blood the previous evening — was only too keen to be unsheathed and plunged into the sorcerer's heart. It whined by Elric's side all day long like a hound begging to be unleashed. It was all Elric could do to stay his own hand and he wondered more than once whether his suspicions about Trypaz (not to mention Gaarek and Kyval Kesh) really stemmed from innate prudence and not from the sword and its treacherous lusts. Was he master of the stealer of souls by his side or merely the human puppet who did its bidding?

The two travelers rested through the middle of the day in the shadow of an outcropping of grey rocks and, while Trypaz dozed, Elric surveyed the desert around him with rapt fascination.

The Grey Lands were never still.

A layer of fine sand swept continually across the hard-baked ground, combing over and over itself in waves, perpetually resculpted by the wind. If ever this restless action paused, it was only an illusion brought on by the hypnotic repetition of patterns that occasionally seemed, in the eye of the beholder, to bring time itself to a temporary halt.

The Melnibonéan was troubled by some of the images that formed fleetingly in that vast expanse of grey. They took on the appearance of warring soldiers, massed ranks of armies, combatants locked in swordplay, burning minarets, screaming women, ships aflame and sinking. Strife and destruction were the themes of that visual symphony, and Elric could not but think that this constituted an omen or, worse, a prophecy of his own future.

The sun passed its zenith. Trypaz stirred from his slumber and the journey was resumed, this time on the horses they had previously been leading, as they were fresher.

It was some comfort to Elric that the sorcerer was so confident of the route they were following, making quick, knowledgeable decisions based on the infrequent landmarks they encountered as to which direction they should be taking. How Trypaz had come by this information Elric was reluctant to ask, for he did not wish to appear over-curious or impolite, especially now that there were just the two of them and it was consequently more important than ever to keep their relations cordial.

He was, moreover, somewhat at Trypaz's mercy. Should the sorcerer for some reason decide to abandon him, it was by no means certain that Elric would be able to make his own way back out of the Grey Lands. So from time to time he would marvel out loud at Trypaz's familiarity with the landscape in the hope that this might lead his companion naturally into an explanation. But as the remarks only ever brought a dry smile to Trypaz's lips or a slight narrowing to his almond eyes or a sly, casual nod of acknowledgement and no more, Elric soon gave up pursuing the matter and committed himself — for better or worse — into the sorcerer's hands.

On they rode through the heat and dust of the Grey Lands. Night fell and they rested, and come dawn they were up and riding again, content to journey in mutual silence and glad, still, of one another's company (though not as glad as they might have been if Gaarek and Kyval Kesh had never joined them in the first instance). And another night passed, and it was on the morning of the fourth day that they rode into a plain more barren and featureless (if that were possible) than any other in the Grey Lands; a broad valley so flat and smooth that it might have been paved with marble, except that it had no lustre.

The sun's heat, having nowhere to hide in this shallow cauldron, boiled the air to an arid and all-but-unbreathable thinness. It was like the atmosphere of a mountain pass at high altitude coupled with the ferocious heat of a tropical lowland: the worst of two worlds. Not a hint of a cooling wind stirred here, not a sound — for the sands were still — disturbed the silence.

Finally Trypaz spoke, having first taken a swig from his water-skin to lubricate his parched throat. "I fear, friend Elric," he said, "that I have not been entirely honest with you."

There was a note of genuine regret in his voice that took Elric quite by surprise and stayed his hand on Stormbringer's pommel. "The quality of truthfulness has been noticeably lacking from this venture from the very beginning," the prince said carefully. "Perhaps now we may speak frankly with one another rather than feint and parry with deceits and subterfuges."

"Well put, friend Melnibonéan," said Trypaz. "You believe that in some way I had foreknowledge of our erstwhile companions' condition. Is that so?"

"It did cross my mind."

"Rest assured, then, that I was as ignorant of it as you yourself. Had I known, I would, of course, never have allied myself with them in the first place. I am no fool, Elric, nor have I ever been in any doubt as to the importance of my personal safety. Self-preservation has been my watchword since I was but an adept, else I would not have requested your company as additional insurance."

Elric nodded. "That is all very well," he said, "but now you are to reveal to me that your motives have been somewhat less than pure."

"I merely wish to make it plain that I erred on the side of mendacity when I said that I knew a way through the Grey Lands. I do not. To the best of my knowledge, no one does."

Elric reined in his horse sharply, as though to go another step might plunge him irredeemably into the unknown, whereas to stop now would keep him just short of an imaginary point-of-no-return. Tyrpaz halted too, and the two men sat astride their mounts for a good few minutes, each waiting for the other to speak.

"Then we are lost?" Elric said at last.

"No, not lost. I am well-versed in the topography of the Grey Lands to a certain point. However, that point now approaches."

"Then our journey has been a quest all along."

"Quite so," the sorcerer agreed. "But then, are not all journeys quests of some fashion or other?"

"Let us not discuss philosophy, friend Trypaz. Let us save that for when we return to that damned Tomesk tavern where first I met you and, meantime, confine ourselves now to the facts."

"You deserve no less."

Elric waited.

"The facts, then, are thus: I seek, it is true, but only that which you yourself seek, that which originally enticed you into the Grey Lands."

The albino frowned.

"Knowledge, friend Elric. Or, more precisely, self-knowledge. A worthy enough goal for any quest, would you not agree?"

"I would agree, yes, but only if the quester were aware that that is what he seeks."

"Quite so," Trypaz agreed, with a slight nod of his head. "Well, the moment draws near when we shall discover whether or not our journey has been in vain." He shifted on his horse, raised one desiccated hand and pointed. "Behold, up ahead."

Following the line of the old man's finger, Elric perceived nothing at first but greyness — grey sand, leaden sky, dulled sun — the horizon shimmering where sand and sky met, the definition between the two blurring and shifting. Then, all at once, he discerned in the middle distance a dark silhouette in the shape of a column, or perhaps a tree-stump, or possibly (Elric squinted harder, his red eyes piercing the heat-haze) a man?

"Come, let us ride," said Trypaz, kicking his drooping steed into renewed life.

Elric had no option but to follow, for a man can no more resist the lure of the solution to a conundrum that he can defy the pull of destiny. Clucking his tongue, he spurred on his own mount, tugging at the reins of the trailing horse to encourage it along, too.

As Elric cantered forward he became aware of a sound, although "sound" may not have been the correct description for what was actually the absence of sound, the denial of sound: a rumble so deep, so low, so subterranean in its intensity that it seemed to suck away the very air rather than to cause it to vibrate. It seemed, indeed, the very antithesis of anything that might be called voluble or melodious: the negative shadow of voice and song; a subtraction from the world's accumulated babel.

The anti-sound began so softly that at first only Elric's mount noticed it, and it flicked its ears in distress and began to toss its head sideways. Elric controlled the horse as best he could, but then the one behind joined in the display of unease. Each on its own would have been difficult to manage but both together proved almost impossible. He could see that Trypaz was experiencing similar difficulties up ahead and, as they struggled on towards their goal and the anti-sound grew louder — or, to be more accurate, emptier — the horses became so refractory that eventually both travelers were obliged to dismount for fear of being thrown. All four horses remained where they were, too scared to bolt, while Elric and Trypaz continued on foot.

VII

As they came within a quarter of a mile of the dark shape in the wilderness, which was now indisputably the figure of a man, the anti-sound bulked around them, deadening their ears until all they could hear was the beating of their own hearts. In Elric's case, this was joined by Stormbringer's ever-insistent siren-song of death and longing.

Elric peered hard at the solitary figure. It was a man, standing with his feet set slightly apart, his hands clasped together at his collarbones and his head bent back as though he were gazing at the sky. His posture was as stiff as any statue's, yet some instinct told Elric that this was no sculpted simulacrum of stone or clay; this was a living human being, frozen in this awkward pose for no apparent reason. He had heard of a certain sect of ascetic monks known as the C'aelthonites who had attained such mastery over their bodies that they could remain stock-still for days on end without food or water — and in the most inhospitable of climates — without apparent ill-effects. But somehow he did not think that this man had chosen to remain out here for reasons of self-discipline and spiritual enlightenment. In fact, he did not think that this man had chosen to remain here at all.

When they were within a hundred yards of the man and the air around them had become a perfect vacuum of sound, Elric noticed that the man's limbs were shaking violently, as though divers invisible hands had hold of him and were treating him roughly. The man's whole body, in fact, seemed to be in the grip of an uncontrollable palsy, from his sandals to the top of his head, and the epicenter of the trembling was the object that his hands clasped at his breast. It was then, too, that Elric realized that the man was standing astride a deep cleft in the earth which ran as far as the eye could see in either direction, east to west, and which was roughly two feet across. The cleft resembled a huge scar in the landscape that might have been cleaved by some immense axe in the days when all was Chaos and the gods fought wars across the length and breadth of the world.

Elric halted, motioning to Trypaz to do the same. "I do not like this," he said. Owing to the strange, draining effect of the anti-sound, his voice emerged faint and metallic, like the buzzing of a fly in a vast, subterranean cavern.

Trypaz's almond eyes were inflectionless. His voice, like Elric's, was a travesty of human speech. "Have you come this far, Elric, braced so much, only to turn back now, when the answers you seek may very well be within your grasp?"

There was an irrefutable logic to his words, but Elric was not content. "There must be some element of danger associated with this lone figure," he said, "else you would not have so craved protection ere you embarked on this journey."

"Protection, aye," Trypaz agreed. "But I am not sure that even your good sword-arm may protect me from my better nature."

"And what does that mean?"

But the sorcerer had started forward again at a swift and determined pace, indicating that no more questions or hesitations would be tolerated.

"Lord Arioch preserve me," Elric muttered, and he hastened after Trypaz.

The anti-sound intensified further and then, when Elric was within five yards of the trembling man, ceased abruptly. It was like walking into the eye of a storm. A sudden calm silence descended all around him, but it was a silence of such profundity that every sound now became magnified out of proportion. A breath drawn in was the crash of a wave on a rocky shore; the rustle of garments the snap of a galleon's sail in a stiff wind; Stormbringer's moan was a massed chorus of keening voices; the juddering of the figure astride the fissure the beating of a dozen drums. But not only sounds were increased. Sight, taste, touch, smell — all the senses seemed sharper and more acute than before, as though the entire world was being brought into focus within the pocket of calm that surrounded the shaking man.

The man's attire marked him out as no more than another traveler, another explorer of the Grey Lands' trackless wastes, but his skin was so dried and charred and withered by prolonged exposure to the elements that it gave him the appearance of a mummified cadaver, agelessly ancient. His eyes were clouded from staring at the sun, their irises almost as pale as their whites; but though he was obviously blind, it was doubtful whether he had actually been looking at anything in the first place. There was something in his attitude that suggested an inward-turning of the senses, a penitential self-absorption, the prayerfulness of the damned.

His uptilted face was pulled into a rictus of suffering, his teeth clenched to splinters, and beneath his chin, at the base of his corded neck where his hands were knotted, he held a talisman the like of which Elric had never seen.

The size and shape of a large saucer, it dangled from a chain of gold which was wound around the man's fingers. It was wrought of gold filigree, ornately inlaid with runes of jet and jade, and appeared to be immune from the trembling that filled the man's entire body — indeed, it seemed to hang immobile in the air, independent of any support. Elric perceived the talisman to be an object of great power and, when he turned to Trypaz seeking answers to unvoiced questions, the light of greed in his companion's eyes suggested great desirability, too.

But almost as soon as that light had appeared, it was extinguished by a look of profound sorrow which crossed the sorcerer's wizened features like the shadow of a cloud on a hillside. As though suddenly remembering himself, Trypaz turned to Elric, gave a small bow and said, "Now it is time for absolute truth."

The words, though quietly spoken, roared and boomed and echoed like cannon-fire. Elric winced but nonetheless leaned forward in polite anticipation.

"This man, this unfortunate creature," Trypaz began, gesturing at the shuddering figure with a bold sweep of his arm, "stands astride the Axis, a fissure which some believe divides the world in two. It is immeasurably deep and its darkness is impenetrable." He walked around the man, looking him up and down but apparently taking great care not to touch him. "Others say the Axis is a crack in the very heart of creation," Trypaz continued, "which affords us a glimpse of other planes, other realities which are normally separated from our own by the laws of time and space. These people hold the Axis to be an alternative manifestation of the Vanishing Tower."

"The — " Elric was startled by the explosion of sound that issued from his own mouth.

"Enough," Trypaz roared in a whisper, holding up his hand. "I alone must talk; you must listen.

"I first learned of the Axis and its guardian — for such is the role of this poor unfortunate — some twenty years ago in the books of the Great Mage Heldengore. The books revealed to me that the talisman you see before you bestows upon the bearer power over the Netherworlds and the beings that dwell therein. But it was not until some fifteen years later that I felt confident enough in my abilities to begin to search for it myself.

"I began acquainting myself with the Grey Lands, entering them again and again from different starting-points, and each time pressing further in a different direction. Eventually, more by error than trial, I finally pinpointed the location of the Axis. Several times on my excursions I came close to death, and it was only the thought that I might obtain the talisman and the power it contains that kept me going."

Elric shook his head, trying to clear the sweeping waves of silence which sought to unbalance him. Trypaz's voice rose and fell in strange cadences and arcane rhythms and it was all the albino prince could do to maintain his ground as the sorcerer continued his tale.

"It was but a few weeks ago that I first stood in this very spot, having penetrated the wall of silence with which the talisman surrounds itself. But I was too timid even then, too scared to seize this mighty artefact for myself. I did not dare so much as touch it. For that, I knew I needed a volunteer — you might say a *victim* — someone intrepid, perhaps even foolhardy, who would take that risk for me. And so I returned to Tomesk to bide my time. Then the Klöef came along and in him I thought I had found the perfect candidate. Sadly, I was not to know of his rash visit to the accursed Isle of Temoraal and of the 'passenger' he carried within him." Trypaz paused and shook his head in annoyance. "Damn me for a fool and a novice! I should have detected the stink of corruption emanating from him the moment I laid eyes on him."

Elric wanted to say that he, too, had been taken in by Gaarek's brash but apparently kindly demeanor, but all he could do was nod sympathetically.

But Trypaz was oblivious to the gesture and, clearly enrapt in his own words, he resumed the tale. "But, no, I was too busy congratulating myself on my cunning and my good fortune even to notice. And then you came along, friend Elric, and, though I knew you to be too cautious a man for my purposes, I encouraged you all the same in your deliberations as to whether you should accompany us. For I recognized in you a kindred spirit and I thought that, if the oafish Klöef should for some reason fail in the task to which I had appointed him, you might be persuaded to take his place. And then, of course, you saved my life, such as it is."

Trypaz, who had been staring at the shaking man throughout most of his story, now fixed his gaze unfalteringly on Elric. "Oh, Melnibonéan, if only you did not have the taint of heroism about you, then, perhaps, my plans and my manipulations might have run a whole lot more smoothly. Either you or Gaarek — or even that adolescent half-wit Kyval Kesh — might now be steeling himself to what I am about to undertake; which, I might add, I approach with no little trepidation. But perhaps it is all for the best, for what use is knowledge and what possible function can power serve save to test the mettle of a man?"

And so saying, the sorcerer reached out for the talisman, his stretched and claw-like fingers first gently, tentatively, brushing the gleaming object and withdrawing, and then resting softly against its shimmering hues.

Elric watched in dumb fascination, his head spinning, his ears still seeming to hear clips and sections of his companion's story, first speeding up like a bird's soaring flight, then falling, deep and resonant, as though heard through pounding water. He saw the gleam in Trypaz's eyes, watched them sparkle and burn as the sorcerer took a firm hold on the object and began to lift it away from the shaking man's clenched hands. The chain slipped easily through the gnarled fingers, almost as though the talisman had been resting there waiting to be taken. And the moment the final link of the chain lost contact with the man's skin, his trembling body began to collapse inward on itself, his blind eyes sinking into their sockets, nose subsiding into his ruined face, head falling into neck, shoulder, arms, torso, all crumbling away — as though the man had been no more than a living shell of dust — to sink with the softest of sighs into the mighty fissure.

There followed a moment of absolute calm, and the two men looked at one another, then down at the last traces of the shaking man as they tumbled into the crack. And then they felt a movement in the ground and heard the vaguest rumble, seemingly miles distant, beneath their feet.

A great belch of smoke billowed up from the fissure, its choking, sulphurous stench driving Elric backwards. Clutching his hood across his nose and mouth, he peered into the roiling, malodorous miasma and, through the blur of tears that streamed from his stinging eyes, he made out the figure of Trypaz bent over the chasm, the talisman in his hand and a look of terror and disbelief on his face. He heard the sorcerer's murmured words as loud as any thunderclap. "Elric," he said, shakily, "I never realized.... I never knew...."

And then Elric saw something stir in the depths of the Axis, something miles down in that rocky slit in the skin of the world shifting its massive, slithery coils. In his mind he glimpsed eyes, a billion eyes, all opening at once, blinking redly and wetly and rolling in their sockets. He saw maws begin to gape stickily and tentacles begin to grope and the slow, lumbersome uprising of something with flesh as pallid and as light-sensitive as his own, something gradually hauling itself up from the pit of darkest imagination, of blackest dreams, towards the distant brightness of the sun.

And he understood that all that stood between this thing and the world was the talisman and the will of he who held it, and that to clutch the talisman was to take on the most fearsome and terrible responsibility the world had to offer — a burden infinitely heavier than the throne of Imrryr — and that whoever grasped the talisman was confronted with the choice of letting loose this appalling, nameless monstrosity on mankind or making the ultimate sacrifice and condemning himself to a trembling half-life, half-death. It was a decision that had to be made within a matter of seconds, a decision that appealed to the scintilla of goodness that resides within the heart of even the most deceitful and self-serving of men.

And he saw, through the billowing clouds that issued from the gaping maw in the ground before them (a crack in which Elric could already see the first signs of long, rubbery arms, stretching), Trypaz turn his head slowly to look at him once more. As their gazes met, Elric felt — as though he himself were experiencing it — the other man's anguish and horror and remorse and despair. But he also felt his acceptance.

Squaring his jaw in grim composure, Trypaz stood erect, placed one foot on either side of the now slowly widening Axis, clasped the accursed talisman to his chest and aimed his eyes heavenwards.

Then he froze in that position, and he began to tremble.

VII

The dusty traveler entered the city just as day was waning, riding one horse and leading another three by their reins. Tomeskians young and old looked up from whatever they were doing to watch him pass by, though none needed to hazard a guess as to what fate had befallen the other three riders.

It seemed to the people who lived out their existence on the edge of the strange, swirling sands of the Grey Lands that the emptiness on whose borders their city stood was an ever-hungry god, continually needing the sustenance that only living, curious flesh can give, but rarely showing appeasement or satiation. And never gratitude. The townsfolk of Tomesk were inured to its appetite and philosophical on the subject of death. If anything, they were a little disappointed that the fourth traveler had survived. His continued existence simply meant that someone else mad enough to venture into those wastes would perish in his search for enlightenment. There was a terrible mathematics to the whole thing — a tally to be reached, a quota to be fulfilled — though they were blissfully unaware of the capricious nature of the gods.

The traveler made his way to the Silver Hand tavern where he dismounted stiffly, tethered his horse and went inside.

It was as if he brought the hissing hush of the Grey Lands indoors with him for, as he crossed to a table in the busy dining area and sat down, the conversations of the dozen or so other diners dwindled away to nothing. A silence fell in the room until all that could be heard was the soughing of individual breaths and the sigh of the fire in the grate. Grey dust drifted down from the traveler's cloak and hood and settled with an almost inaudible patter on the floor.

Recognizing a former customer — and one who had paid him well —Janquil the innkeeper broke into a sardonic smile. "Ho, sir, you have returned sooner than anticipated," he said cheerily as he approached the man's table. Then, reaching the traveler, he leaned forward and added in a softer timbre: "Though there are those as might say no return from the Grey Lands is truly expected."

The traveler nodded, pulled back his cowl and removed his cloak, which he draped across the table-side.

"So, is it a glass of wine you'll be needing? Or food? Mayhap a long draft of ale to quench the dryness in your throat?"

"I require nothing from you," said the traveler, bleakly.

"I cannot believe that," Janquil said. "Eight days you have been gone, and the Grey Lands can drain the life out of a man in half that time."

"I had plenty of sustenance with me."

"That is not what I meant."

"I know."

"Then perhaps...." Janquil reached forward to remove the cloak from the table, whereupon the traveler — as pale a man as the innkeeper had ever laid eyes on — grasped his wrist firmly, squeezing it with fingers that, for all their slender, bloodless appearance, possessed a rare strength.

"You," the traveler said, aware of a dozen pairs of eyes on him and Janquil, a dozen sword-arms ready to rise to the innkeeper's defence, "were not in attendance when my companions and I departed hence."

"It was early," replied Janquil. "I cannot be expected to be at my customers' beck and call at all hours of the day, not least when I had been kept up until the small hours the night before. Besides," he added with a laugh whose heartiness ill-concealed a tremor of fear, "I would hardly call my failure to see you off on your journey an offence deserving of such abusive treatment." He made to extricate his arm from the traveler's grip but the traveler held on tightly.

"Is it merely that you were unwilling to rise at such an hour, or unable?"

"You had best explain yourself fully, sir."

The traveler, still keeping a tight hold on Janquil's wrist, nodded slowly. He lifted his head and glared at the innkeeper, fully revealing the delicate features of a Melnibonéan offset by albino skin and eyes as red as the setting sun. "It was my misfortune," said Elric, "to take up with two companions who hid their evil natures well and a third who disguised his inner goodness yet more skillfully. The Grey Lands eventually exposed the latter, but the first two carried the mark of their untrustworthiness more openly."

"You speak in riddles, sir."

"Do I? Or do you speak in half-truths, landlord?" With that, Elric twisted Janquil's hand over to expose the palm. And there, pulsing slightly like an insect gorged with blood, lay a wart identical to those which had blighted the palms of Gaarek, Kyval Kesh and, briefly, Trypaz the sorcerer.

"A blemish," said Janquil, glowering at Elric. "Nothing more. Quite clearly, your stay in the Grey Lands has left you soft in the head."

"Not so," said Elric. "I must say that I was somewhat confused by the Klöef's remark that the sorcerer was to be his companion's *second* meal, but then it occurred to me that there was one who could have been the first.... One who failed to appear when he should have."

With a strangled scream of fury Janquil drew back and attempted to wrest his arm free, but Elric held fast while his other arm groped for the hilt of Stormbringer.

Throwing back his head, the innkeeper went through a series of coughing, retching convulsions as he summoned the worm-creature inside him up his gullet and into his mouth on a rising tide of bile, but it was too late. By the time the creature's snout was nosing its way past Janquil's tongue, Stormbringer was singing from its scabbard, and no sooner had the black runesword completed an arc through the air than the innkeeper's head was rolling down onto the floor, sheared from his shoulders by a single, clean cut.

There was consternation in the Silver Hand as the other diners responded to the apparently unprovoked slaying of their host with drawn swords and angry voices. But the voices and the swords fell when the worm-creature slithered free from Janquil's still-gaping mouth and writhed on the dusty floor, its truncated stem squirting black blood and its needle-like teeth snapping blindly in all directions. Then their anger turned to disgust, and there was widespread relief when the pale traveler stepped astride the thing and brought down his sword (which seemed almost to have a mind of its own, humming softly as though relishing the exercise) on its head, cleaving its brain in two and stilling the snaky squirming of its body.

VIII

Whether Elric was any wiser when he left Tomesk and the Grey Lands behind him is uncertain. The future beckoning was as unclear as ever, with Destiny's plan for him still a confused knot that could not easily be unravelled. He had learned nothing about himself that he had not already known, and little about the denizens of the Young Kingdoms which he had not already suspected.

But perhaps — and it was a thought so awful that Elric fought with all his might to keep it at the back of his mind — perhaps the Grey Lands *had* held a mirror up to his soul after all... and shown him nothing simply because there was nothing there to show. Because between him and his black sword there was only a barren greyness within which lurked a hideous evil that was only held back from being unleashed by the slenderest, tenderest of restraints.

Perhaps he had seen himself — and his true nature and his destiny — after all, and had mistaken them for the ever-changing but unchangeable grey sands of that most desolate corner of the world.

Only time, a Melnibonéan's greatest ally, would tell.

BEYOND THE BALANCE

B Y   N A N C Y   H O L D E R

The events of a man's life cannot be separated into individual moments; multiversal, they weave in and out among themselves, the strands of fate. If one had done this, then that would have happened. If one had not done that, then the world, the entire world in its past and present, the here and now — all would be changed, altered.

And all could be changed, if one had the means and the will.

So Elric prayed now, tired, defeated, alone. In his rooms, hidden far among the dunes of a forgotten desert, he bowed his head and murmured from the grimoire. Blood ran from his temples with the force of his desire.

Stormbringer lay beside him. The ancient runes etched on the blade seemed to run like sweat, or tears. But the sword wept for no man, no living creature. Stormbringer and its brothers knew nothing of grief, or remorse, nor any tender sentiment.

Outside, thunder rumbled over the landscape, and the wind whipped the sand against the walls of the house. The hangings within gathered and billowed like the crests of waves; the dunes without were the humps of sea dragons. Elric trembled, and longed for all that had been lost.

"Melnibonéan," he whispered to himself, "how did you change? How did you... weaken?"

For he was Melniboné incarnate; he was the emperor by right, and the symbol of the Dragon Isle to the Young Kingdoms and all other planes and worlds. And yet he wept now, and he hoped, and he regretted, so sorely, the evil he had done throughout his life.

With a shaking hand, he turned the thick, dusty page of the grimoire, his legacy from the old woman who had found him in the desert and nursed him back to health; who had told him of the visions she had seen while he lay wracked with pain. Promises had gleamed in the eye of her mind; now Elric, hungry for those promises, chanted anew. He had done so for a long, long, time, after building the pyre for the old woman when she died in her sleep.

"Use this," she had said, her dying words, and given up her treasure — the ancient, hide-bound book.

He had learned the tongue of the grimoire, and chanted night and day. But now he was tired, and sick — having no drugs here, and having no victims for Stormbringer — and he longed for death.

Stormbringer sighed eagerly. Elric touched the blade.

No, not for death. For release. For relief.

⊕

Behold, Elric of Melniboné: emperor of nothing, lover of nothing, friend of nothing.

He who was nothing.

The thunder became a blast, and the sky cracked open with fire. Stormbringer shrieked. All went black, and Elric, suddenly overcome as if he had been struck, tumbled to the floor.

⊕

"Elric, awaken. Elric."

He felt a hand on his shoulder and jerked awake at the same instant that he reached for the runesword. The room was dim; darkness washed the face of the figure who stood before him. Elric's heart clenched and he inhaled sharply: Moonglum, whom he had slain, looked grimly down on him.

"Elric, you must come. Cymoril...."

"My friend," Elric said, touching Moonglum's hand. The man was substantial, warm flesh and coursing blood. Elric swallowed hard. Had the spells worked? Was this part of his answer? The resurrection of his friend — or the appearance of it?.

"Cymoril is in danger." Moonglum pulled on his forearm. "We must hurry."

"But, Moonglum...," Elric began, then stopped himself. Perhaps this was another time, before the dread moment when he had slain Moonglum. An enchanted moment. And perhaps Cymoril rested in her enchanted sleep, in thrall to Yyrkoon. Could it be that this was the source of the old woman's prophecies: *You shall make a choice for yourself, and what you choose shall rule the world.*

Slowly he rose. Moonglum frowned at him and pointed to an ornate wooden table on the other side of the room. "You must fortify yourself, Elric. The way will be hard, and, by the sight of you, you're in grave need."

Elric's drugs were heaped upon the table. His red eyes gleamed with suspicion, but he staggered toward them. He could barely move. As he crossed the room, Moonglum followed, and the hair on the back of Elric's neck rose. All was not well here, not with the room, nor with his friend. The smell of something sinister wafted toward him, curled around him.

The old woman.... Was she what she had seemed, a seeress who foresaw the triumph of Law? Or was she a creature of Chaos, whose duty it was to steer Elric to a false plan? He had considered that before, and deemed it necessary to proceed no matter what her allegiance. He still sought to align himself with Law, to bring it about for the new beings of Earth that were to come. To stop the madness of Chaos and his own time; the world, ravaged; his friends, dead. Many by his own hand.

"Elric, hurry," Moonglum urged.

Elric reached for the drugs, took them —

⊕

— and the room burst apart, and disappeared. The two stood on a narrow wooden suspension bridge swinging high above a vast chasm of molten rock. Unbearable heat sapped the moisture from Elric's white skin. His white hair glowed crimson. His armor branded him.

Moonglum's face was ruddy, his lips blood-red. He nodded, pointing. "She is being held there. If we don't come, they will roast her alive."

"By Arioch," Elric cursed, stunned, and, as if in answer, the lava spewed upward, nearly licking the tips of Elric's boots.

Stormbringer twisted at his side and he brought it up in front of him, like a talisman, protecting it from the heat, though Stormbringer had withstood more fearsome predicaments than this.

"They keep her," Moonglum said, and took a step forward.

"How do you know this?" Elric asked.

Moonglum turned. His face was filled with bewilderment. His lips parted. "Elric? Elric, am I dreaming? I thought I was.... I thought you...?" He stared at his friend.

Elric shook his head. "I don't know, Moonglum. Perhaps I have been dreaming for a long, long time," he said.

Another geyser of lava shot to the left, singeing the planks of the bridge. Both men threw themselves to the right, and the bridge tilted dangerously. Moonglum moved back to the left as the lava geyser dropped back into the molten sea. Without speaking, they waited for the bridge to steady itself.

They continued the crossing.

"Who has Cymoril?" Elric said, raising his voice to be heard above the bubbling rock below.

Moonglum froze. His shoulders hunched. When he turned to look at Elric, his eyes gleamed with fear.

"The same ones," he replied, "who have me."

Elric met his gaze. "And who is that, Moonglum? Who has you?"

Moonglum took a step backward. He put his hand to his forehead, drawing his fingers over his eyes, down his nose, across his lips.

"I live," he said, half to himself. "I live!" He raised his head. "Come," he said tersely, and moved on.

"Ah, but do I live?" Elric murmured, and followed.

⊕

The bridge seemed to stretch across time itself; they walked for hours through the hellish heat. Elric's strength began to flag; he was thirstier than he had ever been in his life; his entire being cried out for refreshment. His blood boiled in his veins. He thought of Cymoril. For so long he had been unable to conjure up her image, so painful was it. His love. The queen of his heart, Zarozinia notwithstanding. Had Moonglum come back from the dead to save the dead? But Stormbringer had eaten their souls, had it not? There was nothing left of them — or so he had believed until now. And that had been the cause of much of his despair.

He held tight to Stormbringer, though he loathed the blade. Moonglum was outpacing him, and he hurried to catch up. As in the old days his friend's legs pumped with vigor as he strode. And yet.... Elric cocked his head. And yet, these were not the old days, and this, was this Moonglum? Was this a vision? Was this truly happening?

He stumbled, and was flung to the left as the bridge tipped. His right leg shot out from under him and he fell, grabbing the ropes. Lava shot up and he gave an involuntary shout as it came within inches of his heel.

"Elric!" Moonglum whirled around and ran to his assistance, helping him to stand on the swinging bridge. Their hands clasped, Elric studied his friend, nodded his thanks, and indicated that they should continue.

"You saved me from a terrible death," Elric said.

Moonglum's face changed. It became a terrible mask of pain and grief. His jaw clenched; his hand around Elric's tightened.

"Would you had done the same for me," he replied, and let go of Elric's hand.

Speechless, Elric watched his friend walk ahead. Faster and faster he strode, until he was practically racing. His figure receded into the distance, growing indistinct... or did tears blur the vision of the once-proud emperor?

"My friend," he whispered, reaching out his hand.

Above him, a great whirring flooded the sky, and he was cast in shadow. He looked up. The heavens were filled with black knights on black, winged horses. They carried battle axes, swords, and shields bearing the ancient runes of Chaos. On their lances heads were impaled, of those Elric both loved and hated, those whom Stormbringer had slain — so many! The mouths of the heads were opened, and, like a chorus, their voices rose in screams of pain and despair. As Elric hefted Stormbringer in his fighting hand and prepared himself for battle, the tallest of the black knights charged him. On his lance, glowing white like the Pearl at the Heart of the World, the head of Elric's beloved was impaled.

"Cymoril!"

She seemed not to hear him; but he knew those eyes, that raven hair tangling with the mane of the steed. Her lips were parted and drawn back slightly, almost as if she were smiling. But a closer look showed that look to be a rictus of pain, and she —

The black knight took advantage of his distraction and slashed at Elric; Stormbringer rose of its own accord to block the blow. Again and again the sword defended him, until Elric roused and threw himself into the battle, hanging onto the rope spans as the knight flew at him and the lava fountained around him. The sky was black with the dark band; they gathered in rows and marched slowly, as if to give their leader enough time to dispatch Elric.

The faceless knight, his helmet low and plumed, aimed his lance at Elric's heart. Cymoril's face bulleted toward him, and he had not the heart to cut it.

But Stormbringer did, and with a lusty bloodshriek it slashed through Cymoril's features and split the lance point in two. And suddenly the blood lust was upon Elric; he was a demon with Stormbringer; the black knight's armor gushed with blood. He tumbled from his mount and plummeted toward the molten lava.

A thousand wails rose from the other knights, a thousand strong. They came at Elric, cantering across the sky, breaking into a gallop.

He hacked, he slashed, taking one down, another. Others worked at the ropes of the bridge. He saw what they meant to do, and he saw that he had no hope, though he uttered spells and called, finally, on his patron demon, upon whom he had sworn to call no more:

"Lord Arioch! I summon thee!"

Then he was falling through the sky, toward the lava, and Stormbringer whipped the air before him. As he fell into the sea, Stormbringer pushed the lava away from him, somehow cutting it into nothingness. Elric fell deeper and deeper; yet he could see, and breathe, and hear the mad cries of the knights, dispossessed of their prize.

⊕

A whirlpool rushed below him, orange flame and red smoke, swirling and mounting, circling faster and faster like a firestorm. Heat beyond his imagining seared Elric's body, and he wondered why he was not dead — or if perhaps he were. He hurt as he had never hurt before, not in the days of long torture at the hands of his enemies, nor in the many times he had languished for want of his drugs. Every nerve, every fiber of his being twisted in searing agony. He was so engulfed by the brutality of it that he stopped breathing. He had no use of his limbs; it was difficult to command his mind. If he were dying, he wished by the bones of his fathers that he would finish with it.

Gasping, he hurtled toward the whirlpool. His white hand was wrapped around Stormbringer and he realized that the sword was dragging him along: He was no longer propelled by the force of his drop. The sword wanted to go there. It began singing of its wish.

Elric hovered on the edge, and looked in. There he saw more fire, and seas of molten rock; black smoke, crimson, and the shadowy figures of a hundred thousand people, screaming and begging and weeping as they stood on small islands of charred earth and scorched trees. Some of the people were aflame; as they wailed and tore their hair, smoke and fire moved along their bodies like the hands of lovers. Others fell to their knees, moaning among piles of blackened skeletons with outstretched limbs.

In the center of it all stood a man with brilliant red skin. He was nude and very beautiful, and his head was wreathed with horns. His eyes were huge, his mouth wide and his teeth very white.

He threw back his head and laughed as Elric flew toward him. Raising his hands, he bellowed, "How now, my penitent?"

And Elric knew who the man was: Arioch, Duke of Hell, wearing human skin. Arioch, whom he had forsworn.

Stormbringer rattled in his hand. What would it be like, Elric thought — not for the first time — what would it be like to drink my lord Arioch's soul?

A column of smoke rose from Arioch's hands. It gathered under Elric's feet and lowered him slowly to the earth beside the red demon.

"Greetings, Prince Elric," Arioch said.

The throngs of people cried out and ran toward them. Hundreds of faces, thousands of outstretched hands. Their faces were filled with frenzy. Elric crouched in a fighter's position and braced himself. Stormbringer moaned in anticipation.

Arioch laughed. "Do you think I brought you here to be torn apart by rabble?" He gestured for Elric to follow him, then turned, took two steps, and disappeared.

Elric quickly followed, only seconds before the wild crowds overran the place where he had stood.

He reappeared in an icy chamber of blue and silver. The stone walls were covered with frost; the floor was solid ice. Icicles hung from the ceiling like dripping candle wax. Shivering, he watched as Arioch reclined on a couch made of ice. It steamed where the demon touched it.

"So, Elric," Arioch said. "You prayed to me, and I answered."

Alarm prickled Elric's flesh. He raised his chin and said, "No, I did not."

Arioch laughed silently. "Ah, but you did. Your savior? She was one of mine." Elric thought of the old woman and swore at her memory.

"What do you want of me?" he demanded.

"You know very well. What I have wanted ever since you turned your back on us and developed that strange fascination for Law."

"Law shall overcome you." Elric sheathed Stormbringer. It protested. But Elric was tired and his arms burned, first with heat and now with cold. He had to reserve whatever strength he still possessed.

"You yourself are a thing of Chaos," Arioch said reasonably. He sat up.

"Why have you chosen this guise?" Elric looked for a warm place. There was nowhere to go in the icy room.

"Chaos prevails in the new world." Arioch rose. "And what a world it is, Elric! The most passionate of people own it. Their battles are something to behold! Their magic, which they call science, is more powerful than anything you can imagine." He cocked his head. "I will make you immortal, Elric, and you will be in this world when it comes to your plane."

"Why do you seek to tempt me, Arioch?" He wondered what had happened to Moonglum. He was nowhere to be seen.

Arioch smiled evilly, as if he had been reading Elric's mind. "Moonglum is here. Many you loved are here, Elric. Alive."

Elric shook his head. "Yes," Arioch insisted. "Oh, yes. Didn't you ever ponder what happened to those Stormbringer took? You believe that it ate their souls, do you not? You believe them to be cast into oblivion. Formlessness."

Arioch clapped his hands once as he fixed his gaze on Elric. Something glimmered behind him. Elric took a step so that he could see better.

"No!" he shouted, pulling Stormbringer from his belt.

Encased in ice, Moonglum flailed and twisted. His face was contorted with pain.

Stormbringer made a victorious sound, then a lower one like the purring of a great beast. Moonglum batted at his frozen prison. Elric couldn't hear him, though his friend appeared to be crying out.

"Look, Elric," Arioch said, and another block of ice appeared beside Moonglum's. And in it, Cymoril. His Cymoril, her eyes wide, her mouth wide with silent screaming. Where she pounded the walls, trails of blood ran, then froze and crystallized.

"They are in constant pain, and have been since Stormbringer slew them. They burn always, within and without. Flames of fire, of ice. It's all the same."

Arioch walked toward the two captives. Cymoril slid to her feet, cowering. Elric thought of what Moonglum had said: *They will roast her alive.*

Then Cymoril saw Elric. Her face brightened with joy. She called out. Still he could not hear her.

Moonglum saw him too, and burst into tears.

"This has been their eternal condition."

"That is a lie," Elric said flatly, unable to tear his gaze away from the two he loved so well. To see them again — his heart nearly burst from his chest. His love, his friend. Without realizing it, he began to walk toward them. His eyes welled. His hands clenched into fists.

"That is a lie," he reminded himself. He had seen Moonglum....

"I will give you one of them back," Arioch said. "That's truly why I brought you here. Oh, I knew you wouldn't come back to Chaos." Arioch smiled. "There was no harm in seeing if I could accomplish it, but, in truth, I simply wanted to present you with a dilemma. Which one will you save? And which will you leave in torment?"

"It's a lie," Elric repeated.

"No. I let Moonglum go to prove to you that I could. I can erase all memory of this pain forever, as I did with him when I sent him to you. I can do it, and you know I can."

Elric knew well of Arioch's vast powers, but this.... He hesitated. Cymoril pressed her palms on the ice, as if she were trying to push her way out of it. Moonglum did the same. Then both fell to the floors of their cells, writhing in agony.

"Why do you do this?" Elric shouted, aiming Stormbringer at the demon. Arioch laughed indulgently. Elric realized he should be saying spells, calling down all the forces of Chaos upon his nemesis. He had defeated Arioch before, even when he was marshaled with allies. And Arioch was all alone in this horrible place.

"I? I have done nothing. This is Stormbringer's doing, not mine."

Elric began to speak an old spell in High Melnibonéan. Arioch waved his hand.

"Don't you know where we are?" he asked, amused. "Elric, I have floated you upon the sea of time. This is the future you dream of. This is the world you believe has been given to Law."

He waved a hand, and Elric stepped backward as the wall nearest him became animated with people and odd machineries. It was a mirror, he saw, and this was a vision, or perhaps a window into the world that now lived and moved above them. People with fiery pieces of metal that shot at one another; people seated in metal boxes, running over others not similarly armored. People starving, their bones protruding from their chests, hands outstretched to others, who passed them by without a look. Youths, lying in a drugged state in filthy rooms, their glazed eyes filled with hopelessness.

"Watch this," Arioch said, and the scene changed: The sky, and then a burst of light so bright that Elric had to cover his eyes. A tremendous fireball billowed up and up, spreading over the world into a toadstool shape.

"The world of Law," Arioch said mockingly. "This is what you would give up your life for, Melnibonéan. This is what you would put all the gods to death for."

"Save you." Elric watched, sickened, as people staggered through the smoke and flame, hideously deformed. Their flesh fell off their bodies; their faces were wiped from their heads.

"I have found my place within the new world," Arioch said. "Here I have a new name."

The scene faded, and Elric found himself staring at nothing but a wall.

He lowered his head for a moment, attempting to compose himself. What Arioch had shown him made him ill to his soul. If it were true, if this were the world he wished to bring into being.... If this were all it was!

"There are new rules here, great emperor. But you could learn them. With a queen at your side, perhaps? Or a trusted ally? A king alone is a powerless king.

You would need a counselor, a confidant, a bodyguard. You would need Moonglum." Arioch chuckled. "They know full well why you're here. I have informed them."

Elric crossed to the icy prisons. First he walked to Cymoril's, and pressed his body against it. She was waiting for him to free her; he saw it in her look. She kissed the ice. Tears ran down her cheeks.

Moonglum stood expectantly, but it was clear he believed Elric would free his beloved.

But which were stronger, the bonds of love, or those of the deepest, most lasting friendship a man could have?

"What do you want in return?" Elric said. Cymoril was so beautiful. He had forgotten just how much so. He had forgotten the paralyzing grief of losing her.

"What I already have," Arioch answered. "Your knowledge that your treachery against the forces of Chaos will come to nothing. You're damned, Elric, and you always will be."

Elric didn't believe him. As he stood looking at Moonglum and Cymoril, he found he didn't care. Let there be a catch. Let his soul be tortured forever. If he could stop the pain for them, for just one of them....

Which one would it be?

With Cymoril at his side, he would live forever. With Moonglum, he would know peace.

If he were immortal, he could fight Chaos and win the day for Law. If not now, then.

He caught himself. If he surrendered to Chaos, then he was what Arioch said: Chaos's creature. No matter that he did it to defeat Chaos.

And if this were truly the time of Law, and this were what Law was? Were any sacrifices warranted for so hideous a destiny?

"I swear by my name and my honor that I tell you the truth," Arioch said in a soft, hypnotic voice.

"But you have a new name," Elric said.

"Nonetheless, I'm telling you the truth. This is the time of Law. This is the victory you fought for. And with it won, Elric, and yourself still alive, you may live for yourself."

Elric leaned his head against Cymoril's prison. She made as if to cup the side of his face. Slowly he raised Stormbringer toward Moonglum, whose eyes widened with surprise.

Then he lowered the runesword, and shook his head at Cymoril, at his friend.

"No," he said.

Arioch stared at him.

"No," he said again. "I choose neither. They must remain."

"*What?*"

He saw it all, in a flash, so clearly: The seeress had not been one of Arioch's minions. He understood that now. She had given him the means for powerful magic. She had allowed him to see beyond his ken. Beyond the ken of all the universes, all the planes.

The events of a man's life cannot be separated into individual moments; multiversal, they weave in and out among themselves, the strands of fate. If one had done this, then that would have happened. If one had not done that, then the world, the entire world in its past and present, the here and now — all would be changed, altered.

And all could be changed, if one had the means and the will.

He must have the will.

"If this is Law, there is something beyond Law," he said. He threw back his head of white hair. His red eyes gleamed with new comprehension. "There is something stronger, and better, that will come after the time of Law. And it will defeat you, and those like you."

Arioch smiled faintly. "There is nothing else."

"Yes, there is something." Elric stood tall, his legs apart, his bearing noble. "There is something that will not permit violence and pain to parade as Law. Something that operates on...." He stopped for a moment, and then the knowledge poured into him.

"Mercy," he finished, exultant. "Love." Yes, that was it! An eternal era of love!

"Love?" Arioch burst into laughter. The room trembled with the force of his hilarity. "Prince Elric, are you mad?"

"And these two will be stars in the new sky," Elric whispered, nearly overcome with emotion. "Their suffering will be over, for love shall avenge... no, love will renew them. But I, I shall be dust."

He turned and embraced Cymoril's block of ice. How he wanted her. How he wished with all his heart that he could free her. But he must not give in. He must not.

He touched the other block of ice. His friend stared back at him. "Moonglum, if you can hear me, know that there is a reason I do... nothing," he said to his friend.

Behold, Elric of Melniboné: emperor of nothing, lover of nothing, friend of nothing.

He who was nothing. Who had, perhaps, set a new wheel in motion; but now that it had moved, could do nothing but let it roll according to a plan he, a child of Chaos, could not comprehend, much less aid.

Arioch had stopped laughing, and studied Elric intently. He bore an expression of puzzlement.

"I had thought to have but a moment's diversion at your expense," he said.

"I wasn't brought to you," Elric replied. "The spell I cast has done its work. You have a new name, demon, but you, too, will become obsolete."

He turned to go. How he would make his way out of there and to his own plane, he had no idea. Yet he knew, in his soul, that he would.

"Wait, Elric! Explain this to me!" Arioch called after him.

"You wouldn't understand," Elric replied. "You never will."

And at least that much had been given to the last emperor of a dead world.

"Thank you," he murmured to the soul of the old seeress.

In the echoes of his heart, he heard her say, "You're welcome, wayshower. You're welcome."

ONE LIFE, FURNISHED IN EARLY MOORCOCK

BY NEIL GAIMAN

> The pale albino prince lofted on high his great black sword "This is Stormbringer" he said "and it will suck your soul right out."
>
> The Princess sihged. "Very well!" she said. "If that is what you need to get the energy you need to fight the Dragon Warriors, then you must kill me and let your broad sword feed on my soul."
>
> "I do not want to do this" he said to her.
>
> "That's okay" said the princess and with that she ripped her flimsy gown and beared her chest to him. "That is my heart" she said, pointing with her finger. "and that is where you must plunge."

He had never got any further than that. That had been the day he had been told he was being moved up a year, and there hadn't been much point after that. He'd learned not to try and continue stories from one year to another. Now, he was twelve.

It was a pity, though.

The essay title had been *Meeting My Favorite Literary Character*, and he'd picked Elric. He'd toyed with Corum, or Jerry Cornelius, or even Conan the Barbarian, but Elric of Melniboné won, hands down, just like he always did.

Richard had first read *Stormbringer* three years ago, at the age of nine. He'd saved up for a copy of *The Singing Citadel* (something of a cheat, he decided, on finishing: only one Elric story), and then borrowed the money from his father to buy *The Sleeping Sorceress*, found in a spin-rack while they were on holiday in Scotland last summer. In *The Sleeping Sorceress* Elric met Erekosë and Corum, two other aspects of the Eternal Champion, and they all got together.

Which meant, he realized when he finished the book, that the Corum books and the Erekosë books, and even the Dorian Hawkmoon books were really Elric books too, so he began buying them, and he enjoyed them.

They weren't as good as Elric, though. Elric was the best.

Sometimes he'd sit and draw Elric, trying to get him right. None of the paintings of Elric on the covers of the books looked like the Elric that lived in his head. He drew the Elrics with a fountain pen in empty school exercise books he had obtained by deceit. On the front cover he'd write his name: *Richard Grey, Do Not Steal.*

Sometimes he thought he ought to go back and finish writing his Elric story. Maybe he could even sell it to a magazine. But then, what if Moorcock found out? What if he got in trouble?

The classroom was large, filled with wooden desks. Each desk was carved and scored and ink-stained by its occupant, an important process. There was a blackboard on the wall, with a chalk-drawing on it: a fairly accurate representation of a male penis, heading towards a Y shape intended to represent the female genitalia.

The door downstairs banged, and someone ran up the stairs. "Grey, you spazmo, what're you doing up here? We're meant to be down on the Lower Acre. You're playing football today."

"We are? I am?"

"It was announced at assembly this morning. And the list is up on the games notice board." J.B.C. MacBride was sandy-haired, bespectacled, only marginally more organized than Richard Grey. There were two J. MacBrides, which was how he ranked a full set of initials.

"Oh."

Grey picked up a book (*Tarzan at the Earth's Core*) and headed off after him. The clouds were dark grey, promising rain or snow.

People were forever announcing things he didn't notice. He would arrive in empty classes, miss organized games, arrive at school on days when everyone else had gone home. Sometimes he felt as if he lived in a different world from everyone else.

He went off to play football, *Tarzan at the Earth's Core* shoved down the back of his scratchy blue football shorts.

⊕

He hated the showers and the baths. He couldn't understand why they had to use both, but that was just the way it was.

He was freezing, and no good at games. It was beginning to become a matter of perverse pride with him that in his years at the school so far he hadn't scored a goal, or hit a run, or bowled anyone out, or done anything much except be the last person to be picked when choosing sides.

Elric, proud, pale prince of the Melnibonéans, would never have had to stand around on a football pitch in the middle of winter wishing the game would be over.

Steam from the shower room, and his inner thighs were chapped and red. The boys stood naked and shivering in a line, waiting to get under the showers and then to get into the baths.

Mr. Murchison, eyes wild and face leathery and wrinkled, old and almost bald, stood in the changing rooms directing naked boys into the shower, then out of the shower and into the baths. "You, boy. Silly little boy. Jamieson. Into the shower, Jamieson. Atkinson, you baby, get under it properly. Smiggins, into the bath, Goring, take his place in the shower...."

The showers were too hot. The baths were freezing cold and muddy.

When Mr. Murchison wasn't around boys would flick each other with towels, joke about each others' penises, about who had pubic hair, who didn't.

"Don't be an idiot," hissed someone near Richard. "What if the Murch comes back. He'll kill you!" There was some nervous giggling.

Richard turned and looked. An older boy had an erection, was rubbing his hand up and down it, slowly, under the shower, displaying it proudly to the room.

Richard turned away.

⊕

Forgery was too easy.

Richard could do a passable imitation of the Murch's signature, for example, and an excellent version of his housemaster's handwriting and signature. His housemaster was a tall, bald, dry man named Trellis. They had disliked each other for years.

Richard used the signatures to get blank exercise books from the stationery office, which dispensed paper, pencils, pens, and rulers on the production of a note signed by a teacher.

Richard wrote stories and poems and drew pictures in the exercise books.

⊕

After the bath, Richard towelled himself off and dressed hurriedly; he had a book to get back to, a lost world to return to.

He walked out of the building slowly, tie askew, shirt-tail flapping, reading about Lord Greystoke, wondering whether there really was a world inside the world where dinosaurs flew and it was never night.

The daylight was beginning to go, but there were still a number of boys outside the school playing with tennis balls: a couple played conkers by the bench. Richard leaned against the red-brick wall and read, the outside world closed off, the indignities of changing rooms forgotten.

"You're a disgrace, Grey."

Me?

"Look at you. Your tie's all crooked. You're a disgrace to the school. That's what you are."

The boy's name was Lindfield, two school years above him, but already as big as an adult. "Look at your tie. I mean, *look* at it." Lindfield pulled at Richard's green tie, pulled it tight, into a hard little knot. "Pathetic."

Lindfield and his friends wandered off.

Elric of Melniboné was standing by the red-brick walls of the school building, staring at him. Richard pulled at the knot in his tie, trying to loosen it. It was cutting into his throat.

His hands fumbled around his neck.

He couldn't breathe, but he was not concerned about breathing. He was worried about standing. Richard had suddenly forgotten how to stand. It was a relief to discover how soft the brick path he was standing on had become, as it slowly came up to embrace him.

They were standing together under a night sky hung with a thousand huge stars, by the ruins of what might once have been an ancient temple.

Elric's ruby eyes stared down at him. They looked, Richard thought, like the eyes of a particularly vicious white rabbit that Richard had once had, before it gnawed through the wire of the cage and fled into the Sussex countryside to terrify innocent foxes. The prince's skin was perfectly white; his armor, ornate and elegant, traced with intricate patterns, perfectly black. His fine white hair blew about his shoulders, as if in a breeze, but the air was still.

— *So you want to be a companion to heroes?* he asked. His voice was gentler than Richard had imagined it would be.

Richard nodded.

Elric put one long finger beneath Richard's chin, lifted his face up. Blood-eyes, thought Richard. Blood-eyes.

— *You're no companion, boy,* he said, in the High Speech of Melniboné.

Richard had always known he would understand the High Speech when he heard it, even if his Latin and French had always been weak.

— *Well, what am I, then?* he asked. *Please tell me. Please?*

Elric made no response. He walked away from Richard, into the ruined temple.

Richard ran after him.

Inside the temple Richard found a life waiting for him, all ready to be worn and lived, and inside that life, another. Each life he tried on he slipped into, and it pulled him further in, further away from the world he came from; one by one, existence following existence, rivers of dreams and fields of stars, a hawk with a sparrow clutched in its talons flies low above the grass, and here are tiny intricate people waiting for him to fill their heads with life, and thousands of years pass and he is engaged in strange work of great importance and sharp beauty, and he is loved, and he is honored, and then a pull, a sharp tug and it's....

...it was like coming up from the bottom of the deep end of a swimming pool. Stars appeared above him and dropped away and dissolved into blues and greens, and it was with a deep sense of disappointment that he became Richard Grey and came to himself once more, filled with an unfamiliar emotion. The emotion was a specific one; so specific that he was surprised, later, to realize that it did not have its own name. It was a feeling of disgust and regret at having to return to something he had thought long since done with and abandoned and forgotten and dead.

Richard was lying on the ground, and Lindfield was pulling at the tiny knot of his tie. There were other boys around, faces staring down at him, worried, concerned, scared.

Lindfield pulled the tie loose. Richard struggled to pull air, he gulped it, clawed it into his lungs.

"We thought you were faking. You just went over." Someone said that.

"Shut up," said Lindfield. "Are you all right? I'm sorry. I'm really sorry. Christ. I'm sorry."

For one moment, Richard thought he was apologizing for having called him back from the world beyond the Temple.

Lindfield was terrified, solicitous, desperately worried. He had obviously never almost killed anyone before. As he walked Richard up the stone steps to the matron's office, Lindfield explained that he had returned from the school tuck-shop, found Richard unconscious on the path, surrounded by curious boys, and had realized what was wrong. Richard rested for a little in the matron's office, where he was given a bitter soluble aspirin from a huge jar, in a plastic tumbler of water, then was shown in to the Headmaster's study.

"God! but you look scruffy, Grey," said the Headmaster, puffing irritably on his pipe. "I don't blame young Lindfield at all. Anyway, he saved your life. I don't want to hear another word about it."

"I'm sorry," said Grey.

"That will be all," said the Headmaster, in his cloud of scented smoke.

⊕

"Have you picked a religion yet?" asked the school chaplain, Mr. Aliquid.

Richard shook his head. "I've got quite a few to choose from," he admitted.

The school chaplain was also Richard's biology teacher. He had once taken Richard's biology class, fifteen thirteen-year-old boys and Richard, just twelve, across the road, to his little house opposite the school. In the garden Mr. Aliquid had killed, skinned and dismembered a rabbit with a small, sharp knife. Then he'd taken a footpump and blown up the rabbit's bladder like a balloon until it had popped, spattering the boys with blood. Richard threw up, but he was the only one who did.

"Hmm," said the chaplain.

The chaplain's study was lined with books. It was one of the few masters' studies that was in any way comfortable.

"What about masturbation? Are you masturbating excessively?" Mr. Aliquid's eyes gleamed.

"What's excessively?"

"Oh. More than three or four times a day, I suppose."

"No," said Richard. "Not excessively."

He was a year younger than anyone else in his class; people forgot about that sometimes.

⊕

Every weekend he travelled to North London to stay with his cousins, for barmitzvah lessons taught by a thin, ascetic cantor, *frummer* than *frum*, a cabbalist and keeper of hidden mysteries onto which he could be diverted with a well-placed question. Richard was an expert at well-placed questions.

Frum was orthodox, hard-line Jewish. No milk with meat, and two washing machines for the two sets of plates and cutlery.

Thou shalt not seethe a kid in its mother's milk.

Richard's cousins in North London were *frum*, although the boys would secretly buy cheeseburgers after school and brag about it to each other.

Richard suspected his body was hopelessly polluted already. He drew the line at eating rabbit, though. He had eaten rabbit and disliked it for years before he figured out what it was. Every Thursday there was what he believed to be a rather unpleasant chicken stew for school lunch. One Thursday he found a rabbit's paw floating in his stew, and the penny had dropped. After that, on Thursdays, he filled up on bread and butter.

On the underground train to North London he'd scan the faces of the other passengers, wondering if any of them were Michael Moorcock.

If he met Moorcock he'd ask him how to get back to the ruined temple.

If he met Moorcock he'd be too embarrassed to speak.

⊕

Some nights, when his parents were out, he'd try to phone Michael Moorcock.

He'd phone directory enquiries and ask for Moorcock's number.

"Can't give it to you, love. It's ex-directory."

He'd wheedle and cajole and always fail, to his relief. He didn't know what he would say to Moorcock if he succeeded.

⊕

He put ticks in the front of his Moorcock novels, on the *By the Same Author* page, for the books he read.

That year there seemed to be a new Moorcock book every week. He'd pick them up at Victoria Station, on the way to barmitzvah lessons.

There were a few he simply couldn't find — *The Stealer of Souls*, *Breakfast in the Ruins*, — and eventually, nervously, he ordered them from the address in the back of the books. He got his father to write him a check.

When the books arrived they contained a bill for twenty-five pence: the prices of the books were higher than originally listed. But still, he now had a copy of *The Stealer of Souls*, and a copy of *Breakfast in the Ruins*.

At the back of *Breakfast in the Ruins* was a biography of Moorcock that said he'd died of lung cancer the year before.

Richard was upset for weeks. That meant there wouldn't be any more books, ever.

⊕

"That fucking biography. Shortly after it came out I was at a Hawkwind gig, stoned out of my brain, and these people kept coming up to me, and I thought I was dead. They kept saying 'You're dead, you're dead.' Later I realized that they were saying, 'But we thought you were dead."

— *Michael Moorcock, in conversation. Notting Hill, 1976*

⊕

There was the Eternal Champion, and then there was the Companion to Champions. Moonglum was Elric's companion, always cheerful, the perfect foil to the pale prince, who was prey to moods and depressions.

There was a multiverse out there, glittering and magic. There were the agents of balance, the Gods of Chaos, and the Lords of Order. There were the older races, tall, pale and elfin, and the young kingdoms, filled with people like him. Stupid, boring, normal people.

Sometimes he hoped that Elric could find peace, away from the black sword. But it didn't work that way. There had to be the both of them — the white prince and the black sword.

Once the sword was unsheathed, it lusted for blood, needed to be plunged into quivering flesh. Then it would drain the soul from the victim, feed his or her energy into Elric's feeble frame.

Richard was becoming fascinated by sex; he had even had a dream in which he was having sex with a girl. Just before waking up he dreamed what it must be like to have an orgasm — it was an intense and magical feeling of love, centered on your heart; that was what it was, in his dream.

A feeling of deep, transcendent, spiritual bliss.

Nothing he experienced ever matched up to that dream.

Nothing even came close.

⊕

The Karl Glogauer in *Behold the Man* was not the Karl Glogauer of *Breakfast in the Ruins*, Richard decided; still, it gave him an odd, blasphemous pride to read *Breakfast in the Ruins* in the school chapel, in the choir stalls. As long as he was discreet no one seemed to care.

He was the boy with the book. Always and forever.

His head swam with religions: the weekend was now given to the intricate patterns and language of Judaism; each week-day morning to the wood-scented, stained-glass solemnities of the Church of England; and the nights belonged to his own religion, the one he made up for himself, a strange, multicolored pantheon in which the Lords of Chaos (Arioch, Xiombarg and the rest) rubbed shoulders with the Phantom Stranger from the DC Comics and Sam the trickster-Buddha from Zelazny's *Lord of Light*, and vampires and talking cats and ogres, and all the things from the Lang colored Fairy books: in which all mythologies existed simultaneously in a magnificent anarchy of belief.

Richard had, however, finally given up (with, it must be admitted, a little regret) his belief in Narnia. From the age of six — for half of his life — he had believed devoutly in all things Narnian; until, last year, rereading *The Voyage of the Dawn Treader* for perhaps the hundredth time, it had occurred to him that the transformation of the unpleasant Eustace Scrub into a dragon, and his subsequent conversion to belief in Aslan the lion, was terribly similar to the conversion of St. Paul on the road to Damascus; if his blindness were a dragon....

This having occurred to him, Richard found correspondences everywhere, too many to be simple coincidence.

Richard put away the Narnia books, convinced, sadly, that they were allegory; that an author (whom he trusted) had been attempting to slip something past him. He had had the same disgust with the Professor Challenger stories when the bull-necked old professor became a convert to Spiritualism; it was not that Richard had any problems with believing in ghosts — Richard believed, with no problems or contradictions, in *everything* — but Conan Doyle was preaching, and it showed through the words. Richard was young, and innocent in his fashion, and believed that authors should be trusted, that there should be nothing hidden beneath the surface of a story.

At least the Elric stories were honest. There was nothing going on beneath the surface there: Elric was the etiolated prince of a dead race, burning with self-pity, clutching Stormbringer, his dark-bladed broadsword — a blade which sang for lives, which ate human souls and which gave their strength to the doomed and weakened albino.

Richard read and re-read the Elric stories, and he felt pleasure each time Stormbringer plunged into an enemy's chest, somehow felt a sympathetic satisfaction as Elric drew his strength from the soul-sword, like a heroin addict in a paperback thriller with a fresh supply of smack.

Richard was convinced that one day the people from Mayflower Books would come after him for their twenty-five pence. He never dared buy any more books through the mail.

⊕

J.B.C. MacBride had a secret.

"You mustn't tell anyone."

"Okay."

Richard had no problem with the idea of keeping secrets. In later years he realized that he was a walking repository of old secrets, secrets that his original confidantes had probably long forgotten.

They were walking, with their arms over each other's shoulders, up to the woods at the back of the school.

Richard had, unasked, been gifted with another secret in these woods: it is here that three of Richard's schoolfriends have meetings with girls from the village, and where, he has been told, they display to each other their genitalia.

"I can't tell you who told me any of this."

"Okay," said Richard.

"I mean, it's true. And it's a deadly secret."

"Fine."

MacBride had been spending a lot of time recently with Mr. Aliquid, the school chaplain.

"Well, everybody has two angels. God gives them one and Satan gives them one. So when you get hypnotized, Satan's angel takes control. And that's how Ouija boards work. It's Satan's angel. And you can implore your God's angel to talk through you. But real enlightenment only occurs when you can talk to your angel. He tells you secrets."

This was the first time that it had occurred to Richard that the Church of England might have its own esoterica, its own hidden caballah.

The other boy blinked owlishly. "You mustn't tell anyone that. I'd get into trouble if they knew I'd told you."

"Fine."

There was a pause.

"Have you ever wanked off a grown-up?" asked MacBride.

"No." Richard's own secret was that he had not yet begun to masturbate. All of his friends masturbated, continually, alone and in pairs or groups. He was a year younger than them, and couldn't understand what the fuss was about; the whole idea made him uncomfortable.

"Spunk everywhere. It's thick and oozy. They try to get you to put their cocks in your mouth when they shoot off."

"Eugh."

"It's not that bad." There was a pause. "You know, Mr. Aliquid thinks you're very clever. If you wanted to join his private religious discussion group, he might say yes."

The private discussion group met at Mr. Aliquid's small bachelor house, across the road from the school, in the evenings, twice a week after prep.

"I'm not Christian."

"So? You still come top of the class in Divinity, jewboy."

"No thanks. Hey, I got a new Moorcock. One you haven't read. It's an Elric book."

"You haven't. There isn't a new one."

"Is. It's called *The Jade Man's Eyes*. It's printed in green ink. I found it in a bookshop in Brighton."

"Can I borrow it after you?"

"Course."

It was getting chilly, and they walked back arm in arm. Like Elric and Moonglum, thought Richard to himself, and it made as much sense as MacBride's angels.

⊕

Richard had daydreams in which he would kidnap Michael Moorcock and make him tell Richard the secret.

If pushed, Richard would be unable to tell you what kind of thing the secret was. It was something to do with writing; something to do with gods.

Richard wondered where Moorcock got his ideas from.

Probably from the ruined temple, he decided in the end, although he could no longer remember what the temple looked like. He remembered a shadow, and stars, and the feeling of pain at returning to something he thought long finished.

He wondered if that was where all authors got their ideas from, or just Michael Moorcock.

If you had told him that they just made it all up, out of their heads, he would never have believed you. There had to be a place the magic came from.

Didn't there?

⊕

"This bloke phoned me up from America the other night, he said, 'Listen man, I have to talk to you about your religion.' I said 'I don't know what you're talking about. I haven't got any fucking religion.'"
— *Michael Moorcock, in conversation. Notting Hill, 1976*

⊕

It was six months later. Richard had been barmitzvahed, and would be changing schools soon. He and J.B.C. MacBride were sitting on the grass outside the school, in the early evening, reading books. Richard's parents were late picking him up from school.

Richard was reading *The English Assassin*. MacBride was engrossed in *The Devil Rides Out*.

Richard found himself squinting at the page. It wasn't properly dark yet, but he couldn't read any more. Everything was turning into greys.

"Mac? What do you want to be when you grow up?"

The evening was warm, and the grass was dry and comfortable.

"I don't know. A writer, maybe. Like Michael Moorcock. Or T.H. White. How about you?"

Richard sat and thought. The sky was a violet-grey, and a ghost-moon hung high in it, like a sliver of a dream. He pulled up a blade of grass, and slowly shredded it between his fingers, bit by bit. He couldn't say *"a writer"* as well, now. It would seem like he was copying. And he didn't want to be a writer. Not really. There were other things to be.

"When I grow up," he said, pensively, eventually, "I want to be a wolf."

"It'll never happen," said MacBride.

"Maybe not," said Richard. "We'll see."

The lights went on in the school windows, one by one, making the violet sky seem darker than it was before, and the summer evening was gentle and quiet. At that time of the year the day lasted forever, and the night never really came.

"I'd like to be a wolf. Not all the time. Just sometimes. In the dark. I would run through the forests as a wolf, at night," said Richard, mostly to himself. "I'd never hurt anyone. Not that kind of wolf. I'd just run and run forever in the moonlight, through the trees, and never get tired or out of breath, and never have to stop. That's what I want to be when I grow up...."

He pulled up another long stalk of grass, expertly stripped the blades from it, and, slowly, began to chew the stem.

And the two children sat alone in the grey twilight, side by side, and waited for the future to start.

BIOGRAPHIES

MICHAEL MOORCOCK

Nebula, World Fantasy and John W. Campbell Award winner Michael Moorcock produced a small-press 'zine of his writings at the age of nine, began writing professionally for Tarzan Adventures at age 16, and has been earning his way as a writer and editor ever since. He's published over one hundred books to date, and few authors have been as prolific in as many different styles at so high a level of quality. His Eternal Champion mythos comprises an influential portion of fantasy and sword-and-sorcery fiction. As editor and consulting editor of the British magazine New Worlds, he fostered the development of science fiction's "New Wave," a period which revolutionized the literary standards of the genre. Michael has toured as a musician with England's

Hawkwind and his own band The Deep Fix, composed music for Blue Ôyster Cult, written about the Sex Pistols, and spearheads lobbies against pornography and censorship. White Wolf, Michael's new American publisher, will reissue his books — some for the first time in the US — in definitive omnibus editions. The Eternal Champion is available September 1994.

EDWARD E. KRAMER

Editor of over a dozen original anthologies, including Dark Destiny: Unseen Architects of the World and Tombs: Tales Beyond the Crypt forthcoming from White Wolf, Ed's short stories appear in a growing number of collections as well. His credits include over a decade of work as a music critic and photojournalist. In 1987, Ed co-founded Michael Moorcock's international fan club, The Nomads of the TimeStreams, and presently serves as Michael's US agent for short and reprint fiction. A graduate of the Emory University School of Medicine, Ed is a clinical and educational consultant in Atlanta.

Richard Lee Byers

is the author of the dark fantasy novels Deathward, Fright Line, The Vampire's Apprentice, Dead Time, and Dark Fortune, as well as the Young Adult horror books Joy Ride, Warlock Games, and Party Till You Drop. His short fiction has appeared in numerous magazines and anthologies. He lives in the Tampa Bay area, the setting for many of his stories, where he teaches Fiction Writing at Hillsborough Community College.

Paul W. Cashman

directed Michael Moorcock's international fan club, The Nomads of the TimeStreams for five years before handing the reins over to some good folks across the Pond. He has served as publications director for America's largest SF convention and remains very active in SF fandom. Age thirty going on seventeen (you can tell by his barbaric musical tastes), Paul discovered the Internet a while ago and has seldom been heard from since. "White Wolf's Awakening" is his first in-genre sale.

Scott Ciencin

authored the critically acclaimed horror trilogy, The Vampire Odyssey, The Wildlings, and Parliament of Blood. He is also the author of several best selling fantasy novels, including The Night Parade, The Wolves of Autumn and The Lotus and the Rose. Under the pseudonym Richard Awlinson, he penned the number one best sellers Shadowdale and Tantras. Currently, he is writing young adult horror as Nick Baron, with six books in the Nightmare Club series. Scott lives in Winter Park, Florida, with his beloved wife Denise.

Nancy A. Collins

is the author of the contemporary horror novels Wild Blood, Tempter, and Sunglasses After Dark. She has worked extensively in comics, predominantly for DC/Vertigo with Swamp Thing (1991-1993) and Wick (1994). She is a winner of the Bram Stoker and British Fantasy Awards for short fiction and has appeared in such venues as Year's Best Fantasy and Horror and Best New Horror. Born in rural Arkansas, she now lives in New York City with her husband, underground filmmaker and anti-artiste, Joe Christ.

Peter Crowther

is the editor of the World Fantasy Award-nominated Narrow Houses anthology series for Little, Brown UK. He is also co-editor of Heaven Sent forthcoming from DAW Books and Tombs: Tales Beyond the Crypt from White Wolf. Pete's short stories, articles and reviews appear regularly on both sides of the Atlantic.

James S. Dorr

is a full-time free-lance non-fiction writer and a semi-professional musician with Die Aufblitzentanzetruppe (The Flash Dance Band). He is a two-time Rhysling Award finalist for his poems "Dagda" (Grails) and "A Neo-Canterbury Tale: The Hog Drover's Tale" (Fantasy Book). His chapbook of horror poetry is entitled Towers of Darkness.

Thomas E. Fuller

is the author of nineteen stage plays, two outdoor dramas, the books to four musicals, and has been produced by theatres all across America. He is perhaps best known for his more than thirty audio dramas written for the Atlanta Radio Theatre Company and as editor of The Centauri Express audio magazine. Thomas is married to artist Bertha Fuller, has four children, and lives in Atlanta.

Neil Gaiman

born November 10, 1960. He has worked as a journalist for a number of UK periodicals and newspapers. His graphic novels include Violent Cases, Black Orchid and Sandman (winner of the 1991 World Fantasy Award as Best Short Story). With Terry Pratchett, Neil co-authored Good Omens, a funny novel about the end of the world and how we're all going to die. He's currently working on lots of things, including a fantasy TV series for the BBC, and currently resides in Minneapolis.

Roland J. Green

is a prolific writer of science fiction, fantasy, action-adventure and historical fiction. He also reviews for the American Library Association and the Chicago Sun-Times, edits, and handles non-fiction projects like the "Concordance" of The Tom Clancy Companion. He is a graduate of Oberlin College and the University of Chicago, and has been active in the Society for Creative Anachronism.

Colin Greenland

won all three U.K. science fiction awards in 1990 for Take Bake Plenty. His other works include Death Is No Obstacle, a book-length interview with Michael Moorcock, and Harm's Way, a Victorian space opera. He is currently working on Seasons of Plenty, the second novel in the Tabitha Jute trilogy, and a graphic novel with Dave McKean, to be called Tempesta.

Gary Gygax

is the author of over a dozen novels and many short stories, and is one of the gaming world's most influential figures. Born in Chicago in 1938, he was playing chess at age six and with miniatures by age fifteen. He is the founder of TSR, Inc., co-creator of Dungeons & Dragons, and has helped develop nine additional game systems as well. His interests include game play, reading, travel, bird watching, fishing, walking, and pyrotechnics.

Nancy Holder's

horror novels include Making Love and Witchcraft, collaborations with Melanie Tem, and Dead in the Water, her first solo horror novel. She has also written over fifteen romance and mainstream novels, forty short stories, and has received the Bram Stoker Award in 1992 for Best Short Fiction. Nancy's credits also include game fiction and comic books.

David M. Honigsberg

works in New York, a city he has lived in almost all his life. His other interests include Jewish Mysticism and he teaches courses in Kabbalah at The Open Center in Manhattan. In addition, David is also a singer / songwriter / guitarist and has appeared in Greenwich village, and as a disk jockey in Hartford, CT. His scholarly pursuits include Arthurian studies and Judaica.

Brad Linaweaver

is best known for his novel Moon of Ice, which won the Prometheus Award in 1989 and, as a novella, was a Nebula finalist. His second novel is The Land Beyond Summer. Brad is also writing, acting and doing interviews for Horror House and Centauri Express; and collaborating on a comic book with Brad Strickland. He is presently collaborating with Fred Olen Ray on film projects and a feature serial, The Daughter of Dr. Moreau, for Argosy.

James Lovegrove

is the author of the novel, The Hope, and several short stories. He is currently working on a musical and graphic novel (with artist Adam Brockbank). James has collaborated with Peter Crowther on several short stories plus Escardy Gap, a twisted, Bradburyesque study in Ameri-arcana.

Doug Murray

began writing at age 13 for movie-oriented magazines like Famous Monsters of Filmland, The Monster Times, and Media Times. In the mid-eighties, he graduated to comic books as the creator and primary writer on Marvel's The 'Nam. Doug has also worked for Comico, DC, and Eternity. His short stories appear in numerous anthologies. His forthcoming novel, The Grand Inquisitor, is based on Carl Kolchak, TV's Night Stalker.

Frieda A. Murray

is married to Roland Green, and has collaborated with him on the fantasy novel The Book of Kantela and several other short pieces. She is a graduate of the University of Chicago, a past member of the Society for Creative Anachronism, and is active in Chicago Women in Publishing. Frieda lives in Chicago with Roland ,their daughter Violette and a black cat named Thursday.

Jody Lynn Nye

began her writing career in role-playing gaming. She wrote The Dragonlover's Guide to Pern and has collaborated with Anne McCaffrey on Crisis on Doona, Treaty on Doona, Death of Sleep, and The Ship Who Won. Jody has co-authored the Visual Guide to Xanth, written additional five novels, numerous short stories, and is working on a Xanth computer game. She lives near Chicago with her husband Bill Fawcett and two cats.

Charles Partington's

short fiction has appeared in Arkham House, New Worlds and New Writings in S.F. He has edited a new-wave sf magazine called Something Else and co-edits New Worlds, the Manchester edition. Charles has also just completed a horror novel, Who Drinks Midnight.

William Alan Ritch

has published numerous short stories collaborations with Brad Linaweaver; a solo tale is forthcoming in Fred Olen Ray's Wierd Menace. A past editor of the Libertarian Futurist Society's Prometheus Journal, Bill also directs and writes scripts for the Atlanta Radio Theatre Company.

Kevin T. Stein

is the author of three novels for TSR, Inc. (two under the pseudonym D.J. Heinrich), numerous short stories, and The Guide to Larry Niven's Ringworld. He is presently writing two novels for the Ultima Underworld series. Kevin has just completed his fifth screenplay at his current residence in Los Angeles.

Brad Strickland

has written or co-written sixty short stories and sixteen novels, including two Star Trek: Deep Space Nine books, The Star Ghost and Stowaways, and a Star Trek Academy novel, Starfall, which he wrote in collaboration with his wife Barbara. His stories have been selected twice for the Year's Best Horror Stories. He teaches English at Gainesville College and lives in Oakwood, Georgia, with his wife and their children Amy and Jonathan.

Karl Edward Wagner

graduated from the University of North Carolina School of Medicine, practicing psychiatry briefly before becoming a full-time writer. He has written or edited over forty-five books, including fifteen of The Year's Best Horror Stories, six books in the Kane series, and two collections of contemporary horror fiction. Karl encountered Moorcock's work as a freshman in high school and sent his early Kane stories to Science-Fantasy, where Elric first appeared. "Can't think why they didn't want them. Probably just a bad hair day."

Robert Weinberg

is the only two-time World Fantasy Award winner to be chosen as Grand Marshal of a Rodeo Parade. He is the author of six non-fiction books, five novels, and numerous short stories. His Louis L'amour Companion was a best seller in trade paperback and was recently reprinted in paperback. His latest fantasy novel, A Logical Magician was published earlier this year. As an editor, Bob has put together nearly a hundred anthologies and collections.

Tad Williams

is a novelist, newspaper journalist, short story author and writer of television and film screenplays. He produces the interactive television show Twenty- First Century Vaudeville, seen in San Francisco and Boston, with his next sights on the UK. His syndicated radio talk-shows One Step Beyond and Radio Free America have focused on controversial political subjects like clandestine intelligence, the drug- and- gun trade, political crimes and assassination. After spending most of his life in the San Francisco Bay Area, Tad now resides in London.